The Widow and the Warrior

Readers are encouraged to go to www.MissionPointPress.com
to contact the author or to find information on how to buy
this book in bulk at a discounted rate.

Published by Mission Point Press
2554 Chandler Rd.
Traverse City, MI 49696
(231) 421-9513
www.MissionPointPress.com

ISBN: 978-1-950659-73-9
Library of Congress Control Number: 2020915171

Printed in the United States of America

THE WIDOW AND THE WARRIOR

JOHN WEMLINGER

MISSION POINT PRESS

This book is dedicated to every widow or widower of any service member lost to the horrors of war. This nation and each and every one of us who enjoy its freedoms are forever in your debt.

FOREWORD

The story you are about to read will be a bit unsettling. It deals with the difficult subject of vigilante justice, which is nothing new for writers, by any means. But 2020 presents itself in a unique and startling way. We are a nation deeply divided along all sorts of lines—political, religious, racial, and even sexual preference is proving to be a basis for division in today's America. As I pen this, we are in the middle of the COVID-19 pandemic. It's everywhere, and the news tracks the number of cases and the number of resultant deaths on practically a minute-by-minute basis. Unemployment is rampant. The stock market is a roller coaster ride of steep highs and equally steep declines. To mask or not to mask has been turned into a political issue—one over which a security guard in Flint, Michigan, was killed. In Brunswick, Georgia, Ahmad Aubery, a man of color out for a jog, was killed by two, maybe three, white vigilantes, ostensibly because he looked like someone who might have been stealing in that neighborhood. The murder of George Floyd at the hands of a white police officer in Minneapolis has ignited the smoldering fires of racial inequality reminiscent of the early civil rights movement of the 1960s.

Dissent is nothing new among us Americans. Thomas Paine famously wrote, *"These are the times that try men's souls."* His words are as profound now as they were at the time of the American Revolution, and in times like these, our differences amplify themselves and actions become more overt as people struggle for answers. We are a nation of laws, but to what extent may new emergency laws be put in place during times of exigency? When are our sacred personal freedoms, guaranteed to each American under The Bill of Rights and our Constitution, too firmly tread upon? And how far may the individual citizen go to secure those rights to which he or she feels entitled?

I lack definitive answers to these questions, but here's what I do know; it's a lesson I learned forty-eight years ago during a tour of duty in South Vietnam. In times of stress, we look to our government, at every level, for solutions. But governments are fallible. James Madison said, *"As long as the reason of man continues fallible, and he is at liberty to exercise it, different opinions will be formed."* The *Widow and the Warrior* deals with what can happen when opinions veer in ugly directions and beget ugly actions. Does the end justify the means? Is justice achieved? My hunch is at the end of this book, the answers to these fundamental questions may prove difficult. Where will you stand?

Enjoy the read!

John V. Wemlinger
August 2020

The Widow and the Warrior

The Fraley Family Tree

Clyde Fraley and Mary Aileen Sullivan
MARRIED, SEPTEMBER 15, 1891

Virgil Fraley and Katherine Sumner Fraley
(1906–1995)   (1915–2000)

William (Billy) P. Fraley   Elizabeth Fraley Swain
and Margaret Rogers   and Roger Swain
(1949–2007) (1949–2017)   (1950–2010) (1951–2005)

Anna Rogers Shane   Ephraim Swain
and Ed Shane   (1972–UNKNOWN)
(1966–PRESENT) (1965–2017)

CHAPTER ONE

But in real life, things don't go smoothly. At certain points in our lives, when we really need a clear-cut solution, the person who knocks at our door is more likely than not, a messenger bearing bad news.

> —*Haruki Murakami,* What I Talk About
> When I Talk About Running

The Monday morning editorial board meeting at *The Washington Post* lasted twice as long as usual, making Anna Shane's morning four times more hectic than its normal breakneck pace. Over the weekend, Donald Trump had announced "that there were good people on both sides" in the wake of the Charlottesville protests, during which a young woman had been run over by a white supremacist. This was 2017, not 1817. Things like this weren't supposed to happen in America now. It wasn't a question of if *The Post* would respond. The wrangling in the meeting was over how strongly the newspaper would react to the pass the new president appeared to be giving to the far right. As *The Post's* national political editor, she would be the point person in crafting the paper's response.

The light on Anna's desk phone was blinking when she returned to her office, alerting her to waiting voicemail. *Christ, what now? I don't have time!* she thought as she deposited her pages of meeting notes on her desk. She was about to pick up the receiver to see who else was demanding her time and attention when her iPhone vibrated in her pocket. *Voicemail can wait,* she thought as she took out her cellphone and saw the call was from Bill Jenkins, the paper's publisher. She answered immediately. The book on Jenkins was that you didn't keep him waiting unless you wanted to work somewhere else.

"Anna, can you come to my office? It's important."

She could count on one hand the number of times she'd been summoned to his office. Jenkins usually worked through her boss. That's just the way things worked at *The Post,* somewhat like it worked in the military. There was a chain of command, and Anna's boss, the paper's editor-in-chief, stood between her and Jenkins in the pecking order. But there was so much going on since Trump's unexpected election, that her curiosity was piqued. Burying her surprise, she managed a confident, "Yes, Bill. Be right there."

Jenkins motioned her into his office as she appeared at the open door. They had been co-workers and friends for over twenty years. Anna had always considered him to be the poster boy for self-confidence. Well-built, about six-feet-four-inches tall, the former All Big-10 college basketball player at Indiana University still retained the lean look of a well-conditioned athlete. Always immaculately dressed, his appearance and his attitude reflected a certain pride for having survived a professional lifetime navigating the shark-infested waters of politics inside the beltway. He was the one most often credited with reviving not only *The Post's* reputation as a profound voice of professional journalism, but its bottom line as well. Most recently he'd been heard, on several occasions, scoffing at the new president, who often referred to the paper as "the failing *Washington Post.*" Nothing rattled him, including the presidential tweets directed toward his paper that seemed to be coming more and more often.

But this morning Jenkins was different. *Subdued,* Anna thought as she stepped into his office. He barely made eye contact with her. Even more puzzling and disconcerting to her, he made no introduction of the other man in the room, a complete stranger to her. Instead, Jenkins focused on the other man and said, "If you will excuse me, I will leave the two of you alone. I have a luncheon appointment, so take as long as you need." He collected his jacket, car keys and phone, offering only a weak smile as he left her with this stranger. *What the fuck?* she thought. *That's rude! Not even an introduction?*

The other man nodded at Jenkins, "Thank you for your help." He was, Anna estimated, in his late '60s, early '70s, distinguished looking with well-groomed silver hair, and dressed in a beautifully tailored three-piece, gray pin-stripe suit. She could not imagine who he was, why he was there or what he might want with her.

"Anna, my name is Charley DeBooker. We have not met, but I am the attorney for your mother, Margaret Rogers." Watching her carefully, he held up his hand and pointed to the couch. "Perhaps you should sit down. I have some difficult news."

Anna's heart raced. *My mother's attorney! Shit! I didn't know my mother even had an attorney.*

As she sat down, he said, "I'm sorry to tell you that your mother has passed away."

Everything in her went numb. Her mind reeled. In moments like this there is no accounting for where our thoughts go. Oddly, her thoughts went back to this morning when she left her husband, Ed, a senior partner in a high-powered D.C. law firm. He'd just come in from a long run and was dripping with sweat. She was eating a piece of dry toast in the kitchen. He'd promised her he'd be home by five o'clock if she could promise the same. They'd go someplace nice for an evening out. *Both of us are overdue for a break,* he'd said. She'd promised him she'd make it home on time. They'd kissed goodbye. And now this ... this terrible news. She'd just talked to her mother ... *how long ago had it been? A week, two weeks* ... she was stunned as she suddenly realized it had been over a month. A pang of guilt swept over her. "I ... I ... " she searched for words. "I'm sorry, Mr ... .uh, what did you say your name was again?"

"DeBooker ... Charley DeBooker. Please call me Charley. May I call you Anna?"

Absently she answered his question with a nod. Still reeling, Anna managed, "I don't understand. How?" She left the question open ended, still struggling to find the right words, the right questions. "I ... I mean she hasn't been sick a day in her life." Another pang of guilt ... *How the hell would you know that? When was the last time you saw her?* Sadly, she couldn't answer the question. She cradled her hands on her lap and hung her head, slowly shaking it back and forth. Once she could gather her thoughts, she looked up at the attorney. "This is all so sudden and ... " she paused again as questions rushed through her mind.

DeBooker offered, "She suffered a massive stroke in her sleep according to the county medical examiner."

Questions came to her randomly. As the next one popped up, she asked, "You say you are my mother's attorney?"

DeBooker merely nodded.

"My mother had an attorney? I ... I never knew that. Why did she need an attorney, Mr. DeBooker? My mother was a woman of modest means. I ... I ... " She continued to shake her head.

"Charley ... please call me Charley. I'm sorry we must meet under these circumstances, Anna. This isn't anything like what your mother and I envisioned for our first meeting, but there is much I must share with you. I also know now is not the time to get into it. I want you to know that all the preliminary funeral arrangements in Michigan are being handled. In fact, I will return there this evening and make sure everything is moving along. In the meantime, I have chartered an aircraft through NetJets. They have a priority reservation waiting for you." He handed her a piece of paper. "All you have to do is call and they will position the aircraft for you at the airport of your choice, but I have tentatively scheduled your flight from the Manassas Regional Airport this evening at 6:00 p.m. Feel free to amend that to best suit your and your husband's schedule."

This is so screwed up. He knows so much about me? He knows I'm married. He knows Ed and I live in Manassas. Until now, I didn't even know he existed.

He handed her his card. "This is my contact information. The flight time from Manassas, Virginia, to Manistee, Michigan, is about two hours. A car and driver will meet you at the airport in Manistee for the trip to Frankfort. I have assumed you will want to stay at your mother's home, but if you aren't comfortable with that, I can certainly make other arrangements. Just let me know your preference when you call with your arrival information. There will be plenty of time to work out the more specific details of the funeral service after you've returned home."

Anna thought his use of the word *home* odd. Frankfort, Michigan, hadn't been her *home* in a long, long time.

She sat motionless on the couch as DeBooker asked, "Is there anything I can get you; a glass of water perhaps?"

His question brought her back into the room. She shook her head.

"Anna, if I might, may I suggest you and your husband plan on staying a few extra days after the funeral? Margaret Rogers was a wonderful woman, a stalwart in the Frankfort community. We all feel her loss deeply. I've talked to Mr. Jenkins. He knows why I'm here and he has advised me that *The Post* is prepared to give you as much time as you need to come home, honor your mother and begin to settle her affairs. They are a very generous employer."

Anna managed a nod in his direction as the first tears began to form.

He reached into an inside coat pocket, removed a white

linen handkerchief and handed it to her. "I'm sorry that I must rush away, but I have a flight in two hours from Reagan National. I assure you, I will be beside you every step of the way once you get back home."

There's that word again—home, she thought.

"For now, is there someone I can have come sit with you—perhaps a colleague here at the paper?"

Absently, she offered the handkerchief back as she shook her head.

"Keep it. I know how very difficult this must be. We'll be in touch soon, Anna." He closed the door behind him on his way out.

She looked around the now empty office, as if she'd find the answers to the list of questions that continued to form in her mind, written on the walls. She began trying desperately to wrap her head around everything she'd learned in the last few minutes. Her mother was dead. She had an attorney. A private jet will fly them to Manistee, Michigan. *How the hell much is that going to cost? My mother was a "community stalwart"? She was just a simple woman. A retired librarian, for Christ's sake.* Shaking her head, she reached into the pocket of her slacks, took out her cell phone and found her husband's number on speed dial. On the third ring, he answered, "Hey, honey, what's going on. I don't usually hear from you ... "

She interrupted him, "Mom's dead, Ed ... " and with those words the tears gushed.

CHAPTER TWO

You feel the last bit of breath leaving their body.
You're looking into their eyes.

> —*Ted Bundy, Convicted and Executed*
> *Serial Killer*

The funeral for Margaret Rogers had been exhausting, and Charlotte Matthews had worked all day, staying well in the background, but making sure that the many details of it went off like clockwork, however. She was a little late in getting on the road to her next important meeting of this long day. The travel distance to her destination wasn't much more than fifty miles, however, construction on northbound US 31 and traffic congestion in Traverse City had further slowed her. She didn't care. It wasn't her idea to meet up here on Old Mission Peninsula, a narrow finger of land jutting into Grand Traverse Bay. *He wouldn't dare leave,* she thought.

The Old Mission Tavern's too-small parking lot was crowded, but she caught a break and waited while an old couple dawdled toward their car. Charlotte tried to pick out which one was theirs. *The black Cadillac,* she theorized. *Rich old bastards.* She was right. She watched the man point the key fob, click it, and saw the Cadillac's taillights blink. He turned to look at Charlotte, and gestured to acknowledge he knew she was waiting for his parking spot. She smiled, nodded, but fidgeted impatiently as the geezer held the door for the old woman who took what

7

seemed an eternity to get in. While she waited, a family of eight—she surmised they were a mix of grandparents, parents and four kids—walked past. *Tourists!* It was late summer, so even at nearly 8:00 p.m., there was still an abundance of daylight that would last for at least another hour or so. In the summertime especially, Old Mission Peninsula is a mecca for tourism, a place dotted with orchards and vineyards, occasional breathtaking views of East and West Grand Traverse Bays, quaint shops, quainter inns and expensive homes.

None of it, however, was of interest to her. Tonight was all about business, her payday. The geezer in the Caddy took another eternity to back out. *Finally!* She pulled into the space, got out, slammed the car door and headed to the restaurant.

"Welcome to Old Mission Tavern," the hostess said.

Charlotte dismissed the bubbly greeting with a brusque, "I'm meeting Mr. Roy Black. He had a 7:30 reservation."

The hostess checked her iPad, nodded and said, "Yes, Mr. Black is here. This way please, I'll take you to his table."

Roy Black was an alias for Ephraim Swain. He was from Bloomfield Hills, a suburb of the greater Detroit area. Balding at forty-five years old, portly, and dressed like someone trying to recapture their youth in faded blue jeans, he wore an untucked shirt that only emphasized his expanding waistline.

She still wore the form-fitting skirt and blouse she'd had on while assisting at the funeral. Her hair, makeup and lipstick were flawless despite the intense day she'd had, and as she approached the table, Swain did a double-take.

This was the first time they'd met face to face. Up until now, everything between them had been discussed over burner phones. If she liked anything about this guy, it was that he seemed to be cautious, with the possible exception of this meeting he'd insisted on. Charlotte had never met any of her other clients in person.

"There you are. I was starting to worry."

Before she settled into her seat across the table from him, she took careful note of the briefcase sitting on the floor next to his chair. They were tucked away in a corner of the dining room near the kitchen. There was a wide aisle between them and the nearest tables to accommodate the wait staff who were constantly bustling back and forth between the dining area and the kitchen. Pulling her chair up to the table, she looked around the crowded room and said, "Kinda' public isn't it, Ephraim?"

"I suppose so, but that only makes our meeting more anonymous. It's like hiding in plain sight." Two waiters hustled past them; one headed to the kitchen, the other to a table with a tray full of food. Their table was noisy, especially when the kitchen's swinging doors were ajar. "Look around, nobody's paying any attention to us. They're all consumed by their own conversations, and this place really has *the* best prime rib I've ever had."

Charlotte knew exactly why he was at this table, tucked away, noisy. He'd already told her he had some things he wanted to discuss with her. He wasn't fooling anybody. These would be things not meant for anyone else's ear. She asked with a hint of disdain, "Come here a lot, do you?"

He stared into her eyes from across the table. "Not a lot, but as often as I can, two or three times a year. You got something against the good life, Charlotte? 'Cause if you do, I can just keep this briefcase." He reached down and tapped the handle with his index finger.

Before she could say what she was thinking, their waitress showed up.

"May I bring you something to drink, besides water?" she asked.

Charlotte quickly checked out Ephraim's drink. Whatever it was, it was full of ice and looked watered down. *A lot like him*, she thought. *Not very strong.* She replied, "Scotch, neat."

"Chivas is our usual. Will that be all right?"

She looked across the table at Ephraim and doubled down. Smiling at the waitress and then at him, she said, "Make it the best single malt you have."

"Yes, ma'am," the waitress said as she smiled back and moved away.

Once the waitress was out of earshot, Ephraim asked, "Are you going to want to count this?" He rested his hand on the case's handle.

In the short time since she'd sat down at the table, she'd already developed a dislike for this guy and that feeble attempt at humor was all she needed to confirm it. Any pleasantness gone from her face, she leaned across the table, her eyes narrow and never straying from his, her voice a low, gravelly sneer, she said, "You'd be a fool to fuck with someone like me. Just slide it over and cut the crap. By the way, this little get-together this evening is on your tab."

"Okay. All business, I get that. But before you get this," he patted the case, "I need some assurance."

What the fuck! After the job's done you're going to sit here and offer conditions. I'll fuckin' kill you. "What?"

"Assure me there won't be any blowback about the old lady's death."

Charlotte glared at him. *You want details, you sorry fuck, I'll give you details.* She leaned toward him, glanced at the surrounding tables to be sure they were still absorbed in their own conversations, lowered her voice and said, "A week ago, I found an open window at Margaret Rogers' house and I snuck in. She was asleep and I surprised the shit out of her when I jumped on the bed, straddled her and slapped a piece of duct tape over her mouth. She struggled, but she was old and feeble. I looked her in the eye as she recognized me. I told her she was going to die. Then, I stuck a needle full of OxyContin laced with fentanyl into the vein in her right arm. She fought it. I watched her eyes as the drugs started to take effect." She shrugged. "It didn't take very long. I made sure she was dead, removed the tape and left. A nosy mail carrier checked on her after her mail piled up for a couple of days. Frankfort is a small town in a small county. The medical examiner is an old codger who got his medical degree about a hundred years ago. He's not real thorough; no autopsy, not even a tox screen. The death certificate shows she died of a stroke ... happens all the time ... leading cause of death among people in their seventies and eighties and all that. So, signed, sealed and delivered." She leaned back in her chair, but kept her voice low, "I did exactly what you asked me to do. I killed her and made it look like death was due to natural causes. There won't be any blowback."

Their waitress brought her scotch, took their dinner order and walked away.

Ephraim Swain stared across the table at Charlotte. He liked what he saw. Charlotte Matthews was, he guessed, early-to-mid 30s, well built, and attractive. He stared briefly at the modest amount of cleavage exposed by her blouse. In another setting, he might have been inclined to make a play for her, but he refocused. Tonight was about business. "That money is mine," he said to her.

She scoffed, "You think so? Not yet, it isn't. Not by a long shot."

"My mother should have inherited ... "

She dismissed the rest of his rant. She knew his family tree, likely better than he did. When he was finished, she coldly stared him in the eye, "But she didn't get any of the Fraley money. So, that makes you little more than the bastard son of Elizabeth Fraley."

"Fuck you, Charlotte."

Waitstaff continued to bustle back and forth. Glancing over at them, she checked in on the people at the nearest table only to find them still engrossed in their own conversation. "Hey, easy there, Ephraim. I don't give a shit who

you are or what your motivation is as long as you pay me."
She knew, however, she'd touched a nerve.

He started ranting again. "My grandparents were fucking crazy. My uncle was even crazier. It's their fault that I was cut out ... "

Charlotte just let him go on, rather enjoying his frustration.

Her smugness angered him more, but he finally realized where he was. His voice still low, barely above a whisper, he asked, "You like the money, don't you?"

She merely nodded and said, "I don't do this because I get to have dinner with nice people like you."

Ignoring her sarcasm, he said, "There's more where this came from." He slid the briefcase across the floor to her side of the table. She reached down and moved it closer.

She knew precisely what he was implying. It was why she'd agreed to this meeting. She needed the cash in that briefcase to pay for future expenses. "Look here, Ephraim, an old lady in Frankfort is one thing. Anna Shane is another matter altogether."

Ephraim shrugged his shoulders. "If it's too much for you, just tell ... "

She put up a hand. "I didn't say that, but let me think this through for you. Anna's not the only stumbling block you have in getting your hands on the money. Her old man is a high-priced Washington lawyer. If something happens to her, as things stand now, he becomes the estate's executor."

One phrase caught his attention. "What do you mean, 'as things stand now'?"

She paused, glad to know he was paying attention. "Old Charley DeBooker is going to be just as big a problem as Anna Shane and her old man. I took the old lady out just in time. DeBooker had the paperwork all set for her to turn over her entire inheritance to something called The

Angels' Overwatch Foundation. If that happens, you'll never see a penny of that money, Ephraim."

Swain grabbed his watered-down drink and drained it. "What's to stop the Shanes from doing the same thing?" he asked.

Me. I'll stop it, you idiot, is what she thought, but she didn't want to overplay her hand. She shrugged her shoulders and said, "Good question. DeBooker hasn't talked to Anna Shane about what he and Margaret were planning, but I know that's on his agenda."

"I'm going to get back what should have been mine in the first place."

Charlotte could hear the hatred in his voice and she continued to play on it. "So, here's the deal, Ephraim. I can take care of all three of your problems, but the price is going up ... way up," and she pointed an index finger toward the ceiling. "Shane and her old man are high profile people. I can get to them, but neither of them can die in Frankfort. The logistics of those deaths are going to be difficult and expensive. Old Charley, he can die in Frankfort, but we've got to be careful. All three of them dying on the heels of the old lady's death might raise some eyebrows, and we may not have a lot of time to get it done. If Shane and her old man want to move forward with this Angels' Overwatch thing ..." she shrugged her shoulders as if to imply she should not need to fill in that blank for him.

"So, you're up for this?"

"If the price is right."

"How much?"

She paused thoughtfully and then said, "Half a million apiece." She saw him wince as she added, "Half now and half when it's done."

"How long?"

She smiled smugly at him, "Nothing starts until I see seven hundred fifty thousand in my offshore account. The balance is due when the job is done."

He nodded and repeated, "How long?"

"Six months and all three of them are dead."

Their waitress brought their dinners: two king cuts of prime rib, rare. As he took the first bite of his, he looked at her and said, "Done. Get it done."

"No worries, Ephraim ... once you show me the money."

Ephraim Swain's hotel was just a few miles from The Old Mission Tavern, but in the short time it took him to get there, he'd worked himself into an emotional state that was half panic and half rage. He didn't have the million and a half he needed to pay Charlotte Matthews for three more murders. Hell, he didn't even have the quarter million to repay the people who'd loaned him the money to get rid of Margaret Rogers. His stomach was in a knot and he felt the deep need to blame someone else. Slamming his car door, he swore to himself, *Mother! You bitch!*

CHAPTER THREE

The very word "secrecy" is repugnant in a free and open society; and we are, as a people, inherently and historically opposed to secret societies, to secret oaths and secret proceedings.

—John F. Kennedy, The President and the Press, April 27, 1961

*D*amn her! Ephraim Swain, his mood changing from foul to fouler, slammed the hotel room door behind him and headed directly for his suitcase. Rummaging through it, he found both things he was looking for. He tapped a line of cocaine out on the bedside table, drew it in deeply through his nose and gave it a minute to work. Aware of the dangers, he didn't use it often, but found it cleared his head quicker and better than a bowl of pot. Heroin was completely out of the question. He'd seen what that had done to his mother and father. He took one of three burner phones in the suitcase and punched in the next number from a list of phone numbers he kept with them. When there was an answer on the third ring, it surprised him. Their normal way of communicating had been for him to place the call, there would be no answer, he would neither leave a voice mail, nor text a message. Voice mail and text messages left trails that could be followed, but the phone would record the caller's number. At a place and time convenient for the person he was calling, the call would be returned. "Uh ... I didn't expect you to ... "

"You caught me at a good time. And I've been expecting your call."

"Then you can talk?"

"Yes."

"Good. Then let me update you. The old woman is dead and buried. Cause of death: natural causes."

"And our money?"

Swain felt the knot in the pit of his stomach tighten. Looking in the dresser mirror, he wiped at the white residue around his nostril and breathed in once again. "I can't get to it just yet."

"When?"

Swain detected a hint of anger and impatience in the terse reply. "There are three people standing between me and what is rightfully mine."

"Ephraim, I could give a shit what you think is yours. What I'm concerned about is the two hundred fifty thousand dollars of our money you already have and the two hundred fifty million you promised us."

He swallowed hard. "Yes, I understand. So, I have a new proposal for you."

"A new proposal? That's gutsy. You want to propose something new when you've failed to come through on the original promise! The Brotherhood will not like this. I don't like this!"

"Hear me out. Our original agreement was you would get two hundred ... "

"I know what the deal was, Ephraim!"

Rightly, he sensed the increase in both anger and impatience. Ephraim stalked back and forth across the hotel room. Gesturing with his hands as if the person on the other end could see, he said, "Okay ... okay ... so how about I sweeten the pot a bit. Your end would become three hundred fifty million."

"And what is it that you want us to do?" the voice asked.

"Advance me three million ... "

A whistle emerged through the phone. "You want me to advance you three million when you haven't made good on the quarter million we've already given you?"

Swain took some encouragement that he didn't say *no*. "Yes."

There was a long pause and then, "Say I would be foolish enough to do this. How long would it be before we see the money?"

Jesus, everyone wants me to show them the money! "A year." There was a long pause. "A year is what it will take for me to have the other three eliminated."

Again, a pause, longer this time, and then, "One year? Seems a bit long."

"You have to spend money to make money and where else are you going to get that kind of return on your investment after only a year? Listen Bob, this is a good deal and ... well ... don't you think ... don't you think you kind of owe me this loan? After all, there is that Vegas thing." Ephraim let that hang there for a minute and then added, "Don't worry, the secret's safe with me." When the pause on the other end drew out too long, Ephraim said, "Are you still there?"

"Yes, I'm still here. Shut the fuck up and give me a minute to think. I'm not buying a pair of shoes here. You're asking me to put my neck on the line for three-and-a-quarter-million dollars." The pause drew out.

Swain kept silent despite the urge to offer more reassurance that he was good for the money.

Then, finally, "It's a deal, Ephraim. But understand this: if you fail to come up with three hundred fifty million dollars a year from now ... " The caller on the other end disconnected without saying goodbye.

Swain removed the burner's sim card and put it in his pocket. Tossing the burner on the floor, he smashed the phone with the heel of his shoe, picked up the remnants and walked them to a dumpster at one end of the hotel's parking lot. Returning to his room, he dialed an expensive escort service he was familiar with and arranged for someone to join him. As he lathered in the shower in preparation for her arrival, he smiled as he ran back over the math. *Three million! A million and a half to Charlotte leaves a million and a half for me.*

On a back road somewhere in South Carolina, Robert Luckridge, the senior senator from that state and chairman of the powerful Senate Intelligence Committee stopped his car, got out, wiped his fingerprints from the phone, threw it to the ground and stomped both it and its sim card. Satisfied that it could never be used again, he kicked the remnants into the water-filled ditch along the roadside.

Ephraim Swain wished his companion for the evening would hurry up and get here. He needed a diversion. He couldn't stop thinking about the deal he'd just brokered with Luckridge. As he stepped from the shower and reached for the towel, he reflected on the very fine line he knew he was walking. Luckridge was not a friend. In fact, he was pretty sure the senator would just as soon see him dead— except for the money the good senator had been promised.

The two first met a couple of years ago sitting next to one another in the first-class section of a wide-body jet flying from Chicago to Las Vegas. Swain was on his way to attend an adult entertainment convention and he advertised himself to Luckridge as a wealthy guy looking to become wealthier by investing in porn. Swain had no earthly idea who Luckridge was at the time ... just another guy with enough money or frequent flyer points to be in first class.

Luckridge, on the other hand, was on his way to speak to a trade group that had multiple companies operating in South Carolina. The trade group was paying his first-class freight.

At the end of the flight they'd exchanged cards. Ephraim was astounded that he'd been shooting the breeze with a US senator.

The next day, on a long shot, Swain called to invite him for dinner. "It's on me, Senator. It's the best steak house in Vegas." To his surprise, Luckridge accepted. Ephraim brought with him two aspiring actresses. It had not been his intention to provide the Senator with a hook up. In fact Swain was rather looking forward to a three-way in his hotel room later that evening. But one of the actresses took a decided interest in Luckridge, so much so, that after dinner they went their separate ways; the implied under-standing—"what happens in Vegas, stays in Vegas"—a verbal contract more important to the married and high profile Luckridge than to the nefarious and single Swain.

About six months ago—a year and a half after they'd met on that trip to Vegas—Ephraim Swain was on the verge of his own personal financial meltdown. He had to do some-thing and that something involved hatching a plan to get his hands on the Fraley fortune—not just part of it—all of it. He began looking for a contract killer—not just some punk, but a professional.

Finding Charlotte had not been easy, and his route to her had been both tedious and expensive. It began with the organizer of some high-stakes poker games he'd managed to get invited to who happened to know a guy, who knew a guy, and on and on. Along the way, each had held a hand out for money in exchange for information—in all, about ten grand. Then there was Charlotte, whose price made the intermediaries seem cheap. He needed a banker, but not the traditional kind.

It was pure coincidence that led him to Luckridge. He'd been browsing some adult porn sites on the web when he made an interesting discovery. One of the actresses—the one Luckridge had consorted with—was making pornography headlines.

Rooting through his desk drawer, he found Bob Luckridge's card. The call dropped almost immediately to voice mail. "Bob, Ephraim Swain here. We met in Vegas a couple of years ago ... shared a meal. Just wanted to touch base again. Something has come up I think you'd be interested in knowing. Please call me." He left his cell phone number. The third time Swain left the same message at the same number, Luckridge called him back.

"Bob, good to hear from you."

"You too ... " Luckridge paused struggling to recall the first name, "uhh ... Ephraim, isn't it?"

Swain thought, *You self-important son of a bitch! Let me refresh your fuckin' memory.* "Uh, yeah. Remember we went to dinner with a couple of ladies two years ago out in Vegas?"

"Yes."

Swain could sense the Senator's caution. "Yeah, well you know I kind of follow the industry ... "

"What industry might that be?"

"The adult film industry, you know, fuck flicks. I just thought you'd like to know the girl you banged that night ... well, she's kind of in the spotlight now. Have you heard of Scarlet Knight?"

"No, can't say that I have."

"Well, that probably isn't the name she was going by back then, but that's her industry name now and she's become quite a star."

"Well, I'm glad for her, Ephraim, but I've got to get going ... "

"Yeah, I'm sure you're quite busy, Senator. But I think

you might want to know that Scarlet Knight is only nineteen years old." Ephraim waited for a response. When there wasn't one, he did the math for the senator. "Which means Scarlet Knight was only seventeen when you fucked her."

There was another pause, this one longer than the last one. "What do you want?"

Ephraim smiled into his cell phone. "Nothing, just thought you should know. Let's stay in touch, shall we?"

A month or so later, Ephraim secured his first quarter-million dollar loan from Luckridge.

Naked under the robe he wore, the knock on his hotel room door brought him back to the present. In anticipation of what lay ahead, Ephraim could already feel himself becoming erect as he answered it.

As Luckridge got back in his car and headed down the deserted road, he hated two things about the way that last call from Swain had ended. First, he hated the fact that this sleezeball had something on him. And second, he didn't like the way his neck was now on the line for yet more money. He was one of the main kingpins of The Brotherhood of American Loyalists, a small and secretive organization of influential government leaders and wealthy businessmen. He controlled the purse strings of it—about two hundred fifty million dollars—all of it in offshore banks. But he knew he'd have to talk to some of The Brotherhood's membership about a loan the size of which Ephraim now was getting. He knew they'd go along. Yet he knew if the investment didn't pay off—well, The Brotherhood was not known for its forgiving nature.

Luckridge suffered no illusions. He knew what Swain was going to do with the money. He'd calculated the risk was worth the reward when he'd loaned him the first quarter million dollars. But Luckridge had a plan for The Brotherhood—a plan for the future—and the money they'd get from Swain. As the government became more and more conservative, there would be a need to enlist help in every state to assist in keeping people in line—*managing the liberals,* is how he referred to it. There was no lack of groups willing to assist in this way, but they would require money for weapons ... which would, in turn, buy their loyalty. That was Swain's value to The Brotherhood—he'd gotten three-and-a-quarter million from them in the last six months, but was now promising a whopping three hundred and fifty million back in a year. *You can't pass this up.* Senator Bob Luckridge wanted to be the one history would record as the guy with sufficient courage to take the necessary risks.

CHAPTER FOUR

You'll leave. And then one day you'll come back, and everything that you once loved about the place will drive you a little bit crazy.

—*Alex George,* A Good American

Anna Shane hadn't slept well and the 4:00 a.m. phone call to her husband's cell phone easily woke her from a not-so-deep sleep. Now she sat at her mother's kitchen table staring into her cup of coffee, the only one she would permit herself daily. Yesterday, she'd buried her mother. At just over fifty years old, she reflected that she was too young to have lost her and now sorrow gripped her, that grip only made tighter by her own guilt. The funeral had been a swirl of a few vaguely familiar faces from her youth and hundreds of complete strangers, all telling her how much her mother would be missed by the community. True to his word, Charley DeBooker had remained faithfully at her and Ed's side during all of it, introducing them to the people that came to pay their respects. Continuing to stare into the cup, she recalled one woman, her name long forgotten, who had her daughter with her. "Your mother has made such a difference in our lives. We loved her so very much." Anna remembered the little girl, about ten or so, was in tears. This vast display of grief across what seemed like the entire community of Frankfort, Michigan, remained unexplained to her. She couldn't understand it—*my mother was the librarian.*

She took a sip of coffee and remembered her upbringing in this town whose population swelled during the summer months with tourists, attracted by the moderate temperatures and the Lake Michigan beaches and breezes. Her mother, a single parent, raised Anna lovingly, but modestly. Anna never knew her father, and Margaret never provided answers to her daughter's questions as she was growing up.

Something had changed. Now, there were private jets to fly them here, chauffeur-driven cars to squire them about and lavish funeral arrangements. It looked as if money were no object. Her husband was curious, but not overly so. He had no basis of comparison. Anna did, however, and she had asked DeBooker to explain how her mother had evolved from the friendly librarian and single mother that Anna had known, to the apparently wealthy community leader so revered by the hundreds of people attending the funeral. DeBooker had been purposely vague. "There's much to explain, Anna. Let's get through the funeral and then I'll bring you up to date."

All of it fueled her guilt. In the thirty-plus years since she'd left Frankfort, while she hadn't avoided her mother, she certainly now felt like she'd neglected her. During her first four years away, as a student at Georgetown University, she and her mother talked on the phone regularly, sometimes long conversations as her mother encouraged her that the long hours of study and preparation would someday be worth it. Christmas during those years was always spent in Frankfort, but not Thanksgiving. There hadn't been sufficient money for her visits home to happen that close together. The first three summers saw her back home, but the fourth summer she'd interned at *The Post*. After graduation, *The Post* hired her and her work there had been all consuming, or at least that is how it now looked to her in the brilliant light of hindsight. She couldn't recall with any clarity the last time she'd been in Frankfort, but was sure that it had only been one brief visit made as a matter of convenience while returning from a business trip to ... *where?* She couldn't recall. *Why didn't she tell me how her life had changed? Where is all this money coming from? Why didn't you come back here? If you had, you could have asked her.*

Another bittersweet recollection was her marriage in DC twenty-five years ago. Her mother had been there, but there'd been hundreds of guests and there hadn't been the time. *Or you chose not to make the time.* Her marriage had not produced grandchildren for her mother to dote on, a conscious decision made by a DC power couple.

And then there were the phone calls, or perhaps better said, the lack of them. As she languished in her grief, this had become her biggest regret. They had been infrequent, mundane, and as she reflected, impersonal. Anna held her head in her hands and wept at these lost opportunities to tell her mother how much she loved her ... *Too late! It's all too late! You were just too self-absorbed! You were just too fucking busy to tell your mother something as simple as 'I love you.' What changed in her life? Why didn't I know about it?*

Today there was to be a meeting. Today she hoped they'd get the answers to the questions that had haunted her since coming home. However, about two hours ago the *they had a meeting* changed to *she had a meeting* when Ed's cell phone woke them, a call from one of the other senior partners in his law firm. Anna didn't want him to go, but that isn't what she'd told him when he'd come sheepishly to her. She asked, "So, who is it you're going back there to meet?"

Anna knew his firm wouldn't have called nor would he have gone unless it was something of utmost importance. Yet she was curious and she was very good at what she did at *The Post*—which usually involved getting information out of people. But all she was able to get from Ed was the man he had to meet was a major client. She'd teased him, "Attorney code for *Big Spender*, huh?" Ed told her he was a politician whose name had turned up on a police blotter in some small town in eastern Maryland. The charges were driving under the influence and possession of a controlled substance. But the police report also contained information about the presence of a passenger in the car at the time, a woman, who was not the married senator's wife, but rather an intern on the senator's staff. Then he'd chided her, "He's a Republican. That fake-news rag you work for will be all over this when it comes out." It made her laugh and she needed that.

At 7:30 a.m. sharp, the chauffeur who'd been their driver for the last three days knocked on the front door. She'd answered the knock just as Ed descended the stairs, luggage in hand. The chauffeur took the bag from him and told Anna, "Mrs. Shane, I will be back here at 8:55 a.m.. That's plenty of time to get you to your appointment with Mr. DeBooker."

Ed asked her when she thought she might be coming home. She shrugged, "I don't know. Let me give you an answer to that after I talk with Charley today." They kissed on the front porch and Anna went back inside, closing the door behind her.

There was the matter of putting her mother's house up for sale; another reason she could not fly back to DC with Ed. She began a slow amble through the home where she'd been raised, a quaint, cottage-like place on the southwest corner at the intersection of Third Street and Forest Avenue, nearly in the middle of Frankfort's downtown residential district. As she walked from room to room, certain things triggered memories. There was the kitchen table where she'd agonized over trigonometry and physics homework, math and science never being her forte; the bathroom mirror that she'd stared into and worried if the pimples and blackheads of puberty would scar her for life;

and the bedroom where her mother had apparently died quite suddenly, just a little over a week ago. She stepped away from that doorway quickly and headed back to the kitchen to warm her now-cold coffee in the microwave. She'd seen her mother's death certificate. It listed cause of death as stroke due to natural causes. She cringed at life's fragility.

Guilt gripped her again as she sat down at the kitchen table. As humans do, she rationalized. Their careers, their lives, Ed's and hers, were bound up in the hustle and bustle that was Washington, DC, and Frankfort was but a memory of distant youth. She knew there was a man out there who was her father, but who he was, where he was, what he might do or have done for a living, were all unknown to her. One of the questions for Charley DeBooker this morning would be, "Was my father at my mother's funeral?" She had the feeling that DeBooker had a lot of information that he was almost bursting to reveal, but was being very particular about when and where he would dole it out to her.

The grandfather clock in the living room, another memory, struck 8:00 a.m. She took her phone from the pocket of her robe and googled *Frankfort realtors*. One of the first to come up was someone she actually recognized as a classmate from high school, and who, on realizing it was Anna, immediately offered her condolences and agreed to meet her at 1:00 p.m. to discuss the sale of her mother's house.

At 8:05 a.m. Anna headed upstairs to get ready for her meeting. After showering, she partially blow-dried her curly, mid-length, increasingly graying hair. She was good-looking in an all-American-girl sort of way. Never one for heavy makeup, she stared into the mirror and pulled at what she thought were bags under her eyes; she was sure they had just become more pronounced. *What did you expect? You haven't slept worth shit since you got the news.* Whatever she felt about her own appearance, the day was shaping up to be a beautiful summer day, so she slipped into a yellow sun dress with a white print pattern, sleeveless, but with a lovely frill that fell just over her shoulders. Her lightly tanned skin contrasted nicely with the dress. She slipped on a pair of tan patent leather, mid-height heels, complementing it all with a single strand of pearls and a bangle bracelet Ed had given her for her birthday. Anxiously she looked forward to her day.

CHAPTER FIVE

*The less I understood of this farrago, the less I was
in a position to judge of its importance.*

    —*Robert Louis Stevenson,* Dr. Jekyll
    and Mr. Hyde

At precisely 8:55 a.m., Anna Shane answered
the doorbell.

"Your husband's plane was waiting. He's on
his way, ma'am. Mr. DeBooker's office isn't
far. If you are ready ... " the chauffeur waved his hand
toward the car.

He'd driven them everywhere since arriving in Frankfort. Yet Anna suddenly realized she didn't know his name.
"Please, call me Anna. And what shall I call you?"

This was the first time it was just the two of them
together. Until now, Charley, his assistant, a funeral
director—someone else—had always been in the car. She
was sure she'd heard one of these people use the driver's
name, but for the life of her she couldn't recall it.

Now standing next to the car, somewhat nervously, yet
respectfully, he removed his hat, extended his hand, and
in a slight Irish brogue, said, "Mrs. Shane, I must tell
you how sorry I am for your loss. I was privileged to have
been your mother's driver for the last ten years, and your
father's before that ... "

He said something else, but none of it registered with

JOHN WEMLINGER

her. Stunned, she interrupted him, "My father? You knew my father?" She hoped he didn't notice the desperation in her voice.

"Uh ... yes, ma'am."

Anna could sense his caution; like a soldier who just realized he was standing in a minefield. There was a long pause, neither knowing exactly where to go from here.

"Mr. DeBooker can explain it all to you, ma'am. His office isn't far. We should be going if you're ready."

As they pulled away from the curb, Anna, still seizing on the fact that this man knew her father, said to him, "You know that I never knew my father. I don't even know who he is."

The rearview mirror reflected enough of him for her to notice that he looked troubled. "Yes, ma'am, I do know that. I shouldn't have said anything." He repeated, "Mr. DeBooker will explain everything to you."

Awkward silence engulfed the big BMW, but not for long. After a couple of stops at intersections and a couple of right-hand turns, he pulled in front of a beautiful home along the Lake Michigan shore, not more than four or five blocks from her mother's house. Looking over his shoulder, the chauffeur said, "Here we are, ma'am."

The trip for Anna had been much too short. This man had known her father and in the past two or three minutes, a dozen questions had queued up in her mind. She wanted more time to ask them. She wanted to know what he knew about the man she didn't know. As he opened the car's door for her and she stepped out, she reiterated, "Anna; please call me Anna. And you are?"

Through a sheepish smile he said, "Big mouth."

As upset as she was ... *apparently some people knew about her father, she just wasn't one of them* ... the chauffeur's wise crack was spectacularly funny to her. Maybe that was exactly what she needed just now. She bent over in a good laugh, and as she straightened up, still giggling, she managed to ask, "No, really. It's okay. What's your name?"

"My name is Mark, Anna. Mark O'Toole."

"Well, Mark, thanks for the ride and the laugh. My curiosity was high in anticipation of this meeting with Mr. DeBooker, but now you've put it through the roof. Thank you."

He tipped his hat, smiled at her and said, "I will be here when you and Mr. DeBooker are finished."

The home's street-side yard was beautifully landscaped. A neatly trimmed, knee-high privet hedge lined both sides of the gently curving walk that meandered up to the front porch. On either side of the walk were two recently mowed, beautifully green, thick patches of grass—not huge in dimension, but sufficiently large that they gave the home a sense of space in an otherwise closely built neighborhood. Anna looked for a sign announcing Charles DeBooker, Attorney at Law or something like that, but there was no shingle hanging out front. She and Ed had several lawyer friends who practiced out of their homes in the suburbs around Washington, and their signs were prominent, often including nighttime illumination.

A woman, Anna guessed somewhere in her late 20s to early 30s, femininely built but appearing fit and athletic, with short hair attractively cut, and professionally dressed, greeted her at the door. "Good morning, Mrs. Shane. I'm Charlotte Matthews, Mr. DeBooker's paralegal," she said.

She led Anna up a flight of stairs into a rather large office, richly paneled in a light bird's-eye maple on two of its walls. Another wall contained built-in bookcases framed in the same exquisite bird's-eye maple. The floor was covered in a thick, deep blue plush carpet. Charley DeBooker sat behind a huge uncluttered mahogany desk. Everything in the room spoke of a level of organization she was unused to in her hustle and bustle office at *The Post*.

Behind DeBooker a wall of windows provided a spectacular view of Lake Michigan, the lighthouse at the end of the northern breakwater and the entrance to Betsie Bay. He rose and stepped from behind the desk to meet his client halfway across the room and extended his hand.

"Lovely office, Charley. Am I correct in assuming this is also your home?"

He smiled and said, "Yes. I've lived here now for nearly forty years."

She pointed to the view and asked, "How do you get any work done?"

"Some days it's harder than others, but I never get tired of this view, Anna. Never!"

"Your clients must really like coming to meet with you."

"Your mother was my only client, and we spent hours in this room going over the many details of the Fraley Family Trust."

Only client? Another revelation of a wealth she did not know her mother possessed. She gathered herself before speaking. "So, I must admit, I am intrigued—and confused. I have so many questions. On the way here, Mark inferred that you knew my father." She let that hang there for a minute, then added, "You know, of course, that I know nothing of him ... who he is, where he's from, what he did for a living ... nothing, Charley. And, I must admit, it seems I didn't know very much about my mother's life either. I know you've been protecting me ever since we first met in Bill Jenkins' office, but it's time we get past that. I'm a big girl. I want to know what went on with my mother. All of this ... the private jets, the big funeral, you as her attorney and she as your only client ... none of it makes sense to me. It's time to take the gloves off, Charley."

"Of course, you want answers and I'm here to give them to you." He waved his hand in the direction of a comfortable-looking leather chair in front of his desk and said, "May I ask how much time you have to spend with me this morning? This is going to take a while. There is much we must cover." As Anna took her seat, DeBooker sat down behind the desk and leaned back.

She could feel the knot in her stomach tighten. Dearly, she yearned for a cup of strong, black coffee, but she'd given it up a month ago, except for one cup a day, "You wouldn't happen to have a glass of water, would you?"

"Certainly," he said as he got up and retrieved a bottle of water from a small refrigerator "Would you like a glass?"

"No, that's fine."

Handing her the bottle, DeBooker settled back into his desk chair. "So, let's start with the complete unknown-- your father." He paused here for a moment and then leaned toward her, "He was a war hero, Anna, if there is such a thing that can come out of a conflict as pointless as Vietnam. He spent six years there, and was heavily involved in the fighting. He was awarded two Silver Stars, four Bronze Stars—all of which were for valor in combat. He was wounded five times and was awarded the Purple Heart each time."

"My mother never ... " A lump formed in Anna's throat. "Why wouldn't my mother tell me about him?"

"She had her reasons, but there was one reason that she told me was more important than any of the others. It stems from his experiences in Vietnam. There is an expression that boys go off to war and come back men."

Anna nodded. "I've heard that malarkey. War doesn't make them men, Charley. It's recovering from it that truly separates the men from the boys."

DeBooker stopped whatever he was going to say next and took a moment to reflect. When he did speak, it was slowly, measuring his words carefully, "I see we are of similar minds on our views of the madness of war, but your statement about 'recovering' pulls me up a bit short. The problem is that your father returned from the war a much different person than he was before he left. If I were to say he was scarred, both physically and mentally, I think I would grossly understate the debilitating effect of William Fraley's six years in Vietnam."

"So that's his name ... William Fraley ... I never knew." She wanted to cry, but fought back the tears.

"Most everyone around here knew him as Billy. Are you familiar with the family name, Fraley?"

She'd been gone for a long time. It was only vaguely familiar. "Had an old house, on the high bluff north of town, I think. Some of my classmates said it was haunted." She shook her head. "Other than that, no, I'm not familiar with them."

"It's an old family name here in Frankfort, but for now, let me finish telling you about your father." He paused briefly as Anna nodded in agreement. "When he did return home from Vietnam, he became a recluse."

Anna was no stranger to war-weary, wounded veterans. Many times, she had covered various politicians as they made visits to Walter Reed National Military Medical Center in Bethesda, Maryland. It was not one of her favorite assignments. She hated to see the service members being treated there with their shattered limbs, but even more, she hated watching the members of Congress. Most of them had never served in the military, and their discomfort was obvious, often marked by remarks that were as awkward as they were disingenuous. The rare exception was the senator or representative who was a veteran, and they were few and far between in the hallowed halls of the US Congress. She said, "I've seen some of the wounded at Walter Reed, Charley. They look at you, but it's as if they don't really see you." She shook her head, "It's haunting. There's a certain lonely hollowness behind their eyes, like something has been lost to them and they have no hope of ever regaining it. I suppose the only good news is that they are in a place where there's help ... "

"There wasn't help in your father's case," DeBooker

interrupted. He'd put that out there as if it were an unde-niable truth.

"I don't understand. If my father's family was wealthy, why didn't they ... "

He interrupted her again. "Anna, the Fraley family is not without skeletons in its closet. Over the next few days, weeks, months, you are going to learn about ... "

Now it was Anna's turn to interrupt. His timetable was beyond her comprehension. "Charley, weeks? Months? I ... I admit that my mother and I haven't been that close over the last ... " She stopped short as a pang of conscience took hold of her. She was ashamed to say it, but she had to admit, "We haven't been that close, but I think she would have told me..." Again, she stopped short. For a moment the pang of conscience changed to anger. *What?* She couldn't fathom what her mother should have told her. She wasn't the retired librarian Anna had thought she was. *The funeral ... all those people ... him, her mother's personal attorney ... the private jet ... the car and driver ...* The litany of her surprises kept running through her mind. Somehow her mother's life had changed dramatically, and Anna had no idea how or why or even when except for O'Toole's clue that he'd become her chauffeur ten years earlier. *Why didn't she tell me?*

Almost as if he were reading her mind, DeBooker contin-ued, "Anna, I've been your mother's attorney since your father died ten years ago. Before that I was her friend. Your mother loved you dearly. Everything she didn't tell you during your childhood was to protect you. Everything she didn't tell you as an adult was to protect you, because she was so very proud of the life you and your husband have carved out for yourselves in Washington. We spoke often about you, but ... " he paused again, "but her death was so sudden, so unexpected. We had only touched on the surface of the role she thought you might play in what she was trying to do here."

Anna felt herself tearing up, but managed to sputter, "What was that, Charley? What was my mother trying to do?" Until just now, she'd not known who her father was. Now that question was answered, but the answer had led to half a dozen or more questions. Anna, the tough political editor for *The Washington Post,* was overwhelmed.

"You have every right to ask that question, Anna," DeBooker said reassuringly. "But, if I might, I suggest that we defer discussion of your mother's plans until later. Let's concentrate for the moment on your father and the Fraley family. It will help put your mother's plans in their proper perspective."

Anna wanted to like this man. She believed that he was somebody whom her mother trusted. Yet, it had been so long since she'd seen her mother, so long since they'd talked about anything in any depth. *Can I really trust this man?* She dabbed briefly at a tear in the corner of her eye, looked at him and nodded, "Okay, Charley, fill me in."

"Your grandfather was Virgil Fraley. I am being kind when I say he was a hard man to work for, and your father, Billy, Virgil's only son, had an impossible task. No one could please Virgil Fraley.

"When your father fell in love with your mother, Virgil did everything within his power to keep them apart, but he couldn't. They would have married, I suppose, if the war in Vietnam hadn't gotten in the way. Billy enlisted in the Army to prove to his father that he was a good man and could live without the Fraley money. Your father was already in Vietnam when your mother found out she was pregnant with you. She sent letters to him, but they weren't answered. She didn't know it then, but he'd become absorbed by the war and was shattered by the friends it had cost him. He spent six years trying to avenge their deaths, volunteering for some of the most dangerous missions: long range reconnaissance patrols, LRRP's for short."

Anna took a sip of water. If she were listening to this

story about someone else, it would have sounded like a beautiful love story. But this wasn't happening to someone else. This was happening to her, and it hurt—it added to her guilt for being such an absentee daughter. She was beginning to deeply regret not pressing her mother harder for answers about her father. Those answers might have made her feel less guilty now, and having her mother give them to her might have helped her mother as well.

"He and his team of four or five volunteers would be inserted deep in the jungle for weeks at a time; their job was to collect intelligence and inflict maximum damage on the enemy whenever possible. He was acknowledged as the best in the messy business of LRRP missions.

"When the war ended in March 1973, your father returned home. He lived up there," he pointed his finger in a northerly direction, "in High Bluff House. You said you'd heard it was haunted?" She nodded. "In a way, I suppose it was." Charley took a sip of tea. "Your father couldn't shake the war. At night, he would arm himself with a rifle and a night vision scope and roam the grounds. He and I talked about this. He wasn't crazy, Anna. But he was possessed by the demons of war and the only way he could get them out of his mind was to roam around the estate in the middle of the night. It was very much like what he did for most of the six years he was in Vietnam."

"You knew him well then, Charley?" she asked.

He nodded. "Quite well actually, but that acquaintance didn't happen until after both Virgil, his father, and Katherine, his mother, had passed. Those two were the real gatekeepers at High Bluff House. The front gate kept others out, but it was Virgil and Katherine who kept Billy in."

Anna could feel the lump in her stomach forming again, only this time it was anger more than anything else. The fact that she had grandparents was a strange and quite foreign feeling for her. Both of her maternal grandparents had passed before she was born. Now she just found out that there were paternal grandparents just a few miles from where she grew up, and apparently all they were good for was to keep her mother and her father separated. *Who would do that? Why?* She couldn't fathom the answers.

DeBooker continued, "Virgil kept Billy sequestered there almost as a form of punishment. He seemed to relish that the war had scarred Billy with so much mental anguish. That torture lasted for two years until Virgil died, and you might as well hear the how-of-it from me. Truth is, no one knows for sure what happened that night. The authorities called it a suicide in the end. They found Virgil, a gun next to him, a gaping hole in his head, but no note. The fingerprints on the gun were Virgil's, but ... "

Anna swallowed. *No! My father couldn't have killed his own father!* It was unthinkable. "So, my father might have ... "

Charley DeBooker merely nodded. "Virgil was a real ... " He searched for the word. "Pardon me, but he was a real sonuvabitch, Anna. He wouldn't have had the guts to take his own life, in my opinion. He was as mean to Katherine, your grandmother, as he was to Billy. My suspicion is that one or the other of them killed him, and again being completely honest, I wouldn't blame either of them.

"Virgil came by his nastiness from his father, who got it from his father. Your father had a legacy, if you will, of three generations of mean—sometimes, violently mean— men. What's worse, their meanness was facilitated by a fortune amassed over the last century and a half. With Virgil out of the picture, I was optimistic that Katherine would seek help for Billy's mental struggles, but she didn't, and I was unable to convince her that there was still hope that Billy could be helped."

"Why wouldn't she want to do anything she could to help her own son? It's incomprehensible ... hell, it's seems criminal to me that she wouldn't ... "

Charley shrugged and offered, "I can only surmise what kept her from acting was fear. She was absolutely terrified to allow Billy off the estate without her for fear he'd hurt someone. That fear stemmed from a single incident." He paused for a moment, then repeated, "Anna, your father was a good man, but the war left him with some terrible demons."

"Tell me, Charley. What happened that frightened my grandmother so much? I didn't know either of them in life, but maybe I can get to know them in death."

"Right after Billy returned from the war, Katherine had taken him into town with her to the grocery store. When they got there, Billy said he'd wait in the car. Katherine told me she was reluctant, but at this point, she didn't know how deeply affected he was by his wartime experiences.

"When she came out of the store, he wasn't there. Obviously, she was concerned, but she wasn't panicked. She went back into the store and found him shadowing a man of Asian descent as he moved from aisle to aisle. Not wanting to make a scene, she let it play out until the man checked out and left the store with Billy still following him.

"Outside, she collared Billy. She told me he'd actually jumped at her touch as if she'd awakened him suddenly from a bad dream. She asked him what he was doing. He muttered something to her about gooks and he needed to keep an eye on this one.

"After that, Katherine said, she never took him with her. Billy's habit became one of sleeping during the day. In fact, Katherine facilitated it. She hung heavy draperies over every window and kept the house as dark as possible during the day. Katherine told me she never told Virgil about the event at the grocery store. She told me she was afraid Virgil would have Billy committed. As to the draperies and the roaming of the estate, she never told me Virgil's reaction to that, although at this point in his sorry life, Virgil was suffering from some dementia. Katherine, on the other hand, knew what her son was doing. She confided in me that she would lie awake in bed listening for a gunshot that never came. As time passed, she became more tolerant of his odd habits. For good or bad, Katherine became his enabler."

Anna's heart bled for her father. She tried to feel his pain based on some of her experiences at Walter Reed, but these veterans were not her father—her blood. She looked up at DeBooker and asked, "Where was my mother when all of this was going on?"

"Good question. Truth is she didn't even know your father had returned from the war and was in Frankfort, until the news of Virgil's suicide broke in the newspaper."

"So, the whole six years he was in Vietnam, he never wrote to her? She didn't write to him?"

"Your mother wrote letters to him until she realized it was an exercise in futility—she never got any letters from your father in return. He was too immersed in the war, too immersed in killing, too immersed in trying to avenge the deaths of his friends." The intercom box on his desk buzzed. "Yes, Charlotte."

"Lunch is here, Mr. DeBooker."

He looked at Anna, "I took the liberty. Chicken salad on croissant from L'Chayim okay with you? They're a local deli. Great sandwiches!"

Anna wasn't really hungry, but she didn't want to dismiss his courtesy and she was ready for a break, a chance to process some of what she'd learned this morning. They made small talk during lunch. Anna talked about her work at *The Washington Post*, but then asked, "What about you, Charley? Been in Frankfort all your life? Married? Kids? Grandkids?"

Charley laughed, "No, never married." DeBooker paused briefly as a smile crossed his face. "Your mother ..." He blushed.

"Charley, you liked my mom?" Anna said that sweetly, with no surprise or judgment whatsoever in her voice.

He didn't answer, but he smiled. "I was born and raised in Frankfort. I knew your mother and father from elementary school. From the time we were seniors in high school, I knew your mom and dad were in love with one another. I went off to the University of Michigan to earn my undergrad and law degree. When I got back, you were just a baby, your dad was in Vietnam and your mom still loved him, of that I had no doubt. I didn't stand a chance with her," DeBooker said as he broke eye contact and looked down as if experiencing regret.

Anna, sensing she might have touched a nerve, changed the subject, "So, what happened then?"

"I started my practice specializing in estate law. Virgil Fraley was one of my first clients. Like I said, he was a tough man to work for. He kept everything compartmentalized. For example, after I earned a certification as a Certified Financial Planner and had a tax accountant working for me, I suggested once to Virgil that he let us do his taxes as well as manage his estate planning. He would have nothing to do with that. No, sir! My job was to provide the info his tax guy wanted and his tax guy's job was to find him every deduction he could. Virgil didn't think that would happen if the two were in business together." Charley repeated, "Tough guy to work for."

She never knew this man Virgil Fraley, but she was becoming more and more sure he was someone she would never have liked, much less come to love as most children love a grandparent.

"When Virgil died, Katherine hired me to do it all, and wanted to be my only client. That surprised me. So I asked her why she'd decided to entrust me with the account. She said I'd been a true friend of the family and she trusted me. She said she'd need more of my time than Virgil had, since she had little business experience and the estate was quite large. I demurred for a while. Then when Katherine died, Billy, your father, asked me again to exclusively devote my practice to the family. Your dad and I had been friends for a long time. I couldn't say no."

Charley checked his watch. 12:30 p.m. He stood, walked to a picture on the wall and swung it open to reveal a wall safe. He spun the dial and said, "I have something for you. I keep it in here because it has some value." He reached in and removed a book, its front and back covers of dark brown leather. It measured about six by nine inches and an inch or so thick, with intricate gold tooling and pages edged in gold.

As Anna took the book from him and turned it over in her hands she said, "It's beautiful." Opening it to the first several pages she added, "It's hand-written. What is it?"

"It's a diary, well over a century old. It was written by Mary Sullivan, or at least that was her name when the entries begin. She later became Mary Sullivan Fraley. She is your great-grandmother."

"Why keep it locked away in a safe?"

"It's in the safe because its contents are ... Well, its contents aren't for just anyone. When you read it, you'll see that they're somewhat scandalous and would not reflect well on the family."

"Of course I'll read it!" her interest now piqued higher than ever. She wanted to know everything she could about this family she'd just discovered she had.

"It's important for you to understand the history of your family, some of the secrets of the fortune, if you will, because it will help you make better sense of what your father and your mother were trying to do at the time of each of their deaths."

Anna glanced at her watch, 12:45. Her time this morning was running out and she had a nagging question, but didn't know quite how to ask it. Finally, she looked at

Charley and said, "I don't know of a delicate way to ask this, but ... "

"Of course you want to know about the money." He smiled. "It's only natural. The fact that you haven't asked it until now, tells me a lot about you."

It was, she thought, a compliment of sorts, given as if he'd been somehow evaluating her over the course of the last few days and she'd passed the test, whatever it might have been.

"Your inheritance is right around a billion dollars."

She held up her hand, "Wait. I must have misheard. Did you say *a billion*, with a *b*?"

"I did."

Anna sputtered, "Oh my, Charley. I had no idea ... "

"Yes, well, Anna, you are heir to an incredible fortune, but ... " He paused, looked at her with what he hoped was a reassuring smile and offered, "My experience in the legal profession is when there is this much money involved, there's always a 'but'."

Because she was married to a successful attorney, she took his point and nodded in agreement.

"There was some opposition from a segment of the family at the time your father became the trust's sole beneficiary. Your father had a sister, Elizabeth Fraley ... her married name was Swain ... who was cut completely out of Virgil and Katherine's will. She passed away in 2010."

"What? Really? Why would any parent just cut a child out of an inheritance? They didn't give her anything at all?"

"As hard as it may be to believe, Virgil hated Elizabeth even more than he disliked your father. As to why Katherine chose to cut her out, I can't be sure, but Katherine rarely mentioned Elizabeth to me, except to express her disappointment in her. At any rate, Elizabeth sued twice; once after Virgil's death, and once again after Katherine's death. On both occasions she sought sole possession of beneficiary rights. The second time, your mother authorized me to settle out of court, which I did."

Anna, a confused look on her face, asked, "So, where's the *but* come into all of this, Charley?"

"During the first trial, Elizabeth tried to prove that your father was mentally incompetent. I was able to prove to the judge, a Vietnam veteran himself, that while your father may suffer from PTSD, he had his full mental capacity. The judge saw Elizabeth for the opportunist that she was and shut the door on her suit. The case was, of course, appealed, but the appellate court upheld the previous decision.

"One of the things that really swayed the judge was Billy's testimony that he intended to have the trust's stipulations changed. He would stipulate that seventy-five percent of any money accruing to the trust in the course of any year be given to a charitable cause or causes. He did this because ... well, first, your father, despite his debilitating mental condition, was a very good man at heart ... and second, he hoped it would make Elizabeth lose all interest."

"So, my dad must have thought his sister just plain greedy?"

"I think so. At one point she was addicted to heroin, both she and her husband, Roger Swain. He was from a wealthy Detroit family and inherited a pretty good-sized fortune after his parents were killed in an airline crash. It should have been more than enough money for them to live on, except for their expensive and unhealthy habit. An overdose actually killed Roger Swain."

"My God, that's horrible!"

"Yes, so you can see why your father wasn't averse to seeing Elizabeth cut out of any of the Fraley money. His decision to donate the sizeable dividends from the fortune into charitable organizations was a cunning move, and both your father and your mother made good on those donations each year. Just as cunning, however, Elizabeth asked the court that she or her designated representative or heir be provided access to financial information to see that Billy was living up to the stipulation."

"Geez, an untrusting lot, these Fraleys, aren't they?"

"I am afraid you are absolutely right. Elizabeth asked the judge to stipulate that if your father should ever fall short of his required charitable donations, then she, Elizabeth or her heir, would automatically be named a joint beneficiary of the family fortune and entitled to fifty percent of its balance. The judge agreed that such a stipulation seemed fair."

"But if Elizabeth is deceased, who's doing the checking now?"

DeBooker's expression changed. "Elizabeth had a son, Ephraim. He was born out of wedlock and was never acknowledged by your grandfather or your grandmother. I don't know very much about him except that during the various lawsuits, he seemed to be the one pushing his mother, Elizabeth, to proceed. I get the requests for financial information from his attorney, like clockwork, every year. I know he's checking to see if the charitable donations are up to snuff."

"So, he, this Ephraim character, still believes he should get some money?" Anna asked.

"I believe he does and he is very vigilant. If it were ever to happen that we miss the seventy-five percent mark in any given year, he could petition the court for half the fortune."

Charley glanced at his watch and pointing to the diary, said, "Our time today is nearly up, and it's important for you to have the chance to come to grips with everything you've learned today about both your mother and your father. I'd also like for you to take a good look at the diary and get a feel for your family history. I warn you, some of it is rather bleak, but with what you have learned today, most of the turmoil you will read about won't surprise you. Having as much information as possible may help inform the decisions you are going to have to make."

Decisions? Anna thought. Her mind went straight to her work at *The Post.* She had told her boss that she would be back as soon as possible; four or five days at the most. "So, when would you like to meet next? I don't have a lot of time, Charley. There's a lot going on in Washington right now ... "

DeBooker held up a hand, "I'm going to leave that up to you. As I said, the Fraley Trust is my only client, so I am completely at your disposal. Just give Charlotte or me a call and let us know when you'd like to meet again."

The intercom buzzed. Charley answered it, "Yes."

"Mr. DeBooker, Mark O'Toole is here to take Mrs. Shane home."

"Thank you. She's on her way down now."

Her head was spinning, but she managed to thank him and, holding up the diary, said, "I will begin reading tonight."

Charley extended his hand and Anna took it. "I look forward to our next meeting."

CHAPTER SIX

The Irish Problem
I am oppressed as a woman, and I'm also
oppressed as an Irish person. Everyone in this
country is oppressed ...

      Irish Republican Mairead Farrell, 1980s

Anna's mother had kept her home nicely updated. The realtor, a former cheerleader, as Anna recalled, greeted her with what Anna felt was feigned cheerfulness. She wrote it off. This was business and time was of the essence. After a modicum of small talk, she proceeded to show herself through the house as Anna sat at the kitchen table clutching a glass of ice water and staring at the diary she'd placed in front of her. She wanted to begin reading, but not while this stranger was here.

When the realtor returned to the kitchen she seemed more animated. "You know this place won't last long on the market. This location is perfect; convenient to downtown, a nice size for that family looking for a vacation home. And that guest room with kitchen and bath above the garage just adds so much value to the property."

Guest room above the garage. She hadn't even noticed. Her guilt returned with a vengeance. *Was that for Ed and me? Why didn't you ever mention it? Maybe you would have if I'd called more often. If we'd talked more.*

"So, I'm thinking somewhere around five hundred thousand ... "

She knew her mother had paid less than fifty thousand, but that had been ... *what?* Her mind boggled at the answer ... *not quite fifty years ago. This was Frankfort. Prices couldn't have gone up that much ... could they?*
"That much?" Anna asked, surprise evident in her voice.

The realtor smiled. "A lot has changed around here since you left." Anna wasn't sure if that was some kind of shot across her bow, or if she was just feeling guilty about the living space above the garage she'd never known about much less ever used. "It's a little over the comps for this neighborhood, but those guest quarters up there set it apart," she said pointing in the garage's direction. "Also, the tiled bathrooms and the updated kitchen are all so beautifully done. Some family from Detroit, Grand Rapids or Chicago will snap this place up, I'm sure of it."

"Okay ... so where do we begin?"

The realtor pulled a sheaf of papers from her bag and began laying them out on the kitchen table.

Anna spent most of the remainder of the afternoon answering emails and talking with her beat reporters back in Washington, the ones who covered the White House, the Senate, the House and, most recently added, the Supreme Court. Her last call was to her boss, Burt Fredericks, the newspaper's managing editor.

"I don't want to say we miss you around here," he said, "but, we miss you. There are more leaks in this White House than in my mother's old spaghetti strainer. We're hearing that there are real troubles between Justice, the FBI, and the White House. People are trying to get the president to read some things, one of which, I'm told is the Constitution. Information we have is that he doesn't read anything he is given by his staff, and that his only news sources are the conservative ones that ballyhoo his election. He seems to think the Department of Justice is his personal attorney and the FBI is his own Sheriff of Nottingham. Personally, I think the guy spends most of the time with his foot in his mouth, but that's only after he has stepped in bigger and deeper piles of shit! There are so many possible stories that require follow up. We need you here to help us wade through the bad shit to get to the good shit."

His comments to her were as troubling as they were flattering. "I need just a couple more days to sort through everything here. I promise I won't be any longer than that."

"Okay, I understand. Anna, I certainly didn't want to sound unsympathetic. We are all very sorry for your loss."

"Thanks, I'll see everyone soon."

At 5:00 p.m. she stepped out onto the front porch of her mother's home as the early evening sun filtered gently through the towering maples that lined Forest Avenue. She toyed with the idea of taking the diary somewhere outside, maybe sitting at the beach and reading it. She'd found a beach chair in the garage, collected her hat and sunglasses along with the diary, but scrapped it all at the last second. She didn't want to read or to think. All she wanted to do was just decompress for a few hours and a walk to the beach would be the best way to do that.

As she turned west on Main Street, the realtor's words floated through her thoughts, *things have changed a lot around here.* There was evidence of that everywhere. All the store fronts were occupied. Cars filled every available parking place along the street. People were already lined up on the sidewalk waiting for a table in Dinghy's, a place where she'd bussed tables during her senior year of high school. She peered in the windows at Betsie Bay Furniture and Design, an upscale store with beautiful furniture and accent pieces. *Expensive,* she thought. *A store like this likely wouldn't have made it back in the day. But now ...*

She came to Storm Cloud Brewing Company, another place filled to capacity with lines stretching down the sidewalk. Tall cloth signs in front of it fluttered in the lake breeze, advertising the company's latest and greatest beer offering. Just down the street from Storm Cloud was the iconic, old Garden Theater that had been beautifully restored and was staffed almost entirely with volunteers. She could smell the popcorn as a line hugged the building, queuing up for the five-thirty showing of *Manchester by the Sea.* She'd seen the previews, but didn't think it was anything she wanted to see right now.

Through the few breaks in the store fronts on the opposite side of Main Street, Anna could see the waterfront and the marina. Huge yachts and charter fishing boats bobbed at their deep-water berths, stretching their mooring lines as if anxiously waiting their masters to turn them loose on Lake Michigan's blue waters. None of this was as she remembered.

The beach was a big surprise. What had once been just "beach" was now a full-blown park, with benches and play apparatus for kids. And there were crowds, throngs of people, walking around both in and out of the water, lying on beach towels, and walking on the breakwater marking the northern boundary of the channel into Betsie Bay. She couldn't remember a single day in her growing up years when Frankfort had ever been this busy. *Maybe Grace was right. Maybe the house won't take long to sell.*

On the way home she came to L'Chayim Deli, the same place Charley had gotten sandwiches for their lunch. She was a bit hungry, so she stepped in and ordered a tuna salad on rye with a cup of their homemade cream of mushroom soup to go.

Next door to L'Chayim she browsed the windows of The Bookstore. She stepped in and soaked up its quaint charm, relaxed atmosphere and welcoming appeal. She met the owners, Barbara and Dwight, who, recognizing her, offered their condolences. She asked Barbara what book she'd recommend for a light read on her way back to DC, not anticipating that the diary she'd been given by Charley would take that long or be that interesting. Anna took her recommendation, told the couple what a charming store they had and promised to return again soon.

Once back at her mother's, she noticed the time as she stepped onto the front porch, six-thirty. *Too early to call Ed.* She noticed some comfortable-looking wicker chairs tucked in a corner of the porch, walked over and placed the sandwich and soup on the wicker table in front of the chairs while she went inside to retrieve the diary.

As Anna savored the first spoonful of soup and the first bite of her sandwich, she reflected on what she was going to tell Ed about the day's revelations. *Well, Ed, we've won the lottery!* was her first thought. *No,* she told herself. While she couldn't yet fathom what they might be, there were going to be some responsibilities associated with her inheritance. He was a lawyer. He liked details and she didn't have a lot of those just yet. *Just tell him Mother was a billionaire. Who knew?* With everything else she'd learned today, she hadn't stopped to think how that might impact their lives. While neither of them thought they were in the one percent that politicians were constantly talking about, they had a comfortable life. Their combined incomes were close to half a million a year. Their investments were growing in the wake of the Great Recession's strong recovery. *If there were ever two people who didn't need to inherit a billion dollars, it's us,* she thought. She figured she and Ed would have to work through this as the details of their inheritance became known to them. After another spoonful of soup and another bite of sandwich, Anna picked up the diary and opened it to the first page.

The hand was a neat script, written in what Anna thought was likely a pen of the type that required dipping into the ink every few words or so. It was a bit hard to read because the indigo ink had faded unevenly with age. But she wanted to savor every word of this, her newly discovered family history.

This is the diary of Mary Aileen Sullivan
Born: October 18, 1867, County Cork, Ireland
Departed Liverpool, England, aboard the Abyssinia.
September 15, 1885
Arrived New York City, October 8, 1885

October 10, 1885
I am, indeed, lucky. I survived a miserable voyage, crammed into steerage with others like myself, desperate to do anything to find a better life than the one we all left in Ireland, a blighted country. Then, a gentleman, I don't even recall his good name, who said he was from Tammany Hall met me after just a few steps onto this country's free soil. Well dressed, polite and offering to help me find work, he said he knew of a likely employer. I told him I had no money to reward his kindness. He said that didn't matter. His benefactor, if he likes me sufficiently to hire me, will pay him a "finder's fee." When I asked as to the line of work, he replied, "Housekeeper."

I started yesterday at the home of Mr. Connor

O'Day. A lovely home it is he shares with his wife and three children. I am his only housekeeper at present, and there is much work as I am responsible to cook and clean for the entire family and care for the youngest child, a girl, still in diapers. But I don't mind at all. I don't know what this "Tammany Hall" is exactly, but it must provide Mr. O'Day with a good salary. Without asking, he advanced me $20, a week's worth of salary. It is frivolous, I know, but I have used a fourth of that to purchase this beautiful book which will be a record of what I know will be success in this new land of plenty.

Anna, a fan of NPR's popular series, *Downton Abbey*, was immediately fascinated. She could almost picture her great-grandmother, sitting on the edge of her bed scrawling out her story in a dim light after working a long day in service to this family. She turned the page.

October 12, 1885

A daily routine is beginning to emerge. The family has breakfast together in the dining room. The two older children, both boys, leave for school. Mr. O'Day departs for work. Mrs. O'Day, who has not warmed to me as well as the rest of the family has, dresses and leaves. If she works, I have not heard mention of it. Perhaps she has friends, other wives of Tammany Hall employees, with whom she visits. The young daughter requires much of my attention as she is colicky, a condition which Mr. O'Day assures me she will outgrow. I have found it best if I carry her around with me as I set about making the beds, cleaning the house and preparing their meals, which thus far is only breakfast and supper. Mr.

O'Day tells me if he will be home for supper or not. Thus far he has been here for only one supper meal. He must work very hard at Tammany Hall. Because it is only me serving the O'Days, I am fortunate that I do not have to shop for groceries. A man comes by in the morning, I place the order with him and he brings it back for me to prepare. America seems to be the land of plenty that I thought it would be.

This move to America, a troublesome decision that took several years to come to, has proven, I think, to be a good one. My mother and father are gone and my only brother has moved to London where he seems to have found some success and happiness. What I have learned is that in these hard times, it is up to each of us to do exactly that—find our own success and happiness.

October 17, 1885
My room is on the third floor. Much of this part of the house is unfinished and used for storage, but my room is private, with its own door. I am provided with a wash basin, but I am permitted to use what the O'Days call a "bathroom," located in the children's wing of the second floor. While I have heard of such new conveniences, I have never experienced such.

The bathroom contains a tub and a faucet from which flows warm water for bathing. I have no idea where it comes from or how it is heated, but I enjoyed my first bath tonight after the children had gone to bed. There is also a stool, made of porcelain. I have never seen such an invention. Andrew, the eldest boy, showed me how it works. To remove the waste, all one has to do is pull a chain and it releases water

from a tank above. I asked him "where does it go?"
He did not know. Until tonight, I have not heard
any of the family after I have retreated to my room.
But just now, I heard voices, those of Mr. and Mrs.
O'Day, that seemed to be coming from the bottom of
my stairs. I could not hear the conversation clearly
and I did not think it was any of my business, but
Mrs. O'Day sounded angry and Mr. O'Day sounded
as if he had had too much to drink. Whatever the spat
was about, it appears to be over. Such things occur in
families. I can easily recall my father coming home
after a pub crawl and my mother expressing her dis-
pleasure. God rest both their souls. Tomorrow I will
turn nineteen. I have much to be thankful for.

October 25, 1885
I must leave this place. I must leave New York City.
Events of the evening leave me with no other choice.
My fear of Connor O'Day is overshadowed only by
my anger towards him. As I was preparing for bed,
he entered my room without knocking, but he was
not menacing at first. He said he wanted to pay me,
but it was not my scheduled date for that. As I tried
to explain it wasn't necessary, he placed his hand
over my mouth and with his other arm pulled me
toward him. I resisted, but he was much too strong.
I know he could see the panic in my eyes, but he was
oblivious, possessed of an animal strength which I
had never experienced. When he was finished with
me, he stood, adjusted his clothing in my mirror and
turned to me as I lay in the bed crying. He stood
over me and said, "My instruction was to find a lass
of solid build and pretty face. I should give my man
an extra commission for finding you." He tried to
stroke my hair, but I pulled away in disgust. His

tone changed to one of utter meanness. He told me if I should speak of this to anyone, he would see to it that I would work the rest of my life in one of New York's worst brothels. He said, "Do not be foolish and think that I cannot make that happen, Mary." With what he left on the washstand tonight, I have $30. I will leave tomorrow after that filthy man and his wife have gone for the day, after the boys have gone to school. I am sorry for the baby, but she will be fine for the few hours she is unattended, and I can think of no better present for me to leave this miserable man than a screaming child with a full diaper.

"Oh my God," Anna murmured. As a woman she was outraged. As a journalist she wanted to devour the rest of this woman's diary. This was her great-grandmother's life she was learning about for the first time. A smirk of satisfaction crossed her face. *I would have loved to have been there when the O'Days came home. Good for you, Mary Aileen Sullivan. Get the hell out of there.* She glanced at her watch. Eight o'clock. She called Ed's cell phone. "Are you home?'

"Yes, just got here before you called."

"You might want to be sitting down."

He laughed, "Let me guess, we're millionaires."

"Replace the *m* with a *b* and you've got it."

She waited for the longest time before Ed finally stammered out, "Uh ... uh ... you can't be serious."

CHAPTER SEVEN

In three words, I can sum up everything I've learned about life: it goes on.

—Robert Frost

Anna Shane could not sleep. It was four in the morning. Her insomnia was to be expected. So much had happened to her the previous day. In a single twenty-four-hour period she'd learned about a father she never knew who had lived apparently just a few miles from her and her mother. She learned that her mother actually had communicated with him over the years, but never had disclosed either his identity or his whereabouts to her. She'd learned that she was now a billionaire. And, after reading the first few pages of her great-grandmother's diary, she'd learned that she was descended, on her father's side, from an Irish immigrant, Mary Aileen Sullivan. Giving up on sleep, her curiosity getting the best of her, she turned on the bedside light, picked up the diary and opened it to where she'd left off.

October 28, 1885
Travel is frightening when you don't know one place from another. I write this in a train station in a place called Erie, Pennsylvania, where I plan on spending the night on a hard bench, but in out of the cold. I have no idea at this point by what means

my trip will progress. If there is anything about my escape from New York and Connor O'Day that makes it easier, it is that there is an abundance of other immigrants like me, most of them it seems, from Ireland, moving westward as well. We are like the blind leading the blind, and we rely on anything that we hear. Some of it is good information, some of it rumor and conjecture, but we move along. Many are headed to a place called Chicago. I will plan to go there, but travel from here will be more challenging as I appear to be at the end of this railway's line. My money is a concern. My train ticket to here took $5 of my $30. A few pennies bought me a crude map, so I am able to tell that I am headed in the right direction. I must continue to watch every cent. I have not eaten in the past day. Perhaps in the morning I can find my way out of here and find something to eat as well.

November 15, 1885

I had no idea of today's date. I had to ask someone not only what the date was, but what day of the week. As quickly as I made it from New York City to Erie, Pennsylvania, it has taken what seems like forever to travel from Erie to this place, Toledo, Ohio.

After what happened to me in New York City, I have made my way from Erie to here by traveling in wagons and only with families whom I judge of good moral values. The trek is arduous. There are few passages that might fairly be called roads. I would liken them more to trails, ruts in many spots. Quite often we have had to dismount the wagon and help the horses pull out of the deeper ones. Cooking is not easy; usually over an open fire. The weather is freezing most of the day now and certainly at night. I can't remember the last time I would say I was warm.

I have thus far traveled with five families. Four of them had children. Two of the mothers were pregnant. These women, three of them Irish, two Italian, were truly appreciative of my help with their children on the trek westward. Communication with the Italian families was a challenge as their English was little and my Italian nothing, but necessity spawns creativity and we learned to manage together. Last night, as we made camp at a favored spot just outside of town, I was able to speak to several other women whose families gathered here for the evening.

One of them told me she and her husband were heading north from here to a place called Manistee, Michigan. She said the place completely burned to the ground in 1871. Apparently, there was a dangerous storm with very high winds that swept across this part of America. The storm that burned Chicago to the ground is the same storm that burned down Manistee. Now, according to the woman I spoke to, Manistee has rebuilt. It has become a center for lumber which is cut, milled, and then shipped to Chicago as that city rebuilds. She spoke with her husband. They have agreed that I might join them on their trek north.

No one is exactly sure how far it is to Manistee. As I look on my map, Manistee is not shown, but we believe it will be about three hundred more miles; a bit farther than Chicago is from here. But, in all honesty, I have no desire to return to a big city. The last one did not treat me well. Why would Chicago prove different? Perhaps the smaller town of Manistee will be more to my liking.

December 15, 1885

It has taken us a month (I know this because I began keeping a crude calendar after my previous entry), but we have reached Manistee. Everyone is exhausted. The trip was daunting due to the snows and freezing temperatures. There were several days when we made no progress at all because of the snow. On those days we would huddle close to a fire, our only source of warmth. Our job then was to gather enough firewood to survive, though food was plentiful. Deer seem to be quite well populated in this part of America and Mr. Milligan is an excellent shot.

Tonight, we are able to take shelter in a boarding house in Manistee. The owner is a widow whom I have paid $5 for all of us to stay here and to take an evening meal with her. The family I have traveled with, the Milligans, would take no recompense from me before this. So, I am glad that I can provide all of us the comfort we enjoy this evening. We have become quite close and this is a friendship I hope will continue as we each establish our lives in Manistee, Michigan.

January 1, 1886

It is quite ironic. There is not a day goes by that I don't remember that loathsome Connor O'Day threatening me with a life in "one of New York's worst brothels." I ran away from New York ... I ran away from him ... because I would never submit to him again nor do such work as he promised for me if I should refuse him.

Yet, today I took a position in Manistee's finest whorehouse, or so I am told by its owner and the women who work here. I will not be one of the "working girls" though Miss Franny DeVine, the owner of DeVine's Delight, assures me I would have no dearth of customers should I want to try my hand at it. It was Mr. Milligan who recommended that I make a call at Miss DeVine's. In fairness to him, I should point out that he is not a patron, but that a co-worker of his told him of the place and that Miss DeVine was apparently looking for someone to work as housekeeper, laundress and seamstress to the ladies of the evening employed there by her.

Today I met most of the women who work here and they all seemed nice enough. Miss DeVine told me that is because the chores that I will do for them have been their responsibility for the last month since the last housekeeper left her employ. She also said that since I will not be "working," none of them felt me a threat to their clientele. So, I will take this job out of necessity (I am down to the last $1 of the $30 I left New York City with) while looking for something more respectable, although I am sure Miss DeVine's promised salary of $30 a week, room and board included, will be very difficult to match. I know from Mrs. Milligan that her husband makes only $20 a week at the mill where he has found employment.

Smiling, Anna closed the diary, but kept her index finger on the page. *Damn, my great-grandmother worked in a whorehouse. Hell, she lived in the damned place!* As Anna lay there, she found herself amped up by her great-grandmother's story. She toyed with the idea of picking up the phone and telling Ed about it, but it was five a.m. and she knew he would be sound asleep. This news was such a revelation to her though. Her great-grandmother had *chutzpah*. Anna was tempted to skip to the last few entries. She wanted to know right now how this would end. *No! Don't! Let her tell you this story piece by piece all these many years later.* She stacked another pillow behind her, shifted around until she was comfortable again and opened the diary to where she'd left off.

January 31, 1886
Miss Franny (a compromise: I called her "Miss Devine." She wanted "Franny." We settled on "Miss Franny") has been a most wonderful employer. She pays me well and faithfully the promised amount each week. The difficult trip to get here has proven to be well worth the sacrifice. Make no mistake. The work is hard. There are anywhere from 12 to15 women I must take care of daily, but I am not afraid of hard work. In fact, I consider my work less hard than the work they must do to earn their way in this world. But most of them, I have found, have tender hearts. Even the ones whose hearts seem hardened by the work they must do, still seem grateful for the work I do for them.

Miss Franny was one of them in Chicago. She was there during the Great Fire. She told me she barely escaped with her life. She said recovery from the fire there was slow. There was little to rebuild with. That is how she wound up in Manistee. She says she came to the source of the rebuilding supplies. In Manistee, lumber is king and the town is filled with the men who cut it, mill it, load it onto ships that will cross Lake Michigan to Chicago with it and the seamen who work on these many ships. Miss Franny realized the need for services like hers in this town, and hers is the finest establishment for the services these men want, providing they can pay the prevailing cost. I am told by several of the girls that the cost at Miss Franny's is nearly three or four times greater than at other like establishments.

She is very particular about the clientele she will allow her girls to serve. If a lumberman from one of the camps decides that he wants to pay the extra cost to be with one of Miss Franny's girls but he carries with him the "stink of the camp" (as Miss Franny calls it), he must first pay for a haircut, beard trim and bath, all of which Miss Franny is more than happy to provide at additional cost. I cannot be sure, but I would guess that the number of people in her employ on a daily basis is near 50 souls.
DeVine's Delight serves all manner of clientele, most through a public door. However, there is a private entrance at the rear of the business. I have not been permitted to go there. One of the girls who serves clientele through the public door said she hoped she would one day be able to work in this private area. She told me that it is accessible only to members ... members who have paid a fee to belong. Curiosity getting the best of me, I asked what the fee might be. She said she didn't know, but thought it was over $1000 a year on top of the cost of what one would do after entering. I cannot imagine having that kind of money to waste. There are, as best I am able to determine, only five or six girls who work in there. I do for them everything that I do for the other girls, but Miss Franny delivers everything to them including their meals. These girls are not allowed to associate with the other women at DeVine's Delight. The hopeful girl said that the men who come and go there do not want anyone to know who they are or

what they do there. She said she asked Miss Franny one day about working there and Miss Franny scolded her ... told her that no such room exists and she should never ask about it again ... that she didn't want rumors to spread.

While I can only suspect what must go on in the private area, I do know that it exists. In the kitchen a week or so ago, I met a huge man.. I had not seen him before; he said his name was Harold and that he'd just been hired as the doorman for "the back door." I will not ask Miss Franny about any of this. I do not want to anger her. But the private area is a curiosity to me.

February 15, 1886

It is late, I am exhausted and a full day of work lies ahead tomorrow, yet I cannot sleep until I write this. I have just returned from dinner with Michael and Estelle Milligan at their home. Estelle and I have remained close since our arrival together in Manistee. I see her frequently as she works at the millinery shop where I buy sewing supplies two or three times a week. I am very grateful for the Milligan's friendship, especially Estelle's. She has not judged me even a single second for where or for whom I work.

We were joined at dinner this evening by a man I judge to be about my same age. His name is Liam. He works with Michael at the mill. It was a wonderful evening and I found myself quite attracted to this new acquaintance, and I feel he was equally attracted to me; so much so that he walked me home to DeVine's Delight. I will not hide this from him. I work in a whorehouse. If he were to judge me because of this, then there is nothing for either of us to look forward to. As near as I can tell, he knew exactly where he was and he lodged no objection with me because of it. I hope I hear from Liam in the future.

February 16, 1886

I do not record my thoughts here every day. There isn't time. But tonight I must write that Liam contacted Estelle today at the millinery shop and indicated to her that he would like to see me again, unless I was being courted by another gentleman. Estelle tells me she assured him I was not. She told him that the best way to contact me would be to simply go to DeVine's Delight and ask to see me. I hope he will do exactly that.

February 17, 1886

Liam called on me today at work. Tomorrow evening he will call again and we shall go to dinner together. I am thrilled. I have put behind me what happened in New York City. It is over, in the past. My life must go on, and though we are just recent acquaintances, I can see a future with Liam.

The reading was slow going. The ink coloring was inconsistent—the result of one hundred thirty years of age. The script was thick and lavish, almost a type of calligraphy. Each letter was perfectly formed—the kind of penmanship taught back then by writing the same letter in countless repetitions—the kind of lessons all but abandoned in schools today, replaced by computers, iPads, iPhones, email and text messages.

As Anna studied the letters and words, she realized she

was, in all likelihood, looking at a soon-to-be extinct art form. It had taken her nearly an hour to wade through these last few passages and digest what she'd found there, but she was hooked.

She thought about her schedule for the remainder of the week. She wanted to be back to work by week's end, so that meant she could spare only two more days. That was it—that's what she'd tell Charley. Besides there was already an abundance of things she and Ed would need to talk about and she was sure DeBooker would add to that list today. She fluffed the pillow behind her and returned to reading.

February 27, 1886

I am this day a bit at odds with Miss Franny. This morning she came to me to tell me a particular gentleman has inquired after me. I reminded her that I have been seeing Liam. She knows who he is as he calls here to pick me up for our time together. She was quite brutal in her assessment of what I should do. "Forget him," she told me. "He is but a common man. The gentleman who has inquired after you is wealthy. He could provide for your every wish." When I asked the other suitor's name, Miss Franny would not tell me. I imagine he is a patron of the back door. Perhaps I can inquire of Harold, who sees to the back door. He has become my friend.

Liam, while not rich, is a good man and we get along well together. I have told Liam about what happened to me in New York City. He has been patient, kind and understanding. Why would I want to give that away for the likes of someone who wastes his money on private entrances and the women who await him on the other side of the back door?

March 2, 1886

I saw Harold today in the kitchen as he was eating his lunch. He offered up that I should be flattered that a very wealthy gentleman has inquired about me. When I asked his name, Harold, like Miss Franny, would not tell me. I dislike this entire situation very much. I am not interested in any man that must work through their agents to get to me. That was my downfall in New York City and I refuse to fall into the same trap again, so I told Harold that I am not the least bit interested in any further discussion about this man.

March 10, 1886

Tonight, Liam and I took dinner together at a local restaurant patronized by lumbermen. He has many friends among them and is well liked. I liked them too. Their humor is rough and their language is coarse, but they are without false airs of importance. They made me laugh.

Afterwards, I allowed Liam to take me to his apartment. His accommodations are spartan to say the least. A small single room with a bed, and a small wooden table with two straight-backed wooden chairs, but he keeps it neat and clean. A small coal-fired stove sat in the middle of a westward facing wall just below the room's only window. A smokestack vented out one of the window's panes. Liam started the coal burning, and as the room warmed, we sat at the table and he began to discuss a future he saw for us. I must say that I liked what he saw. For the first time I allowed him to kiss me and his touch was so gentle and warm that I consented to *his desire comfortably and without regret. I am in love with this man and he is in love with me.*

Anna thought this might be a good place to stop, but as she caught the first sentence of the next entry, she found its call irresistible.

March 21, 1886

The first day of spring this year is not a pleasant memory for me. As I stood in the kitchen preparing lunch for some of the women, a man approached me from behind and when he spoke, the surprise of it frightened me so that I nearly jumped onto the table-top. He said Harold had told him he might find me here. Polite enough, he apologized and proceeded to introduce himself. Mr. Clyde Fraley was dressed in an expensive black waistcoat with beaver-trimmed lapels. A diamond stick pin, as large a diamond as I can ever recall seeing, adorned the ascot around his neck. He wore gray slacks accented with black stripes that made him appear taller than he likely was. Everything was tailored to perfection.

He wasted no time in asking me if he could call on me this evening and perhaps take me to dinner at The Hapsburgs, a place I have heard of, but could never go because of its cost. Was this the man that Miss Franny and Harold mentioned to me? I still am not sure. Later I sought each out looking for confirmation. Both refused to say. I told Mr. Fraley that I was seeing someone. He asked if I was betrothed, to which I responded that I was not, as of yet. His response to my answer took me aback. "Then hope springs eternal in my heart." After that he turned on his heel and, without saying anything else, departed.

I have no interest in him. Further, I hope to never engage Mr. Clyde Fraley in conversation again. Something about him frightens me.

At seven, Anna placed her bookmark between the yellowed pages of the diary and gently closed it. She regretted having to stop there, but it was to be a busy day. Though she bore a great sense of pride in this woman she was coming to know, this last passage left her with an overwhelming sense of foreboding.

First she called Ed and told him her plans for the remainder of the week. Then she hurried through her work email, answering those requiring her immediate attention. She interrupted this task with a call at eight to Charley DeBooker. Charlotte Matthews answered the phone. "Charlotte, this is Anna Shane. Would Mr. DeBooker be available to meet with me at nine this morning?"

"Yes, of course, Mrs. Shane."

"Anna ... please call me Anna."

"Certainly, Anna. I will let Mr. DeBooker know you will be here at nine. Mark will pick you up."

"That won't be necessary. It's a short walk and it's a beautiful morning. I'll see you then."

CHAPTER EIGHT

Sometimes you'll get hurt and you won't get an apology ... that's fine because you're strong enough to move on without it.

—Sonja Parker, Children's Advocate, Perth, Australia

I t was a beautiful morning for Anna to walk the six or so blocks that separated her mother's home from Charley DeBooker's. Along the way, no fewer than three neighbors saw her and offered their condolences. Though she tried to remember, Anna just couldn't be sure if they had been among the many attending the funeral. She smiled remembering from her growing up years here that such kindnesses were common in the small towns that dot this part of Michigan, and she drew comfort from their thoughtfulness. In Manassas, Virginia, where she and Ed had lived for over twenty years, she knew only one of their neighbors and—when she stopped to think about it—she had to admit, they didn't know them very well beyond a passing wave as their lives rushed by.

As she opened the front door of DeBooker's office-home, Charlotte Matthews greeted her, "Good morning, Anna. Pleasant walk?"

"Good morning. Yes, very pleasant. I had forgotten how wonderful Frankfort can be this time of year. I spoke to my husband just an hour ago or so. He told me it's already ninety degrees in Virginia and it may reach one hundred today. It will be miserable there with the humidity."

"This is the time of year to be in northern Michigan, that's for sure. Before you go up, may I bring you something? Mr. DeBooker has already asked for his usual tea."

"That's very nice of you and, yes, I'll have a cup of coffee, black, please," Anna said as she realized that she had not yet had her permitted daily cup.

"I'll bring it straight away." She motioned up the stairs toward the attorney's office, "Mr. DeBooker is expecting you."

The office door was open and DeBooker sat in his desk chair, swiveled toward the windows, facing Lake Michigan. The high chairback blocked her view of him. She knocked lightly and announced herself.

Without turning to face her, DeBooker said, "Beautiful morning, isn't it?"

"Magnificent, Charley. How are you?"

Anna noticed a lag in his reply, and then the chair swiveled toward her. "On days like this your father and I would meet occasionally, and I would take him out on the boat."

His melancholy not lost on her, she asked, "So, he did come out of his shell at some point?"

"After your grandmother passed, he slowly gave up roaming the grounds at night."

"So, eventually he led a normal life?"

"Well, as normal a life as can be expected of a Fraley man."

Had she not been reading Mary Sullivan's diary this remark would have been very cryptic. But she recalled her sense of earlier foreboding. "I started reading Mary's diary."

"But you're not through it completely?"

"No, so be careful not to give away the ending. It reads like a novel."

He chuckled, "Okay." Then he became more serious, "I'm glad you've taken my advice to read it, though. It's important for you to know about those beginnings, so you can understand how your mother and father wound up where they did."

Charlotte Matthews sat in front of her computer. The bug she'd planted earlier was state-of-the-art. The ear bud in her right ear allowed her to listen to every word of the conversation between attorney and client.

"Was he ever happy?" Anna asked.

"There was a time ... " DeBooker paused before answering. "He and your mother ... "

Anna seized on his words. "So, they were together?" She let her voice trail off as grief's long tentacles gripped her throat. A tear formed and trickled down her cheek.

Charley passed her another sparkling white linen handkerchief like the one he'd passed to her in Bill Jenkins's office at *The Post* a week or so earlier. "It was after Katherine's passing that your father started to come out of the darkness that Virgil and Katherine kept him in. I think your mother's presence in his life was a key factor in his healing in the seven years he lived after Katherine's death."

"How did he die, Charley?" She recognized her bluntness, but she wanted to know everything and she had precious little time remaining here in Frankfort.

"Cancer. His doctors believed it was his exposure to Agent Orange for all those years in Vietnam."

Anna knew about Agent Orange. She'd actually talked with some veterans at Walter Reed who suffered from its effects. Their conditions were painful and, in many cases, eventually fatal. "Mom was there when he died?"

"She was." The room fell silent.

Anna stared past him, out the window into the endlessly blue sky. A wave of guilt, this one tsunami-sized, swept over her. She had taken her mother for granted and, now, she was gone. And, this man, her father—whom she never knew, whose life was filled with such tragedy—was gone as well. "Did he know about ... " It was a question that kept popping up in her mind, but she was almost afraid to hear the answer. "Did he know about me?"

"He did, but not until you were already a successful reporter at *The Post;* long after you'd been gone from Frankfort. When he was struggling with his PTSD, your mother tried to protect the both of you by keeping each of you secret from the other. After he got better, she told him about you. He read *The Post* every day after that. He never missed one of your by-lines once he knew you were his daughter. He was so very proud of you, Anna."

Anna was in tears and jumped when the buzzer on the intercom sounded.

"Yes, Charlotte?" DeBooker said.

"Mr. DeBooker, Mark's here."

"Thank you. We'll be right down." DeBooker said to Anna, "If you don't mind, there's a place I'd like to take you this morning. There are some folks I'd like you to meet."

"Sure, Charley, but before we go, I must tell you I plan on leaving tomorrow. I have to get back to Washington." Anna could see that this came as a surprise to him.

"I see."

"May I ask Charlotte to schedule with NetJets for me?"

"To be honest, I wish we had more time together, but I do understand." He smiled warmly. "We can give Charlotte your details on the way out."

Anna reached over and took his hand in a gesture of pure gratitude. "Charley, I don't know how I would have ever gotten through this without you. Thanks for introducing me to my family."

CHAPTER NINE

*I have found that among its other benefits, giving
liberates the soul of the giver.*

—*Maya Angelou*

"Good morning, Anna," Mark O'Toole said in his light Irish brogue as he opened the car door for her.

"Good morning, Mark," Anna replied cheerfully and then asked, "Did you know my great-grandmother was from Ireland?"

Glancing first at Charley, as if he was looking for permission to answer her question, O'Toole replied, "Aye, Anna, I did."

After they'd settled in the car and O'Toole pulled away from the curb, Anna asked him quite innocently, "Did my father tell you about her?"

Both Charley DeBooker and Mark O'Toole had served the Fraley family for most of their adult lives. It would not be wrong to say they were both indebted to the family for their livelihoods. So, information about what they knew about whom was almost never revealed; suspicions, rumors and innuendo were taboo. But this was Anna, Margaret and Billy's daughter. O'Toole looked in the rearview mirror first at Charley and then at Anna. "Your father let me read her diary."

"Ohhh," his answer surprised her. "So, you know all the juicy family history."

A rather awkward silence fell over the passengers in the big BMW as it motored its way out of Frankfort, north up M-22.

Charley broke the silence by changing the subject, "Anna, I'm taking you to High Bluff House. I think a tour of the place will give you a good sense of what it is your father and mother had in mind. I know you told me you have never actually been there. So, you have no basis of comparison, but let me set the stage just a bit for you.

"Your father passed some ten years ago now. For most of that time the place was unoccupied. To say it was in a care-taker status would be an overstatement. Virtually no one ever went up there except me or the occasional contractor or a security guard from the firm I hired to keep an eye on the place after we had some minor vandalism. Just kids horsing around. After the first incident, we caught them on a security camera and their parents dealt with them; nothing more after that. Honestly, I am very thankful you never had to see it in the condition it had fallen into.

"Two years ago, your mother came to me with an idea ... an idea she said your father and she had been considering for the last seven or eight years of his life. She was finally ready to move forward with it."

Anna interrupted him, "What took her so long to decide?"

"Do you remember me telling you that your father, during Elizabeth's first attempt to get control of the Fraley Family Trust, made it a stipulation the trust must donate seventy-five percent of its annual income to charity?"

"I do. I believe you told me that was one key factor in the judge's decision to honor Katherine's wishes bequeathing the entire fortune to my father and leaving Elizabeth out in the cold."

"That's correct, and both your father and your mother were faithful about living up to that commitment. But they knew what they were planning would eventually impact the charitable organizations they had been supporting. Even as much as four or five years before your father died, they gave these organizations warning that the Fraley money was going away. So, they kept the donations going to those organizations up until 2015 in order to give them time to find replacement dollars." He handed her a folder. "You don't need to deal with this now, but here is a complete accounting of who those organizations were and how much they received year-by-year."

"Okay." She took the folder from him and put it in her handbag. "So, where we are going now is where the money has gone since then?"

DeBooker nodded, "At your mother's direction, I created a non-profit organization. Your mother was the chief executive officer, I am the secretary and Tom O'Brian, a CPA, is the treasurer."

"Did that raise some eyebrows with my cousin ... what's his name?"

"Ephraim, and yes, it did. I received several threatening phone calls from his attorney. I supplied him with all the documentation we'd gone through to establish the non-profit. After the third or fourth phone call, I heard nothing else.

"One of two things happened. I can't be sure, but either Ephraim Swain's attorney advised him there was nothing he could do, or Ephraim ran out of money to pay him for additional billable hours. I assure you, this is all completely on the up-and-up. The salient point is that for the last two years, all of the money generated by the trust's holdings plus a small amount of its corpus has gone into paying for what you will see today."

Mark slowed the car, pulled into a driveway, and stopped in front of a chain link gate that spanned the width of it. On either side of the drive's entrance were impressive field stone columns. Embedded in one of the columns was a bronze plague that read, HIGH BLUFF HOUSE and then under that, 1898. The other held a newer plaque reading, ANGELS' OVERWATCH; under that, ESTABLISHED 2015. Both columns were topped by magnificent bronze lamps. Tacked to numerous trees bordering the road near the driveway were yellow signs with large black print warning NO TRESPASSING, CONSTRUCTION SITE, VIOLATORS PROSECUTED. The dilapidated chain link gate looked terribly out of place between the two regal columns.

The signs were unfriendly, foreboding, and the chain link gate was just plain ugly. DeBooker immediately apologized for all of it. "When construction is complete, this atrocity will come down. Those signs will go away. The grounds, then, will be completely open to the public, but for the time being it is necessary to keep people out of the construction site and provide the contractors a measure of security for their equipment." Mark lowered his window, punched in a code and by way of a series of chains and amid the clatter of rattling and clanking, the gate slowly retreated from left to right.

The drive wound its way for nearly a mile through rather dense hardwood forests on both sides. Anna imagined her father roaming through these woods stuck in the throes of his PTSD. Then suddenly, around a final turn, they emerged into a huge open area across which they could see the vast expanse of Lake Michigan and the unblemished blue sky above it. It looked to Anna as if this might have been a well-cared for lawn in an earlier time. Now it was like an unattended pasture, dotted with grasses of different varieties and lengths with weeds springing up here and there.

DeBooker said, "Anna, eventually this will be greenspace, a park if you will, with all sorts of playground equipment, picnic tables, and again, all of it open to the public."

High Bluff House stood in the middle of this open space.

Most of the original structure was natural fieldstone, but it was now covered in scaffolding that supported half a dozen workers, while at least that many labored on the ground preparing more stone and mortar to be hoisted up to them. Toward the front of the old house, the side closer to Lake Michigan, Anna could see what looked like new construction that appeared to be attached to the old house. She was no expert, but roughly she estimated it would increase the house's square footage, which was already impressive, by at least five or six-fold. The outside of the new construction appeared to be nearly complete. A bronze-tone metal roof covered the entire structure, its color perfectly complementing the cedar planks workers were installing over the silver sheathing that clad the entire exterior of the new construction. Anna, trying to take all of this in, could only say, "Oh, my!"

O'Toole pulled the car to a stop at the apex of a semi-circular drive in front of two massive, gracefully arched wooden doors, which formed the entrance to the older part of the house. "Welcome to Angels' Overwatch at High Bluff House, Anna," DeBooker said, as he opened his door and O'Toole got out to help Anna.

As she got out and looked up, the front doors swung open. A woman and a little girl emerged from the house onto the front porch. Anna immediately recognized them—they were the mother and daughter who'd offered their tearful condolences at her mother's funeral. A third person, a man, was with them; Anna made the immediate assumption they were a family. She smiled at all of them as Charley did the introductions. "Anna I'd like you to meet Nora Schneider and her daughter, Jenny."

"Mrs. Shane, Jenny and I are so sorry for your loss, but we are very glad you were able to make the time to visit us this morning."

"Nora, thank you. It's nice to see you again. Please call me Anna." After shaking her hand, Anna bent down and offered her hand to the little girl. "Jenny, it's very nice to see you too."

"Mrs. Shane. I miss Grandma Margaret."

Nora caught the confused look on Anna's face. "That's what Jenny called your mother. We all miss her very much."

Charley introduced the gentleman. "Anna, this is Brian Gilbert. Brian is the architect who did the design work for this project."

"Good morning, Mrs. Shane," he said as he extended his hand.

"Anna, Brian. Please call me Anna."

The architect nodded and after shaking her hand, reached over and shook Charley's. "Good to see you again, Charley." Then to everyone he said, "If you will all follow me ... "

Nora asked Charley, "Could Mark take Jenny to day camp? She wanted to be here to meet Anna, but she has asked if she could go after that."

"Certainly."

Playfully she patted her daughter on the back and pointed in the direction of Mark and the waiting car.

Anna said, "Thanks for being here, Jenny." The little girl waved at her as Nora took her other hand and the two headed toward the waiting car.

Nora, over her shoulder, said, "Thanks, Charley. I'll join you inside after I get her on her way."

They entered through the front doors into a spacious, but, as yet, unfurnished room with what looked to be rooms, perhaps offices, Anna quickly speculated, along the outside walls. They were small, maybe twelve feet by twelve feet, but each with its own window looking out onto the grounds. In the northwest corner a massive fieldstone fireplace ran from floor to ceiling with a raised hearth and a mantel made out of what looked like an old barn beam skillfully set into the fieldstone. Brian stopped after only a few paces, spread his arms wide and said, "Imagine this room as a library filled with shelves of books."

DeBooker tapped Anna on the shoulder. "Yes, and a public library at that. It will be named the Margaret Rogers Branch of the Frankfort Public Library System."

Anna smiled at him and said, "How perfect is that!"

The architect continued by pointing to the offices along one wall and waved his hand down the length of it, "And these offices will be filled with the residents of Angels' Overwatch, hard at work on building bright futures. Each resident family will have one of these. They might be small business incubators, or they might be study spaces for job retraining, or whatever the residents need them to be while they are here with us. Each office will be equipped with a computer, telephone, and internet service." He pointed an index finger toward the ceiling, "Above us, in this older part of High Bluff House, are two floors of residences: four apartments on each floor. These will be the larger ones with three bedrooms for those families with more than two children." Pointing to the silver doors of an elevator, he continued, "The entire complex is handicap accessible. This is one of three elevators serving the floors above us."

Anna's mind was in overdrive. *'Building bright futures' ... families ... children ... he's not talking about senior housing ... is this going to be low-income housing ... this is being built by a non-profit ... can't be high end condos ...*

Pointing to the west, the architect continued, "The new construction on the lakeside of the existing structure will contain twenty-four two-bedroom residences." By now they'd reached a hallway at the other end of the library. "Let's go to the conference room. I'd like to show Anna the drawings for the new wing."

As he spread architect's drawings over the conference room table, Anna's alert eye captured the square footage for each in the lower right-hand corner. This new space added just a little over five thousand square feet per floor, an astounding addition to the old mansion.

Using both hands to smooth out the first-floor drawing, he said, "The first floor contains a community center that is meant to be a meeting place, not only for residents, but for any non-profit organization within a five-county area who may schedule its usage without cost. It will contain a complete commercial kitchen and dining area accommodating up to one hundred fifty people for banquets, meetings, etc." Pointing to another space, he continued. "This is the residents' dining area. Residents will have the option of dining here, or if they should prefer, they may prepare meals in their own apartments." He focused their attention on another area, "In this area are the offices for the support staff. We envision a full-time nurse, three or four counselors, perhaps some job training and job placement staff. Again, these offices will be fully equipped." Then moving to the other two drawings, he said, "These are the two-bedroom residences: twelve on each of the two upper floors. Each residence, including the larger ones in the older section of the house, are independent living areas with two full baths, complete kitchens including granite counter tops, stainless steel appliances and garbage disposal. Every apartment will have cable TV and internet service. Each resident, ten years old and older will be supplied with a laptop which they may take with them when they make the decision that it's time to leave High Bluff House. All furnishings will be provided to the residents. I had hoped the interior designer could be here, but her business has her in Chicago today. I have seen her preliminary plans, however, and they are exceptionally good and, I might add, below budget," he said with a glance in Charley's direction from whom he got a nod and a smile. "These living spaces will be the homes our residents deserve while they are here with us."

Anna was impressed, but still had a nagging question. She asked, "I hope I don't sound like a complete fool, but who are these *residents* to be?" She saw Brian glance at Charley, who, then glanced at Nora.

DeBooker said, "Nora, I think you're the right person to answer that question, don't you?"

"Yes, Charley, I am."

Anna shifted her attention to the thirty-something Nora Schneider whose long, brunette hair was pulled back into a ponytail, giving her a youthful appearance that exuded confidence. Dressed in tan slacks, white blouse and tan shoes with a modest heel that added nicely to her already tall and slender build, Nora smiled warmly at Anna and began, "High Bluff House will be for people like Jenny and me." She let that sit there for the briefest of moments, averting her eyes from everyone in the room as one might do before telling a story that is deeply personal. She took a deep breath and began again, "Two years ago, my husband, Sergeant First Class William Schneider ... everyone called him Billy ... was killed in Iraq. Jenny and I were here in Frankfort. This is home for us. Billy and I were born here. Well, to make a long story short, I didn't know how Jenny and I were going to make it after we lost Billy. I was a stay-at-home mom and there were bills to pay. I was on the verge of losing our home when your mother found out about my situation. She met with me ... and Jenny. She had an idea and she wanted to know if I might be interested in helping her pull it off. She wanted to take an old, dilapidated mansion that she'd inherited and turn it into a haven for people like me who have lost the love of their life to war.

"She wanted this place to be full of all the essential services that someone struggling with such a loss might need; affordable housing, transportation, counseling, medical care, job training, access to things that otherwise might be financially out of reach. She asked me if I wanted to help others like myself. She asked if I'd take on the job of being the first family to test her theory.

"It wasn't easy at first. Jenny didn't want to move out of our house. She felt like it was losing her daddy all over again, until your mother took her directly under her wing. She was like the grandmother Jenny doesn't have. Billy was raised in foster care and my parents are both gone. Your mother was great!" Nora's voice began to crack a little.

Anna's throat tightened and she blinked back tears. The room was quiet except for the muffled sounds of construction going on outside.

"By this time next year, there will be thirty-two single-parent families living here. The terrible thing we will all have in common is that we have lost a spouse to war. The wonderful thing we will have in common is all the time and support we will need to climb out of the hole that a loss like that puts you in. This is a place where people like Jenny and I can begin to move forward in our lives. Residents will be able to stay here for as long as they need in order to be on their own again. I worried about slackers ... someone who might move here and never have the ambition to leave. Your mother dismissed the idea. She said to me, 'Nora, it will be the job of you and every other resident not to let that happen. Encourage them, challenge them, don't let them rest until they wake up and seize the day'."

Anna was shaken to the core by Nora's story. She could not hold back the tears. *Why even try?* Anna stepped around DeBooker, who was standing between them, and held out her arms. As the two women embraced, Anna whispered, "I am so very sorry for your loss. I had no idea." She held on to her for a long time as her mind went back to Walter Reed and all of the victims of war she'd seen there. When she stepped back from Nora, she had to wipe away the tears rolling down her cheeks. Then she said to everyone, "What you are doing here is amazing. I don't know exactly what I have to do at this point to support you, but Charley and I will talk about that."

Nora wasn't quite finished. "It warms my heart to hear you say that, because your mother and I envisioned High Bluff House as the prototype for Angels' Overwatch. Anna, there are people like Jenny and me all over this country. Every state needs a High Bluff House and an Angels' Overwatch. Some could even use two or three. Angels' Overwatch is a project like no other."

On the drive back to Charley's office, Anna asked him, "My mom saw a lot of her own situation in Nora and Jenny, didn't she? I mean, even their names ... Billy ... "

"The idea for Angels' Overwatch came about well before your mother ever met Nora Schneider. But you're right. After your mother heard of Nora and Jenny's situation, she was struck by the similarities. She took it as a sign that she really needed to commit to the idea of Angels' Overwatch. A year ago, High Bluff House was basically an abandoned old house. Today ... well, you saw for yourself."

Charlotte Matthews sat at her desk, earbuds in each ear, fingers poised over the keyboard as if she were about to begin transcribing something. She stared into the empty computer screen as she listened to the conversation taking place in the office above her.

"So, tell me, Charley, what do I need to do?"

"Just before your mother passed, we were working on the idea of creating an Angels' Overwatch Foundation and doing away with the non-profit organization we currently operate under."

"Okay, I'm guessing there is a reason for making that move."

"There is, but with the plan your mother and I discussed, there are some financial ramifications that you need to consider."

"Such as?"

"Currently, The Fraley Family Trust merely contributes to Angels' Overwatch, a separate non-profit organization, which has no legal connection to the trust. Your mother and I were in the process of drawing up papers that would, first, liquidate the non-profit organization, and second, transfer all of the money in the Fraley Family Trust to The Angels' Overwatch Foundation. This would forever guarantee that the facility you saw today and others like it would be the sole recipient of the Foundation's money. It would also guarantee that neither Ephraim Swain nor anyone else could ever get their hands on the money in the Fraley Family Trust, which would be liquidated by the transfer of funds from one to the other."

Anna nodded, "Shrewd."

"We ... that being, your mother, Brian Gilbert, Nora Schneider, and I ... also think it will greatly aid in our ability to attract grants. Other charitable foundations, for example, the Kellogg Foundation in Battle Creek, Michigan, gives grants to organizations benefiting children, and Angels' Overwatch certainly does that. But, when an organization like the Kellogg Foundation does their due diligence and sees that the money goes to another foundation, one entirely dedicated to helping kids and their families, and one that has solid finances behind it, they are much more likely to approve the grant. Your inheritance is nearly a billion dollars and that makes Angels' Overwatch very sustainable. Other foundations contributing to it don't have to worry that their money might be going to something that might not be around in five or ten years. They like it that their money would go to something that will last ... " he paused, looking for the right word, "well, frankly, something that will last forever."

"So, what you're telling me is that mother was going to divest herself of any further interest in the Fraley Family Trust and turn the money over to Angels' Overwatch."

"Ah ... yes and no. The Angels' Overwatch Foundation would be controlled by an executive board and your mother was going to be that board's chair. Which brings me to my proposition that *you* would now be the board chair?"

One floor below, Charlotte waited for the answer.

Anna stared out the window behind DeBooker's desk into the azure blue sky and the blue-green waters of Lake Michigan below it for quite a while before she said, "I ... I can't answer that question, Charley, not without talking all of this over with Ed. I am in full support of Angels' Overwatch. I don't think I have a problem turning the trust into a foundation. My mother didn't, obviously, so why should I? I think you may go ahead and begin drawing up the necessary paperwork." She paused. "I ... I don't know when I'll get back to Frankfort. I hope you understand. I need to get back to work. There's so much going on in Washington these days."

"Take whatever time you may need. Tell Ed to call me with any legal questions he may have. I am at your complete disposal. I hope you know that."

"I know that. I can't thank you enough for all your kindnesses over the past week. It's been difficult, but you have certainly done your share to ease the burden. Ed and I will take a look at coming back over the Labor Day holiday."

Charlotte quickly glanced at the calendar lying next to her computer's keyboard. That gave her about six weeks to eliminate three people.

That evening Charlotte sat in the kitchen of her small apartment above a gift shop overlooking Frankfort's Main Street. Below her, tourists bustled about looking for their dinner, some ice cream treat, that perfect beach souvenir, beach read, or beach T-shirt. She picked up the burner phone lying on the table in front of her and punched in a number. An hour later, the burner rang and she answered it.

"Didn't expect to hear from you so soon," Ephraim Swain said without introduction.

"Didn't expect to have to call you so soon," was her reply.

"What's up?"

"The price, Ephraim."

"We had a deal, Charlotte ... "

"We did and that deal said I had six months to kill three people. The problem is that I no longer have that kind of time. I have six weeks. So, it's going to cost you a million more for me to do this job."

Swain seethed.

"They are going ahead with the plan to move the money from the trust to a foundation. If they do that, you will be locked out forever. Killing three people this quickly and this close together increases my risk, and let's face it, I'm the one who's got it all hanging out here. So, the cost of my increased risk gets passed on to you. That makes it two-point five million. What's it going to be?"

"What happens if I refuse?"

"The money passes you by."

"Give me back the $750K I've advanced you!"

"Nope."

"You bitch!"

She laughed. "Sucks to be you, Ephraim, and the answer is still no."

"Charlotte, you better not ... "

She interrupted him, knowing he had no choice in the

matter, "Ephraim, if you want to get your hands on that money, you'd better put another half a million in my offshore account in the next couple of days or you will lose your only chance." She hung up on him. The phone rang. She didn't bother to answer. Nothing else needed to be said. Either the money would show up or it wouldn't. If it did, she'd kill three more people in the next month or so. If it didn't, then she'd just made the easiest million dollars ever. She opened her laptop, connected to the internet and began to follow an idea she had. She googled the deceased golfer, Payne Stewart.

CHAPTER TEN

*I weep for the liberty of my country when I see
at this early day of its successful experiment
that corruption has been imputed to the House of
Representatives and the rights of the people have
been bartered for promise of office.*

— *President Andrew Jackson, 1825*

Burl Smyth pulled his black Cadillac CTS into the parking lot of The Southern Cross Restaurant in Biloxi, Mississippi, just before 4:00 p.m. on Wednesday afternoon. His wife thought he was in Oxford, Mississippi, for a meeting. This gathering was supposed to be clandestine, and most of the time he took pride in his vanity license plate, but right now he wished it didn't read, CHJUST1. He didn't care much for Biloxi. *Dirty place!* he thought as he got out of the car. *Fuckin' hot too.* The Southern Cross wasn't directly on the Gulf of Mexico, only a mere two blocks away. But on this late August day in 2017, it wouldn't have mattered. There wasn't a breath of air blowing off the Gulf. The water was as flat and smooth as a mirror.

The owner of The Southern Cross, Judd Cross, was a fraternity brother. Fifteen years ago, shortly after they'd graduated from the University of Mississippi, or more simply as it was referred to by everyone in these parts, Ole Miss, Judd inherited this business from his family. Burl Smythe had matriculated to law school, graduated, passed the bar and become a prosecutor in Jackson. In 2008 he made a good run for State Attorney General but failed, and then in 2009, he ran for the Jackson district's seat on the state's Supreme Court and won. Five years ago, after a spate of unexpected early retirements by other justices, he became the chief justice of that court as its most senior member.

"Judd, how ya doin'?" Burl bellowed, extending his hand. Smythe was a true son of the south and a verbal chameleon. If the truth were known, he much preferred talking in the deep rich drawl that could switch pronouns and verbs around easily or sometimes even just leave them out all together to create a sense of downhome at-ease not duplicated in any other of America's regional dialects. In Jackson, however, he would have said, *Judd, how are you?*

"Great, Burl. How you been?"

"Fine. Jus' fine."

"I've got your room ready. It's jus' the four of you, right?"

"Yep. I'm early. Coupla things I need if possible. This group ... " he paused, choosing his words carefully, "well, this group is special. We gonna be discussin' some things that ... " another pause, "well, let's just say they somewhat sensitive. We don't want any interruptions."

"I understand, Burl."

"I knew you would, Judd." Then, trying to lighten things up a bit, he said, "But these guys like to eat too. Know what I mean?"

Judd laughed and nodded.

"So, what I'd like to do is order a bunch of food and just have you put it in the room for us. Have it in there say about 5:30 this evening. We jus' eat family-style like it was a buffet or sumthin'. We all scotch drinkers, so send in a bottle of Chivas, some glasses and some ice and we be all set, Judd. Put everythin' on one bill and give it to me," Smythe said, playing up his role as this group's leader. "Tell your waitress she be well taken care of. Give us a pretty one, please, Judd. You got one of those around, don'tcha?" Smythe winked.

"Same ol' Burl. Room's this way," and he motioned for the judge to follow him.

Smythe hadn't been alone in the room for more than a minute, two at the most, when there was a knock at the door. "Come in," he bellowed. The waitress opened the door. "Well, ol' Judd did good," the lechery obvious in Smythe's voice.

"Pardon me?" she asked even though she'd heard him and caught the quick up and down the old fool had given her.

Unembarrassed, he gave a wave of his hand, "Nothin', darlin'. Lemme look at that menu and I'll tell you what we gonna have to eat tonight."

She handed him a menu. He looked it over and ordered an amount of food that would have been sufficient to feed eight people. She asked, "There're only four of you?" as she pointed to the table set for four.

"Yes, darlin', but them other boys are big eaters."

Noticing his sizeable girth, she merely nodded.

"Now, listen here. I don't know if Judd told you or not, but we have some sensitive matters to discuss here tonight. Your sign is going to be that room door, right there," and he pointed to the open door. "If that door is open, you can come on in and check on us. But, if it's closed, I'd like you to stay out. Don't even knock. I'll let you know if we should need anythin'. Is that clear, darlin'?"

She hated his condescending attitude, his thick southern accent and the way the word *darlin'* slithered off the end of his tongue. *You lecherous ol' cracker. Bet you runnin' a Klan meetin' here, aren't you?* Yet she took a breath and said, "Yes, sir. I understand."

"That's good. So, have the food in the room at 5:30 along with that bottle of spirits that I asked Judd for. Get that done and there's a nice tip in it for you, darlin'."

"Yes, sir."

"And would you mind closin' the door on your way out? I got a little preparation I have to do before the others get here."

"Yes, sir."

Alone now, Smythe reached in his briefcase and pulled out a scanner. He swept the room for any kind of listening device or other electronic gadget that might possibly allow anyone else to hear what they would be discussing.

An hour later, the others began to arrive. Burl Smythe greeted Walter Thompson, state representative from Alabama's 42nd District, then Bill Roth, State Senator from Georgia's 4th District and, finally, Steve Miller, who owned fifty car dealerships spread across Florida and Georgia.

Smythe closed the room door and announced, "Okay, gentlemen, you all know the drill." He held out a bag. "Cell phones off. Put 'em in here." Then he took the same scanner he'd used to sweep the room and scanned each of his companions. No one objected. These precautions were part of their routine at these quarterly get-togethers. When they were each satisfied that the other wasn't trying to record or in some other way attempting to eavesdrop on the other, Smythe waved his hand toward the waiting food. "Let's eat, and then we can talk."

The main item of discussion this evening was whether or not the Southern Sector of The Brotherhood of American Loyalists was going to recommend to the national headquarters another member, Mr. Lane Stubblefield, Missouri's Congressman from the 5th District, to the U.S. House of Representatives.

But before Smythe could get to that agenda item, Miller had something he had to get off his chest. "Burl, can I just say I'm not at all happy that Luckridge seems to be playing fast and loose with three million of the Brotherhood's dollars. Did you know he was doing that?"

Smythe, his paranoia showing a little, asked, "How did you hear about that?"

"Relax ... heard it from a brother on the national board, Henry Barker. He sells cars too. A fuckin' bunch more than I do. He's probably got a hundred dealerships spread across New England. We were at a conference. Took dinner together one night."

Not happy that things about the Brotherhood were being discussed outside the regular— and well secured—meeting rooms, Smythe thought of calling Miller to task for it, but decided to relent. After all, Miller had just made a two-million-dollar contribution to the Brotherhood. Smythe replied, "Bob Luckridge called me. It's an investment opportunity. Pretty good one ... some risk ... but I trust Luckridge. If he says we should invest the money, then I told him to go ahead. He had my support as the chief of the southern sector."

"Okay, but mind telling me what the return on investment might be?"

This was one of the things Smythe didn't like about Miller. He was a businessman, always wanting to know the money to be made. That wasn't what the Brotherhood was about. It was about making America great again,like the president says. "ROI's strong."

Miller persisted, "How strong?"

The other two were paying attention now. Smythe lowered his voice, "We invest this three million now and a year from now, we get three hundred fifty million."

"Jesus, Burl. That's not strong, that's fuckin' crazy. Never heard of such an investment. What's Luckridge got to do to get that kind of pay back, kill somebody?"

Burl Smythe tried to laugh it off, but Miller persisted. "C'mon, Burl, you can tell us. What's Luckridge got up his sleeve to get that kind of ROI?"

Smythe took on a serious look, glancing at each of them. "Listen, gentlemen, Bob Luckridge is *the* single most important conservative law maker we got in Washington right now. He's the insurance we have against Trump fuckin' things up for every conservative everywhere. Let's face it. Trump's really a foul ball down the third base line that the umps just happened to miss. Yeah, sure, he's brought true conservatism back into Washington again. But which one of you, at this point, is willing to bet a million dollars he'll get reelected in 2020?" When no one offered to pony up to that challenge, Smythe continued, "Even if he does manage to get reelected, we only got him until 2024 at the most. What the Brotherhood stands for has only just begun to take root. We gonna need somebody beyond 2024. Mark my words, Luckridge will be there for a long, long time after that, and he will be the one who drives the kind of conservative government we all want for the long term ... long after Trump's out of the picture. I'll be honest with you, I don't specifically know what this investment is, but I trust Bob Luckridge's decisions. If he decided this three million is a good shot, then I'm all in. You should be too."

Miller started to say something, but Walt Thompson interrupted him. "Give it a rest, Steve. Burl's right. I trust Luckridge." To which Bill Roth offered his support. Miller quieted.

Smythe said, "All right then, gentlemen. Shall we get on with discussing Mr. Stubblefield's nomination for membership into the Brotherhood?"

Somewhere around 9:00 p.m., Smythe gave his platinum credit card to Judd Cross who ran it. The judge included a one-hundred-dollar tip, signed it and handed it back. "That little waitress you gave me tonight is a cutie. You tappin' that, Judd?"

Cross, now a quiet, hardworking family man, despite

those years at Ole Miss and the frat parties, shook his head. During those years, if Cross had been a partier, Smythe's reputation put his to shame. "Thanks for the business, Burl. Keep us in mind if you should come down this way again."

"Will do, Judd. Will do." Once Smythe reached his car, even before starting it, he reached in the glove box, retrieved the burner phone he had in there and placed a call. It went to voice mail. Per protocol, Smythe disconnected and began the drive back to Jackson and home.

An hour later, the loud ring of the phone jolted him out of his road trance. "Bob, thanks for getting back."

"What can I do for you, Burl?"

"We had a meeting tonight to discuss a new member we are going to be recommending to you."

"Okay."

"But that's not the reason I'm calling."

"What *is* the reason, Burl?"

People overly impressed with their own importance often react to others with impatience and Smythe knew that Robert Luckridge was one of these people. "One of my guys, Steven Miller, asked some rather pointed questions tonight. Seems he and Henry Barker were at some kind of car dealers' convention and talking about the three million dollars the Brotherhood loaned out the other day."

Luckridge immediately took up the defense. "That money will earn us more ... "

Now it was Smythe's chance to become impatient. "Relax, Bob. I assured him the ROI was beyond comprehension. He bought that. I just thought you might want to know that there were at least two of our members who were questioning what you'd done. I didn't like it and I sure don't like membership talkin' about The Brotherhood outside of our secure meeting rooms. I'm sure you don't either."

There was a prolonged silence and then, "Burl, thanks for the call. I appreciate it and you're right; I don't like it."

"I didn't get into it with Miller, but he *is* one of my guys. If you'd like me to, I'm more than happy to set him straight. I know we need these business people in with us. They bring us a lot of money. But he's just a fuckin' car salesman, for cryin' out loud. I eat guys like him for lunch once a day and twice on Sunday in court. Happy to do it, Bob."

"No, Burl. Not necessary."

There was a long pause. Smythe said, "Bob ... you there?"

He wasn't. Luckridge had disconnected the call.

"You're fuckin' welcome, senator," Smythe snarled to no one. Checking the car's navigation system, he saw he had another hundred miles to home. "Hope you remember those of us who had your back when the time comes, you self-important prick."

CHAPTER ELEVEN

When you know what a man wants, you know who he is, and how to move him.

—*George R.R. Martin,* A Storm of Swords

It was mid-afternoon when Anna returned to her mother's home after visiting Angels' Overwatch. The first thing she noticed is that the realtor had already placed a lock box on the front door and a For Sale sign was prominent in the front yard. These things shot another ripple of guilt through her. *You couldn't come back here to visit your mother. Now that you're back, you just can't wait to get out of this town, can you?* She was never more than a moment away from guilt's grip, it seemed. It wasn't so much that she wanted to leave as it was a matter of having to leave. She watched the cable news feeds. She could see what was going on back in DC. Besides, she had already given her travel requirements to Charlotte who had confirmed with NetJets that the aircraft would be in Manistee at 10:00 a.m. tomorrow. She had checked with Mark just now as he dropped her off that he would pick her up here at 9:00 a.m.. She quickly packed her suitcase with everything except what she would wear home tomorrow, and the few toiletries she would require between now and then. Checking her phone messages and emails, she discovered there was nothing that couldn't wait, but she did take a moment to send a group email to her office telling everyone she'd be at work the day after tomorrow.

Her great-grandmother's diary was calling to her, yet she wasn't quite ready to close herself off in Mary Sullivan's world, not after what she'd seen and heard on the morning's tour. What her mother was doing was a wonderful thing. That's what she'd tell Ed. *We can't simply turn our backs on what my mother and father started.* She stood at her bedroom window looking up at a cloudless sky and decided to take another walk to the beach, probably stop at L'Chayim on the way home and pick up another sandwich and maybe some more of their great mushroom soup.

At 6:30 that evening she spoke to Ed while he was driving home from his office. She told him she had much to tell him, but she didn't want to do it over the phone. They agreed that he'd be home by six tomorrow evening and they'd go to dinner and discuss everything. At 7:30 p.m. she crawled into bed, put three pillows behind her back, and opened the diary to her bookmark. She recalled the sense of foreboding she'd had as she closed it earlier that morning. *Clyde Fraley has come into your life. What's he want?* She suspected she already knew, but wanted to hear it from her great-grandmother. Anna opened the diary and picked up where she'd left off.

April 1, 1886
Liam told me tonight that he has been asked to become a lumber looker for the company that owns the mill where he has been working. He is very excited because the job will pay him a lot more money than he makes even as a foreman at the mill. When I asked what a lumber looker does, he became quiet and I became concerned. Their job is to go out

into the wilderness and find tracts of lumber to be cut the following season. I foresaw the issue. He will be gone for months at a time. When I asked where he will stay, where he will take his meals, he laughed at my naiveté. On good nights he will sleep under the stars. On stormy nights he has a canvas tent for shelter. He will pack some basic supplies, but food will be what he hunts. I asked if this is something that he really wanted to do. I told him that I will worry about his safety the entire time he is gone.

I know from my trek from Toledo to Manistee how rough Michigan can be, and the country north of Manistee where he will be looking is, I believe, some of Michigan's densest wilderness. I asked him if this is really worth the extra money he will make. He told me that he hates the idea of being gone from me, but he is willing to put up with that hardship so he can better provide for us later. He said he will make enough in a year doing this work, that he can buy us a home here in town. He told me his company has promised him he can revert to his foreman's job after a year if that is what he'd like. I have many fears about all of this, but I love him. He wants what is best for us and I trust him that his plan for us is a good one.

April 10, 1886

I am sad today. Liam has just departed Manistee headed into northern Michigan's wilderness, looking for new stands of trees to be cut for lumber. He has with him a mule, Amos, who bears all his supplies and will be his only companion for the next three months. We have talked of marriage. We

*would like to wed in the summer of next year. I love
this man so very much and I will miss him dearly.*

July 4, 1886
*My head is light from the beer I drank tonight with
Michael and Estelle Milligan as we celebrated Independence Day. This is the first time I have been able
to share in the kind of joy that marks the founding
of this new country of mine. My heart is also light
tonight, because Liam should be home in the next
few days ending his first 90 days as a lumber looker.
I hope he and Amos are safe and that he has found
many acres of trees for his company.*

July 15, 1886
*Liam has not yet returned. My hope is that he has
had such success that his travels took him perhaps
a week or two farther into the wilderness, which will
require a week or two longer for his return to me. I
can be patient, but I so long to see him again and
hold him in my arms.*

July 21, 1886
*Mr. Clyde Fraley sought me out again at work.
Again, he asked me to Hapsburgs for dinner. I
reminded him I was promised to another. That piece
of information did not seem to dissuade him. He
said he can be patient. This man continues to dis-
turb my thoughts.*

August 1, 1886
Liam has not yet returned. I have begun to worry.

Michael has asked around the mill if anyone has any news of Liam. All he has been able to discern is that lumber lookers go out and come back with little information in between.

August 13, 1886

As I began work this morning, Miss Franny came to get me. She pointed to the front door and said there was someone here to see me. It was Liam. My heart nearly leaped from my chest as I saw him and Amos standing there at the foot of the steps. Words cannot express my relief. He was paid earlier this afternoon for the information he brought back to his company. It is a king's ransom. Liam told me it is twice as much as he expected; $2000. He has agreed to another round of lumber looking. I was not thrilled at this news, but he reminded me that I had agreed to a year of it. It is part of his plan. So, I cannot dwell on his departure back into the wilderness a month from now. I must live in the moment and cherish this time we have together.

As I write this, Liam is asleep in the bed behind me. We have just made beautiful love. We are staying in a spare room at Michael and Estelle's. They are both at work and their son is at school. Liam was not comfortable staying in my room at Miss Franny's, a position I understood completely. The Milligan's know we will be wed, so they turn a blind eye to what some would call sinful. Perhaps it is because of where I work, but I do not care what other people may think. His absence has made me realize how much I am in love with him, so I am more than comfortable granting him liberties that are, in the sight of God, reserved only for married people.

Anna smiled in relief. To her, everything seemed to be right in the world again.

September 12, 1886

Liam and Amos left today. The last month has passed in the blink of an eye. He promised to be home for Christmas, but I know that the time between now and then will pass much more slowly.

November 20, 1886

I am pregnant with Liam's child. Miss Franny has offered the services of the doctor she uses here at Devine's Delight who is quite familiar with such occurrences. It was disturbing to me when she suggested that this doctor might be able to "fix things." Apparently, he does this with some frequency for the girls who work here. I told her that I would entertain no such idea. This is Liam's and my child. Miss Franny laughed at me. Sometimes she can be terribly cruel.

December 5, 1886

I have started to show my condition. Today, as I was in town shopping, I crossed paths with Mr. Clyde Fraley. I had hoped he hadn't seen me, but such was not the case. He feigned congratulations and then was quite snide. Pointing to my stomach, he said, "Perhaps you should consider marriage as soon as possible." His comment struck me as odd. It was cold today. I was wearing gloves. How did he know that I did not have on a wedding ring? He does not know Liam by name. I have been careful not to disclose the name of my suitor to him. Yet he acted as if he knew exactly that I was not married yet to the baby's father. He is, I fear, watching me somehow and that continues to frighten me.

December 25, 1886

I celebrated Christmas today with Michael and Estelle. Tonight, as I write this, it is snowing heavily outside. I think of Liam and Amos huddled somewhere in the wilderness making a future for us and our child. I long for him to be home. I want him here when the child he does not yet know about is born. I will insist that this is his last trek as a lumber looker.

January 1, 1887

New Year's Day and no Liam. He was late the last time. I have no reason to expect different this time.

January 31, 1887

A month has passed since my last entry. The baby grows bigger inside me, but beyond that there is little in my life without Liam's safe return to us.

February 15, 1887

Liam where are you? Are you and Amos safe? You are nearly two months overdue. Please come home to us.

Anna glanced at the clock on the bedside table; two hours had passed. There was a lump in her throat, a knot in her stomach and she could feel the first tear roll down her cheek. It was as if the diary were alive in her hands. Through it she could feel the baby growing in her great-grandmother's womb and the pain increasing daily in her heart. Anna got up, went to the kitchen and took a drink of ice water. *What happened to Liam?* She let the investigative reporter inside her emerge. *Does Fraley have something to do with this?* Returning to the bedroom, she fluffed the pillows behind her, crawled back in bed and began reading again.

March 15, 1887
The winter has been a terrible one. I have a dreadful fear that Liam has in some way fallen victim to it. The doctor says that our baby is due in mid-June. I desperately want Liam to be here when the time comes. Liam, my love, where are you?

April 12, 1887
Harold, whom I have always thought of as a friend, came to see me today in the kitchen. He said Mr. Fraley had asked him to inquire as to my "availability." The audacity of both men! I told Harold my "availability" was to be no concern of his. As to Mr. Fraley, I have but few words for the man and all of them are loathly.

June 20, 1886
A week ago, our baby was born—a boy, healthy and strong, like his father. I have named him Liam. Without his father here with us, my heart is only half full with this birth. Miss Franny and the other women at Devine's Delight have become my life-line. They dote on me and more so on baby Liam.

These women, whose lives must be so devoid of true love, never cease to amaze me with their tenderness towards us.

July 4, 1887

I recall a year ago celebrating this nation's independence with Michael and Estelle and hoping for Liam's return. This year, I fear that my love will not return. Today I also learned through Michael, as we talked about his work at the mill, that the mill and the lumber company that supplies it are owned by the same person, Mrs. Isabelle Fraley. I asked him if he knew if she was of any relation to Mr. Clyde Fraley. I told him that Mr. Clyde Fraley had sought to be a suitor, but I refused him because of my devotion to Liam. He said he did not know, explaining these people were too far removed from his work as a mere foreman at the mill. But he did promise to make a few discreet inquires.

July 6, 1887

Michael told me today that Mr. Clyde Fraley is Mrs. Isabelle Fraley's only son. She is the widow of Mr. Silas Fraley and is the only woman to head up any of the lumber companies operating in Michigan today. He got this information from the mill's supervisor who told Michael that while Mrs. Fraley is a very good businesswoman and employer, her son, Clyde, is less so and that I should be careful if he continues to pursue me. While this is frightening, I feel I must speak to Mrs. Fraley about Liam's disappearance.

July 10, 1887

I was granted a few minutes today to speak to Mrs. Isabelle Fraley about my Liam. She was of no help except to tell me that her son handles that end of the business that employs lumber lookers and that I should speak to him. I despise it that I must talk with Mr. Clyde Fraley, but he may be the key to unlocking Liam's whereabouts. I have watched the girls at Miss Franny's manipulate men to do things for them. I am not so naïve as to lack understanding of what it is that attracts him to me. I am not the powerless woman I was when Mr. Connor O'Day assaulted me that night in New York City. I will use my power to find out where my Liam is and then I will go to him. Through Harold, I have left word that I would consider having dinner with Mr. Clyde Fraley at The Hapsburgs if he might be so inclined as to invite me again.

Anna could feel the urge to sleep overtaking her. It had been a good day, an informative one. She didn't want to stop reading, but as she thought ahead, there would be time tomorrow on the trip back to Virginia. She yawned, reluctantly picked up her bookmark, placed it between the diary's pages, and within a minute or two, fell asleep.

CHAPTER TWELVE

... and what is a good weapon but a good idea made murderous flesh?

—*Paul Hoffman,* The Last Four Things

Four days after her conversation with Ephraim Swain, Charlotte Matthews was able to see another five hundred thousand dollars in her off-shore bank account. She celebrated with dinner at Rock's Landing, a hip little restaurant located just north of Frankfort, wedged between the edge of M-22 and Crystal Lake at a fork in the road locals call Chimney Corners. Now back at her apartment, she sent a quick text to a New York number on her iPhone. Innocuous enough, it read, *Long time since we've spoken. Is now a good time?* Minutes later came the reply, *212 417-9902.* She picked up one of the burner phones Ephraim had supplied her and punched in the number.

"Hello."

"Mick?"

"Yeah. Charlotte. That you? How are you, sweet cheeks?" The voice was deep, harsh, and heavily accented with a New York City/ Brooklyn brogue.

Mick Janes was the biggest chauvinist pig she knew, but he was also the best "fixer" in the business. It didn't matter what or who you needed to pull off a job, Mick always *knew a guy.* "You ol' fucker. You always know the right things to say to a girl," she said in her most sarcastic tone.

"What's it gonna take to get you back to New York? I enjoyed our dinner together the last time you were here, and it turned out to be profitable for both of us. Maybe the next time we could take things to the next level."

From her previous dealings with him, Charlotte knew this sonuvabitch wanted to get in her pants. She also knew that was never going to happen, but he was a valuable resource in her line of work and not someone she could just tell to fuck off. So she played along. "I don't know, Mick. I'm kind of busy, but I'll keep you in mind. For now though, I need a real specialist."

"Specialist, huh? Shit, Charlotte, specialists are my specialty."

"Need an explosives guy; a really good one. The job is going be on an aircraft, but there are some strict requirements for the job."

"For instance?"

"For instance, the fuckin' thing has to keep on flying after the bomb detonates," she paused, realizing the difficulty of what she was asking. Then she added, "It has to fly until it runs out of fuel."

"What the fuck, Charlotte? Who you workin' for now, Al Quaeda?"

"Privileged information, Mick. You know that. But my source has some pretty deep pockets."

"Well, you gonna need those too, girlfriend." Mick paused, then said, "I gotta guy ... "

"Knew you would, Mick."

"Used him a coupla times before, but nothin' quite as technical soundin' as this job. He was expensive before, or so I'm told. He prefers to work out the financial details with the one who's employin' him directly. Know what I mean, Charlotte?"

She did. "Yeah, Mick. So, what's your end if me and this guy hook up?"

He laughed, "If you and this guy hook up, just let me watch."

Jesus, you never give up, do you? She shot back at him, "Fuck you, Mick. Stop jerkin' off and tell me how much."

"My end's fifty K. Twenty-five before I make the call ... non-refundable. Twenty-five after he's done what you need him to do."

It was highway robbery. All Mick was going to do was call the guy, give him this number and some idea of what she was looking for, and then his job was done. In other words, fifty thousand dollars for about two minutes' worth of work. But she had little choice in the matter. This wasn't like looking up a plumber on Home Advisor. "Okay, you son of a bitch." Charlotte heard him chuckling. "Have him call me on this number, it's a burner. What's his name anyway?"

"Charlotte, you know better than that. What the fuck other explosives guy is gonna call you and say he's callin' about blowin' up an airplane 'cept the one I'm gonna call?"

"Okay, okay," she relented. "I'll transfer the money tomorrow. Same account?"

"Yep, after I see the money, you'll get the call. Good luck with this one, darlin'. Sounds like a bitch of a job to me."

"Goodbye, Mick."

Charlotte had read everything online that she could find on the airplane accident that killed professional golfer Payne Stewart, two of his agents, a golf course architect and two pilots. On October 25, 1999, Stewart's rented Lear Jet 35 took off from Orlando, Florida, on a flight to Dallas, Texas. The flight was routine until reaching a reporting station over Cross, Florida, at thirty-nine thousand feet, at which point it should have turned from a northerly direction to a westerly one. When that did not happen and no radio contact could be made with the pilots, air traffic controllers declared an emergency. Over the course of the next three hours or so, the nation followed the flight of the ghost plane as it was shadowed by U.S. Air Force F-16s, whose pilots reported the Lear did not appear damaged, with the exception of an opaque windscreen and dark passenger cabin windows. Despite getting precariously close, the F-16 pilots could detect no life on board and there was speculation that everyone had to be dead. At this altitude, if the thing had depressurized, the temperature inside the airplane was somewhere around minus forty degrees Fahrenheit. They shadowed the doomed aircraft until it ran out of fuel over Edmunds County, South Dakota, where it spiraled to the ground. The final report by the National Transportation Safety Board concluded there was likely a pressurization problem, and a subsequent failure of the pilots and passengers to access the supplemental oxygen system before they succumbed to the effects of hypoxia and hypothermia.

It was equally easy to research the aircraft that would likely fly Anna and Ed Shane back to Manistee from Virginia. Ed Shane's law firm, Shane, Lawson & Keats, leased a Gulfstream G650. The firm's website freely advertised this information to include a flight schedule as it became known. Other attorneys and businesses in the Washington area could schedule a seat on any flight or even charter the aircraft from Shane, Lawson & Keats. While they were far from a scheduled airline, this was a way of offsetting the cost of leasing the G650.

Charlotte correctly calculated that use of the law firm's aircraft was important because NetJets operated a fleet of aircraft that would make it impossible for her to tell her *mechanic* which airplane to target or where that airplane might be located in time for him to get in, rig his explosive charge and get out. The law firm's aircraft, on the other hand, was hangered at Reagan National Airport when not in use. If the Shane's couldn't come up with the idea to use the law firm's aircraft to come back to Michigan, then she could make the suggestion. The idea made perfect sense. She was sure she could convince them.

That was it; her way to kill Ed and Anna Shane at the same time. They would board the G650 together enroute to Manistee. Her mechanic would get access to the aircraft before taking off, the "how" of this, left up to him as part of his exorbitant fee. The explosive charge would detonate at altitude and be sufficiently strong to depressurize the aircraft and disable the supplemental oxygen system, but not disable its flight control systems, including the aircraft's autopilot. At a cruising speed of nearly six hundred miles per hour and a range of over three thousand miles, on nearly a due westerly heading from DC to Manistee, she calculated it would run out of fuel somewhere over the Pacific Ocean. The likelihood that there would be any wreckage for the NTSB to sift through following the crash was near zero. All she needed now was to let her mechanic know when the Shanes would be returning to Frankfort. She had no idea at this point when that might be, but she didn't think it would be very long. DeBooker was eager to gin up the paperwork and make the Trust go away and Angels' Overwatch Foundation begin. *Get these two out of the way and ol' Charley will be a piece of cake.* She leaned back in the kitchen chair, poured a shot of scotch and let it slide warmly down the back of her throat, content she had everything well under control.

CHAPTER THIRTEEN

When we try to develop an understanding of things we can do and the powers we have, we will have several revelations about our real self.

—Dr. Prem Jagyasi

Anna watched Mark O'Toole pull to the curb, glad he was fifteen minutes early. Dragging her suitcase behind her, she stepped out onto the front porch. She caught O'Toole's eye and he immediately got out and headed up the walk to help. "I'm early."

"Yes, and since you are, I have a favor to ask. Would it be possible to take me to my father's grave before we head to Manistee?"

O'Toole took her luggage and smiled. "Sure, it's just a wee bit up the road."

They stood in the shade of a huge oak tree. The bronze plate at the foot of the grave read:

WILLIAM P. FRALEY
SSG, 25TH DIV VIETNAM
25 JUNE 1949 - 3 OCTOBER 2007

Anna stood over it, staring down, a complete range of emotions coursing through her, but guilt not among them. *I can't feel guilty that I never knew you. You could have* ... there was a lump suddenly in her throat. *Dammit, you and Mother took the decision to know you or not to know you completely out of my hands. How is that right? I would have liked you. I know I would. You weren't like your father ... or your mother either. Look at what you and Mother were going to do with all your money. I'm sorry we never met, but I had no say in the matter.* She suddenly was a little ashamed that she wasn't crying; so much had been denied her, but she didn't shed a single tear.

"The Fraley family plot is up there," Mark said, pointing in a northerly direction, up a hill in front of them. "Your dad wanted no part of being buried with all of them."

Absently, she asked him, "What's the P stand for?"

Mark smiled and replied, "Phineas."

Anna looked at him and laughed, "You're kidding?"

"No, ma'am. Your father hated that name. The only reason it's on there is that the Army wouldn't let him enlist with just his initial. They told him if he had a middle name, it had to be spelled out on his entry paperwork. When he tried to tell them he didn't have a middle name, his recruiter had already seen the P on his driver's license and didn't believe him. He made him produce a birth certificate. I'm sure he's up there in heaven, thankful that they only put the P on his bloody grave marker!" Mark was laughing.

"You knew my dad pretty well."

A mischievous smile and another chuckle, "Well, good enough that when I wanted to get under his skin all I had to do was call him Phineas."

"Is it some kind of family name?"

"If it is, neither Charley, your father nor I ever heard of a Phineas. We both decided that it was just another way your grandfather messed with your dad." There was a rather long pause and then Mark added, the humor gone now from his voice, "Virgil was a real sonuvabitch." Then he caught himself, "I ... I'm sorry, ma'am. I shouldn't say things like that."

"No, Mark. It's okay. Believe me, I've heard much worse around the newsroom, and besides, Charley's told me much the same thing about Virgil."

Mark looked at his watch. "Nine-fifteen. We'd best be going. Your plane is scheduled for a 10:00 a.m. departure. It'll take us thirty minutes to get to the airport."

Before she left, Anna bent down and touched the grave marker. "Sorry. I wish I could have gotten to know you better than this, but I'll be back."

Anna was the only passenger aboard the NetJets flight. The co-pilot got her settled into her seat, and told her the flight time today would be right at two hours. As the plane taxied for takeoff, she retrieved the diary from her handbag and opened it to where she'd left off.

July 15, 1887

Tonight, I dined at The Hapsburg with Mr. Clyde Fraley. It was all very elegant. He is quite the dandy. Quite charming, I would have to admit. Though I tried to be discreet in my inquiry about Liam and his whereabouts, it was easy for him to see through me. He said when he had hired Liam as a lumber looker he did not know he was my suitor. He asked if Liam was the father of my baby and I told him the truth. Finally, he told me that he has no idea why Liam has not returned to Manistee after his departure last October. With little regard for my feelings he also offered that it is not unusual for lumber lookers not to return. Often, he said, they become traitorous to the company that sent them out and they sell their information on valuable tracts of lumber to other companies who simply pay them more for the information they have collected. I told him Liam would not do such a thing. His half-smile, half-sneer look at me was irritating.

July 20, 1887

Mr. Clyde Fraley and I dined together again at another elegant restaurant, The Lake House. The buggy ride there was quite nice and the view of Lake Manistee as the sun was setting was beautiful. On the ride home, Mr. Clyde Fraley tried to hold my hand. My refusal irritated him and he asked if I was still holding out hope that Liam was coming home. He said he'd made some discreet inquiries of other lumbermen and was told that Liam had done exactly what he'd suspected him of doing. He'd sold his information elsewhere. I still believe Liam incapable of such treachery and deceit as it applies not only to his employer, but to me as well, the mother of his child, although he has no way of knowing that he is a father. Little Liam continues to thrive at Miss Franny's. The women there are so kind to him ... and me.

July 26, 1887

A curious discovery today. I spoke to Harold as he came into the kitchen for lunch. He asked how things were proceeding with Mr. Clyde Fraley. I didn't care for the insinuation in his tone and told him so. I told him that I am still promised to Liam. He did not relent, instead telling me that Mr. Fraley has long been interested in me and I should be careful that I not discourage him.

In the course of our exchange, it came out that Harold thought Mr. Fraley had been very patient with me. He added that he would not be so patient. The idea that I would ever be with the likes of Harold was quite repulsive to me. But that is not the salient point. When I pursued the topic of Mr. Fraley's patience, Harold told me he'd given Mr. Fraley Liam's name months ago. Harold also disclosed that Mr. Fraley, some time ago, had told him he knew Liam was an employee of his at the mill here in town. Apparently, Mr. Clyde Fraley knew that Liam and I were in love even before he hired him as a lumber looker. I will inquire of him regarding his lie to me that he did not know Liam before sending him into the wilderness.

July 30, 1887

This will be my last entry for some time. At dinner two evenings ago, I asked Mr. Clyde Fraley if he took me for a fool. I asked if he didn't think I would find out that he knew about Liam from the outset. He asked about the source of my information, but I refused, although I don't know why I should feel obliged to protect Harold. Quite unashamedly, Mr. Clyde Fraley told me he'd paid Liam the sum of $5000 to go elsewhere and that Liam had been quite eager to do so. He asked me if I knew how much $5000 was, as if I should be very pleased that it took that much for Liam to leave me.

I am so very confused. I cannot believe Liam would betray me like this. I am so very angry and I have so confessed. Father Patrick told me I must say three Hail Marys and as many Our Fathers. Having done so, they have not diminished my desire to take revenge.

"Jesus," Anna murmured. She turned the page. The passage of time between diary entries was, by itself, dramatic and she could not help but wonder how Mary Sullivan had coped during the four years since her last entry. It wouldn't take her long to find out.

September 15, 1891

I married Clyde today. His mother despises me. She hoped he'd marry better, another wealthy lumberman's daughter perhaps. There are plenty around here. But Clyde is now mine and I will complicate his life as much as possible. I have started by spending his money. Our mansion here in Manistee will be completely electrified. He has ordered a horseless carriage for me. He denies me nothing, much to his mother's consternation, and this conflict pleases me to no end.

October 12, 1891

Clyde is so stupid. He thinks that I do not know, but Miss Franny and I have become good friends over the years, especially during the years I made Clyde court me. Everything I know about manipulating Clyde, I have learned from her. She is a master at it. Miss Franny and I speak often and I know that I am the only one with whom she breaks the confidence of the back door at Devine's Delight. I believe that is because she knows that I am now in the inner circle of the wealthy here in Manistee. I know Clyde still frequents the place. I delight in knowing that which he thinks I do not.

January 12, 1892

Today I am pleased to write that Mrs. Isabelle Fraley passed away just a few hours ago. Her stone-cold body still lies in her bed, the undertaker coming shortly to take her away. There will be a large funeral, many mourners, and though I will be among them, I will not be mourning her loss. I despise her as much as she despised me, but I was able to exact my revenge upon her just before she died. I told her it is my intention to bear Clyde a child, a repulsive condition that I must endure to exact my full revenge. Be it boy or girl, I told her just before she breathed her last that it will be my life-long intention to turn this child into the exact same kind of monster that her son is. It was gratifying to watch her twitch and struggle to breathe. She does not see her son as that monster. Of course not. She has spent a lifetime doting on him, spoiling him. Clyde is gone somewhere. I knew she would die before his return. I laugh because even if she'd wanted to warn someone of my deceitfulness she couldn't have. I controlled completely who came and went from her bedside during her last hours on this earth, and I made sure I was the only one she saw ... the last person she wanted to see would be the last person she saw. How ironic!

Anna stopped reading and flipped backward through the last few pages. *Jesus, Mary and Joseph ... how bad can things get for her? My great-grandmother, in four years, has transformed from a sweet, naïve young girl to a woman absorbed in ... what ... vengeance?* She returned to where she'd left off.

May 4, 1892

Today I bid farewell to Michael and Estelle Milligan. They are leaving Manistee to become farmers in Iowa. Michael says that the lumber will run out. He complains that men like Clyde have raped the land, never planting a single seedling as they cut acre after acre of virgin forest. I have no doubt he is right. Their son studies agriculture at The Agricultural College of the State of Michigan. What he learns there, Michael is sure, will sustain them in Iowa. I have remained close to Estelle even though I have seen much less of her over the last four or five years. She has told me she fears for my sanity. In honest conversations I have told her of my wish for revenge on Clyde. I still do not believe he has told me the truth about Liam's disappearance, but I will get to the bottom of it one day, I am confident. Estelle says she prays for me daily and lights candles for me at Guardian Angels Church. Ironically, this is the church that I have given a lot of Clyde's money to over the past few years. His money should do some good someplace.

January 3, 1893

Little Liam is six years old. He attends Catholic school and his marks are good. He studies without too much prodding. One day, he will attend seminary school, away from all the deceitfulness and hatred I bear for Clyde. As much as I love him, I must get him away from all of it, lest he become as ensnared in it as am I.

November 16, 1894

Clyde is as lucky as he is pathetic. He has expanded the family's business interests into banking. He is ruthless in this business, even more so than he is in the lumber industry. In that industry he kills forests. In banking, he eviscerates people's souls. I believe he loans money with the intention to fore-close on the borrower rather than to be repaid. He offers the debtor no room for error. No one likes him, least of all me. Yet everything he does results in more and more money. As hard as I try, I cannot spend it all.

May 5, 1895

This has been a tragic time for Clyde and I am buoyed up by his sorrow. A week or so ago, the family's mansion here in Manistee burned to the ground. The fire captain has blamed it on the electrification and some shoddy work that may have been done at the time of installation. Clyde believes that expla-nation, so I passively agree with it, even though I know it is incorrect. I took great pleasure in setting the horrid place ablaze. I have decided that I want to start anew and this is the first step. Little Liam is nine, still achieving high marks in school, but is still too young for seminary school. I must shield him as much as possible from Clyde, who is overly critical, unloving, and sometimes even hateful toward the boy.

August 30, 1895

I have told Clyde that I will not live with him in Manistee. Instead we will build a new mansion along Lake Michigan just north of Frankfort. He is not happy with the decision, but he has now decided he wants an heir. When I asked if he did not consider little Liam an heir, he remorselessly replied he did not. It is of little consequence to me. I have long planned for little Liam to be given to the church when he comes of proper age. The price of my new mansion is my agreement to produce an heir for Clyde, but I will give him one and only one. I am aware the Church tells us we should marry and procreate. But perhaps my promise is to Satan. None of this truly matters. He has agreed to the move north to Frankfort. I will take a suite of rooms at the Frankfort Inn and will oversee the construction of my new home. I will miss Miss Franny and some of the women at Devine's Delight, but I will not miss the boorish mix of the wealthy here in Manistee who are more Clyde's friends than mine. Where I used to work, my immigrant roots, my penniless background are all topics of hushed discussion among them. I am happy to leave them behind. As for Clyde, his offices are in Manistee, both for the lumber business and the banking end of things. He will find an apartment to keep here in Manistee and come to Frankfort when he can. I know he still maintains his membership to Miss Franny's back door. All of this is fine with me. I will only have to deal with him occasionally and, once an heir is produced, he will never touch me again.

November 29, 1895

I cannot spend the money Clyde makes. He has just made a major investment in westward rail expansion and already it is yielding him returns. Costs thus far on High Bluff House have exceeded half-a-million dollars and this is with lumber provided nearly free. Electrification, hot and cold running water, indoor plumbing, glass roofs that can be opened in warm weather, an indoor swimming pool, imported marble tile for floors and counters, the finest fabrics from Italy and France, and natural gas used to cook with and fire the massive boiler heating the mansion, have not made noticeable decreases in his accounts. The architect and the engineer have both been told, "price is not an object." Yet, I never hear from Clyde about these expenses. He visits Frankfort three, sometimes four times a month. He has sex with me when he is here. I hate this. These occasions are painful reminders of Connor O'Day. Yet I tolerate him. I will take my revenge in good time.

November 15, 1898

I am not sure if finding the diary today after nearly three years is a blessing to me or a curse. Little Liam and I moved into High Bluff House this past summer. I have only this day found the diary in one of the endless boxes I must unpack as we settle into this great house. Time passes slowly, so I have taken the time to read what I have written. It saddens me to see the woman I have become, but I am still gripped with overwhelming disappointment and anger. My beautiful son, Liam, is like a cut from a double-edged sword. On one side I bleed more love for him with each passing day. The other side of the wound, reminds me of what I lost when his father did not return to us and how much I hate Clyde's deceitfulness... and my own. Liam is of sufficient age to ask questions of his heritage. I avoid the issue with him. I tell him he is a child of God, and in a few years he will begin his studies to learn exactly what that means. I shield him as much as I can from Clyde, whose attitude reflects his rejection of this child. Liam is not his and it is apparent he believes he bears no responsibility to raise the boy. That attitude is fine with me. I can think of no redeeming trait that Clyde could teach him. I remain barren, likely because Clyde repulses me. However, I must bear him a child. It is part of my revenge ... and that has become my duty.

May 1, 1900

Today I learned of the death of Miss Franny Devine when I heard two women of means discussing it at tea. There was, I thought, both revile and relief in their voices. I suspect we share something in common. All of our husbands tended to Miss Franny's back door. I approached and asked if either of them knew the particular details of her demise. They acted as if they had no idea what I was talking about. It was a particular pleasure for me to inform them of Miss Franny's wonderful qualities of generosity, feeling and caring especially for those who were of her employ. One of them asked me how I knew of such things. Clyde's wealth has placed me at a much higher social standing in the Frankfort community than either of these two connivers. I told them that I used to work for Miss Franny and then without further explanation I left them standing there, mouths agape. It was some of the most fun I have had in years.

June 15, 1900

Liam is 14. It is time he sees the world. I have told Clyde that we are leaving Frankfort next month for that very purpose. We will begin by touring all of Europe. How long we will be gone is undetermined and Clyde has not bothered to ask. With all his money at our fingertips this will be the grandest tour.

August 21, 1904

I am saddened to the depths of my soul today. Liam has left for the Seminary. He is in God's hands now. I need not worry about him at all. I am at peace with this choice for him and for me.

July 12, 1905

I am 38 years old and now carry Clyde's progeny. My age makes this a dangerous condition, but I must bear this child. My revenge depends upon it.

January 4, 1906

Clyde is jubilant. I have given birth to a son he has named Virgil after some uncle he apparently admires. If Clyde admires the man, I would surely despise him. Now my revenge begins. I will not love this child. His care will be given over to nannies and I will pick the strictest of the lot to care for him. What he learns about life he will learn from Clyde and I am sure those lessons will be all about self-interest and deceit. To anyone who may read this account years from now, I apologize in advance for my abject bitterness. I know you must struggle with

*my complete rejection of a child I carried inside
of me for nine months. You must wonder how bitterness can build to such a crescendo. I am not able
to answer your question except to say that I have
become more bitter with each year that has passed
since I lost the only man I have ever loved, Liam.*

Anna turned the page just as she heard the jet's landing gear deploy. It was only a minor distraction as she had
already caught the first line of the next entry.

June 1, 1906
*This is the last entry I will make in this journal. My
desire for revenge is stronger now than ever. I have
often wondered if my anger has been misdirected.
I know now it was not. Clyde and I had an awful
argument this evening. He was drunk and I was in
no mood for his abusive advances. In the course of
the shouting he said he should have let Liam live.
He said I did not deserve the life of privilege he has
given me. I asked him what he meant by "let Liam
live." In his drunkenness, he admitted that he did
not pay Liam to leave me. Instead he paid two men
to follow him into the wilderness and murder him.
With this bit of information, I now curse this family
and all of its progeny. Anyone who touches the
Fraley wealth will live a tortured life.*

Anna sat in complete disbelief. *A curse! Virgil's life, Katherine's, my father's ... my mother's.* She had never believed
in such things. She didn't want to believe now ... *but look
at what happened to them.* She was jolted back to reality
as the jet's wheels touched down at Manassas Regional
Airport.

CHAPTER FOURTEEN

*A lot of people don't believe in curses. A lot of people
don't believe in yellow-spotted lizards either, but if
one bites you, it doesn't make a difference whether you
believe in it or not.*

—*Louis Sachar*, Holes

"Anna, honey, I'm home."

She was in the study at the rear of the
house, the diary, open to the last few
pages, lay in her lap. Quickly she closed it
and ran to Ed. "Oh my God, I am so glad you're home," she
said as she flung herself into his open arms.

They were an affectionate couple, often seen walking with
their arms around one another or holding hands. After
twenty-plus years of marriage the glow had not worn off.
Ed was glad she was home, but they'd been apart before,
for much longer periods of time, and he was a bit surprised
at this greeting. "Whoa, girl. Is everything all right?"

She looked up at him. "Can we go somewhere for dinner?
Somewhere quiet. I have so much to tell you."

He sensed a certain tension in her as he continued to hold
her against him. "Sure." He thought for a minute, "How
about that little Italian place in town on Main Street. I
can't remember the name, but I remember the last time
we ate there we had a nice little table in the corner all to
ourselves. And the food was good. Don't know about you,
but I'm starving."

Into his chest, she murmured, "Sounds perfect."

The waiter poured each of them a glass of wine and then sat the squatty, straw-covered bottle on the table between them. As he walked away, Ed looked at Anna, raised his glass and said, "Billionaire, smillionaire ... you can't beat this cheap Chianti with a plate of spaghetti and meatballs." They tapped glasses together. "So, tell me everything."

Anna had been planning what she'd say to Ed since she finished reading the diary, but now that she was at the point where she had his rapt attention, she faltered for a moment, took another sip of the wine and instead began telling Ed about her father. He listened without interruption. He was good at that. *It must be a skill that goes with his profession,* she thought.

When she was finished, he could only say, "All that time you were growing up in Frankfort he was right there." Ed shook his head, "But you didn't know it."

It was a bit hard to believe. And it hurt. She wanted to hold it against her father, but she wasn't oblivious to his pain either. She'd seen plenty of it in the eyes of vets at Walter Reed. She nodded at Ed and then began to tell him about Mary Aileen Sullivan. Their salad came. Ed ate his while she picked at hers and told the story. Their main course came and went. By the time Ed poured the last of the wine into her glass, she'd reached the end, "She put a curse on the Fraley money, Ed."

He looked at her in disbelief. "Anna, you don't really think ... "

"I know. I know. But look at them. Virgil, my grandfather, was as mean as they come. He made my father's life miserable. His wife, my grandmother, Katherine, lived in silent fear of both her husband and her son. And one of them ... either my father or Katherine ... probably shot and killed Virgil. And my poor mother! Can you imagine living and loving someone, bearing their child for Christ's sake, but never able to be together because your lives ... " She searched for the right words before finally shrugging and giving into profanity, "Can you imagine living like that because your lives are so fucked up?"

That night, after they'd gone to bed, Anna snuggled close to her husband. "You think I'm crazy, don't you?"

"No, I don't think that at all. You've been through a lot in a very short period of time. Think about it; a few days ago, you thought it was just you and your mother. Now you're a billionaire with a father you are just learning about and a whole family tree ... a full grown sonuvabitch ... with roots extending back to Ireland almost a century and a half ago. Sweetie, that's a lot to come to grips with."

She would rather have had him simply say, *No, you're not crazy*. But he didn't.

Weeks passed. Labor Day weekend came and went. Things at *The Washington Post* were crazy. It didn't matter if it was foreign policy or domestic policy, the Trump administration seemed to be all over the place. Anna's reporters would return from White House press briefings just shaking their heads.

Under the two previous administrations, there had been a solid working relationship between the White House and the press that allowed for contentiousness from time to time, but for the most part, it was a good conduit for information to pass back and forth. Anna had played a role in creating that. Now, under the Trump administration, the relationship was rapidly turning adversarial. It looked like the press was going to be spoon-fed only what the White House wanted to give it. Announcements were made from the press room dais as if they were facts not to be challenged. Questions by reporters were met often with anger and frequently went unanswered. If Anna had had a dollar for every time she'd had the thought, *America isn't supposed to be like this,* she could have retired an even wealthier woman. So, what was happening back in Frankfort, though important, wasn't always on her front burner.

She had managed frequent email contact with both Charley DeBooker and Nora Schneider about the progress at High Bluff House and Angels' Overwatch. Anna was particularly excited that Nora had forwarded to her the applications of four widows and one widower of soldiers killed in combat. Ed and Charley were in contact over the paperwork and the precise language that would establish Angels' Overwatch Foundation and the transfer of funds in their entirety from the Fraley Family Trust to the new foundation. This was lawyer work, and while Ed tried to go over all of it with Anna, between her duties at the newspaper and her interest in identifying the families who would live at Angels' Overwatch, she honestly had little interest and even less patience for the legalese. But both she and Ed knew it was time to get back to Frankfort, get papers signed, notarized and filed.

Anna called Charlotte Matthews on October 1, 2017, and said they'd like to arrive in Manistee on October 5 and they could stay until October 8. She confirmed Charley's availability and then told Charlotte NetJets would not be necessary. They would arrive via Ed's law firm's corporate jet, which was chartered by another Washington law firm to carry three other lawyers on to Bozeman, Montana. Anna was quite pleased to inform her that there would be no charge for their use of the jet. The other law firm was paying the freight for this trip. They would stay at Anna's mother's home. Though several offers had been made on it, Anna had refused them all. She planned on telling her high-school-now-turned-realtor-friend she was going to take it off the market, for a little while at least.

Immediately after the call from Anna, Charlotte Matthews told Charley she was going to break for lunch and asked if he'd like her to bring anything back for him. He'd declined. She didn't go to lunch. Instead, from the privacy of her apartment, she called her mechanic on a burner phone. "They are flying on the 5th from Reagan National…the corporate jet I told you about."

"You have got to be fuckin' kidding me. That's four days from now."

"What's the problem? You've known about the what and the where … you just needed to know the when, and I just gave that to you."

"Listen. I'm in Miami and I have to drive to DC. I can't just hop a flight, not even a private jet. They object to bringing on board the kind of shit I need to do what you want me to do."

She hated his condescending attitude. "For what I'm paying you, you should be getting on the road pretty soon, then."

"Fuck you. This short notice is going to cost you more."

Charlotte, even though she'd played the same game with Ephraim, was furious. She thought, *If I were face to face with you, you prick, I'd put one through your head.* But she wasn't and she needed this guy to do what he'd said he could do. She tried to call his bluff, "A deal is a deal … "

"Another hundred thousand."

"You sonuvabitch … "

"Okay, lady, but who you gonna call?"

He had her by the short hairs. "First off, you better come through. Second, you better hope you and I never meet face to face," Charlotte said.

"Listen, you're wasting my time. I ain't movin' out of Miami until I see another $100K in my offshore account. Get that done and I'm gone to DC."

Charlotte, still furious, hung up, opened her laptop and made the transfer.

October 1, 2017, was a day that did not end well. Within hours of Anna's call to Charlotte setting up their trip to Frankfort, some whacko in Las Vegas had begun spraying automatic weapons fire into a crowd below a high-rise hotel. In just a matter of minutes he'd killed fifty-eight people and injured another four hundred thirteen. Hospital emergency rooms looked like war zone hospitals. The nation looked to Trump to begin the healing while the cries for gun control measures started to proliferate on the nation's airwaves and in the print media.

On October 5, Anna Shane was on her way out the front door of their home to meet Ed at Reagan National for their flight to Manistee, when she got the call from her boss. "We just got word that the president is planning some big announcement. Typical, we have no idea what the substance is except it's about the Las Vegas shootings. I need you here, Anna, in case this turns out to be something we need to get on. If it turns out to be more of Trump's bullshit, then you can get out of here, I promise."

It was her job to cover this. Gun control had long ago moved from the category of *policy* to the realm of *politics* inside the beltway. "Is it Trump or someone from the NRA who's going to be briefing the press?" she said, only half jokingly.

He took from this that she was going to be heading into the office. Relief evident in his voice, he repeated, "Thanks, Anna. I promise if it's nothing, you can get out of here."

She called Ed, who was already at the airport. "Trump's promising something on the Vegas shootings. The paper's asked me to stick around and see what he's going to do. I need to be here for this, Ed."

There was a rather long pause. "Okay, honey. I get it, but I can't hold this flight up. These other three guys are on a tight timeline to get out to Bozeman."

"Sure, I understand. Go ahead. As soon as I get my arms around this, I'll take a commercial flight to Traverse City. Hopefully I can be there on Friday, but Saturday for sure. I promise."

"Okay."

She sensed his disappointment. She knew he'd been looking forward to this long weekend with her. "Sorry."

"No, it's okay. Really." Then he said, "Remember: Fair and Balanced."

It was a private joke between them, the Fox News byline, *Fair and Balanced*. "Fair and Balanced, it is," she replied laughing. "I love you. See you as soon as I can get there."

CHAPTER FIFTEEN

*When things can go wrong, they will go wrong
and at the worst possible time.*

　　　—Murphy's Law

The TV in the newsroom at *The Washington Post* was constantly tuned to MSNBC. Anna froze in front of it. "This is an NBC Special Report: A private jet enroute from Washington, DC, to Bozeman, Montana, has just been intercepted by U.S. Air Force jets after air traffic controllers declared a state of emergency when the jet missed a mandatory reporting point and failed to respond to numerous radio calls. Reminiscent of the tragic accident that killed professional golfer Payne Stewart, Air Force pilots report that both windscreens in the cockpit appear to be broken. The aircraft, a Gulfstream G650, leased by a Washington, DC-based law firm, continues in flight on a westward course at thirty-eight thousand feet. At that altitude it could take only a matter of seconds before the effects of hypoxia would cause unconsciousness and the temperature inside the aircraft to drop well below zero. There are six people on board including the two pilots. It is doubtful that anyone on board survived the aircraft's decompression. This has been an NBC Special Report. We will continue following this event and will update you as more is known."

Her hands were shaking almost uncontrollably, as her co-workers gathered around her. She retrieved her iPhone from her hip pocket and called Ed, but the call dropped to voice mail. She didn't leave a message. More people gathered around her.

In Frankfort, Charlotte Matthews clicked open her internet browser to search for an answer to a legal question Charley had posed to her earlier. As it opened, she read the headline: *Ghost aircraft heading west; 6 on board believed dead.* A smile crossed her face briefly, until she quickly determined the body count didn't add up. Anna had told her that it would be the three attorneys heading to Bozeman, along with her and Ed and the two pilots. That should be seven on board. The headline was reporting only six. *What the fuck ... ?*

Anna pushed her way past the crowd that had gathered around her in the newsroom. She was physically ill.

Her boss undertook crowd control duties, "Okay, everyone. Let's get back to work." As they slowly began to disburse, he pulled a young woman aside, a new reporter that he'd observed Anna had kind of taken under her wing. "Judy, go ... " he pointed after Anna. "Help her. Let me know what I can do." She nodded and went off. He turned to another reporter who was standing next to him. "Jesus, she was supposed to be on that flight ... first her mother, now Ed ... this is so fucked up."

The Gulfstream G650 spiraled into the Pacific Ocean over five hundred miles off the coast of British Columbia sometime in the late afternoon of October 5. A Canadian coast guard C-130 surveyed the crash site, observed some debris on the ocean's surface, but reported no signs of life in the vicinity. The aircrew tried desperately to pick up the ping from the aircraft's black boxes, but to no avail. The water here was deep—very deep—and they speculated that might be why they couldn't pick up any signal. They tried until their fuel situation required them to return to base. After that, no further effort was made to search for anyone or anything.

By 9:00 p.m., Charlotte's mechanic was calling her. "Where's the rest of my money?"

She snarled back into the phone, "You've gotten all the money from me you're gonna get, you sonuvabitch. The job's not done. The woman is still alive."

"That's not my fuckin' fault. My job was to take the plane out. I did that. Your job was to get everyone on board. You fucked up, not me."

Charlotte disconnected the call. The mechanic called back. She refused the call. Fifteen minutes later she had a text on her personal cell phone: *Need to talk to you. Call 212 636-4705.* It was Mick Janes, she was sure. *Shit!* She went to the kitchen drawer, found the burner phone and punched in the number.

"Charlotte, I've got a rather unhappy guy in Miami callin' me and sayin' bad things about you."

"Not payin' that fucker another red cent. He held me up for another hundred K above what we originally agreed on and then he didn't get the job ... "

"Shut the fuck up and listen to me. I could give a shit less about the financial arrangements between you and him. I told you from the beginning it was up to you and him to negotiate that. You're hurtin' my reputation with folks like him. Know what I mean?" He didn't give her time to answer. "If it gets around that Mick Janes hooks people up with other people who don't pay their bills, then people are gonna stop workin' for ol' Mick. I can't let that happen, Charlotte, not even for a nice piece of ass like yourself. Pay this guy what you owe him. Don't think about stiffin' 'im, 'cause if you do that, you're gonna make an enemy out of me and you won't like bein' in that position. Oh, yeah, and don't forget the twenty-five K you owe me on the backend of our deal. Gotta pay your bills, girl. Know what I mean?" This time he expected an answer.

"But, Mick ... "

"No fuckin' *'but Mick,'* Charlotte. Pay the man what you owe him. Pay me too." He hung up.

Mark O'Toole had been on the road since about 8:00 a.m. on October 5, taking Nora Schneider to a face-to-face interview with a recent war widow just over the Michigan-Indiana border. The car's radio was tuned to a Sirius XM station that played nothing but music and when it was turned off, the car was filled with conversation between the two; neither seemed to miss hearing the day's news.

It was about nine in the evening and he'd just dropped Nora off at High Bluff House. Hungry, he decided to stop at Dinghy's Restaurant & Bar for something to eat and a quick beer before heading home himself. On the TV above the bar, he heard the news about the ghost jet for the first time. By now, the news feeds were disclosing the names of the passengers. As he heard Ed Shane's name announced as one of the victims he could feel his stomach knot. He listened intently for Anna's name and when it didn't come, he felt a sense of relief which quickly turned to a deeper feeling of compassion for her. *First, your mother. Now, your husband.* It was late, but he found Charley DeBooker's number in his phone's directory and punched it in.

"Mark, I'm guessing you're calling because of the news?"

"I am, Charley. How can this be? Have you talked to Anna?"

"I have. She's at home and inconsolable as you might expect. I spoke to a young woman by the name of Judy. She's a co-worker of Anna's. She's with her now and will stay with her for as long as Anna wants."

Mark O'Toole wasn't necessarily a suspicious man, but he was a cautious one and a dark thought had crept across his consciousness. "Charley, you don't think someone might be trying ... " he tried to be delicate, but the thought he'd had was about as far from delicate as one could get. "I mean, there's a lot of money at stake here. You don't suppose that this thing that's killed Ed was some kind of an attempt ... " he gave up on being delicate, "to kill them both, do you? I mean Anna was supposed to be on that flight as well. Right? I remember you telling me you were going to pick them up at the airport in Manistee because I was on the road today with Nora."

"I don't know, Mark. I just don't know what to make of it right now. You're right, Anna was supposed to be on that flight. She canceled at the last minute because the paper needed her. I spoke only briefly with her. She is devastated, so I didn't want to press, but ... "

Mark O'Toole's mind was running a hundred miles an hour. "If someone's trying to kill her ... "

"Mark, it's too soon to—"

Mark started to voice his disagreement, but he backed off as another idea crossed his mind. There was someone he needed to talk to and after that he would reengage with Charley, perhaps as soon as tomorrow morning. As soon as he closed out his call with DeBooker, and in the quiet of his car parked at the curb in front of Dinghy's, he punched in a number from memory. When the call went to voice mail, he left a message, "Shawn, it's Dad. Call me when you get this. It's important."

CHAPTER SIXTEEN

*The key to risk management is never put yourself in a
position where you cannot live to fight another day.*
　　—*Richard S. Fuld, Jr.*

Ephraim Swain held the burner phone away from
his ear as Senator Robert Luckridge railed, "Are
you fuckin' crazy? Couldn't you find a more
public way to kill somebody?"

Swain didn't have many answers. He'd been trying since
the news broke to contact Charlotte and find out what the
hell was going on and why only Ed Shane was dead. He
knew the plan called for Anna Shane to be on that plane.
He desperately wanted to know what had gone wrong. Why
wasn't she dead as well? Swain had even gone so far as to
break the cardinal rule of no voice mails, leaving several on
a couple of her burners. But Charlotte continued to keep
him in the dark. "Look, Bob, I don't know what's going
on. I thought sure this was going to solve two of our three
problems. Yeah, I guess it was a bit showy ... "

Luckridge angrily broke in, *"Our three problems?* Let me
remind you, Ephraim, I don't have *three problems,* but you
sure as hell do!"

"I've got a call into Char—"

"You've got a call." Anger had now changed to con-
tempt in Luckridge's voice. "That's just fucking great!
Listen, Ephraim, my ass is on the line here. A couple of
the members of The Brotherhood have been asking some

questions about the loan I made you. Get hold of your girl, find out what the fuck she's doing and get back to me. Let me remind you, if there's no margin for error on my part, there certainly isn't any on your end."

A few days after his angry phone call with Ephraim Swain, Robert Luckridge sat alone at a corner table in the Senate Dining Room, thumbing through the newsfeed on his cell phone while he waited for the breakfast he'd just ordered. He was moving rapidly through the various articles looking for something in particular. In his haste, he skipped past what he'd been looking for; an article reported by CNN. Reversing the direction of his search, he stopped on it and began reading:

October 10, 2017

The Manchester New Hampshire Union Leader

Mr. Henry Barker, owner of numerous car dealerships throughout the northeast was killed last evening in a one car accident between Manchester and Hooksett, Massachusetts. Hooksett firefighters and EMS responded to the scene, but found Mr. Barker unresponsive. He was declared dead at the scene. There were no witnesses. The cause of the accident remains under investigation, but it is suspected that the driver may have fallen asleep at the wheel. Mr. Barker is survived by his wife and ...

Luckridge stopped reading. He could give a shit who Barker was survived by. *Fell asleep my ass! My guy did a good job with this one!* Looking up, he smiled broadly at the waiter as he placed his breakfast in front of him.

Two days later, at the same table, waiting again for his breakfast, Luckridge got a text on his personal cell phone from Burl Smythe asking him to call. The text included the number for Smythe's burner phone. This breach of The Brotherhood's security infuriated Luckridge. If a busy day of committee hearings didn't lie in front of him, he would have gone outside, called Smythe and taken him to task for it.

Late that evening, a still-angry Robert Luckridge called Burl Smythe from the privacy of his car parked next to the Tidal Basin with the illuminated Washington Monument in his rearview mirror. "Burl?" Luckridge snarled as Smythe answered.

"Bob, yes ... "

"Dammit, Burl, what the fuck is the matter with you. Do not ever contact me on my personal cell phone again for any reason. Why the hell do you think The Brotherhood gave you these burners, for Christ's sake?" The question was purely rhetorical. Smythe had no time to provide even the flimsiest of answers. "What the hell is so important that you'd breach security like that?"

"I ... I'm sorry, Bob, but I thought you should know."

"Know what?" was the impatient reply.

"Steve Miller's dead."

Luckridge didn't know, but wasn't surprised; just curious.

"What happened?"

"Don't know for sure. They found him drowned in the pool in his backyard in Columbia."

"Really?" Luckridge said, now trying to feign surprise.

"Odd, don't you think, both Barker and Miller turning up dead, so close to one another?"

"What the fuck are you tryin' to say, Burl?"

"I ... I didn't mean to offend ... "

Smythe's timid response, told him he had Smythe right where he wanted him. Luckridge asked, "Who else knows about Barker and Miller's conversation at that car dealers' conference?"

"Walt Thompson and Bill Roth were at the meeting where Miller brought it up." There was a pause and then Smythe added, "But you don't need to worry about those two guys, Bob. They told Miller to stop asking questions. Both of them know if you think it's a good idea, then loaning that money is good for The Brotherhood."

Luckridge relented, "Okay, just watch the security from now on, Burl." He paused, and then said, "Listen, I've been meaning to give you a call ever since I heard about Henry Barker getting killed in that car crash up there in New Hampshire. He was going to handle this for me, but that's obviously not going to happen now. I've got some important work that needs to be done that I can't do myself. So, maybe I could count on you. I don't want to talk about this on the phone ... not even this burner. Can you make some time to come to Washington?"

"Absolutely, Bob. Just say when and where and I'm there."

Luckridge could hear the relief in his voice. He smiled. Exactly the response he was hoping for. "Okay, let's have lunch tomorrow at the president's hotel here in DC. I'll make a one o'clock reservation at the restaurant there, BLT Prime. Can you make that, Burl?"

"I'll be there, Bob. Thanks."

Luckridge had long ago pegged Smythe as an ambitious suckass, but that was exactly the kind of person he needed to do what he was going to ask of him.

CHAPTER SEVENTEEN

Don't be afraid to ask questions. Don't be afraid to ask for help when you need it. I do that every day. Asking for help isn't a sign of weakness. It's a sign of strength.

—*Barack Obama*

"Where's Charlotte?" Mark O'Toole inquired as he made himself a cup of coffee in Charley DeBooker's kitchen.

"Gave her a week off," DeBooker replied. "She asked. First time off she's taken since she got here. Now's as good a time as any. Unfortunately, Anna's a mess."

O'Toole hung his head, "The funeral had to have been really hard ... no casket, no urn, just his picture. Sure doesn't help her get any closure on this thing, does it?" Then he asked, "I know it's probably way too soon to ask this question, but what do you think she's going to do?"

"That question, Mark, has so many different ramifications, I have no idea how to answer it. They love her at *The Post*. I'm sure they don't want to lose her. Selfishly, I'd like to see her just come home to Frankfort and become the Foundation's CEO. I know she has a great interest in Nora's work at Angels' Overwatch. Lord knows, she doesn't need

144

to worry about money. She's directing all the questions from Ed's law firm about buyouts, insurance settlements, and all of that to me. I'm going to have to refer some of it out to lawyers around here who are experts. Her tax implications alone are staggering."

Mark O'Toole had done something he wasn't at all sure Charley DeBooker would like. He drew a deep breath and asked, "Can we talk about something?"

"Yeah, sure. Let's go up to the office."

As he settled into the chair in front of Charley's desk, O'Toole began, "I may step on your toes a bit here, Charley. I don't mean to do that, but I have a gut feeling ..."

DeBooker held up a friendly hand, "You've been a friend of the Fraley family for many years, Mark. I'd be a fool if I didn't listen to you."

"Yeah, okay, Charley, but I've gone ahead and done something." Mark rubbed his rather sweaty palms down the seam of his pants.

"Whatever it is ... well, I will never doubt your good intentions."

"It's Shawn." O'Toole gave that a moment to sink in. "He's on his way here from Utah."

"I see." DeBooker said, caution and curiosity apparent in his voice.

"I know you're worried about Anna. I am, too, Charley, but while *you're* worried about her *mental* health, *I'm* more concerned with her *physical* well-being. Margaret's sudden death, now Ed's ... and what really bothers me more than anything else is that Anna was supposed to be on that plane with him. What if ..." O'Toole just let that hang there.

"What are you proposing, Mark?"

They had been friends for a very long time. DeBooker could be direct. Mark could too. More often than not, Mark demurred to the attorney, but not this time, "Charley, I'd like to ask Shawn to keep an eye on Anna. If someone is trying to kill her ... "

"Have you talked this over with Shawn?"

"He knows I think she might be in danger. He knows I think she needs someone to keep an eye on her. Beyond those two details, the answer is no. I told him I haven't talked it over with you." Mark knew DeBooker was well aware of the details of his son's sudden retirement from the Army a little over a year ago.

"You think Shawn is ready for something like this? I mean, after what's happened to him, will he be okay doing this?"

O'Toole shrugged. "Damned if I know, Charley. I just know that if Anna Shane should need someone providing her personal protection, there's nobody I'd trust more than Shawn to do just that. He's due here this evening. How about joining us for dinner? We can talk more about this."

Shawn O'Toole arrived in Frankfort a little after four in the afternoon on October 12, 2017, along with his two-year old border collie, Rusty, a rescue from a sheep farm not far from Shawn's home on the edge of Fishlake National Forest, about fifty miles due east of Koosharem, Utah. His new Chevy Silverado crew-cab truck was filthy after the trek from nowhere to Frankfort. He found a drive-thru carwash and ran it through just to get the big pieces off, and then spent fifteen or twenty minutes toweling off some of the hard-to-get-to places. At just a few minutes before five he was hugging his dad in the driveway of his home just outside of town.

"Who's this?" Mark asked as Rusty stood next to the two of them, tail wagging excitedly.

"Rusty, meet your grandfather. Dad, meet Rusty."

Mark bent down and rubbed the dog's ears. "He's a beautiful dog, Son."

"Can you believe they were going to shoot him?"

"What?"

"He's got a touch of dysplasia. He can't run the sheep anymore. Those farmers out there … it's all about the business, and a dog that can't earn its keep … well, they were just going to shoot him. I know the guy, a bit of an asshole really, but I worked on one of his rifles, so he likes me. I told him I'd pay him for Rusty, but he gave him to me. He's on a daily supplement … Tri-COX … it's really helping his joints. Follows me everywhere. Couldn't leave home without him."

"Well, he can come along with us. We're meeting Charley DeBooker at Storm Cloud Brewing Company. Good beer. Nice night too. We can sit outside." He quickly checked his watch. "Almost five. We'd better be on our way."

"So, you and Charley gonna fill me in?"

"Yep, but that can wait. I'll drive. You can tell me about the ranch."

"Okay, my favorite subject these days." Shawn patted his leg and said, "C'mon, boy. Let's go."

Charley DeBooker had known Shawn since he was a baby. When his mother died in childbirth, DeBooker asked Virgil Fraley if he thought the family could see their way clear to help Mark out. It may have been the only compassionate thing Virgil Fraley had consented to in his entire lifetime. Mark got a twenty-five-thousand-dollar bonus that year. All of Mark's childcare expenses were paid by the Fraley family and a college fund was established for Shawn. Mark had long ago cashed that in and returned the money to the trust. It hadn't been needed for college expenses. Though Shawn had been a standout running back at Frankfort High School and had been offered several football scholarships at Division 1 schools, college was not in Shawn's cards. In 1996, he'd enlisted in the Army. By 1998, he'd completed the tough Army Ranger training and the tougher Special Forces training. He served on the elite Delta Force until 2005. After that he was assigned to the Central Intelligence Agency working exclusively on the most clandestine of missions including the one in 2011 that took out Osama bin Laden.

When Shawn and Charley saw one another at Storm Cloud, for the first time in over twenty years, their handshake quickly collapsed into a hug. "My God, Shawn, it's good to see you, son."

"You, too, Charley. Thanks for taking such good care of my dad."

DeBooker felt a lump rise in his throat. "What are you drinking, Shawn? Your money's no good here."

The three men settled around an outside table under a propane warmer as a cool breeze off Lake Michigan began to set in, so cool in fact that they were the only ones sitting outside. Rusty, after coaxing a few ear rubs from Charley, curled up at Shawn's feet under the table. Beers and pizza were ordered. Then Charley and Mark laid out their thoughts about Anna Shane.

The discussion ended with Charley saying, "Shawn, this could be nothing. It could be something. Your father thinks we should protect against the *something*."

Shawn looked over at his dad, chuckled just a bit, but was dead serious when he asked, "When did you get so suspicious?"

"Tell me you think I'm crazy and we'll just call this an overdue homecoming," was Mark's quick reply. When Shawn didn't say anything, Mark turned to Charley and said, "See, he doesn't think I'm being too cautious. Listen to me on this, Charley. I'm only trying to help."

DeBooker looked at Shawn. "You sure you're up for this?"

Shawn hung his head for a brief moment and then met Charley's eyes. "Absolutely. This is kind of what I do."

"Shawn ... "

Shawn knew what was making DeBooker hesitate. "Charley, I know what you're thinking, but it's all right. Let me tell you the truth. That would probably be a good place to start, so you know everything. I did exactly what the Army said I did. I got information out of a couple of Taliban operatives. They were double agents; worked for us as translators. Turned out they were passing along information to the bad guys and were taking money from both sides. To make matters worse, they were bomb makers. I made their lives extremely..." He paused, searching for the right word and then said, "I inflicted a world of pain on the bastards. What I got out of them was good information that wound up saving a lot of lives—and avenging a few they'd taken.

"When I was done with them, I had to make a decision. Making them prisoners of war wouldn't have solved anything. They weren't important enough to get an all-expenses-paid trip to Guantanamo. They'd have gone to some prison in Kabul and after a few months and a few bribes, gotten out. They would have eventually wound up right back out there, doing exactly what they did that killed four of my guys. Not a lot of people knew about what I did, but some guy looking to get ahead in the Agency started asking questions. So, my boss warned me. He did me a favor, something he didn't need to do. I didn't have a lot of options. I took retirement rather than face an investigation and likely court martial. The Army's got a million things going on now, so they were waiting on the CIA to do something. My boss made sure the pending investigation got squelched at the Agency, so it all just went away when I retired." Shawn paused and then added, "I'd do it all over again, if I had to."

DeBooker was silent for a long time, then said, "I don't know what to say."

"Charley, just know that I have no regrets," Shawn's steely blue eyes were focused on him.

"Okay, what are your rules of engagement? I believe that is what you call them in the military."

"Yeah, that's right. ROE for short. Best rule is KISS ... Keep It Simple Stupid. So how 'bout we all agree that nobody except the three of us knows what I'm up to. That includes Mrs. Shane. Hate to say it, but she's the bait in this trap to maybe catch a killer." Shawn searched both of them for a reaction. Clandestine operations were his specialty. They were nodding. "If she knows I'm watching her, it might spook her. And we don't want to do that. If someone's watching her, what they likely don't know is that we're watching out for them. It wouldn't take much to tip our hand. Any kind of a wrong move, any misstep, anything that looks different, might just be the thing that upsets the applecart, and we lose any advantage the element of surprise might give us. So, just us, no one else knows we are surveilling her."

Their flatbread pizzas arrived and the three of them began to eat in silence. Shawn couldn't be sure if DeBooker was just digesting his suggestion about keeping their suspicions from Anna or was he asking himself, *Do I really trust him on this?*

After a piece of pizza and a long pull on his draft beer, Shawn said, "I'll keep the two of you posted on what's happening, but let's agree that the mission is to protect Mrs. Shane ... nothing more, nothing less. If there's a killer out there, then we can decide what to do with them after we've secured the main objective ... Mrs. Shane. Clear?" Both men nodded. "Dad, can you keep Rusty?" At the sound of his name, the dog jumped up, tail wagging. Shawn slipped him a piece of pizza crust. "He's no trouble. I've got everything you'll need."

A thought crossed Mark's mind. "I'm happy to do that, but would you mind if he spent some time with a woman and her daughter who are friends of mine?" He looked over at Charley. "Her name's Nora Schneider. Her daughter, Jenny, is ten. Nora is a widow. Her husband was killed in Iraq. She's working on a project that I will show you at some point, but trust me when I say you will be impressed. I assume Rusty likes kids?"

Shawn chuckled. "Rusty likes anyone who might have a treat in their hand."

Mark asked, "Then, it's okay with you if I take him out to High Bluff House sometime and let Nora and Jenny keep an eye on him? Dogs you know ... well, they can be therapeutic."

Shawn thought for a while, then said, "I ... I was in a bad way until this guy came to live with me. So yeah, dogs, especially this one, can be quite therapeutic and that's the voice of experience talking."

CHAPTER EIGHTEEN

The dog was created especially for children.
He is the god of frolic.

—Henry Ward Beecher

Mark O'Toole pulled to a stop at the front door of High Bluff House. Just as he opened the car door for the dog, Nora Schneider stepped out onto the porch. Rusty went running to her as Mark announced, "His name's Rusty."

She knelt down, "Mark, he's beautiful! I didn't know you had a dog."

"I didn't until last night. He belongs to my son, Shawn. I'm just watchin' him until he gets back here."

Still kneeling and petting Rusty, Nora looked up at Mark and smiled. "So, something else I didn't know ... you have a son? Why didn't I know that?"

Mark had known Nora for the two years she and Margaret Rogers had been working together on the Angels' Overwatch project. There was a reason he hadn't told her about Shawn. He was retired from the Army, a weird sort of coincidence that could mark a period in their lives that Nora and Billy Schneider had once looked forward to themselves. But, for the last year or so, he watched Nora slowly emerge from grief's abyss, and Mark hadn't wanted to do or say anything that might trigger painful memories of what might have been. So he simply told her, "Out of sight, out of mind, I suppose. He has a ranch out in the middle of nowhere in Utah; doesn't get out this way often. But he's on a business trip out east and stopped here long enough to drop Rusty off for me to watch while he's gone. If you and Jenny are of a mind ... "

"Absolutely," she answered, anticipating his request. "Jenny's been asking me if we could get a dog. She says she will take care of it—you know, feed it, walk it, play with it. This will be a good test of her dedication." Nora took Rusty's head in her hands. He stared into her eyes. "You want to stay with me and Jenny for a while, Rusty?" The dog gave a gentle whine as if he were saying yes.

Jenny burst through the door just as Nora stood up. "Mom, where ... who's ... "

"Okay ... okay, little girl. Get a grip. His name is Rusty. He belongs to Mark's son, but Mark has asked if we would like to watch him for a while. I've told him we would, if you are willing to start living up to all the promises you've been making about caring for a dog."

"Mom, I will. I will. You know I will."

"Ummm ... we'll see. Take him out in the yard. Find a stick. Let's see if he can fetch." Jenny and Rusty were off like a shot. Turning back to Mark, Nora asked, "Haven't talked to Charley in a few days. How's Anna doing?"

Mark stared after Rusty and Jenny. "She's a mess, as you'd expect. I asked Charley if he had any idea what she was going to do. The answer was no. He was honest with me; told me he wants her to come here and work with you on what you and Margaret started, but ... "

"I feel so damned helpless." It was the first time he'd ever heard her curse, but she'd expressed quite plainly how everyone felt at this point. "I just don't know what to do. I want to call her. I want to tell her I know exactly how she feels. But I also know it's way too soon for that. She has to get through the utter emptiness she's feeling right now."

Reassuringly, Mark replied, "There'll be a time when

Anna will talk to you. I don't know when, I don't know where, but there'll be a time."

"Mom, watch this," came the shout across the broad expanse of land that surrounded High Bluff House. Jenny threw a stick, Rusty charged after it, brought it straight back to her, dropped it at her feet, then stood staring up at her, tail wagging, ready to go again. "He's learned how to fetch already."

"He's a smart boy, darlin'," Nora shouted back. "Mark, we'll keep a good eye on Rusty. How long do you ... "

"I don't know. Can I get back to you on that? Shawn isn't sure how long his business will take, but he said he'd keep me informed. In the meantime, Rusty's better off out here in the wide-open spaces with you and Jenny than he would be cramped up in my small house. If he gets to be too much ... "

Nora held up her hand. "Look at them," she pointed to Rusty and Jenny. "They're already great friends."

Mark smiled, "I'll let you know as soon as I hear anything from Shawn."

Nora went the rest of the day, unable to shake her conversation with Mark about Anna. Later that evening, after she'd tucked Jenny in with Rusty draped across the end of the bed like a blanket just waiting to be pulled closer, she sat down at her kitchen table with pen and paper and began to write.

October 13, 2017

Ms. Anna Shane
12932 Compton Heights Court
Clifton, VA 20124

Dear Anna,

I want desperately to talk to you; to tell you I know exactly what you are feeling right now. It hasn't been that long since I was in the same place you are. I want to tell you that things will get better with time. With time comes healing. But I know now isn't the time for me to be telling you any of this. So, that is why I am writing. I didn't want to call your cell phone, or text you, or email you ... no, this isn't a time when the modern conveniences should be used. So, I'm doing this "old school." This letter will take a week to reach you. That isn't enough time, but it's a start. Read as much of this as you want, when you want, then put it away and come back to it when you are ready.

Charley tells me The Washington Post is being most gracious in your hour of grief. He also tells me they want you to return to the paper when you are ready. If I were them, I would want the very same thing. I also know that you love what you do and that you are called to do what you do at The Post.

This letter is my call to you. Anna, I want you to consider returning to Frankfort, living here, and working with me as we breathe life into High Bluff House and Angels' Overwatch. This is something that I believe nearly 150 years of family history is calling you to do. Yes, I have read your great-grandmother's diary. I know you have as well, Charley has told me so. There are only a few of us who have been privileged to know her story: your father, your mother, Charley, Mark, me, and now, you. I do not believe your grandparents ever read it ... possibly they didn't even know about it. Your grandfather likely would have destroyed it had he known of its existence. Your mother gave it to me to read, just as she would have given it to you had she lived. Together we shared many cups of coffee and many glasses of wine talking about Mary Sullivan. Both of us concluded that she was perhaps the strongest woman we've ever known ... yes, I used the word known, because one cannot help but believe you've come to know her after reading her diary. But the two of us also concluded that neither of us would want to have lived as she did all those years, consumed by the deceit and hatred that ate away at the fabric of the Fraley family.

As your mother was helping me climb out of my grief, she would often tell me about your father. She loved him deeply, Anna, so deeply in fact, that she saw it as her duty to shield him from you ... yes, that's right ... shield him from you. He was so disturbed by his experiences in Vietnam, that if he had known about you during your growing up years, it would have disturbed him even more knowing he had a child he'd abandoned during all the years of the war. In many ways your mother's life was much more difficult than mine as a war widow. When the Army's casualty officer showed up at my door to tell me my Billy had been killed, I knew I would never see him again, never feel his tender touch. That wasn't the case with your mother. She knew your father was just a stone's throw away, but that she could be no part of his life after his return from Vietnam. I can only imagine the anguish that caused her as she shielded him from you and you from him. You were the two people she loved most in the world, but could never bring together without fear of making each of your lives more difficult.

In his later years, after you'd left for college and started to build a life of your own, your mother told me his mental health improved and the two of them became closer. The idea for something like Angels' Overwatch was born out of their mutual desire to see Mary Sullivan's curse come to an end. Both thought putting the money to a noble cause was the only way to do that.

So, Anna, I am asking you, when the time is right, to objectively consider your options. The first would be for you to keep the Fraley fortune and do nothing. Recalling your visit here, I think this an unlikely choice. A second option would be for you to turn over the Fraley fortune to the Angels' Overwatch Foundation, but choose to stay away from the place and the people here. My fear is, with this choice, you would never see the good your money is doing. Seeing the good in what we can do will help you heal, just as it has me. And so, I reiterate, a third and final option is for you to come back to your roots and oversee all the good that we can do together. I pray that this will be your choice.

Standing with you at this terrible time, I remain,

Very truly yours,

Nora

She began to fold the letter, but as she ran her finger over the final crease, she had another thought. Unfolding it, she retrieved her pen and entered,

PS: I should probably tell you that I have not discussed this letter's contents with anyone, including

Charley. I am not trying to be deceitful. There certainly has been enough of that in the past as far as the Fraley fortune is concerned. I am familiar with the emotional rollercoaster you are riding right now. Many people will be offering advice; just as I have here. Some decisions though, are yours and yours alone to make. Always know I am here for you.

She mailed it the next morning after dropping Jenny at school.

CHAPTER NINETEEN

People don't usually regret doing something;
they regret getting caught.

— *Thatonerule: #1940*

Charlotte Matthews checked her watch, 11:55 a.m. She'd been sitting in her rental car parked along the curb at the entrance to the cul-de-sac on Compton Heights Court in Clifton, Virginia, staring at the front of Anna Shane's home for the last thirty minutes. Deep in thought, the burner phone in her bag startled her as it rang. It was Ephraim Swain. His calls had been coming about twice a day for the last two days. She'd dodged the earlier calls but decided now was about as good a time as any to deal with this prick. "What?"

"Where the fuck are you?"

"Ephraim, this has got to stop. I'm sitting outside her home right now. You want this done, then get the fuck off my back and let me do my job."

"Listen, Charlotte, for what I'm paying you, I can call you every fifteen minutes if I want to. What's the latest?"

Realizing he wasn't going to give up, she answered, "She's not alone. A woman is staying with her. Kind of to be expected, don't you think? She did just lose her husband." *You micromanaging little sonuvabitch. All these calls aren't going to get the job done any sooner,* is what she wanted to say to him, but she didn't. There was no point in further antagonizing the jerk.

"What are you going to do?"

"What the fuck kind of question is that? What can I do except wait? I don't think it's a good idea to kill both of them, do you?"

"Who is this woman, anyway? I'm expecting ... "

She'd had enough. A pickup truck had just passed her and slowed in front of the Shane house. It had no sooner circled through the cul-de-sac and passed her on its way out, when a woman emerged from the Shane home with a suitcase. The woman opened the door of the Prius parked in the driveway, put the suitcase in the seat behind her, got in and drove away. Charlotte had no idea who she was, just a friend probably, staying with her while the widow endured her first few days of grief. *How sweet,* she thought sarcastically. She'd observed this woman coming and going over the past couple of days. But now, the suitcase told her everything she needed to know—she was leaving for good this time. Abruptly, Charlotte said into her cell phone, "There's something happening."

"Charlotte, don't you ... "

She'd already hung up on him.

Shawn O'Toole had been on the road for fourteen straight hours. He was tired, but he wanted to get the lay of the land around Anna Shane's house. Turning left off Compton Heights Circle, he followed it to Compton Heights Court, made a left and almost immediately took note of a car parked along the curb with Massachusetts plates on it. A woman sat behind the wheel talking on a cell phone. It struck him as odd for several reasons. First, it was the only car parked on the street, and second, in an upscale neighborhood like this one, cars normally parked in driveways or in three-car garages with elaborately designed garage doors shielding them from view. He quickly took note of the license plate, BUH 789 as he drove past to the apex of the cul-de-sac. In front of Anna Shane's house he slowed, but did not stop, noting on his initial drive-by a Toyota Prius with Virginia plates parked in the driveway, and an ADT Security sign stuck in the ground in front of a shrub. Continuing around the cul-de-sac he exited the way he'd come, passing the woman in the car who was still on the phone.

Two miles down Compton Road, heading back toward Manassas, he pulled into a gas station, but before he got out to fill the tank, he placed a call. "Robbie, it's Shawn O'Toole."

"No shit! Shawn! Where the hell are you?"

Robert Blackmon was *the* sharpest analyst the Central Intelligence Agency had, in Shawn's estimation. Certainly the sharpest he'd ever had the privilege to work with at CIA's headquarters in Langley, Virginia. "How's it going there at spy central, buddy?"

"Same old, same old, Shawn. Where are you? Are you in town?"

"Yeah, I am, Robbie. Got a little thing I'm working on for my father and a friend of his; kind of a personal security gig." He knew he could tell Robbie all the details, but he also knew in this case it might be better for Robbie to know only that which he needed to know. "Was wondering if you could run a license plate for me?"

They were old friends. Robbie probably more than anyone else at Langley hated to see Shawn retire from the military. Robbie had actually called in a few favors owed him, and lined up an analyst's job at Langley for him, but Shawn wanted no part of sticking around. At the time, he viewed his retirement as forced, bordering on disgraceful, so he sought solace and solitude. "Not a problem. Give it to me and I'll call you back."

Sitting in a Waffle House, because he was hungry and wanted breakfast even though it was just after noon, Shawn O'Toole answered his cell phone. "That was quick!"

"You call, I haul, buddy. It's a rental car, Avis; rented to a Shelby Masters. She picked it up in Muskegon, Michigan, and is supposed to return it on Sunday. I've got a copy of her Michigan driver's license. Want me to send it your way?"

Shawn jotted down the name on a napkin. "Hey, that would be great. Thanks, man. You know I appreciate it."

"No problem. Hope it helps. If you got the time, let's get together for a beer."

"Love to, Robbie. I'll give you a call. Thanks, again."

A minute later Shawn had an image of Shelby Masters' driver's license on his cell phone, which he forwarded to his dad with the following message:

Long shot, but any idea who Shelby Masters might be? She's parked just down the street from Anna's house in a rental car.

Mark O'Toole was on his way from High Bluff House to Charley DeBooker's office with some invoices that needed payment when his iPhone dinged telling him of an incoming message. The picture was a bit blurry, but there was no mistaking the image of Charlotte Matthews on the Michigan driver's license. The address was Grand Rapids, Michigan. The leisurely trip back into town suddenly became an urgent one.

"Charley, take a look at this," O'Toole said as he opened Shawn's message.

"That's Charlotte," DeBooker said, the confusion evident in his voice. "Who the hell is Shelby Masters?"

Mark asked, "Where did Charlotte say she was going?"

"She said she was going south to the Gulf. Someplace called Watercolor. I don't understand."

"Neither do I, but look at Shawn's text. Charlotte's parked just down the street from Anna's home. I didn't want to get back to Shawn until I showed this to you."

"Should I call Charlotte and ask her what she's doing?"

O'Toole thought for a minute. "I don't know. Let's give Shawn a call."

Charlotte Matthews had dismissed the pickup truck that had slowed in front of the Shane home. Before she pulled from the curb, she said to herself while thumping both hands on the steering wheel, *Finally, a fuckin' break.* It was time to think about what would happen next. *Friday, October 13, is going to be a bad day for you, Mrs. Shane. I can knock on the door. You'll let me in. The interior alarms will be off. Likely, you're already on some sedative. I'll just add to that a little bit. Don't want to have to fight you ... no marks on your body. String you up. No suicide note: cops'll just figure you're depressed after your husband's death.* She started the car and pulled the transmission into drive. She'd wait until dark to come back.

"No shit, she's your paralegal, Charley?"

"Yes, and I have absolutely no idea what she's doing there. I certainly didn't send her. She told me she was headed south for a few days of rest. I can't make any sense out of this at all." DeBooker paused and then asked, "Maybe I should give Anna a call."

Shawn thought for just a few seconds. "Hold off on that. I need to get back in that neighborhood and check out a few things before we give her any cause for alarm."

After disconnecting the call, Shawn headed back to Compton Heights Court. As he drove, he tried to determine what good reason this paralegal could have for being here, especially since her boss had no clue either. He could come up with no *good* reason, but several *bad* ones immediately came to mind. Turning onto Anna's street, he noticed the rental car was gone. There was no point in asking Robbie Blackmon to try to track her, something that was certainly within the CIA analyst's capability. But Shawn reasoned if Charlotte had a fake driver's license, she was probably using credit cards under an assumed name or paying cash for everything. Besides, he knew where the bait was. The thing he had to decide now was how to intercept Charlotte before she got to Anna.

Once again, he made a slow drive past Anna's home, but this time his attention was focused on security measures in such a posh neighborhood. With hardly any exceptions he noted every home had a sign somewhere prominently displayed indicating the place was protected by one security service or another. He also noticed that a lot of them had security cameras surveilling their entrances and driveways. A few were trained on the front yards, covering the street in front of the home as well. He noted, however, that Anna's home was not one of these with external cameras.

He tried to put himself inside Charlotte's mind. *She'll know there's security inside, but not on the outside. She'll know which houses to avoid because of their outside security cameras. It won't be hard to get to Anna's front door undetected.*

Could she come in from the rear of the house? he asked himself. Shawn drove around to see what lay behind the Shane home. On another street he found equally upscale homes backing up to her property. There was enough space between houses that someone, at night, could easily sneak between them. There were fences that would have to be negotiated, but none that couldn't be overcome if one were intent on coming in from that way. Again, nearly every home had some security company's sign in front of it. Similarly, some had exterior security cameras. He made a calculated guess. *She's not going to go after her in broad daylight. No, she'll wait until dark. It will be harder for her to be recognized if one of the external cameras should pick her up.* But he had a dilemma. *She can come at her from either the front of the house, or through the back, and I've never been any good at being two places at once.* He decided he couldn't take the chance that he'd be in one place and Charlotte would go to the other. Pulling to the curb, he called Charley DeBooker back. "I think you need to give Anna a call and tell her I'm going to be knocking on her door."

"I hate to do that. She's been through so much."

"I know. But I've looked that neighborhood over pretty well. It won't be hard for Charlotte to get to her. She'll wait until it's dark. I'd almost bet on that. I also think she will count on Anna recognizing her and just letting her in. I need to be inside that house if Charlotte comes calling."

"How much do I tell her?"

"Good question. You know her better than I do, but no matter how tough a person is, if they get news that some-one may be trying to kill them—well, how would you react? Maybe just tell her you sent me with some papers for her to consider. Tell her I was visiting Dad in Frankfort and then heading this way to see a friend and you asked me to drop them off. Tell her I was happy to do that."

"Then you'll have to tell her what's really going on?"

"Yep. She may not believe me, but if that's the case I'll call you."

"I hope this is all just a false alarm."

"Yeah, me too. But have you been able to come up with

another reason why Charlotte would be here after telling you she was going south?"

Shawn heard him sigh. "No."

"Yeah, me either. So, best to be prepared. Call me back.

Shawn waited a respectable amount of time after hearing back from Charley that he'd talked to Anna and he was expected. It was about five in the evening when he swung onto Compton Heights Court and drove past the Shane house again, making one last reconnaissance of the area. There was no sign of the rental car or Charlotte Matthews. Exiting the neighborhood, he drove to a busy intersection and parked his truck in the rear of a restaurant parking lot and walked back to Anna's, again being cautious for any sign of Charlotte. He rang the doorbell and a rather haggard-looking Anna Shane answered.

"Mrs. Shane, I'm Shawn O'Toole, Mark O'Toole's son. Mr. DeBooker asked me to stop by."

She stepped back from the door, "Yes, Mr. DeBooker said you would be stopping. Please come in." Anna pointed to the bag slung over Shawn's shoulder and said, "Charley told me you have some things for me to look over."

For the last several hours, Shawn had played out in his mind several scenarios about how this next part of their conversation would go. Each scenario began with the same words. After telling her how sorry he was for her loss, Shawn looked at her and said, "Mrs. Shane, Mr. DeBooker, my dad and I all think you may be in some danger."

"What?"

"Do you know Charlotte Matthews?"

"Of course," she answered cautiously. "She's Charley's paralegal."

"Do you know of any reason why she might be here in Clifton?"

"No, but shouldn't that be a question for Charley?"

"He didn't send her."

"Uh ... well then, Mr. O'Toole, I would have no idea why

she might be here. Is she here? I haven't seen her." Shawn took out his cell phone and showed her the picture of the driver's license with Charlotte's picture on it. Anna looked at it and said, "Well, that's Charlotte all right, but I don't recognize the name on the license."

Shawn pointed to the picture. "She was parked just down the street earlier today. Mrs. Shane, I must admit that I am not here to leave papers for you. I am here to possibly protect you from this woman."

Anna held up a resistant hand. "Listen, I don't know what kind of cockamamie thing ... "

Her disbelief was anticipated. Shawn found DeBooker's number in his cell phone directory and punched it up. Three rings later he said, "Charley, I need you to tell Mrs. Shane why I'm here." He couldn't hear what DeBooker said to her, but he didn't really have to. Anna Shane gave out a cry and slumped to the floor. Picking his phone up, he said, "She's fainted. Let me call you back."

Gently, Shawn tended to her, checking to be sure the fall hadn't hurt her. As she came to, he saw the terror in her eyes. He helped her to her feet and led her into the living room. As she sat down in a wingback chair he asked, "May I get you something; a glass of water?"

She ignored his courtesy, "This can't be happening. You think Charlotte may have killed Ed, my mother and now is coming after me. Why? Why would she do that?"

"Mrs. Shane ... " Shawn took a second to collect his thoughts. "None of us are sure at this point. But you must admit it does appear suspicious."

"Why? My mother, my Ed ... " she broke down in tears.

"I can't answer that question yet. My job right now is to make sure you are safe. So, when you are ready, we need to talk about some 'what if's.'"

She stood up, a bit shaky at first, but soon regained her composure. "I don't know about you, Mr. O'Toole ... "

"Call me Shawn, Mrs. Shane."

She nodded, "Okay, Shawn. I'm Anna."

They were making progress, but news like he'd just brought her isn't easily sloughed off. He watched her closely to be sure she'd overcome her fainting spell. He felt more reassured when Anna offered, "I could use a drink." She led him to a great room at the rear of the house overlooking the pool area.

Pouring herself a scotch, "What would you like, Shawn?"

He held up a hand, "Nothing right now, thank you."

After she'd swallowed, Anna said, "So, let's talk about these 'what if's' of yours."

"Okay. Let's begin with what if she knocks on your front door?"

"You really think she's that brazen?"

"Think about it, Mrs. Sh ... Uh, Anna."

"That's better."

He smiled, "I think that is going to be her likely play. You wouldn't be expecting her. You'd look through the peephole to see who it is, but once you saw it was Charlotte, you'd open the door, even let her in. Am I right?"

Anna nodded.

The other option for her is to break in—maybe through one of those sliding glass doors," he said pointing to them. "I think she'll take the path of least resistance though, and rely upon you recognizing her as a friendly face. The bottom line is that if she shows up, I'd like to get her in the house. I won't let her hurt you. The element of surprise is on our side. Once she's subdued we can start asking some questions."

"Okay. You sound like you have some experience with all of this."

He nodded, "Yep. Army Special Operations. Don't worry, Anna. She isn't going to hurt you. I won't allow that to happen."

Shawn sat in the darkened living room, able to observe

anyone approaching the home from the front. It was just past eight o'clock when he saw a lone figure walking up the center line of Compton Heights Court, proceed up the driveway and to the cement walk leading to the front door. As the doorbell rang, he motioned for Anna to answer it as he took up a position against a wall next to the living room's entrance off the foyer.

She and Shawn had rehearsed the reception. Feigning complete surprise, Anna opened the door, smiled and said, "Charlotte, what in the world are you doing here?"

"Mr. DeBooker asked me if I would ... "

As if she was chiding him, Anna said, "Mr. DeBooker? Why didn't he call me and tell me? Well, no matter. Come in, please."

Charlotte wasted no time. As soon as Anna turned her back on her, Charlotte grabbed her from behind and that was Shawn's signal. Emerging from the living room into the foyer, approaching Charlotte from the rear, he grabbed her by the waist and pulled her from Anna.

Long ago, Charlotte had imagined she might someday require some martial arts training, and she'd kept those skills well-honed over the years. She was strong and pumped up on adrenalin. She quickly recovered from her surprise and elbowed Shawn in the groin hard enough to loosen his grip sufficiently so she could escape his grasp. Athletic and agile, Charlotte quickly followed up the elbow jab with a vicious whip kick that hit Shawn in the shoulder and staggered him. Had it hit its intended mark, his head, it would probably have knocked him out.

He realized he'd underestimated his opponent. Behind Charlotte, he caught a glimpse of Anna, her eyes were as big as saucers, her hands over her mouth. She would not be able to help him. This was a fight he could not lose. Charlotte was coming at him with her fists raised. Just before she got to him, he pulled his Taser from its holster, lunged past her fists and pressed it against her neck. Charlotte fell to the floor, immobilized, jerking spastically from the voltage she'd been hit with. Gathering the bag he'd brought with him, Shawn found the roll of duct tape and began wrapping Charlotte's wrists, then her ankles, and then her mouth.

When he was done, he sensed Anna standing directly behind him. "The bitch!" she managed to say. Then again, "The bitch!" only louder this time. Then, a third time, louder still, "The bitch! She killed Ed! She killed my mother!" She stepped around Shawn and delivered a solid kick directly to Charlotte's midsection that caused her to groan through the duct tape.

Anna, her rage apparent in her eyes and her posture, was poised to deliver yet another kick, when Shawn stepped in. "Whoa. I know how good that must feel, but we need to get her to talk." He grabbed Charlotte at the elbows and roughly yanked her to her still-unsteady feet. "Come on, lady. We need to have a little talk." He dragged her into the kitchen and shoved her down onto a straight-backed kitchen chair.

Just for a moment, he flashed back to a decrepit mud hut in Afghanistan, a bomb maker strapped to a chair, a cloth and a five-gallon can of water.

Coming back into the present, Charlotte resisted as he duct-taped her to the chair. "Sit still, dammit!" When he was sure she was securely lashed down, he ripped the duct tape from her mouth.

"Who the fuck are *you*?" Charlotte shouted at the top of her lungs.

Shawn grabbed a dish towel from the kitchen counter and stuffed it in her mouth as Charlotte struggled helplessly against him.

Anna walked over, leaned down in front of her and screamed, "Why? Why did you kill them?"

Shawn grabbed the end of the towel protruding from her

mouth. "Better answer the lady's question, Charlotte," and he pulled the towel out.

"Fuck you," this time not quite so loud.

Anna slapped her as hard as she could across the face. Charlotte's head snapped sharply to the left from the blow, but as she recovered, she spit on Anna.

Shawn intervened, trying to be a voice of reason, "Charlotte, we know you killed Margaret Rogers and Ed Shane. We know Anna was supposed to be on that plane with Ed. So let's have it—all of it—why? Who's paying you? Where's the money—all of it?"

She just sat there stone-faced.

"You fucking bitch," Anna said from somewhere behind him, and then quick as a cat she stepped up and slapped Charlotte again. "You are not going to get away with this!"

Shawn offered, "Come on, Charlotte. You're caught. There's no point in holding back."

Nothing.

Shawn motioned for Anna to follow him and they retreated to a corner of the great room far enough away from Charlotte that she couldn't hear them, but close enough he could still keep an eye on her. "She's not going to tell us easily what we want to know," Shawn said.

"Let's tell her we're going to turn her over to the cops and see what she says then."

Shawn replied, "Stay here for a second. I want to get something." When he returned, he brought with him the bag Charlotte had over her shoulder when she'd entered the home. With Anna watching, he removed from it a length of half-inch thick rope, a syringe and a bottle of something Shawn recognized as a sedative. Looking at Anna, he said, "So this is what we have," holding up the four items. "My guess is her plan was to subdue you, inject you with some of this stuff and then hang you to make it look like a suicide, which ... " he paused trying to find a way to spare her feelings, and when he couldn't, he proceeded, "given what has happened to you so suddenly with Ed's death, it would have been chalked up as a suicide by the police."

"That's fucking crazy. I would never do that."

Acknowledging her, he said, "I know that. But do they? I really am not sure turning her over to the police is the right thing for us to do. I think someone hired her to kill you. Why? We don't know. But she does and she's not ready to tell us. She won't tell the cops either. There are a lot of limits on them and once she gets an attorney—which you know she will ... " Shawn just let that hang there.

"So, what are you suggesting?" There was a commotion in the kitchen and both of them looked just in time to see Charlotte struggling so hard to get loose that she tipped the chair over. "I hope she cracked her head good!" Anna said.

"During my time in Special Forces I was attached to the CIA. I know some things I can do that will loosen her tongue."

"Torture? You want to torture her?" Anna asked, incredulous.

Shawn did not answer her questions. He figured whatever naiveté Anna may have once had, that it had to have been shattered by the evening's events.

"Can I have a crack at her?"

Shawn waved a hand in Charlotte's direction, "Be my guest."

Anna walked back to Charlotte while Shawn moved in that same direction, but stayed back in an attempt to communicate to Charlotte that it was clearly Anna she was dealing with now. "You fucking bitch! You've ruined my life. I don't know why you did it and at this point I don't really fucking care. But I want you to know this, if you don't answer my questions, I'm going to turn you over to this guy. Trust me, he knows what he's doing and I am more than willing to let him ruin your life like you've ruined mine if you don't answer me. So, Charlotte, or whatever the fuck your name is, why did you kill my husband and my mother?"

When there was no response, Anna turned to Shawn and said, "She's all yours. I don't give a fuck if you kill her."

After he made sure Charlotte was well secured to the chair, he gave Anna his Taser. "If she tries anything, just point this at her and pull the trigger. I'll be right back. I'm going to go get my truck. I'm going out through the garage so just leave the door open. I won't be long."

When he returned, he pulled inside the garage and closed the door behind him. Anna watched him cut her loose from the kitchen chair. Shawn checked the tape around her wrists and ankles and then picked her up and carried her to the garage. He took little care as he slammed her down on the truck's tailgate. Anna watched all of this intently. Shawn wrapped her eyes with duct tape, removed the dish towel from her mouth and immediately took multiple wraps of duct tape to keep her silent. He used the syringe and sedative Charlotte had brought with her and injected her. As it took effect, he asked Anna if she had some blankets. "Where she and I are headed, it's cold this time of year."

When Anna returned with the blankets, she asked, "Where are you taking her?"

Shawn wrapped the blankets around Charlotte and pushed her up into the bed of the truck before he replied, "It is probably best if you don't know that bit of information."

Somewhere just west of Toledo, Ohio, around 7:00 in the morning, just before it became fully light, Shawn pulled into a rest area and parked at a deserted end of the parking area. He had been driving all night. After he'd reinjected Charlotte with some of the sedative he'd brought along with him, Shawn called his father.

"Everything okay, Son? Where are you?"

"Toledo. Did Anna talk to Charley?"

"She did. Charley called me and told me what happened."

"I've got Charlotte Matthews in the back of the truck." He chuckled, "She's asleep or I'd let you say hello."

"Are you headed to the cabin? Anna told Charley you were taking her somewhere where it was cold. Charley and I put two and two together."

"Yep. Charlotte's one tough bitch."

"Anna told Charley, Charlotte wouldn't say anything about motive."

"That's correct."

"So, what happens next?" After a long pause, Mark asked, "Shawn, you still there?"

"Yeah, Dad. I'm still here. It's probably best I don't answer that question—first, because I'm not quite sure, and second, because you may not like the answer."

"Shawn, don't put yourself ... "

"Hey, Dad," Shawn interrupted, "this bitch has killed seven people already and was going to kill Anna. Don't feel sorry for her. We have to get to the bottom of this. Someone, I think, was paying her for these murders. We have to find out who that is. We've taken Charlotte out of the picture, but she's not the only contract killer in the world. What's to stop whoever hired Charlotte from finding someone else once they've discovered Charlotte's out of the game?"

There was another long pause and this time it was Shawn's turn to ask, "Dad, you still there."

"Yeah, Son. Be careful will you?"

"I will, Dad. I will. Don't worry."

CHAPTER TWENTY

Whoever fights monsters should see to it that in
the process he does not become a monster.

—*Fredrich Neitzsche*

S hawn O'Toole was in the kitchen area of the cabin, a one-room affair measuring about twenty feet wide and thirty feet long, with built-in bunk beds along every wall. A fireplace with a fieldstone chimney running from the floor out through the peak of the roof was the only source of heat. There were a couple of windows; one above the kitchen-area sink and the other directly across the room. He'd built a fire and the place was just beginning to warm when he heard her begin to come out of the effects of the sedative. He'd already removed the duct tape that had gagged her on the trip here.

"Where the fuck am I?" she yelled.

Walking over to her, he purposely removed the duct tape that had her blinded. She hollered as he roughly yanked it off, taking with it some of her hair. Unflappably calm he answered, "Hello, Charlotte. Welcome to the upper peninsula."

"Who the fuck are you?" she screamed at him.

She was tightly strapped with multiple wraps of duct tape to a straight-backed wooden chair he'd moved from the kitchen table. The chair sat on a wooden platform about four feet square and about six inches high that Shawn had removed from one of the nearby deer blinds. Underneath all this was a piece of plastic sheeting measuring about ten feet by ten feet. The edges of the plastic were rolled up as if to create a barrier. On the cabin's floor, sat a bucket of water and, next to it, a folded towel. These things were placed where Charlotte could see them. He wanted her to anticipate what was headed her way. The only thing she couldn't see was a second wooden chair similar to the one she was in. Shawn had placed it on the cabin's floor a few feet behind her, tipped over on its front. In between Charlotte's fits of screaming, the only sound came from the hum of a generator just outside the cabin's front door that powered the cabin's sparse light fixtures.

Calmly, he answered her, "I'm your worst nightmare, Charlotte."

She struggled violently against the wraps of duct tape until the chair she was bound to fell over. She yelped as it tipped over the edge of the platform and she hit the floor. Her arms and legs tightly bound, she had nothing to break the fall.

Shawn was surprised it hadn't knocked her out. Picking her and the chair up, he slammed her back down on the platform. "Go ahead, Charlotte, get all of that out of you and then we'll get started." He walked away as she screamed expletives at him. It didn't matter. Where they were now, she could scream her head off and no one could hear her, except Shawn.

The cabin sat in the middle of nowhere about twenty miles east of Lake Gogebic in Marenisco Township. Unless you knew of it, finding this cabin would be almost impossible. There were no road signs in this part of Michigan's upper peninsula, and you'd have to make multiple left and right turns from one unnamed two-track trail onto another to get to it. In fact, it had been so long since Shawn had been here that without a handheld GPS, he wouldn't have found the place. He and his dad had built it practically with their own hands nearly three decades ago. There was no indoor plumbing. The only thing they had needed help with was the well, which was connected to a hand pump that stood alongside an old, stained porcelain sink in the kitchen area. It had taken nearly all of the bottled water he had with him to prime it, but he'd gotten the ice-cold well water to flow. He wasn't sure how long it had been since the cabin had been used by his dad and his select group of friends for their deer hunting extravaganzas, a truly fond memory from his growing up years. A portable propane tank provided gas for cooking on an old two-burner hot plate. For the last three hours of their trip from Virginia, Shawn had not seen another living soul.

He left her there, screaming at him while he went outside. He could still hear her screams as he grabbed an axe and set out to find suitable firewood. He needed some time to think.

Fifty yards or so from the cabin was a pile of unsplit firewood placed there by his dad, or perhaps some of his buddies who may have used the cabin at some point and piled the wood here as payment for time spent. He stood the first piece on its end on the "splitting stump" and deftly swung the axe into its center. While his hands and his eyes were in perfect sync and the piece split smoothly down the center, his mind was someplace else altogether.

What are you going to do with her? He tried to mentally list his options. *Turn her over to the cops,* but before his mind could get to the second option, it turned to the consequences of doing that. *Then what? She's got money. She can hire a good attorney. What proof do you have that she killed Margaret Rogers? What proof that she killed Ed? You're fairly sure you know what she was planning to do to Anna. You've got the rope, the hypodermic and the sedative. What will she say she was going to do with that stuff? What will she give the cops as an excuse for being at Anna's? She'll tell them you coerced her confession; that she lied to save her own life. She'll accuse you of kidnapping her.*

Now you're on trial. He swung the axe harder and harder with each question, frustrated with the answers he came up with for them. He recalled the two bomb makers. The option he'd used with them was looming as the more likely one for this situation as well.

He finished stacking a couple of day's supply of freshly split firewood near the cabin's door, refilled the generator's gas tank and went inside out of the cold. Snow lightly covered the ground, and more was predicted. He would have to dig the hole soon, or the ground would be frozen more deeply than it already was.

Inside the cabin, he turned on the propane burner, heated the coffee he'd made earlier and poured himself a cup. She began screaming at him again, only now she was becoming hoarse. Ignoring her, he sat down at the kitchen table and waited.

"Who the fuck are you?"

An hour or two passed and she'd kept asking him that. *Well, maybe it's time I gave her the answer.* She was screaming at him as he laid her back until the chair she was strapped to rested against the other chair. He steadied them with his free hand and his legs as she struggled against him. Then he placed the towel over her face and drenched it with water from the bucket. He didn't keep her in this position very long, intending to give her only a taste of what she was in for.

He snatched the towel from her face and sat her back up on the platform. She choked hard and then sputtered her first attempt to reason with him, "I...I've got money ... lots of it. We can work something out. You and me ... "

Shawn stepped in front of her and bent down. "I know you've got money. What I want to know is who's paying you, and why." She spit in his face. He stood up, turned his back to her as he wiped the spit off and then coolly, calmly said, "All right. I expected this is how it was going to be."

Waterboarding is a highly effective means of producing

the sensation of drowning within seconds. The subject is leaned backward with their nose and mouth below their feet, a towel is placed over their face and then water is slowly poured over the towel. It only took a second experience, this one slightly longer than her first, before she'd given up Ephraim Swain as the man who'd employed her to kill Margaret Rogers, Ed and Anna Shane, and Charley DeBooker.

The next question was *why?* When she refused an answer, he repeated the process, holding her back for just a second or two longer.

"He thinks he'll get the money once they are all out of the picture," Charlotte sputtered.

"Now we're getting somewhere. Where's the money he's paid you, Charlotte?"

"Fuck you." He leaned her back in the chair again and waterboarded her a third time ... a fourth ... a fifth ... each one longer, more painful than the last. She was weak from retching and gagging. He gave her a moment to recover and wasn't prepared for the question she managed to eke out. "Who the fuck's paying you to do this?" she asked him, still struggling for breath. "You're no better than me. In fact, you're just like me ... just another killer for hire."

It angered him to the point he wanted to smash his fist into her face. *Why not? You're going to kill her anyway.* But something inside him, some shred of decency conquered his inhumanity, allowing him to resist the easy temptation. He asked her again, "My patience is wearing thin, Charlotte. Where's the money Ephraim paid you?" When she didn't answer, without another word, he leaned her back, oblivious to her pleas for him to stop.

As he sat her upright, her head flopped violently to one side and hung there. He thought for a moment he'd overdone it, he thought she was gone, but then she gasped for a breath. He backed off momentarily before asking again about the money and when she didn't answer, he walked away from her in frustration. *The bomb makers weren't this tough,* he thought. He muttered just loud enough for her to hear, "I am nothing at all like you, Charlotte."

When he returned to her a few minutes later, she stared groggily at him. He asked, "You got people, Charlotte?" She didn't answer. "Who cares about you? Who's going to come looking for you when you drop off the face of the earth?"

She tried again to negotiate with him, this time the desperation in her voice more evident. "Listen, you and me, we're alike ... a couple of loners on this earth. It doesn't have to be that way. We think alike. We're both killers. Together we could make a lot of money ... "

She kept rambling on. Shawn, however, was thinking about what she'd said, *we're alike ... loners ... killers.* The information about the money she'd been paid wasn't important. The only reason it might come in handy, he thought, was in a criminal prosecution of Ephraim Swain. But he'd never encountered someone quite as stubborn as she was. She'd endured many more "trips to the well" than either of the bomb makers had before they gave him what he was looking for. He drew the conclusion she was willing to take her money to the grave with her. *What are you gonna do now?* Again, his thoughts ran back to the bomb makers. *She's right ... dammit, she's right.* Reluctantly, he had to admit she was absolutely right about the *killer* part. And the more he thought about it, she was right about the loner part as well. He'd bought the ranch near Koosharem because it was in the middle of nowhere. He'd killed two people. Granted both of them were sonsovbitches! Nonetheless he'd killed them. His retirement hadn't exonerated him of that, only stopped any investigation into what he'd done. He fled to Koosharem because he didn't want to be around people after that. He'd been perfectly happy there in his self-imposed exile and it was his intention to return there after doing this little job for his dad and Charley.

As he leaned her back for what he thought would be the last time, she broke. "No ... No ... wait ... stop ... please, no more. I'll tell you what you want ... just don't ... don't ... no, please, no more. Please."

He sat her upright and got a notebook and pencil from the kitchen table. "Okay, Charlotte, give me the banks, account numbers, passwords. I'm gonna drain every one of them."

White City, located at the southern tip of Lake Gogebic, was nearly deserted at this time of year. He pulled into the parking lot of the Dollar General and called Charley DeBooker.

"Where are you?" Charley asked.

"The *where* is less important than the *what* and the *why*, Charley. I've got some information for you. Somebody by the name of Ephraim Swain hired Charlotte."

"Sonuvabitch!"

Shawn knew DeBooker to be pretty strait-laced so he was surprised when he heard him swear. "So, you know him?"

DeBooker's response surprised Shawn. "He's Anna's cousin."

Shawn told him, "Apparently, he thinks if he could eliminate Mrs. Rogers, Ed and Anna Shane and you, Charley, he could get his hands on all that money."

"Me ... she was going to kill me too?"

"Ephraim apparently thinks you're a threat."

"What about Charlotte?" DeBooker asked.

"Uh ... " There was a long pause in the conversation, and then Shawn said, "Maybe it's best you don't know the answer to that question. She's still alive, if that's what you're worried about."

"Shawn, I didn't mean it like that."

Dismissively, O'Toole replied, "I know. Truth is I don't know what I'm going to do with her. The bitch doesn't deserve to live. All she'll do is kill someone else for money."

DeBooker replied, "I don't know, Shawn ... vigilante justice ... "

"Listen, Charley, there isn't time to debate the *good* and the *bad* of it. Sometimes it's just a matter of necessity. If you know this Swain character, then give me an address or some clue as to his whereabouts and leave the rest up to me."

"Shawn ... I ... I ... "

"You know this isn't over until we run Ephraim Swain to ground. Charlotte Matthews isn't the only murder-for-hire person out there. Let's find out what the hell he thinks he's doing."

O'Toole stayed quiet, knowing DeBooker was going to have to come to this on his own, so he gave the attorney the time he needed to think. Finally, DeBooker responded, "Okay, here's the address. He's in Bloomfield Hills."

Shawn copied down the information. "Thanks, Charley. I'll keep you up to date."

When he'd finished with DeBooker, Shawn took his iPad, inserted his portable "hot spot" and googled the banks Charlotte had given him. He was amazed at how easy it was. In a matter of thirty minutes he'd transferred just over three million dollars from her offshore accounts to an account he'd just established at the same Cayman Island bank, leaving Charlotte nearly penniless. He made a quick stop at an outfitter's store before he headed out of White City back to the cabin in a rapidly-building snowstorm.

It took him nearly an hour longer to get back as the storm grew in intensity. When he opened the door to the cabin he was not surprised to find that Charlotte had again tipped over her chair. She lay shivering in the pool of water that had gathered in the plastic sheeting Shawn had spread on the floor. The fire had dwindled to just a few embers. He picked her up, chair and all, plunked her down in front of the fireplace and added some wood which quickly caught fire.

As she began to warm, he casually said to her, "Well, Charlotte, I'm happy to report you are now officially penniless. I can't believe how easy it was to open an account down there. All I had to do was send them a picture of my driver's license and then I robbed you blind."

She practically spit the words at him, "Fuck you, whoever you are. I told you, you're no different from me."

"Yeah, well, that's where you're wrong. I'm not going to kill you, Charlotte, but before it's all over you might wish you were dead."

"What are you going to do?"

Shawn took out his duct tape, wrapped a few extra wraps around her ankles, wrists and her torso which strengthened the bindings holding her in the chair. "I'm going to take a nap. I suggest you do the same thing. You've got quite an ordeal ahead of you." He opened the cabin's door and pointed to the raging snowstorm outside. "They say this is going to drop about eighteen inches of snow up here before it's over. How good are your survival skills, Charlotte?"

Shawn's "nap" was more like a night's sleep. When he finally awoke, the cabin had a distinct chill. Charlotte was asleep in the chair in front of the fireplace. Prodding her roughly, he said, "Wake up. You've got a big day ahead of you."

For the next hour he went about closing up the cabin. He shut down the generator and moved it inside, turned the valve on the propane bottle that fed the hot plate to *off*,

cleaned up the plastic sheeting and the water it had collected, and got her ready for their departure. Still bound
tightly to the chair, he removed the duct tape around her
ankles and fashioned a kind of shackle out of the stuff.
Charlotte would be able to take shuffling steps, but little
else. He checked the duct tape around her wrists and
added a few wraps for good measure. He stirred the last
few embers in the fireplace and produced no flames, just
a few wispy puffs of smoke which quickly drafted up the
chimney. Satisfied the fire was all but out, he cut the binding that held her to the chair and ordered her to stand
up. When she didn't he grabbed a handful of her hair and
pulled her up. "Don't fuck with me, Charlotte." He led her
to the cabin door, opened it and stood her on the threshold.
Pointing to a now snow-covered hole in the ground roughly
the size of a grave he said, "That was meant to be your final
resting place."

Pulling her back inside, he took a winter coat out of a bag,
along with a pair of coveralls, a pair of winter gloves and
a pair of high-top hiking shoes. She watched him put the
gloves in the pocket of the coat, along with a single book
of matches. Shawn took off the shoes she'd been wearing
since he'd apprehended her in Virginia and replaced them
with the hiking boots. Using the remote starter on his
truck, he started it and said to her, "Let's go." She fell once
on the way to the truck in the deep snow. He gave her no
help. "Get up. No one is going to help you." Snow-covered,
she struggled to recover. At the truck he opened the passenger side front door and told her to get in. She managed,
but not easily. He pulled the seat belt across her and then
wrapped duct tape around her eyes and mouth. He pulled
a floppy hat down over her head and placed the winter coat
around her neck. It was unlikely they would pass too many
other cars on the road, but this was assurance that no one
could see she was blindfolded and gagged.

For the next six hours Shawn drove around in an erratic

pattern generally headed in a northwesterly direction into one of the most remote sections of Michigan's upper peninsula. The snow covered everything including most of the roads they navigated. The storm had moved east and was now creating havoc on the eastern seaboard. The sky was a magnificent blue, the sun was out, but the temperature outside the vehicle hovered between twenty and twenty-five degrees Fahrenheit. Just as important, it had been five hours since they'd seen any sign of another human being.

They stopped only to relieve themselves—a much easier task for Shawn than for Charlotte. He told her they were stopping for that purpose. "Take care of it now, Charlotte, or pee your pants, I don't give a rat's ass which." He would not unbind her, but merely pull her pants down and turn away, saying, "Okay, I'm not looking. Grunt when you're finished." Necessarily, she would be quick, the frigid temps hurrying her along.

Sometime around four in the afternoon, Shawn pulled to a stop, got out, walked around the truck, opened her door and commanded, "End of the line, Charlotte. Get out." When she didn't, he pulled her from the truck and she plopped down in a foot and a half of fresh powdery snow. He stood her up, cut the tape from her eyes and gave her a minute to adjust to the dim light remaining. He placed the coat and the coveralls on the snow next to her and reached in his pocket pulling out a pocketknife. He held it up in front of her eyes. "Watch carefully, Charlotte. You're going to want to go get this in a minute." When he was sure he had her rapt attention, he tossed the knife about twenty-five feet away in a snow-covered bush that seemed to gobble it up. "You're free to go, Charlotte," but as she began to move toward the bush and the knife, he stopped her and gave her a final warning, "If you should decide to find me, or to ever bother Anna Shane, Charley DeBooker, or anyone else I know, I will find you and kill you—probably something I should have done this time around." He got in his truck and drove away. In his rearview mirror, he watched her fall face down in the snow as she fought the duct tape shackles too aggressively on her way to try and find the knife. The temperature had dropped to under twenty degrees. "Better find that knife, cut yourself loose and get a fire built. It's going to be cold tonight."

Cell phone signals in this part of the Upper Peninsula are spotty at best. It took him an hour to find a place where he had sufficient signal strength to make a call. He called his dad.

"Everything okay, Son?" Mark O'Toole inquired upon answering.

"Yep, just fine. Have you talked to Charley?"

"I have. He filled me in."

"Listen, Dad, I'm going to be gone a little bit longer. Everything okay with Rusty?" Shawn asked in an attempt to delay the questions he knew were inevitably coming.

"Uh ... Yeah ... he's fine, Son. Just fine. He's staying out at High Bluff House with Nora Schneider and her daughter, Jenny. That little girl and your Rusty are fast friends."

A smile crossed Shawn's face. "Good to know the ol' boy's safe, sound and being loved. He deserves that. When you see her again, tell her to give him a hug from me."

"Sure, Shawn, will do."

"Has Charley talked to Anna? She was pretty shaken up when I left there a couple of days ago."

"He has. She's angry. She asked him if he knew what happened with Charlotte. He told her about Swain. Anna agrees with you. She thinks you need to go after him. So what happened with Charlotte?"

Shawn could hear the anxious edge in his voice. "She was alive the last time I saw her, Dad."

"She's not with you now?"

"No," Shawn's delivery short, unexpansive. He hoped his dad had taken the hint that he was not going to be much more forthcoming about Charlotte.

"So, are you on your way to Bloomfield Hills."

"I am."

"You be careful. Okay?

"Always, Dad. Always." It was hard for him to hold back with his dad, but it was his training. Everything in special operations, everything in the CIA was handled on a strict need-to-know basis; if you needed to know, you did, if not, you didn't, and you didn't ask questions. He thought his dad understood, but it's not always an easy thing to live with, especially when someone you love is heavily involved in the "needing-to-know."

CHAPTER TWENTY-ONE

Some debts are fun when you are acquiring them, but none are fun when you set about retiring them.

—*Ogden Nash*

Mick Janes sat at the table he was always given as a regular here. This was his favorite Italian restaurant in all of Brooklyn. He liked this table because it was out of the way, quiet, someplace he could just sit and enjoy his food and at the same time, as necessary, conduct business without fear of interruption or someone overhearing. It was a place he liked coming to. Today, however, he stared into his plate of spaghetti and meatballs, furious. He'd just transferred two hundred fifty thousand dollars from one of his off-shore accounts to the mechanic in Miami, Florida, who'd engineered Charlotte Matthews' plane crash that took the life of Ed Shane. He looked up and said to the two men sitting opposite him, "I want you to find someone."

Janes had spent three decades building his business and his wealth. For the first ten years, he had to supplement his income with the incidental "hit" here and there as he built a list of people who were good at accomplishing a wide range of nefarious acts for whomever could pay the going price for such things. In the second ten years, his reputation grew, as did the range of people he knew who would do almost anything—kidnappings, murders, arson, bombs of all varieties—you name it and Mick Janes knew someone

THE WIDOW AND THE WARRIOR

who would do it for money, and do it well. Now, for the last ten years he'd grown accustomed to simply answering the phone, hearing what was required and connecting two parties. For this he was paid exorbitant fees for very little work, as had been the case with his most recent dealing with Charlotte.

The problem was that Charlotte had crumped on both the remaining debt she owed him, twenty-five thousand dollars, as well as the two hundred fifty thousand dollars she owed the Miami mechanic he'd hooked her up with. The mechanic told him, "I don't want to talk bad about you, Mick, but I expect better from you when you put me in touch with a client. If you tell me they're good for the money, then I believe you. She wasn't, so you gotta set this right with me, or I'm gonna spread the word: 'Mick Janes does business with people who don't pay their bills,' and honest, Mick, I don't wanna do that." Janes' business was a real niche industry and the Miami mechanic was right— it depended on trust—and cash, of course. So he'd paid the mechanic what was owed him and now he was ready to deal with Charlotte.

He slipped a picture of her across the table to one of the men on the other side. "Her name's Charlotte Matthews and don't let them good looks fool you. She's a stone-cold killer. But she's put me in a bad spot. Find her and bring her back here. I got some plans for her," he said as he cast them a lecherous glance.

The man looked at the picture and asked, "Okay, Mick, but it's gonna cost you."

"How much?"

The two men looked at one another and then the man holding the picture replied, "A hundred grand plus expenses. Any idea where she might be?"

Janes nearly lost it, but caught himself. The restaurant was busy at this lunch hour. Leaning across the table he said, "You fuckin' idiot, if I knew the answer to that, I'd go get her myself. No, I don't have a fuckin' clue. That's your job, and for a hundred K, you'd better be pretty fuckin' good at it."

The man holding the picture looked at his partner and said, "Let's get outta here." Then to Janes he said, "If that's the way it's gonna be Mick, then you can find someone else to do your dirty work. We don't need your shit!"

They got up to leave when Janes said, "Okay, Louie, okay. Don't be that way. I'm just really pissed that this bitch has cost me over a quarter of a mil. C'mon, sit down and let's talk about this."

The two partners exchanged glances and Louie, who was standing next to the table said, "Okay, Mick, but if you have anything, anything at all, that might help us, we might be able to get things done quicker. That's all I meant, Mick. So, how 'bout it? Think about it for a minute. You got anything that might get us headed in the right direction?"

As the two sat back down, Janes thought and then said, "Honest, I don't got nothin', but the mechanic might." Janes took out a pen and wrote a number down on a cocktail napkin. "I can't give you his name, but here's his number," he said as he slid the napkin across the table to them. "I'll call him and let him know you're gonna be callin' and I'd appreciate it if he'd cooperate with you. I don't know how much he and Charlotte talked about this job he did for her—you probably heard about it in the news—the plane crash that killed that DC lawyer and five others. That was Charlotte's gig. I put her in touch with the mechanic who rigged that plane to explode, but keep on flyin'. Maybe he can get you started. I don't know, but it's all I got fellas." He paused and then stuck out his hand, "So, whaddya say? We got a deal?"

They shook on it. Janes smiled at both of them. "Great!" He took a bite of his spaghetti and a sip of wine and said good naturedly, "Now get the hell out of here and find this bitch for me. I don't care what kind of shape she's in when you get her here, just as long as she's alive. Go ahead and have some fun with her if you want to on the way back from wherever the hell you find her. I could care less. Whatever you do to her will seem like nothin' by the time I'm through with her. I'll transfer fifty K to you as soon as I'm finished here. The rest plus your expenses will come when you deliver the goods. Okay?"

Both of them nodded in agreement and left.

CHAPTER TWENTY-TWO

Weakness of character is the only defect which cannot be amended.

—Francois de la Rochefoucauld

It was nearly five hundred miles from where Shawn O'Toole had dropped Charlotte in Michigan's remote upper peninsula to his destination in Bloomfield Hills, Michigan. He was about three hours into that trip—sometime around seven in the evening—when his cell phone rang. His caller ID said, "Unknown" but he recognized the area code, so he answered.

"Shawn, it's Anna Shane."

With some surprise and caution evident in his voice he said, "Anna ... yes. Is everything okay?"

"I'm fine, thanks to you. But I've spoken at some length to Charley DeBooker," she paused for a moment and continued, "He's told me everything ... " Her voice trailed off.

He thought the call had been dropped, "Anna, are you still there?"

"Yes ... yes, I'm still here. This is hard for me."

"What is it?"

"I told you when you left here with Charlotte that I didn't care what you did with her ... "

"Anna ... "

She abruptly interrupted, "I ... I didn't know about Afghanistan ... about the bomb makers when I told you that. It was wrong of me ... "

"Anna, I didn't kill her."

"I know. Charley told me you'd called your dad and said Charlotte was alive when you last saw her. Charley warned me I shouldn't ask what you did with her."

"That's right. My experience tells me it's best if you don't know that precise detail."

"Now you're going after Ephraim Swain?"

"Yes. I don't think you're safe until he's been dealt with."

"Shawn ... I ... I ... don't want to keep putting you in ... "

Now it was his turn to interrupt her, "It's okay, Anna. I honestly don't know what to do at this point. We don't have enough evidence to turn either Charlotte or Ephraim over to the police, not yet, anyway. Maybe I can get something out of Ephraim that will make that change. We'll have to see."

"Please, be careful."

"I will. Thanks for your call." He paused as he struggled with what he wanted to say next, and then, "Anna, I have killed men for information before, but I'm not like Charlotte. I took no pleasure in it then and I certainly would take no pleasure in it now. I know I'm hard against the law's guardrails with what I did with Charlotte, and likely what I'm going to have to do with Ephraim, but sometimes the limits of the law force more extreme measures."

"I know, Shawn. Mom and Ed didn't deserve to die like they did—over money. I appreciate what you're doing for me, but, please be careful," she repeated.

"Count on it, Anna."

Ephraim Swain was not hard to find and even easier to take down. Two nights after dumping Charlotte, Shawn O'Toole caught up with him. Waiting in the shadows of an overgrown arbor vitae tree next to Swain's garage door, he saw the car's lights as it came up the driveway, watched the garage door roll open and got his first glimpse of Ephraim Swain as he drove in. Shawn merely stepped from the shadows, entered the garage staying clear of the car's rearview mirrors, waited until Swain opened the car door and, then rammed a 9mm pistol into his startled face. "Do exactly as I say and you won't get hurt."

A frightened Swain stammered, "What do you want? I've got money. It's inside. Don't hurt me, please. I'll give you whatever you want."

"Hold still." Shawn plunged the hypodermic into his arm. "This will take just a couple of minutes." He watched as Swain became limp. Retrieving the duct tape from his backpack, Shawn taped Swain up just as he'd taped Charlotte. By the time he was finished, the sedative had taken effect and Swain was asleep. He searched for and found his mark's billfold, looked at his driver's license, verified Swain's identity and now satisfied the man he'd come after wasn't going to move, Shawn said under his breath, "Wait here. I'll be right back." He retrieved his truck from its parking place and returned. Swain was dead weight, but Shawn was strong. He lifted him up to the tailgate, wrapped him in the same blankets he'd used on Charlotte and pushed him into the truck's bed. He snatched the remote control from Swain's car and lowered the garage door as he backed down the driveway. Shawn estimated, with stops to administer additional sedative, for gas, bathroom breaks, etc., he would arrive at the cabin in the upper peninsula sometime just after sunup tomorrow morning.

Compared to Charlotte Matthews, Ephraim Swain was weak; a character trait Shawn despised in him but had to admit made his job easier. Like Charlotte, Swain's initial gambit was to pay him off, "I've got over a million dollars. I'll pay you. I won't say anything. Just don't kill me!"

All Shawn had to do was poise a knife over one of Ephraim's index fingers for him to spill his guts. Yes, he'd paid Charlotte. Then came the big surprise. He'd had to borrow the money.

"From who?" Shawn asked. A reluctant pause ensued until Shawn exploited Ephraim's weakness again. The knife came back out. Swain literally screamed, "Robert Luckridge."

Shawn knew the name from his time in the CIA. "Senator Luckridge?" he asked his victim.

"Yes, that's him."

"Interesting. Tell me more, Ephraim."

"What? What do you want to know?" Swain was almost exuberant, thinking he might have found something that would save his life.

Weak asshole! Play along and see what it gets you. Calmly, almost sympathetically, Shawn prodded, "Okay, Ephraim. Now we're getting someplace. Tell me how Luckridge became your banker."

Ephraim gave chapter and verse on how the two met and how he'd used their meeting in Vegas to exploit the senator, but it didn't make sense ... *Why not just blackmail him?*

Shawn asked the question. Swain didn't hesitate, "Luckridge is scary. The money wasn't his. It came from something he called The Brotherhood."

"What's that?" Shawn interrupted sharply.

"I ... I don't know."

Shawn interpreted Ephraim's hesitancy as an unwillingness to disclose. He picked up the knife. Ephraim freaked.

"No ... no ... no ... don't ... " He was an absolute puddle.

"Tell me, Ephraim. What's The Brotherhood?"

"You've got to believe me. I honestly don't know.

Whatever it is, I ... I'm not a member of it. I never asked him. Luckridge ... he ... he never told me what it is or who they are. Honest. Oh, Jesus Christ, you have to believe me ... I don't know ... " He was sobbing uncontrollably and shaking his head. Shawn knew Swain didn't have an answer to his question. He was about to give up when Swain frantically offered, "But I ... I have the sim cards ... all of them."

"What?"

"The sim cards ... from the burner phones. I kept them."

"So that's how you communicate with Luckridge?"

"Yeah ... burner phones."

Again, Ephraim must have thought he'd found some kind of a bargaining chip.

"I can show you where they are."

"Better yet, you can tell me where they are."

"No ... no ... "

Shawn reached for the knife. "Ephraim, you aren't in any kind of a position to refuse."

He freaked again. "Top drawer ... chest in my bedroom. Burner phones are in there. Chips are in a baggie. Go ... you'll see."

"I will. Now, where is the money from Luckridge?"

Shawn watched Swain gulp. He reached for the knife, but before he could turn back around he heard, "No ... No. I'll tell you." Banks, account numbers and approximate amounts in each account couldn't come out of his mouth quick enough.

Shawn had what he needed. As Ephraim continued to beg for his life, O'Toole threw a few more logs on the fire and without a word put on his coat.

"Where are you going? You can't leave me tied up here like this. Please let me go. I promise ... "

"Shut up, Ephraim. There's enough wood on the fireplace that you won't freeze before I get back."

"Where are you going?" he asked again.

Shawn pulled the cabin door closed behind him, remotely started his truck, got in and departed for the outfitters in White City.

Emerging from the last two-track onto the paved highway leading to White City, Shawn put in a call to Anna Shane.

"Shawn? Are you all right? Is everything okay?"

"Yes, I'm fine, just fine. I've been entertaining Ephraim Swain. It's been interesting. I'm calling to ask if you know Senator Robert Luckridge?"

"Uh ... well, not personally, but I'd say professionally, yes. He's one of the bigger birds on Capitol Hill who likes to preen in front of the cameras and reporters."

"Yeah, I've seen him on television. Have you ever heard of something called The Brotherhood?"

She thought for a moment and then, "Can't say that I have. Why do you ask?"

"Well, it seems Ephraim got the money to pay Charlotte from Senator Luckridge who got it from this outfit that calls themselves The Brotherhood—he was able to tell me that the full name is The Brotherhood of American Loyalists—does that help at all?"

"Nope," was Anna's quick reply. Then she asked, "Do you think Luckridge knew what Swain was intending to do with the money?"

"Yes. He told me Luckridge has been badgering him about why you didn't die along with Ed in the plane crash. Luckridge knew exactly what Ephraim was up to. Swain told me Luckridge knew your mother had been taken out of the picture. Apparently there was a first loan for that. The money to kill Ed, you and Charley was a second loan."

"Why would Luckridge go in on something so evil? The man's a sitting US senator."

"Well, there are a couple of ways to answer that. First,

Ephraim has some dirt on the Senator. It seems there was a night in Vegas some time ago and the Senator and Ephraim entertained a couple of porn stars for the evening."

There was a whistle into the phone and Anna said, "The senator's a happily married man and a pillar of morality."

"It gets even more intriguing. Luckridge and this thing calling themselves The Brotherhood would get three hundred fifty million once you and Charley are dead, and Ephraim becomes the next in line to the fortune by blood."

Anna's blood was near the boiling point. She shot back, "You have got to be shitting me. First of all, I'm not at all sure that Ephraim has any right to the Fraley money even if he managed to kill all of us off. And, second, what the hell does The Brotherhood intend to do with that kind of money?"

"Those are the questions I've asked Ephraim. He says his attorney has convinced him that he does have rights to succession. I don't know if that's true or not. Maybe the guy just wants to bill some hours. As to what The Brotherhood intends to do with the money, he doesn't know, Anna. I know he doesn't know. He's so scared he'd tell me if he knew. There's no doubt in my mind."

"So, what do we do next?" she asked.

"I don't know. Let me think about that for a while. I'll be back in touch."

"What are you going to do with Ephraim?" After a pause, Anna said, "I've put you in another bad situation and I don't want to keep doing ... "

"Not to worry, Anna. I will leave him alive."

"But you're not going to tell me exactly what you're going to do, are you?"

"Remember those guardrails of the law I told you about the last time we talked?"

"Yes."

"Best you don't know exactly how hard I'm rubbing up against them."

"Okay. I trust you know what you're doing."

"Yeah, well, thanks. Let's just leave it at this: I've got no regrets about how I've dealt with either Charlotte or Ephraim."

In the parking lot of the outfitter's store in White City, Shawn plugged in the hot spot to his laptop, connected to Ephraim's bank in Nassau, The Bahamas, and drained all of his accounts depositing them into the Cayman account he'd created for himself before emptying Charlotte's accounts. Again, he marveled at how easy it was to move all of this illegal money around. Then he went into the outfitters and bought the same things he'd bought for Charlotte, only in larger sizes to accommodate Swain's much larger frame.

Shawn had been gone from the cabin for a little over three hours. He knew exactly what he was going to do. He'd been here before. When he opened the door and stepped in he found Ephraim sobbing almost uncontrollably. He began pleading, "Please, I don't want to die. I don't want to ..."

"Relax, Ephraim. I'm not going to kill you." It was late in the afternoon—no point in leaving the cottage now. As he had been with Charlotte when he'd reached this point in his interrogation of her, he was tired. "I'm going to get some sleep, Ephraim. I suggest you do the same. You have some tough days ahead of you, starting tomorrow."

In a different northwestern upper peninsula location, but one equally as desolate as the one he'd chosen for Charlotte, Shawn stopped the truck, got out and walked around to open the passenger side door. "Get out," he commanded. The weather had not changed much—still frigid, deep snow on the ground and there was a storm in the forecast. When Swain didn't move, Shawn reached in, hooked his hand through the duct tape binding his wrists together and pulled him out. Swain fell into the snow with a plop; Shawn stood him back up and removed the tape over his eyes and mouth. He looked in Swain's eyes after throwing the pocketknife into a snow-covered bush and didn't like what he saw, but he took no pity on this man who was every bit the murderer that Charlotte was. "You're going to need that knife and these," he said as he placed the coat, gloves and coveralls on the ground next to him. There's a book of matches in the coat pocket. Don't waste them."

"You can't just leave me out here."

Offering the same admonition as he'd given Charlotte, Shawn said, "If I ever find out you are trying to get to Anna Shane, Charley DeBooker or the Fraley money again, I will find you and kill you, Ephraim. Do you understand?"

"You can't ... "

Roughly he grabbed Swain's head with both hands and asked again, "Do you understand?" This time he literally shouted it.

Swain nodded weakly.

Shawn turned his back on him and returned to his truck. As he had done with Charlotte, he glanced in the rearview mirror as he drove away. Swain had slumped in the snow, his head bobbing up and down as if he were sobbing. Shawn thought, *He's not even trying to save himself.* He turned his eyes back to the deserted two-track in front of him and drove away as fast as he could in the deep snow.

As soon as Shawn had sufficient bars on his cell phone he called his dad, who immediately asked, "You comin' back here to Frankfort?"

"Umm ... not just yet."

"What's up, Son?"

"There's something I want to check out. Likely it's going to take me back to DC."

"Okay," Mark said, the resignation evident in his voice as he was acutely aware that, try as he might, he wasn't going to get much more information from him.

"Rusty and Jenny still hitting it off?"

"Saw them both yesterday. One hardly goes anywhere without the other."

"That's good, Dad. That's good. Take care of yourself?"

"You too."

Shawn drove for the next several hours, his eyes on the road, but his mind elsewhere. He was wrestling with a decision, and finally, after he'd come to it, he went to his cell phone's contact list and found Robbie Blackmon's number.

"Shawn! You in town?"

"Not yet, but I'm headed your way. How 'bout dinner tomorrow night? Four Sisters in Falls Church okay with you."

"Sounds good."

"Hey, Robbie, got a question for you. Robert Luckridge still head of Senate Intelligence?"

"Sure is. He's become a real pain in our ass since Trump's become president. One day the senator's singing our praises, the next day he's suckin' up to the president, who, in case you haven't noticed, isn't exactly a fan of the CIA. The boys on the top floor don't know whether to shit or go blind."

Shawn laughed, "So I've heard, but then that's nothing new, is it?"

"Nope," Robbie replied.

"I got an interesting tip on Luckridge and I might need you to do some follow up if you are able ... and willing. We can talk about it over dinner ... on me."

It was well after dark when Shawn arrived in Bloomfield Hills. He used the garage door remote control to get into Ephraim's house. In the top drawer of the chest in the master bedroom, he found four burner phones and half a dozen sim cards exactly where Ephraim had told him they'd be. He put all these things in a Ziploc plastic bag and headed for northern Virginia.

Terrorist and criminals, especially drug dealers, had begun using cheap burner phones for single uses a decade ago. In those ten years, law enforcement and intelligence agencies had worked hard on cracking the information found on these phones when the bad guys became careless in destroying them. So, he thought what he had might be of some value, and he also knew if there was anything worthwhile there, Robbie Blackmon would find it.

CHAPTER TWENTY-THREE

*In the struggle for survival, the fittest win out at
the expense of their rivals because they succeed in
adapting themselves better to their environment.*

—*Charles Darwin*

Charlotte Matthews had survived three frigid nights in the most desolate and rugged part of Michigan's upper peninsula with nothing more than a book of matches and a pocketknife. It had taken her a full hour to ferret the knife out of the bush where Shawn had tossed it. Her hands were on the verge of frostbite by then, unable to put on the gloves she'd been given because her hands had been bound together. She'd barely been able to hold on to the knife as she'd cut her duct tape bindings. She had shivered terribly as she pulled on the coveralls, the coat and the gloves he'd left for her, but once she'd found the knife, freed herself from the duct tape, pulled on the warm clothing and begun vigorously gathering firewood, she'd begun to warm up. She'd kept that first night's fire going for twelve hours before setting out—somewhere, anywhere—she had no fucking clue where the hell she was, but she'd reasoned she could build another fire if she didn't stumble upon someone or someplace she could exploit for her survival. Toward the end of her third day, she'd found herself on a two-track road, recognizable in the deep snow only because of the swath it cut through the dense forest on either side of it. She'd used her last remaining matches to build a fire for the night.

It was just after sunrise on her fourth day when she'd seen the truck's headlights rolling toward her. Flagging the driver down, she portrayed herself as a hiker who'd gotten lost. She'd profusely thanked him for saving her life, telling him how she'd used her last match to build the previous night's fire. She'd told him how lucky she was he'd come along just in the nick of time. Unsuspecting, the man had offered to give her a ride into some town she'd never heard of.

She'd no sooner settled into the truck's passenger seat than she took the concealed, opened pocketknife and plunged its four-inch blade as deep as she could into the driver's ear nearest her. Ever the methodical killer, she'd quickly decided against simply reaching across and slitting the driver's throat. *Too much fucking blood and I don't know how long I'm going to need this truck.* She'd kept her hand on the knife's handle for a few seconds making sure that it was as deeply embedded as possible before twisting the blade quickly from side to side. When she'd let go, he'd immediately swiveled his head toward her, the look in his eyes one of disbelief, the knife's handle protruding grotesquely from the side of his head. He'd begun to jerk spasmodically, trying to move toward her as if trying to defend himself against the attack that had already predetermined his less-than-immediate and painful death. But he was bound by his fastened seat belt, so he'd posed no real threat to her. As the brain bleed continued and shock set in, he'd quickly lost consciousness. His coat and shirt underneath had soaked up most of the blood emerging from his ear canal. She'd reached over, unfastened his seat belt, opened the truck's driver-side door, pulled the knife from his ear and swiveled her feet around in order to push him out. The blood from his wound spread in the pure white snow like red ink spilled across a sheet of white parchment. Charlotte had slid across into the driver's seat and drove away, leaving her victim to the ravages of his wound, the cold and the area's plentiful carnivorous wild-life. Taking stock of the truck, a newer model, she'd real-ized it was equipped with navigation software. A few miles down the two-track she'd stopped, put in her Frankfort address and proceeded.

It was near midnight by the time she arrived in Frankfort. As she pulled to the curb in front of her building, she took careful stock of her surroundings. There was only one other vehicle parked along Main Street, a van. It was at the far end of the block and appeared to be unoccupied. She quickly got out of the hijacked pickup and headed upstairs to her apartment where she located the briefcase with the one hundred twenty-five thousand dollars Ephraim had given her that night they'd met at the restaurant on Old Mission Peninsula. She opened up her computer, logged into her Cayman bank accounts and, as she expected, found them empty. Swearing under her breath, she quickly packed a suitcase with a few things, grabbed it and the briefcase and headed back to the truck. As angry as she was at the unknown man who'd robbed her of her fortune and left her for dead in the upper peninsula—a man she thought was likely to be somewhere here in Frankfort—a man who old Charley DeBooker likely knew—she also knew she could not take the chance of sticking around. They were on to her and her murderous plan. No, she needed to be on her way somewhere—anywhere—*killers for hire can work from any fucking place*, she thought. *I'll go somewhere else, do a few jobs, build up my bank account again, then maybe I'll come back here and see if I can find that mother fucker.*

Exiting the building, she was putting the suitcase and briefcase in the passenger side of the stolen pickup, when a Taser jolt knocked her to the ground, unconscious.

Mick Jane's employees had been told by the Miami mechanic whom Charlotte had employed that he didn't know for sure her whereabouts, but he'd been told that the plane he was to disable, had to be taken care of before it reached Manistee, Michigan. With that single clue, they'd begun their investigation. They'd dove into both local newspapers — *The Manistee News Advocate* and *The Traverse City Record-Eagle*—and hadn't needed to go back too far in time before they'd found several days-worth of articles about the rather sudden death of a wealthy Frankfort, Michigan heiress, Margaret Rogers. Then they'd been able to piece together that Margaret Rogers was the mother-in-law of Ed Shane, one of the passengers killed in the mysterious plane crash engineered by the Miami mechanic. It wasn't much, but they took a chance and headed to Frankfort where they casually passed around the picture of Charlotte that Mick Janes had given them, identifying themselves as brothers who were looking for their sister whom they thought might be here. Someone had tipped them off as to where her apartment was located. Their two-day surveillance paid off as they'd watched her pull up in the pickup, go upstairs and return with a briefcase and a suitcase.

The suitcase full of money was a bonus, or at least that was their initial thought; theirs for the keeping. But as they discussed things on their way out of Frankfort, they reconsidered keeping the money all to themselves. If Mick Janes found out about it—well, neither of them thought it a good idea to cross Janes. They decided they would simply give it to him with the suggestion that since they'd been up front with him, maybe a fifty-fifty split would be appropriate, but ultimately they'd go along with whatever Mick might offer. They had a good payday coming soon no matter what.

When Charlotte awoke, she found herself completely naked, stretched out on her back and bound by chains which were attached to each ankle and each wrist, then secured to eye bolts welded to steel ribs inside the van's window-less rear compartment. Only a flimsy mattress offered her some relief from bumps in the road. All she could discern was that the van was moving. "What the fuck?" she stammered, still groggy from the Taser's jolt. Then she realized she was shackled. Terrified, she began to struggle weakly against the restraints.

"Good evening, sweetness. Mick Janes sends his regards and says he's looking forward to seeing you," said the man in the van's passenger seat. "In the meantime, make your-self comfortable. Here's a little something to help your disposition," he said, as he got up and stepped into the rear of the van. Holding up a syringe, he tapped it with an index finger before mainlining her with a dose of heroin. Charlotte struggled, but he was strong, she was still weak from the Taser and helpless in her shackles. "Don't worry, sweetheart," he told her. "There's plenty more where this came from. Ol' Mick'll see to that. It won't be long until you'll be beggin' for somebody to fuck you just so you can get your next jolt."

He watched her slip into semi-consciousness. Turning to his partner at the wheel, he began removing his clothes and said, "I'll take first crack at her." The driver turned his head slightly and frowned. The other man, now nearly naked, barked back at the driver, "Don't worry, I'll clean her up for you."

CHAPTER TWENTY-FOUR

Experience hath shewn, that even under the best forms of government, those entrusted with power have, in time, and by slow operations, perverted it into tyranny.

—*Thomas Jefferson*

Shawn O'Toole arrived in McClean, Virginia, at midday and checked into a Holiday Inn Express. Exhausted from the long trip, he collapsed into bed. It was 5:00 p.m., after he'd showered and dressed, when he placed a call to Robbie Blackmon. It was just a little after six when the two settled over large bowls of pho, a rich Vietnamese rice noodle soup. Their waitress at The Four Sisters Restaurant in Falls Church, Virginia, sat two large glasses of 333 beer on the table. "Here you go. Is there anything else I can bring you?"

Shawn smiled at her. "I think we're good, thanks." As she walked away, he raised his glass to Robbie, "To *Ba Muoi Ba* beer and good times, ol' buddy."

"God, I miss you. Work just isn't the same ... "

Shawn chuckled. "Jesus, Robbie. Take it easy. You'll make me cry."

"I'm serious, man. The place just isn't the same. Especially right now ... " He didn't elaborate and Shawn didn't press.

Getting right down to business, Shawn began, "Listen, I think Luckridge is mixed up in something," he paused, not knowing exactly how to describe it. "I don't know what to call it, but I think it's very wrong. Ever heard of something called The Brotherhood?"

Robbie thought for a moment, then shook his head.

"Yeah, me either." Shawn filled him in on Charlotte Matthews, Ephraim Swain, the seven murders they'd committed, the Fraley fortune and the information he'd gotten out of them.

Robbie asked, "Where are these two fucks now?"

Shawn shook his head. "They were both still alive when I left them, if that's what you're asking."

Blackmon, more than familiar with the circumstances that led to Shawn's quick retirement, put his head down and shook it. "Sorry, man. I ... I didn't mean to imply ... no offense intended."

"Naw, it's okay, Robbie. None taken."

Robbie said, "Fitzhugh retired about a year ago," referring to the CIA officer who was Shawn's accuser at the Agency.

"Oh yeah," Shawn replied trying to sound noncommittal. He wasn't. Fitzhugh was one of those who would climb over as many bodies as he could, if it meant he could get recognition and a promotion out of it.

Robbie said, "Don't know exactly what happened to him. Just heard a rumor he'd pissed off someone on the top floor. He's down in south Florida. Got a fishin' boat, I'm told. Perfect place for that sorry ol' fuck. Down there with a bunch of old people and the only thing he can hurt is himself and a few fish."

"Too bad for south Florida and the fish."

Robbie nodded. "You got that right." Then he moved on, "So, how can I help with Luckridge?"

"There's some risk ... "

"Shawn, stop it. There's risk to everything. But, if we manage it well, maybe it can separate right from wrong."

"Wow. You've become a philosopher."

Robbie looked around the room to see who might be watching, and then flipped off his old friend. "Yeah, we both know better than that. Seriously, what do you need?"

Shawn smiled and then said, "I need to get to the bottom of this Brotherhood thing. Swain implicated Luckridge, but knew nothing about The Brotherhood except that is what Luckridge called it. Whatever it is they're up to, they are cautious about it. They communicate with burner phones. I've got the phones that Swain had and a bunch of sim cards. So, I'm assuming they're hiding something, but exactly what that might be is a mystery."

Robbie pulled a long strand of noodles out of his pho with chopsticks and half pushed, half sucked them into his mouth. "Wow, I've really missed the food here. Haven't been back since you left."

He was stalling for time, Shawn realized, and he used that time to eat a few of his own noodles.

Robbie said, "So, am I to assume that whatever I do at this point has to be on the down-low?"

Both men knew the answer to the question. Blackmon didn't wait for Shawn to answer. "Well, we've come a long way on cracking the code with burner phones since 9/11. I don't understand all the technology, but if the bad guy has a burner phone activated, we can trace the call. Typically, they will only use the phone once and then destroy it and the sim card. But with the phones and sim cards that you've got, I think we can reconstruct call history. The Anti-Terrorism Task Force has busted up a lot of terrorist plots using this stuff. If Luckridge is using burner phones to conduct *Brotherhood* business, I think we can snag him."

Shawn knew he had a reliable ally in Robbie Blackmon, but was also relieved to know that, as he hoped, there was technology that could be used to assist in this delicate investigation. Excitedly he said, "That's exactly what I need."

"Yeah, okay, Shawn. But to take advantage of all of that, I'll need some help. I've got a friend in the FBI, on the Task Force. You okay with that?"

As a special operator, Shawn had spent a professional lifetime as part of a lethal team in which each man trusted the other with his life. Then he went to work at the CIA where military people were spread thinly across the work force. He'd learned to trust Robbie while working on a lot of clandestine operations involving US Special Forces and CIA field operatives. He got to see first-hand Robbie's dedication to the people he was backing up. Since his unfortunate experience with the two bomb makers and his rather forced retirement, Shawn only trusted a handful of others. Robbie headed that list. "If that's what you need to do, then I trust your judgment completely."

They ate some wonderfully seasoned pork and shrimp served on jasmine rice and talked about old times. Then, over another 333, Robbie asked Shawn, "So, let's say Luckridge is dirty. What then, bro?" He leaned over the table, closer to Shawn. "Luckridge is a high-profile target, dude. He can't just disappear without people asking questions ... lots of them."

Shawn leaned back in his chair and shook his head. "That's a really good question and one I don't have a good answer to yet. If your guy at the FBI gets caught helping me, people will ask questions, especially if he's doing it with highly classified methods. But he ... "

"He's a *she,* Shawn," Robbie interrupted.

"Sorry, a ridiculous assumption on my part." He gave Robbie a look, "Is she somebody ... "

"Naw. Just a good friend."

It was the way Robbie said it that made Shawn pursue the matter. He knew his good friend had gone through a tough divorce four or five years ago, the breakup caused by strong personalities and two people more devoted to their work than to each other. He'd seen Robbie withdraw into a shell for the first year. If this was someone he cared for, he wasn't sure if he should ask his friend to mix business with pleasure. "Hey, Robbie, this is Shawn talking to you. If this is someone you care for, do you think it's a good idea ... "

Robbie waved him off. "We've been out a couple of times. We enjoy each other's company. But she's got the Bureau, I've got the Agency. That's too much like the last time I let myself fall for someone, so no, she's just a good friend, but thanks for asking."

"Well, she might be sitting on a powder keg if The Brotherhood turns out to be what I think it might be."

"You thinkin' it might be some kind of high-level, well-funded Ku Klux Klan?"

Shawn nodded. "Something like that."

"Can I tell her that?"

"If you think it will help."

"She's black. Grew up in the south. Hates the fuckin' Klan. It'll help."

"Great!"

"How long do we have to run this little op?"

Shawn thought for a moment and replied, "The people I needed to keep safe are safe at this point. Whatever it is Luckridge is up to is long-term, so no rush, I think. It's more important for you and the lady at the Anti-Terrorism Task Force to be careful ... minimize your risk. I'll give you a call periodically if I don't hear from you. You can call me anytime you get something that you think is significant. Okay?"

"Works for me. Great to see you, Shawn! Even better to be working with you again!"

CHAPTER TWENTY-FIVE

*Friendship isn't about whom you have known the
longest. It's about who came and never left.*

—Unknown

Nora Schneider had just pulled into Frankfort's Family Fare Supermarket parking lot after dropping her daughter off at school when her cell phone rang. The caller ID indicated *unknown caller*, but she recognized the area code, 202 as Washington, DC. She hoped it might be Anna. She answered, "Nora Schneider."

"Nora, it's Anna Shane."

Nora dropped her hand from the car key. It was cold for early November, she hoped this would not be a short phone call, so, she kept the car running. "Anna, it's so good to hear your voice. How are you doing?"

"Better, thanks to your letter. I'm sorry it's taken me so long to ... "

"Anna, please, no apology necessary. Believe me, I know what a difficult time this is."

"I still don't know ... "

"I understand completely. I didn't either ... " she paused as she remembered those dark days after her husband's death. "May I tell you something?"

"Yes, of course."

"There's every likelihood I'd still be stuck in my grief had it not been for your mother. Jenny and I owe her so much." It was still painful for her to talk about Margaret's passing. "Anna, I want to pay your mother's friendship forward. I want to be that friend to you."

"Nora, I ... I ... "

The conversation had gotten intense quicker than Nora had intended for it to, so she tried to lighten things up a bit. "Charley told me the other day that you're back to work."

"Yes. I'm driving in now, but thought I'd give you a call."

Nora sensed Anna had more to say, so she stayed quiet.

"It's a good diversion—work, I mean. Ed and I ... well, we weren't home a lot, but we did enjoy our time together ... " Anna's voice cracked. She had told herself she wasn't going to get emotional, but she had and she searched for the words she wanted to say. She settled for, "The house is so quiet now without him there. So, yeah, work is a good diversion."

"That was your mother's advice to me. But I was so scared back then. I told her I didn't have any skills. No one would ever hire me. To be honest with you, I think that is when she became really serious about Angels' Overwatch."

"So, that's one of the things I'm calling you about. I want to thank you for sending me the copies of the applications for residence. Among other things they have helped me put my situation in perspective. When I get down in the dumps ... " Anna paused, her sorrow palpable. "I've been there many times in the past month. I pull those applications up on my computer and reread them. How are you coming with identifying who the first residents will be?" Before Nora could answer, Anna added, "That poor woman from West Virginia, with the four boys. I can't imagine what her life must be like ... "

"Anna, she's already here. She's the first. The larger suites, those above the library ... do you remember?"

"Yes, I do," her voice filled with a new excitement. "She's there; moved in already?"

"Yes, I should have updated you. Those larger suites are ready and she was desperate. Eviction was imminent. Food was scarce. Cold weather was closing in on the mountains. We had to get her out of there. Charley and I discussed it and, bottom line, she's here now and she and her boys are getting settled in. She is so very grateful, Anna."

"Oh my God, Nora, you're a miracle worker!"

"Not me, Anna. The Fraley Trust is making all this happen. You are the miracle worker."

"Which leads me to another reason I wanted to talk to you. I'm going to sign the paperwork to turn all the money over to Angels' Overwatch Foundation. I think it's appropriate that I tell you before I tell anyone else. I haven't even told Charley."

"Anna, you're making me cry. I hoped and prayed ... "

"It really wasn't that difficult, but when Ed died ... "

"I know. Something like that puts the brakes on life, for sure. Believe me, I know."

"Well, it's time I move forward with this. So, here's the final reason I'm calling you this morning. What are you and Jenny doing for Thanksgiving?"

"Well, we really haven't given it much thought. Last year we just stayed at home and fixed a small bird ... just the two of us."

"So, how about we have a big celebration this year? I'd like to have everyone over to mom's house for Thanksgiving. And when I say everyone, I mean Charley, Mark, Brian, and our new residents at Angels' Overwatch, of course. What do you say?"

"You're coming home for Thanksgiving?"

"Yep. I took the house off the market. Can't sell it. Too many memories."

All of this was music to Nora's ears. "Oh, Anna. This will be so much fun. I can't wait to tell Jenny. Do you want me to tell Charley?"

"No, I'd like to do that. And I want to tell him to draw up the necessary paperwork to create the foundation as well."

Quite innocently, Nora offered, "Did you know Charlotte isn't there any longer."

One of the things that was on the top of Anna's list of things to discuss with DeBooker after telling him of her Thanksgiving plans was to determine exactly who knew about Shawn O'Toole's work. So, she played it cool, "Yes, Charley told me that when we talked about another matter a few days ago." She left it at that, not wanting to have to lie to Nora any more than was necessary to protect Shawn.

Nora offered, "So, I'm kind of filling in for Charlotte until Charley can find someone else. May I make a Net-Jets reservation for you?" There was a pause, and for a moment Nora thought the call had dropped. "Anna ... you still there?"

"Yes ... uh ... sorry ... but the thought of getting on an airplane ... "

Nora almost slapped herself for being so oblivious to what would obviously be a touchy thing for Anna. "I'm so sorry. I should have considered that before I opened my big mouth."

"No, don't apologize. You know what? Ed would kick me right in the butt if I said I didn't ever want to fly again. I have to move on. So, yes, please make that reservation for me after all; the earlier the better. I'm looking forward to getting back home."

"So, an early morning departure out of Manassas Regional Airport the Wednesday before Thanksgiving?" Nora asked just to confirm.

"Perfect."

Then Nora thought of one last question, "Oh, there's one more thing. It's not just me and Jenny anymore. We are keeping an eye on Mark O'Toole's son's dog. He's back east on some business. Mark asked if we could watch Rusty. It was only supposed to be for a week or so, but that has come and gone. Apparently, some other things have come up and Shawn is still back east. Jenny and Rusty have become inseparable. May Rusty come for Thanksgiving as well?"

Though she didn't know it, Nora had just confirmed for Anna that Charley had not told Nora anything about what was going on with Charlotte or Ephraim. She replied, "The more the merrier, Nora. Tell Mark, if his son happens to be in town, he's invited to Thanksgiving as well."

As Nora disconnected the call and headed into the Family Fare, she was overjoyed that Anna seemed to be overcoming her grief well, after such a tragic loss.

CHAPTER TWENTY-SIX

Whoever said the pen is mightier than the sword never encountered automatic weapons.

—General of the Army Douglas MacArthur

Burl Smythe manipulated the court's docket so that Thanksgiving week, 2017, was unscheduled. Benevolence was not his intention—merely a by-product. His juggling of the schedule allowed the associate judges to make plans for their holiday, and all of them were scattering to be with family and friends, which in turn allowed all of their support staff to have the week off with pay. Needless to say, Burl was extremely popular among those who depended upon the Mississippi Supreme Court for their daily bread. The Judge, however, needed to make a day trip and since it was a short week anyway...

On Tuesday, November 21 , 2017, Judge Smythe was in his car headed for a bar just on the northern outskirts of Yazoo City. His wife thought he was in Oxford. Truth be known, Oxford and Yazoo City were about one hundred fifty miles from one another geographically, but light years apart in other ways. About twenty-five thousand Mississippians call Oxford home, a large number of them affiliated with the urbane University of Mississippi, or Ole Miss, as it is more popularly known. Yazoo City, by comparison, is a small Mississippi delta town remarkable for clinging to life since 1824, surviving Yellow Fever epidemics, Civil War destruction and most recently, tornadoes that threatened to wring the very life out of the place. Smythe was to meet with another "reliable militiaman," this one personally recommended to him by Robert Luckridge himself.

This was Smythe's third such meeting with militia leaders and each had been a learning experience for him. A month ago, he'd traveled to Maine to meet with a militia leader in Cornish, Maine. The two had been distrustful of one another from the outset. Smythe's southern drawl clashed with the other's deep "Mainer" accent. Reporting back to Luckridge on the meeting, Smythe was only half joking when he'd told the senator, "Hell, Bob, I thought I was going to have to get a fuckin' translator!"

Two weeks ago, he'd been in some map-speck of a gully-town in West Virginia, even smaller than Cornish, Maine, had been. This guy had brought three of his friends along and Smythe had had to insist that the friends leave. What he had to say was highly sensitive and important to the country's future. There had been some stiff resistance and for a moment it had come down to, "Whatever it is you've got to say to me, you can say in front of these boys." But Smythe had invoked the Holy Grail, *national security*. The three friends bellied up to the bar, while Smythe and the guy he'd come to see got down to business.

Robert Luckridge had assigned the judge the mission to develop what he'd euphemistically called, "local relationships." Smythe had asked him to be more specific. Luckridge told him, "Burl, we're coming into a helluva lot of money in the next year or so. The Brotherhood can use these militias to our advantage, down the road, after we've established ourselves. So I want to sow a little seed money with these guys. Let's get them armed up, so that when the time comes they can help people see things our way. Know what I mean?"

Smythe was moving fast on this even though Luckridge had told him, "Be thorough and discreet. We need good, reliable men to carry our cause forward." But Smythe was ambitious and he wanted to move up as Luckridge moved up, so he'd pressed ahead. He believed the senator would be president of the United States one day and Smythe was bound and determined to be there alongside him when that day came.

From the moment he swung his nearly new Cadillac into the dusty parking lot of the Down River Bar, Smythe was a fish out of water. There were five pickups in the lot, none newer than the 2000 model year. The two Ford 150s and three Chevy Silverados, appeared to be held together by the dirt and grime that covered them, along with random pieces of duct tape and wire here and there. Smythe got out of his caddy in a cloud of dust and watched as particles of red Yazoo clay settled over its shiny black finish. *Fuckin' Delta rednecks.* He was dressed in blue jeans with a Columbia shirt, the shirt's tail, of course, worn stylishly out. The final complement to his wardrobe was a pair of well-shined, black Weejun loafers. For the judge, this was dressing down.

As he stepped through the door, all heads turned his way. It took a minute for his eyes to adjust to the dim light inside the Down River. The place stank of stale beer and staler smoke. Four good ol' boys were draped over the bar like pieces of old flannel, each with a cigarette burning and two ashtrays in front of them heaped to the brim with ashes and butts. If there was a law against smoking in bars and restaurants in Mississippi, the patrons of this place were oblivious to it. A replay of last Saturday's Ole Miss's SEC showdown with Alabama was playing on the TV behind the bar, the sound muted, the outcome already known. The Tide had rolled decisively.

Smythe just stood there backlit by the open front door. The bartender looked at him with a smirk, rather enjoying the discomfort he read in this stranger's body language. The furniture that dotted the room was a hodge-podge of '50s era chrome and linoleum tables and chrome and vinyl chairs. Some of the upholstery had rips hastily repaired with the standard silver colored duct tape. Most of the metal parts were more rust than chrome. Down the center of the room ran a row of five ceiling fans with spiraling lengths of fly paper dangling from them, each strip abundantly peppered with the remains of flies gone by. Smythe had no idea what the man he was meeting looked like. Equipped with only a name, he stepped toward the bar.

Radford Cox hailed from Eufaula, Alabama. He'd been in Yazoo City once or twice before, but this was his first visit to the Down River Bar. The place had been recommended to him by his attorney, Edsel Walcott who, coincidentally, was from Yazoo City. Ten or so years ago, when they'd first met, Walcott asked Cox why he wanted to do business with an attorney that was four hundred miles away and in another state. Cox's simple explanation was, "Want a good attorney, but not who's so close that he's all up in my bidness."

Cox had complete trust in Walcott, who'd pulled him back from the ledge of legal purgatory more than once. He'd called Walcott to inquire about Judge Burl Smythe after Smythe had called Cox to set up this meeting. Smythe wanted to meet in Jackson, Mississippi, but when Walcott told him who Judge Burl Smythe was, Radford had bellowed into the phone, "What the fuck do you think he wants with me, Edsel?"

"Your guess is as good as mine, Radford, but if you want my suggestion, don't go to Jackson. That's his turf. Meet him someplace that's more like where you're from. There's a place just outside of town here that might be to your likin'..."

Cox saw the stranger in the doorway and just as the judge moved toward the bar, he hollered from a dark corner, "You Smythe?"

The judge stopped in his tracks and moved in the direction of the voice. At the table, he stuck out his hand and said, "Burl Smythe. Are you Radford Cox?"

"You late," was the abrupt reply, Smythe's hand ignored.

"A few minutes. This isn't the easiest place ... "

"Listen, I come farther than you did and I was on time, so don't give me that fuckin' shit."

Burl Smythe was not used to being treated with this kind of belligerent disrespect. He mustered up some courage despite the unfamiliar surroundings and asked, "You know who the fuck you're talkin' to, mister?"

The man got up, drained the liquor in the glass sitting in front of him and said, "Yep. You Burl Smythe, Chief Justice of the Mississippi Supreme Court. I gotta piss," and he walked away.

Smythe sat there fuming, but completely without resources to do anything about it. He watched the overweight Cox waddle away from him, dressed in a once-white, now dingy-gray short-sleeved T-shirt that was stretched to its limit in the arms and chest. His bib overalls were no better. He wore a pair of cowboy boots, run down at the heel, the toes pointed nearly skyward and the leather scuffed and cut. When he returned to the table, Cox laughed, "You still here, Burl? You must want somethin' pretty bad."

"I have a proposition for you, but your smart-ass attitude is telling me that I should get the fuck up and get outta here."

"Well, you could do that, but then you'd be losin' out on what you want, I reckon."

"And just exactly what is it that you think I want?"

"Militia."

It was succinct, to the point and one hundred percent correct, but Smythe was shocked that his purpose was apparently so transparent. "How the fuck did you know that?"

"Me to know ... you to wonder. But I'm right, ain't I?" It had been a shot in the dark, but Cox knew he'd hit the mark.

Smythe didn't answer.

"Yeah, I am. The look on your face tells it all." Cox was pleased. This whole thing was about two roosters strutting around, each one trying to convince the other it was meaner—Cox had won; now he could move on. "Well, Burl, I've got militia, about a thousand good ol' Alabama, Georgia, and Florida boys." He looked over at Smythe with a glint in his eye. "Ain't got no Mississippi boys in the mix. There's kinda a dividing line. I stay on my side of it and ol' Abel Potts stays on his side. Right now, I'm way across that line bein' over here in Yazoo City, know what I mean, Burl?"

Smythe didn't, but acted like he did by nodding. "You and Abel Potts friends?"

"Don't know you could call us friends, 'zactly, but we acquaintances."

"He sounds like somebody I should talk to sometime."

Cox replied, "Ummm ... maybe. I don't know much 'bout his boys, but mosta' my boys been trained by the Army and the Marines. All of 'em kind of skeptical of anythin' that got to do with the gobment ... any gobment ... state or federal ... don't matter. We train a lot. Urban tactics mostly. We could be the best guerilla fighters in the world, better than the Viet Cong or North Vietnamese Army. We a damned sight better than the Taliban, Al Qaeda or those rat fuckers that called themselves ISIS over there in Iraq and Syria, bustin' up all that cultural history o' theirs. What kind of rat fucker does that, Burl?"

Cox had described exactly the militia The Brotherhood

was looking for. "So, are you well supplied? Got everything you need to train with?"

"Fuck no. I was hopin' that's what you were offerin'. We don't need trainers. We don't need someone tellin' us what to do or how to do it. We need guns, ammo, shoulder-fired anti-tank and anti-air weapons. We got good tactics. What we need is better weapons. Can you help with that, Burl? 'Cause if you can, then we should keep talkin'. If you can't, then conversation over."

It was well after midnight before Burl Smythe left Yazoo City for the drive back to Jackson and home. Like the other two militia leaders he'd talked to, he felt Radford Cox had bought into The Brotherhood of American Loyalists. As he drove home, he wondered who Luckridge was working with to supply the kinds of exotic weapons Cox was looking for. Somewhere just east of Yazoo City he decided, *Not my fuckin' worry!*

On the same day, the Tuesday before Thanksgiving, 2017, Senator Robert Luckridge stood at a staffer's desk discussing the details of a bill that was coming up for vote soon. In the background, a TV tuned to CNN was playing, the sound just sufficient for Luckridge to hear. "Welcome to the midday news roundup. Here with me today to talk about President Trump's latest push to fund the controversial border wall is Anna Shane, national political editor for *The Washington Post* and CNN political analyst ... " Luckridge felt a surge of adrenaline and blocked the rest of it out. It had been over a month since he'd heard from Ephraim Swain. The last he'd heard was that this woman should have died with her husband in that plane crash, but that his contract killer was working on it and Shane's death was imminent. After her, only one person stood between

Swain and a billion dollars. He muttered under his breath, "What the fuck?"

"Excuse me, sir?"

Luckridge turned his attention back to the staffer, "Nothing. Go ahead. I'm listening." He wasn't. He was furious at Swain. He wanted to know why he couldn't get hold of him and what the hell was taking so damned long to get Anna Shane out of the way.

CHAPTER TWENTY-SEVEN

Blessed is the season which engages the whole world in a conspiracy of love.

—Hamilton Wright Mabie

Shawn O'Toole arrived back in Frankfort, Michigan, from Virginia, the Sunday before Thanksgiving, where he was greeted warmly by his dad and Charley DeBooker. They were all looking forward to spending some time together. The question of how long he could stay had been asked and answered cryptically, and when Mark had attempted to delve deeper, Shawn had shrugged his shoulders and said, "Not sure. Waiting on a call from a buddy back east." Even if he had more details, he wouldn't have given them up. He had the feeling he was playing with fire on this one and if everything went up in smoke, he didn't want anyone else to get burned.

He spent some time every day looking online at a few upper peninsula newspapers—there weren't many to choose from—checking for any news of either Charlotte or Ephraim. Finding nothing, he gave up looking beyond Wednesday's editions. Anna Shane was to arrive in Manistee at 9:30 a.m. this morning and Shawn was going to accompany his father to the airport.

"You're here!" she said to Shawn as Mark gathered her bags from the aircraft.

"Got back last Sunday."

As the car departed the airport, Anna asked him, "Have

you discovered anything more about Luckridge or The Brotherhood?"

He shook his head, "Not yet. I have a good friend who's working on it—just have to be patient."

Anna nodded, "Well, it's the holidays. I'm glad you're here, home, where everyone should be during this time of year. You're coming to Thanksgiving tomorrow." She hadn't phrased it as a question.

"I am, thanks. Looking forward to it."

Mark and Shawn arrived at Anna's at noon on Thanksgiving Day. It had been carefully coordinated with Nora Schneider that they would continue to watch Rusty because Shawn might be called back east at any time and—well, why cause either Rusty or Jenny to be separated now when Shawn's pending departure was so up in the air. When they rang the doorbell, they heard Rusty barking and then Jenny answered the door. Rusty, recognizing Shawn, barked, wiggled, wagged and pressed into him as he bent down to greet his dog. Jenny silently took all this in. Though she'd never met him, she knew who Shawn was—the man who would eventually take Rusty away from her. Nevertheless she was polite, "Come in. We've been cooking all morning. There are all sorts of things to eat."

The home smelled of everything good about the holidays. Rusty ranged around the group as they moved into the hallway. Out of the corner of his eye, Shawn watched Jenny silently retreat from the group. As he removed his coat, he saw Rusty leave them as well and head in the direction Jenny had gone.

Mark made introductions as he and Shawn moved through the home to the kitchen where Anna, Nora, and Jenny were studying the turkey they'd just hefted out of the oven. Rusty lay in the corner watching everyone. By the time Mark had introduced Shawn to Nora, Jenny and Rusty had disappeared. Perhaps no one else in the kitchen had noticed this, but Shawn had. The elder O'Toole asked, "How much does that bird weigh?"

Proudly Anna announced, "Twenty-two pounds. The biggest fresh bird Nora could find. She did good, didn't she?" Anna read the meat thermometer sunk deeply into the bird's breast, "Not quite done yet, but we'll leave it uncovered, baste it and let it brown. Dinner will be about 1:30. What would you guys like to drink? The bar is right over there," she pointed to a corner of the kitchen counter where an assortment of bottles and mixers stood. "Help yourselves."

After the bird had gone back in the oven, Nora walked over to Shawn who was pulling the top off a Storm Cloud Rainmaker ale. "Shawn, it's nice to finally meet you."

"Same here, Nora. Dad's told me a lot about you and Angels' Overwatch."

"Yes, well, thanks for *your* service."

It caught him by surprise. His dad had filled him in on what had happened to Nora's husband. Here she was thanking him for *his* service. Hell, he should be thanking her for her sacrifice. "Nora, I ... I ... "

"It's OK, Shawn. Jenny and I are in a good place now. We've a lot to be thankful for this Thanksgiving." There was a pause and Nora started to say something about Jenny, but the doorbell rang. Nora looked at Anna, "I think that's the Harmons. I know they can't wait to meet you."

Nora opened the front door and warmly hugged Delores Harmon and her four sons. Motioning them inside she said, "Delores, so glad to see you. Please come in and let me introduce you to everyone."

As Nora introduced Anna, Delores teared up. "Mrs.

Shane, I don't how to thank you. West Virginia seems like a hundred years ago!"

Anna, a bit glassy-eyed herself, said, "Welcome, and please call me Anna." She then introduced Charley, Mark and Shawn to the new arrivals, interjecting that the Harmons were "High Bluff House's first resident family." When she introduced Shawn, Anna told the Harmons that he was a retired Army master sergeant. Delores and her sons, including the youngest, a ten-year old, each in their turn, thanked him for his service. Humbled, he thought, *Jesus! What do I say? How do I thank them? This woman ... lost her husband ... these kids ... lost their dad. How do you make that up to them?* As everyone moved into the house and individual conversations sprung up here and there, Shawn looked for Rusty and Jenny, but neither were to be seen.

At 12:45 the doorbell rang again. It was a three-person news crew from the Traverse City NBC affiliate. Anna again made the introductions, and asked everyone to gather in the living room for a moment. At Anna's invitation, Charley took up a position behind a coffee table in front of the sofa. Anna stood proudly next to him. The news crew began filming at her first word. "My good friends, today is a special day. Yes, of course, it's Thanksgiving, and we all have much to give thanks for today. But it is a special Thanksgiving for me." She pointed to the coffee table. "In a minute, we will sign these papers. The first one will officially establish The Angels' Overwatch Foundation. The second, will dissolve the Fraley Family Trust. And the third ... " Anna's voice cracked, "this third document transfers nearly one billion dollars to Angels' Overwatch. That means that Angels' Overwatch is now its own fiduciary, fully funded and not reliant on any other person or organization." Nora had all the papers spread neatly on the table with yellow sticky pointers where signatures were needed. Charley signed first, then Anna. With each signature, the room erupted in applause, whoops, hollers and whistles. Rusty, who along with Jenny, had joined the crowd in the living room, barked at everyone's excitement. The reporter interviewed Anna, Nora, Jenny and Delores Harmon and her sons. The news crew was invited to stay for Thanksgiving dinner, which was about to be served, but they declined.

The reporter told Anna, "We have to get back and get this edited. It's going to be on the national news tonight."

By five o'clock it was only Anna, Nora, Charley, Mark, and Shawn left. Daylight was starting to fade and Jenny asked if she and Rusty could go for a walk. Nora allowed it. Shawn watched the pair walk down the sidewalk. He saw Rusty, unleashed and in front of Jenny, turn every now and then to make sure the little girl was there. The two headed for the beach area which, this time of year, was all but abandoned.

A harsh winter wind whipped off Lake Michigan, skittering sand across the roadway into the now empty parking lot, obliterating the lines between parking spaces and piling up against the curb stones. Jenny sat down on a bench, patted the cold wood next to her, coaxing Rusty to jump up. Obediently, he sat beside her. She put her arm around the dog's neck, snuggled her face against him and said, "Rusty, I love you. I don't know how I'm ever going to be able to let you go."

In Anna's living room, over coffee laced with Baileys Irish Cream, the adults sat basking in the warmth of what had been a great day. For the first time in over a month, Anna had not thought about Ed's unfortunate death—his murder. She looked around at all the guests. She knew everyone had read Mary Sullivan's diary, with maybe Shawn as the one exception. "I think we have finally put an end to my great-grandmother's curse."

DeBooker nodded, looked in Nora's direction and asked, "Whose idea was it to invite the press?"

Feeling a bit sheepish, Anna answered. "Mine, Charley. Kate Snow's a friend. She'll be doing the nightly news tonight on NBC. I clued her in on Angels' Overwatch. She jumped at it. Sorry, I guess I should have told you, but I also kind of wanted it to be a surprise."

He smiled at her and raised his glass, "Well done."

Jenny and Rusty walked in the front door at 5:30 just as everyone was preparing to leave. Shawn watched the two head upstairs. He'd made a decision. He pulled Nora aside. "Listen, I've been watching Jenny and Rusty. They're inseparable."

She nodded, "She's surprised me. I told her Rusty coming to stay with us was a test to see if she was mature enough to have a dog. She's begged me for one for the last year or so. I wasn't sure she was ready, but she's proven she is."

"You haven't picked one out yet, have you?"

She shook her head and smiled at him, "No. We'll take care of Rusty until you tell us it's time for you to take him back."

"Yeah, well, that's the thing, Nora. Rusty seems to be as devoted to her as she is to him." He paused, not sure he should say what he was thinking, but decided to go ahead with it. "The two of you have had enough loss in your life. She shouldn't have to lose a dog that she obviously loves."

Nora could see where he was going with this. "Shawn, what about you? Your dad's told me how Rusty came into your life."

"Yeah, he's a really good dog. But you know what? That sheep rancher out there in Utah will have another border collie or Australian shepherd that he wants to get rid of and when that happens, I'll be his guy. No, I want Jenny to have Rusty."

She looked up at him—deep into his eyes—as if she were trying to peer into his soul. "You're sure?"

"Yep."

Nora stepped forward, threw her arms around his neck and pulled him close to her. She whispered into his ear, "Shawn O'Toole, I don't know how to thank you. I wasn't at all sure how I was going to handle the breakup when you took Rusty back."

It surprised him. He hadn't been this close to a woman in ... he couldn't remember how long. Everything in his life had been so ... what was the word he was searching for ... he couldn't find it. He put his arms around Nora and held her there for a brief moment. Then, as quickly as they'd come together, they both stepped back, as if they'd been caught doing something wrong.

She was blushing. "Do you want to tell her?"

"No, I think you should do that. Tell her after we've left."

"Okay, but one condition," she said.

He feigned a frown, "What's that?"

"Tomorrow ... you choose the time ... come out to High Bluff House and let me show you around. Jenny and Rusty will be there. I want her to thank you."

His dad came up from behind him and said, "Ready to go, Son?"

Shawn looked at Nora. "Noon-ish, okay? Maybe I can take you and Jenny to lunch."

"It's a date," Nora said, and then turned beet red.

"See you tomorrow." Shawn liked the sound of the word *date.*

Robert Luckridge sat alone in his study at his home in Charleston, South Carolina. Thanksgiving dinner for him had simply been another meal. His wife and two daughters were someplace in the sprawling waterfront historic home, doing something that he could care less about. He was anxious to get back to Washington, to the Senate, to the divisive politics playing out across the country. Kate Snow was wrapping up the NBC evening news on the TV in front of him.

"Our final story this evening is the perfect one to close out this Thanksgiving edition of *NBC Nightly News.* In Frankfort, Michigan, today, Anna Shane officially transferred one billion dollars of her family's money to the Angels' Overwatch Foundation, a project serving the needs of the families of some of America's most deserving heroes, those killed in war ... "

Whatever the rest of the story had to say about the event was lost on Luckridge who suddenly felt sick to his stomach. Ephraim Swain was not answering any of his calls. It appeared that the money he'd been promised would come to The Brotherhood of American Loyalists was now going elsewhere ... and he didn't have the three-and-a-quarter-million dollars to stuff back into the dent he'd made in The Brotherhood's treasury. He'd been playing fast and loose with their money since embarking on this scheme to get two hundred fifty million, and then again to get three hundred fifty million. He'd not only gotten into their coffers for three-and-a-quarter-million dollars to have Ephraim's relatives killed, he'd taken out another half million to kill the two car dealers who seemed to be questioning his authority to make financial decisions in the best interest of The Brotherhood. He was in some deep shit and he wasn't exactly sure what his next move should be. People, very influential people, would soon be asking him questions about what he was going to do about all the money he'd drained from their cause.

CHAPTER TWENTY-EIGHT

*I'm sorry, Dolph, but around here you gotta
earn respect.*

—*Randy Orton, Professional Wrestler*

The week after Thanksgiving had flown by for Shawn. Mark, Charley and he were nearly inseparable during this first post-holiday week. They'd caught a sunny, but cold day when the gales of November relented sufficiently that they could venture out onto Lake Michigan to fish. Later, they'd feasted on their catch with Anna, Nora, Jenny, and of course, Rusty, who'd gotten his own personal filet. The three of them had gone to a hockey game in Grand Rapids, followed by dinner at Ruth's Chris Steakhouse in the Amway Grand Hotel where they'd checked in, because none of them thought the other should be driving all the way back to Frankfort that night. And while Shawn thought he'd been very careful not to send any wrong signals, Mark and Charley were aware, perhaps even thrilled, that he'd seen Nora and Jenny not just once following their introduction at Thanksgiving, but three times since then. Shawn had noticed a distinct twinkle in his father's eye and that wry smile of his when he told him about giving Rusty to Jenny.

But Shawn was getting restless. He hadn't heard from Robbie Blackmon. So, when his cell phone rang on Sunday evening, December 3, and he saw Robbie's name appear in caller-ID, he quickly snatched up the phone, excused himself and stepped outside onto his father's front porch. "Robbie. I was going to give you ... "

"Great minds think alike, ol' buddy."

"What you got for me?"

"Well, not as much as we'd like, but it's a start. My contact at the FBI has had to be careful. Trump's mad as hell about leakers so every department of the federal government has been required to put measures in place. Bottom line, some of the systems she'd hoped to be able to use to find out who's using these burners and what they are saying aren't available to her. She'd have to log on, identify a specific case, on and on and on. They'd know she was snooping and they'd want to know why."

This wasn't the news he'd been hoping for, but he said, "Okay, I understand. I don't want her or you to get into any hot water over this."

"But she was able to wicker together a sort of system of her own. Actually, this woman is a fuckin' genius. She's triangulated the cell towers that the calls ping off. I may not have names and conversations for you, but I can tell you roughly where the calls are coming from and where they are going."

"I'll take whatever info you've got, Robbie."

"Well, first, we think Luckridge is desperately trying to get hold of Ephraim Swain. The burners you gave me have rung at least a dozen times, most of those just since Thanksgiving. When she triangulated the caller's location, the calls were originating from the Senate Office Building, the Senate parking garage and most recently from Charleston, South Carolina. Luckridge's home is in Charleston."

While this wasn't earth-shattering news to Shawn, it did confirm that Luckridge and Swain were mixed up in something together. "Got it. Good information."

"Yeah, I know, but nothing you didn't already know. So, here's some new stuff for you. Luckridge is calling someone in Jackson, Mississippi; two calls since she's been monitoring his cell phone usage. Those calls were from burners rather than his personal cell phone. She's on him like a blanket. Anytime he makes a burner call, she can track it. She's not bothering with his personal cell phone. We don't think he conducts any business on it that might have to do with this Brotherhood thing."

"Any idea to whom?"

"Not specifically. But we think the guy in Jackson must work somewhere in or around the Mississippi Supreme Court Building. She's triangulated in on the location, but again, we can't use the technology that would allow us to source a name for you."

"Still, it seems like the dominoes are lining up."

"We've got the guy at the Mississippi Supreme Court using burners to call Luckridge, or at least we are pretty sure that's who he's calling. She tracks the calls to a general location. If I check the good Senator's public calendar, he's in the vicinity of those calls every time. Now here's the interesting thing: this same guy in Mississippi is using the same burners to call a fuckin' peanut farmer not too far north of Eufaula, Alabama."

"Can you search property ... ?"

"C'mon, Shawn. Give me some credit. Did that already. Got a paper and pencil?"

Good ol' Robbie. "Ready to copy."

"The peanut farm belongs to a guy name of Radford Cox. The name mean anything to you?"

Shawn thought for a moment, then replied, "No, it doesn't."

"Yeah, me either, so I ran Mr. Radford Cox through some of our files here and had our friend at the Task Force do the same with FBI files. We got some hits. He's been on an FBI watch list as a member and organizer of militia down in that part of the country for some time now. You know the kind ... good old boys that like to get together on the weekends, drink beer, shoot at things, tell war stories, and generally hate everyone and everything that aren't a part of their little group."

"I'm familiar with the type."

"Radford's name has come up during some FBI investigations of hate crimes in that part of the country, but he's not been charged. ATF appears to be keeping an eye on his arsenal, but hasn't found anything that's conclusive. On the plus side, he's a Vietnam vet. Holds the Silver Star and a Purple Heart. My bet is that Radford Cox just might be the next domino you should make fall. I'll bet dinner at The Four Sisters you could get the name of whoever he's been talking to at the Mississippi Supreme Court building. Hell, he might even tell you what they've been talking about. All I can give you is GPS coordinates of the Cox farm. The old guy doesn't have an address, just a PO Box at the Eufaula Post Office."

"Text 'em to me, will ya, Robbie? Listen, you and your friend back off for a while. You've given me enough to work with for now. I'll let you know if I should need more."

"I'll send the coordinates straight away. As to backing off, you're the one running this little op, Shawn, and it's sure good to be working with you again."

"You, too, Robbie. Thanks, and thank your friend at the Task Force."

Mark knew his son was leaving early, but when he heard him moving down the hallway at 4:30 a.m., he swung his legs over the edge of the bed, grabbed his robe to ward off the early morning's chill and went downstairs. "Want some breakfast before you leave?"

"No, thanks, Dad. I'll grab a bite at a McDonald's somewhere along the way."

"Where you headed?"

"South Alabama."

Mark wanted more, but he knew he'd probably gotten as much as he was going to get. He changed direction. "Want me to tell Nora anything?"

The question surprised Shawn. "Uh ... uh ... I guess you could just tell her that my business has called me back east. Anna has told me Nora doesn't know what I've been up to. I think we are all in agreement that's best."

"Look, Son, Charley and I both ... "

Shawn suspected he knew where his father was headed with this. He put up a hand and said quite firmly, "Hey, Dad, don't you and Charley turn matchmakers. That woman and her daughter have gone through enough in the past few years to last a lifetime. They don't need to be getting mixed up with the likes of me, and you shouldn't be encouraging something like that."

Mark knew his son to be as tough mentally as he was physically; some would even call it *stubborn*. He put up both hands in mock retreat. The two loaded Shawn's truck and Mark waved goodbye just before 5:00 a.m. on Monday, December 4.

About the same time as Shawn was leaving town for Alabama, Anna was packing her suitcase for a 7:00 a.m. Net-Jets flight from Manistee's Blacker Airport. Leaving this morning was not something she was looking forward to. Before leaving DC to come home for Thanksgiving, she'd made some rather life-altering decisions. Now her presence back there was required to follow up on those decisions. There were also some last-minute signatures needed at Charley's office, so Mark took her there first before heading to the airport. Anna thought it a bit odd that instead of just waiting at the car for the few minutes the signatures would take, Mark followed her into Charley's. As the two descended the stairs from DeBooker's second floor office, Mark emerged from the kitchen, cup of coffee in hand, and said, "I thought I'd better let the two of you know Shawn left this morning for someplace in southern Alabama."

"Is this about Luckridge?" Anna asked.

Mark confessed he didn't know. "All I know for sure is he got a call last night at my house, and immediately packed his bag—left early this morning. But I'm guessing whatever it is, Luckridge is mixed up in it."

"Dammit," Anna swore. Her tone was a mixture of regret and rage. "Does he have anyone with him? Should one of us have gone along? Luckridge is a powerful guy. Shawn shouldn't be the only one grabbing this tiger by the tail."

"He's alone," Mark replied. "I know him. He knows what he's doing, and he didn't give me a lot of specifics because he knew if he would have, all of us would be wringing our hands even more than we are now. We need to trust his judgement, I think."

DeBooker was nodding.

"I'm going to call him," she said as she began rummaging through her purse for her phone.

"And say what?" DeBooker asked. "You're not going to convince him that he needs someone with him and you're not going to convince him he needs to stop what he's doing."

Now it was Mark who stood nodding.

She looked back and forth between the two of them, stopped rummaging and said, "Okay, dammit, but if either of you hear anything, I want to be the first to know—and tell him I said to be careful."

It was about eleven hundred miles between Frankfort, Michigan, and Eufaula, Alabama. Shawn was somewhat familiar with that part of the country, having spent some time at Fort Benning and Dahlonega, Georgia, while attending the Army's Ranger School. There hadn't been a lot of time during training, but following that brutal nine weeks, he'd taken some time and casually roamed down to Panama City Beach, Florida, to recover. It was the deep south where, especially in the rural areas, staunch Republican conservatism was covered with a thick layer of Christian fundamentalism to create a kind of American sub-culture that kept big cities at arm's length, liberal ideas at bay, and friendships were tinged with a healthy skepticism of anything that sounded too much like "big government." His GPS led him right to the front gate of Radford Cox's farm where he found a two-track dirt driveway behind a padlocked cattle gate. It appeared Cox didn't want just anybody coming or going. It was late afternoon and Shawn was tired from the long trip south. *Radford Cox can wait*, he thought. He found a Days Inn in Eufaula, checked in, took a shower, grabbed a bite of dinner and fell asleep.

Refreshed, the next morning he was on his way back to Cox's peanut farm when his cell phone rang. "Robbie?"

"Hey, Shawn, I know you asked us to back off. And we have, but our girl at the Task Force was looking at some satellite photographs of Cox's farm and found some interesting plant life. Seems Mr. Cox is growing another cash crop besides peanuts. He's clever about it. He's got about a thousand acres down there. It's a big spread. He's got some really nice marijuana plants growing in small plots all over the place. Unless you were really drilling down on the acreage, it's not likely you'd detect them, the plots are that small, but there must be a couple of hundred of them. I just thought you might find this bit of information helpful."

Anything he could find out about Radford Cox was potentially helpful. He thanked Robbie and continued on towards the ranch. All he wanted to do was talk to the man. This wasn't an op like the ones he'd run against Charlotte and Ephraim. There was no point in being clandestine. Once he arrived at the entrance to Cox's farm, he pulled to the side of the road opposite the cattle gate. It was a beautiful late fall day, so he lowered the truck's windows, opened up the local newspaper and waited.

It was after dark, about 8:00 p.m., when a late-model pickup rolled slowly past, its driver staring hard at him. The truck swung onto the two-track's entrance and pulled to a stop in front of the gate. A rather large man in bib overalls got out and stared through the dark at Shawn while slowly, intentionally, as if to send a clear signal, removed a shotgun from the gun rack inside the pickup's rear window. Laying it over one shoulder, he gave Shawn one last look and then moved to unlock the gate's padlock.

No sooner had Shawn gotten out and closed his truck's door than he heard in a loud, firm voice from across the road, "Stop right where you are or you're gonna be wearin' a load of birdshot."

"Mr. Cox, my name is Shawn O'Toole and I'd like to talk to you. It's important."

"Yeah, sure it is. Why don't you just send me an email? Here's my address: RadfordCox@fuckyou.com." He laughed at his own joke.

"Seriously, Mr. Cox, it's about Senator Robert Luckridge and The Brotherhood."

That caught the old man up short. "You a friend of his or that fancy judge he's got runnin' around ... that Smythe feller?"

Fancy judge! Smythe! Cox had already given Shawn more than he'd hoped for during this first meeting. "Neither of them is a friend of mine..." he paused and then added, "and they aren't friends of yours either. One of 'em promise you a bundle of money?"

It was another surprise flung on a man who detested

surprises, "Who the fuck are you anyway? You with the gobment?"

Shawn allowed himself to slip into an easier vernacular in an attempt to win Cox's confidence. "Nope. I'm a private investigator." He accented the word *private*. "I was hired to protect some money. I've done that, but along the way Senator Luckridge's name came up. I suspect he's tryin' to fool some folks into thinkin' he's got that money I was protectin' to spend on this fuckin' thing he calls The Brotherhood. But fact is, the well he was thinkin' he'd dip into has already come up dry." Shawn paused to give Cox a moment to think. Then he said, "So can we talk? Guarantee you won't regret the conversation."

He watched Cox put the shotgun back in the rack and climb into his truck. He lowered the window and said to Shawn, "We'll talk, but in a public place. I like to see a man's face when he's talkin' to me. I'll lead the way. You follow."

They drove for about ten miles, Shawn estimated, the last five miles of which were down a dark, narrow, half gravel, half dirt road before Cox slowed and turned into what looked like a shack set back under a stand of live oak trees. Lights were on inside and Shawn could see other people in there, but there was no sign, nothing to identify this place. He felt behind him in the waistband of his jeans for the 9mm pistol he had there. *OK, Radford, this might be your home turf, but if you try to get tough ...* He got out of the truck and followed the old man into the dingy bar.

Inside Cox was greeted warmly by everyone, women and men alike. The genders were slightly unbalanced, numbers favoring the ladies, and if he had to guess, Shawn speculated that the women were the more heavily tattooed. The air was a most unusual mix of sweat, smoke and cheap perfume. Several of the women gave Shawn a smile and a nod of the head. All of the men regarded him with skepticism even though he appeared to be with one of their own,

Radford Cox, who parked his ample ass at a table that magically emptied for him in a corner of the room.

"So, now, here we are. First things first. You know who I am. Who the fuck are you, Mister?"

"Shawn O' ... "

"The fuck you say ... " Cox roared, bringing the room to a dead quiet. All eyes were focused on them. Some of the men moved toward the table. Cox held up a hand. They stopped. "Don't treat me like a fool, Shawn O'Toole. I got your name back at the gate to my farm. I want to know who you work for, how you got my name, how you know about Luckridge and Smythe."

Shawn had no sooner started to give Cox the information he was looking for when someone Shawn recognized stepped up to the table. He was a bit heavier, but still well-muscled, more tattoos, but there was no mistaking him, and their history had not been good. Shawn looked up at the man, nodded and said, "Buzzer."

Buzzer Bradford looked past Shawn to Cox, "Mr. Cox, don't know if you know who you got here or not."

"Don't know yet, Buzzer. You know him?"

"Yes, sir, I do."

Cox liked being talked to like this—like he was the man in charge. He gave Buzzer a broad smile, pointed at Shawn and said, "Well, why don't you tell me how you know Mr. Shawn O'Toole."

"Didn't know him as mister, sir. Knew him as Master Sergeant, US Army Special Forces assigned to Delta Force."

Cox was familiar with Bradford's military service. "The two of you serve together in Special Forces?"

"Almost together." There was a pause as Bradford stared hard at Shawn. "Never did quite understand why he didn't want me as part of Delta. I'd sure like to get an explanation now, Mr. Cox, if you wouldn't mind."

Radford looked over at Shawn and smiled, "Why, no, Buzzer. In fact, I might like to hear about that myself."

Shawn exchanged looks with both men and then said, "There was a picture ... "

"Fuck you, Sarge. You fuckin' bet I took a picture. I posed for it. That fuckin' family deserved what they got. They deserved to be killed. Their fuckin' little boy had just strapped a bomb on and walked into the compound. What kind of fuckin' parents do that to one of their kids? Suicide ... it was fuckin' suicide. I'll bet the little sonuvabitch didn't even know what was gonna happen to him. We lost six good men that day. His family knew what that boy was going to do. The father fuckin' admitted it to me. So, don't preach to me about the picture ... not you, of all people, Sarge. I know what the fuck happened to you. I know you took the retirement and ran so they wouldn't investigate you for doing the same thing to those bomb makers as I did to that family."

Cox didn't say a thing. Instead he stared hard at Shawn.

O'Toole, his fists clenched, looked up, "You through, Buzzer?" He didn't wait for an answer. "Not sure how you know so much about my retirement, but I'll not deny what I did. I sweated two bomb makers to death for information. I used that information to conduct a raid. I took a retirement to avoid an investigation. But I never took any pictures of what I'd done, like I was proud of it. I pegged you as a natural killer, but it took the picture for me to decide that you enjoyed killing way too much to be a part of Delta. My estimation of you is that you'd be takin' pictures of the havoc you'd wreaked on somebody instead of payin' attention to what the fuck is goin' on during an op, maybe while one of your teammates needed you to have his back."

"Fuck you, Sarge. You and I are alike."

This was the second time someone had compared him to themselves and Shawn hadn't liked it either time. He stood up, "No, fuck you, Buzzer. We ain't nothin' alike."

Buzzer was ready to throw the first punch when Cox ordered, "Buzzer, you best be gettin' along. You got to say

what you wanted to say. You got to hear the man's answer.
Go have another beer and calm down." Buzzer stared at
Shawn and didn't immediately move. At this point, Cox
stood up and hollered, once again loud enough to quiet the
entire place, "Get the fuck away from me, or I'll have you
taken outside and stomped." Bradford looked around at
the group of twelve or so men moving his way and quickly
decided that discretion was, in fact, the better part of
valor. He walked toward the bar and never looked at the
corner table again for the remainder of the evening.

"Thank you, Mr. Cox. There was no need for us to tear
the place up and we would likely have done that had you
not backed him down."

"No thanks necessary. So, you were Delta?"

"Yep. Eight years. Then I worked clandestine ops at the
CIA until I retired."

"So, still got some connections in the CIA, have ya?"

"Yep, and the FBI. That's how I come upon your name
and Judge Smythe's." Shawn did not have a clue as to who
Judge Smythe was, but he figured if Radford didn't tell
him all he had to do was check the internet as soon as he
got back to his hotel room. In the meantime, he thought he
could play like he knew a lot more than he did.

Cox began, "I ain't gonna lie to you. Ol' Burl Smythe and
I met a week or so ago. He promised me some big money
for guns and stuff. Was a little vague on what he expected
in return, but I figured it had somethin' to do with the
gobment. We ain't big on big gobment down here, as you
might already know."

O'Toole felt like Cox was cozyin' up to him a bit. "Yeah,
well, you know that money I told you I was hired to
protect?"

"Yep. Is that the money Smythe is promisin' to me?"

"One and the same, Radford. Sorry." *Sorrow* really
wasn't the emotion Shawn was feeling, but he could feel a

connection starting to form between him and Cox. He used his first name to help cultivate that.

"How do I know you tellin' me the truth, Shawn O'Toole?"

He was prepared for this question. "It's on YouTube." He took out his iPhone, opened up the link and played the tape of Kate Snow's *NBC Nightly News* Thanksgiving story for Cox.

"Luckridge and Smythe know that the money has been signed over?"

"Pretty sure Luckridge does. He's been tryin' to get hold of the guy he loaned money to. That guy was supposed to use the loan to hire someone to kill the people who stood to inherit all that money. But I got in the way of that. I don't know if Smythe knows or not. Depends on how truthful Luckridge has been with him." Shawn paused and rubbed his chin, "But if *you* don't know anything about the money going away, then I'd say it's one of two things. Either Smythe don't know, or he knows and he don't want to tell you the truth."

"What's happened to the guy that Luckridge made the loan to?"

"Not gonna go into the exact details, but let's just say he's unavailable."

"Well, I'd ask for picture proof of that, but based on the earlier conversation, it doesn't sound like you are the picture-takin' kind," Cox laughed.

Smiling back, Shawn replied, "No, I'm not, Radford."

The militia leader put both hands on the table and looked at Shawn, studying him, as if he was coming to some kind of decision. Then he raised one hand and snapped his fingers. A minute later a bottle of Maker's Mark Kentucky Straight Bourbon showed up at the table with two glasses. Radford poured a generous shot into each one and said, "I hate a lot of things, but the thing I hate the most is when someone tells me somethin' and then can't follow through on it." The two men reached for their glasses, clinked them together, swallowed the shot down, and then Cox asked, "What can I do to help you?"

He'd already been a bigger help than Shawn had hoped. He had Smythe's name, but he was a big fish, a lot bigger than either Charlotte Matthews or Ephraim Swain. Shawn knew it was time for caution. He looked across the table and said, "Radford, could I ask you to stand down for now? I know that's not what you were hopin' I'd ask, but I think maybe that's best."

"How so? Luckridge ... Smythe ... they're fuckin' dirt bags."

"Yeah, I know. But they're high-profile dirt bags. These are the kind of guys that hire a bunch of high-priced lawyers who pull all kinds of courtroom shenanigans and the dirt-bags walk away scot-free."

"So, let's just take the law into our own hands. There's places down here where nothin' can be found. Missin' bodies are hard to litigate." Cox said with a mischievous twinkle in his eye as he looked at Shawn and arched his eyebrows.

Shawn shook his head and reemphasized, "They're high-profile, Radford, and we can't forget that. Either one of these two boys goes missin', there'll be an investigation for sure. You don't want the feds or the state snoopin' around. Besides, we don't know enough yet about who's in this thing they call The Brotherhood. Nope. I think we need to be more cautious. Find out more about who they are."

"Okay. It ain't easy. Backin' off is a hard thing for me. Just ask some of these ol' boys in here. But you've earned some respect tonight. I'll wait to hear from you." They downed one more shot of the Maker's Mark and shook hands. Just before he left, however, Shawn stepped closer to Cox and whispered, "Radford, that other cash crop you growin' out there on the farm ... really hard to spot with all those little plots spread all over the place. Secret's good with me. Just thought you'd appreciate knowin' that."

The old man screwed up his weathered face, rubbed his gnarled hands together and simply nodded. "Your people in the CIA tell you about that?"

"FBI."

"Yeah, well, guess it's good to have them contacts." He smiled sheepishly at Shawn, "Thanks. That shit's gonna be legal one of these days, even down here in south Alabama. I'm gonna be ready when that time comes. Till then, just gotta be a little more careful and hide it out there among the peanuts."

CHAPTER TWENTY-NINE

If you get all the facts, your judgment can be right.
If you don't get all the facts, it can't be right.

—Bernard Baruch

O n the drive from Eufaula to Jackson, Mississippi, Shawn thought about his plan to confront Burl Smythe. Completely unfamiliar with the geography around Jackson, he'd reached only one definite conclusion: he would not confront the judge in the Mississippi Supreme Court Courthouse. That was Burl Smythe's territory, as was all of Jackson, for that matter. All the more reason to be slow and methodical, but he had to pick up the judge's trail at some point.

Shawn remembered what Radford Cox told him. *He drives up to this ol' Delta bar tryin' to look like a local. No fuckin' way!* At this point he recalled Cox throwing back his head and laughing uproariously. *He looked like a fish out of water if ever I'd seen one ... could tell by the way he was dressed, he'd never been to a delta bar. Then I notice when he's leavin' he's drivin' this shiny black Cadillac. So, I notice his license plate; CHJUST1.*

Shawn arrived just after first light and drove around downtown Jackson before rush hour traffic started to build. Sometime just shortly after eight, he found a parking spot along George Street where he could observe cars pulling into the parking garage he was pretty sure served the Mississippi State Supreme Court building. Sure enough, it wasn't long before he watched a black Cadillac with the CHJUST1 license plate pull in. He had his mark. Assuming Smythe was just starting his workday, Shawn pulled from the curb, found a restaurant and had breakfast before checking into a Holiday Inn Express. He used the internet to find a photo of Judge Burl Smythe, figuring it would be helpful if he could recognize the man as well as the car. After that, he decided to catch a nap before heading back to the courthouse.

It was about four-thirty on December 7 when he returned to nearly the same parking space he'd had earlier that morning. By 7:00 p.m., the black Cadillac had not yet emerged from the parking garage. Shawn thought about going in to see for himself, but dismissed it, figuring every inch of the parking garage was surveilled by camera. *Slow and methodical.* He stayed in the truck until nine before returning to his hotel. *Dammit, he must have left early today.* It was a day lost, but he reminded himself that he needed to be patient. He didn't know exactly how much; he just knew there was a lot at stake here. *Slow and methodical.*

At eight-thirty the next morning, he watched the black Cadillac pull into the parking garage. Today he would stay where he was for as long as it might take. If the judge left work early, he'd be here to pick up his trail. At 4:30 p.m., Smythe exited the garage. Shawn fell in behind him, hoping he might stop somewhere and he might be able to approach him and ask a few pointed questions. But when the judge pulled into the driveway of an upscale home in a neighborhood just north of Jackson, Shawn figured he was home, and just going up and ringing the doorbell was an idea that didn't appeal to him. *Another day lost,* Shawn thought.

Back at his hotel room, Shawn used his cell phone to call Robbie Blackmon. "How risky is it for you and our friend at the FBI to start monitoring burner calls again? I'm specifically looking for calls that Luckridge might be making to burners in Jackson, Mississippi."

"No problem, Shawn. You got any leads on the Mississippi guy?"

"Chief Justice Burl Smythe of the Mississippi Supreme Court."

Robbie gave a long, low whistle, "Wow. The net you're casting is catching some pretty big fish. Best be careful in those waters, Shawn."

"I'm trying, but getting to Smythe is proving to be a bit of a problem. I'm betting Luckridge is going to be calling him sometime soon. Any chance I could get you to let me know when those calls are taking place?"

There was a pause and then Robbie said, "Yeah, I think she and I can do that. I'll give Gail a call right now and ask."

It was the first time he'd ever used her name and Shawn caught it. "Gail, huh?"

"Uh ... yeah. We had dinner last night ... just to talk about this op."

"Listen, Robbie ... "

"Shawn, don't make a big deal out of it. It was just a working dinner—nothing more nothing less."

"Okay, my friend, but the two of you be careful. No need to call me back unless there is some problem with letting me know when the burner calls are flying back and forth."

"You got it."

At seven the next morning, after not hearing anything from Robbie, Shawn's impatience got the best of him. He needed to shake up the judge's world a little bit, so he called the public telephone number listed for Judge Burl

Smythe on the Mississippi State Supreme Court's website. The recording was a woman's voice and invited the caller to leave a message. "This call is for Judge Smythe. I'm a private investigator and I've been monitoring the calls between you and Senator Robert Luckridge. I know about *The Brotherhood of American Loyalists*. The money you were expecting isn't coming. Perhaps we should talk?" He didn't leave a call back number. As he disconnected the call he thought, *So much for slow and methodical.* Half an hour later he was parked on George Street, near the parking garage, looking to see if he'd managed to get the good judge's attention.

Smythe arrived at his office at his usual 8:30 a.m. time. At nine, Smythe's secretary—as was her habit—prescreened the judge's public telephone messages. She typically deleted those she thought were nuisance calls and she had been inclined to dump the one from Shawn, but the mention of Senator Robert Luckridge made her change her mind.

At 9:15, Burl Smythe listened to Shawn's message and immediately began to feel queasy.

At 9:30, Shawn saw the black Cadillac leave the parking garage and drive past him. He fell in behind it at a safe distance, but they didn't go far. The judge pulled his car onto the grounds of The Greenwood Cemetery just around the corner from the State Supreme Court's courthouse. Shawn hung back, but watched him come to a stop under the shade of a huge live oak. As he drove past the parked car, he saw Burl Smythe making a cell phone call. *Let me guess ... Luckridge maybe.* He proceeded well past Smythe to a spot on the opposite side of the cemetery where he could observe Smythe's parked car, but sufficiently far away that his presence would not be of any concern to the judge. All Shawn could do at this point was wait.

Frantic, Smythe broke The Brotherhood's security

protocol and left a voice mail on Luckridge's burner phone. "Bob, we got trouble. Some guy calling himself a private investigator left a message on my office phone. Says he's been listening to our calls. Says he knows about The Brotherhood. Says there isn't any money coming. What the fuck, Bob? Better call me back ASAP."

Shawn continued to watch the Cadillac, still parked in the cemetery, where it had remained for over two hours. He wished he had binoculars to see what Smythe was doing during this time. Then he got a text from Robbie and it became clear to him. *There was a call from Jackson to Luckridge just about two hours ago. Luckridge just called back. Sorry I don't have numbers or what was said, but it appears that your judge and the senator are talking to one another.* Shawn had no sooner answered Robbie's text with a "thumbs up" emoji than Smythe pulled away from the curb under the live oak, headed toward the cemetery's entrance and returned to the parking garage.

The call to Luckridge had not gone well. It began with an ass-chewing over leaving another voice mail. Smythe, pissed, angrily interrupted the Senator, "Listen, Bob, stop shooting the messenger. What I want to know is do you have any idea who this guy is—and what's this he's saying about there not being any money?"

Luckridge snarled into the phone, "Shut up, Burl, and let me think for a minute."

Smythe didn't shut up. "Listen, Bob, I've been out there talking to some pretty tough characters. They will not like it if I have to go back and tell them there is no money."

"Dammit! Listen to me. Stop panicking. I've got some connections. Don't do anything stupid. Let me see if I can find out who the fuck this is we're dealing with. Give me some time. I'll be back in touch."

"What do I tell the militia ... "

Luckridge cut him off, "Don't tell them a damned thing. We didn't promise them any money tomorrow for Christ's sake. Will you settle down?"

"I ... I don't like it, Bob. We're supposed to be a secret society. No one's supposed to know, but this guy knows. He knows about you, me and The Brotherhood. I just don't fucking like it. You worry about me leaving a voicemail on your burner. Fuck it! I'm getting voicemails on my office phone. How's that secure, Bob?"

Luckridge could sense the panic. He tried to be reassuring, but when the call ended, the senator was deeply concerned that Smythe was coming apart at the seams.

Sunday, December 10 broke bright, sunny, but somewhat chilly in Madison, Mississippi, a well-heeled community about fifteen miles north of the greater Jackson area. At 9:00 a.m., Burl Smythe sat at the breakfast table with his two daughters while his wife finished preparing pancakes and bacon for all of them. He was drinking a glass of orange juice with his head tilted back toward the wall of glass overlooking the pool area. The solar effect of the sun through the glass was producing a perfect warmth in the kitchen. The high-powered rifle round struck directly at the crown of his head. There was less than a second between the time it broke through the glass and the instant it impacted his skull. The bullet went completely through his head, exiting on a downward trajectory under his chin, then through the center of the table's wooden top until it buried itself in the tile floor. Blood splatter covered both of the daughters and reached as far as the stove top where breakfast was still being prepared.

Police responded within three minutes to the wife's 911 call. Every law enforcement agency within fifty miles of Jackson was notified within minutes of what had happened to Chief Justice Smythe. At the Mississippi Supreme Court Courthouse, the chief bailiff arrived within the hour and secured recordings of the last seven days from every security camera in and around the building.

Senator Robert Luckridge received a call to one of his burner phones notifying him the job was done and advised him final payment was now due.

By 3:00 p.m., a forensics analyst with the Mississippi State Police watched a security camera video and noticed a pickup truck, with a man sitting behind the wheel, parked just outside the parking garage serving the Mississippi State Supreme Court's courthouse. The timestamp on the video showed it was parked there for an extraordinarily long time and at one point appeared to follow Judge Smythe as he departed the garage. By 4:00 p.m., the truck was identified as registered to Shawn O'Toole. By 5:00.p.m., they had a credit card record indicating Shawn O'Toole was registered as a guest at a nearby Holiday Inn Express. At 5:30 p.m. he'd been taken into custody as a person of interest in the murder of Chief Justice Burl Smythe.

At 8:00 p.m. that evening, Shawn was allowed to make a single phone call. Mark O'Toole answered his phone. "Dad, listen. I don't want you to panic. Listen very carefully. Get a paper and pencil. I have a number for you or Charley to call." Deputies were standing on either side of him. He gave the number to his dad and had him read it back. He watched one of the deputies write the number down as well.

"What's going on, Son?"

"I'm in Jackson, Mississippi. I've been arrested for the murder of Mississippi Supreme Court Chief Justice Burl

Smythe. I didn't do it. Here's what I need you to do. Call that number." There was no point in trying to be careful here. In a matter of minutes, they'd know it belonged to Radford Cox. "Be sure you tell Radford that line is no longer secure. The deputies here just wrote it down." He watched the deputy make another note. "Tell him I need his help." Shawn watched the deputy take more notes. "I'm okay. Don't wor—"

From behind him he heard, "Time's up." The other deputy disconnected the call.

Shawn looked at both of them. "You both know that I was entitled to make that call in private, don't you?"

Neither one of them said anything. The bigger of the two pointed in a direction.

Shawn shrugged his shoulders and muttered, "Fuckin' rednecks. You got the wrong guy for this."

CHAPTER THIRTY

I get by with a little help from my friends.
    — *The Beatles*

Mark O'Toole was normally a very level-headed guy. It had always been kind of his life's mantra: *Keep your cool. Panic clouds the brain. THINK!* But Shawn's phone call pushed him to the edge. Mississippi was, if not *the* worst, at least the *second* worst state, possibly behind Alabama, for a Yankee like Shawn to wind up in jail. He immediately called Charley DeBooker and, after telling him Shawn was in jail, drove the short distance from his house to DeBooker's.

Thirty minutes later, the two of them placed a call to the number Shawn had given them. They used Charley's cell phone. Since Shawn had called his dad from the prison, both correctly assumed the authorities already had Mark's cell phone number and were probably getting the necessary warrants to begin monitoring it. The call to Cox dropped almost immediately to voice mail. "Hello, this message is for Radford Cox. Your name and number were given to me by Shawn O'Toole. My name is Charley DeBooker. Shawn asked me to tell you he's been taken into custody in Jackson, Mississippi, for the murder of Mississippi's Supreme Court Chief Justice. He said to tell you he needs your help. He said to tell you your number probably isn't secure any longer."

THE WIDOW AND THE WARRIOR

Five minutes later, Charley's iPhone rang. The caller ID showed, *Unknown Caller,* but the area code was the same as the one they'd just called. "Hello, Radford Cox here. Saw the news about ol' Burl Smythe gettin' greased. Sad thing. Right there in his own home in front of his family and all. Nobody should die like that ... just ain't right."

Charley had put his phone up on speaker so Mark could hear the conversation as well. "Mr. Cox. This is Charley DeBooker. I'm Shawn's attorney. First things first, Shawn wanted us to make sure you know the authorities in Mississippi have your cell phone number and your line isn't secure any longer."

"Yeah, I figured—already dumped that phone. This is a new one. I'm assuming this here number you're calling from ain't one them rat fuckers at the county jail have gotten their sticky fingers on."

"This number should be okay. I wanted you to know I'm leaving within the next couple of hours to go to Jackson to meet with Shawn and find out exactly what's going on. I'm sure he has more information he'll want me to pass on to you. I'll call you after I talk with him."

"That sounds good, Mr. DeB— What did you say your last name was again?"

"DeBooker, but please call me Charley."

"Sure, call me Radford. Met Shawn a couple of days ago. Seems like a straight shooter. He didn't do this, I know." There was an awkward pause. Radford had more to say. "Don't take this the wrong way. Ain't tryin' to tell you how to do your business, but ... well ... you might want to get a lawyer more familiar with the law in Mississippi, if you know what I mean, Charley. I got a good one ... one you can trust. Let him do all the talkin' with the police and especially in the courtroom. You should stay in the background. Ain't your fault you ain't from around these parts."

"Good advice, Radford."

"All right. Let me give him a call. Lawyer's name's Edsel ... Edsel Walcott. One of us'll call ya back. I promise."

"Thanks, Radford."

"Yep."

Mark O'Toole dreaded the conversation he was about to have. The caller ID on his phone told him it was Nora Schneider on the other end. He knew why. The assassination of Burl Smythe had been picked up nationally. Shawn's name and an old Army photo of him were all over the news. "Hello, Nora."

"Mark, what the heck is going on? This thing that's in the news—why is Shawn in Jackson, Mississippi? That's not back east. That's down south."

"Nora, I ... I am not sure where I should begin ... "

"Mark, it's me, Nora Schneider. Remember me? Whatever this is, I want to help. Shawn ... he ... he didn't do this ... did he?"

"Where are you?"

"High Bluff House. I just dropped Jenny at school. She's seen the news. She's asking questions. You know Jenny. I can't just dismiss her."

"I'll be right there. Put on a pot of coffee. I have a lot to tell you."

"Has anyone talked to Anna?"

"Charley's doing that. We tried to keep this away from you, not because we were trying to hide anything ... " He paused, because he knew how dreadfully untrue that sounded. "We were just trying to protect ... "

"Mark, it's okay. Just get out here and tell me what's going on."

"Anna, it's Charley DeBooker ... "

"I was about to call you. It's all over the news."

"I'm about to get on a NetJets flight to Jackson. I'll call you from there after I've talked with him."

"Charley, don't spoon feed me like you did with my mom's death, my dad, the inheritance, the curse ... all of that stuff. I'm tougher than you think."

"I know, but honestly I don't have a lot of information at this point except that we all know Shawn didn't do this."

"Luckridge behind it?"

"I ... I don't know, but I have my suspicions."

"It's all somehow linked together. We have to figure out the links for Shawn's sake. When do you expect to be back from Jackson?"

"In a day, two at the most. I've spoken with a local attorney who will defend Shawn. Once he's arraigned, I'll come home."

"Can we post bail? Can we get Shawn home?"

"Realistically, no. The charge will be first degree murder. The judge won't allow bail for a couple of reasons, not the least of which is Shawn will be considered a flight risk."

"Will he be okay in jail?"

"Yes. It won't be easy for him, but Shawn's a tough guy."

"Charley, I got money. You know that. Whatever it costs to defend him ... " She hated how that sounded, like money could assuage everything. But, she felt like this predicament Shawn was in was entirely her fault. One thing had led to the other after he'd rescued her from Charlotte. She should have just stopped it after that—all of it—Ephraim—this wild goose chase with Luckridge—it had all led to this horrible mistake.

"I know, Anna. I know. Let me get down there, make

sure he's got good counsel, and find out more about what's going on."

"I'm coming home," she declared.

"But, you ... you just got back to DC, to the paper. I don't think you need ... "

"No, Charley," she interrupted. "I'm coming home to stay."

There was a long pause and then, "But what about your job, what about your life ... "

"It's been a good run, but without Ed, I've no reason to stay here. In Frankfort, I've got you, Mark, Nora, Angels' Overwatch—and I'm no good here right now with Shawn in this kind of trouble. You realize he's there because of me, right?"

"Anna, I don't think Shawn or Mark think ... "

"Charley, they may not think that, but I know differently. No, Shawn's in prison because of me. Call me from Jackson after you've talked to him. Tell him I'm sorry and that I will do everything within my power to make it up to him."

Robbie Blackmon sat at his desk at CIA headquarters in Langley, Virginia, and was so frustrated he pounded a clenched fist on top of it. He had information, valuable information, he thought, but he'd seen the news. He knew Shawn was in jail, out of communication. He was stuck. He didn't know who to contact and he hated this feeling of helplessness.

The two attorneys, Charley DeBooker and Edsel Walcott, met at a coffee shop a few blocks from the Hinds County

Jail. They were on their way to their first meeting with Shawn. The contrast between the two was dramatic; DeBooker, well groomed, stylishly legal in his three-piece gray suit and shined wingtips. Walcott, on the other hand, wore a wrinkled sport coat, open-collared shirt and a long mane of gray hair that screamed *would someone please comb me.* DeBooker spoke in an unaccented precise style, while Walcott spoke in a slow southern drawl developed from a lifetime of living life at a much slower pace in Mississippi's delta. What they shared was a deep knowledge of the law, all aspects of it, but Walcott was definitely the more experienced in criminal law cases and especially in the ways of those cases in Mississippi.

DeBooker extended his hand. "Mr. Walcott, Charley DeBooker. Nice to meet you."

"And you as well, sir. Please call me Edsel. Radford Cox sends his best."

"I go by Charley. Radford speaks highly of you."

"Have you met Radford?"

"Only on the phone."

Walcott ran a hand through his wild hair, "He's a bit of a radical, to say the least. One of my most ... " he paused, and then smiled at Charley, "Let's just call him 'interesting' clients. One thing I will say for him though, is if he likes you, his loyalty will know no end. And he likes Shawn O'Toole."

"So, tell me, Edsel, where do we stand right now?"

"They ain't got a lot on our boy, but that prosecutor sure actin' like it's some kinda slam dunk. Arrogant little weasel. I fuckin' hate it when he acts like that ... and he acts like that a lot." Charley nodded. Edsel continued, "Listen, Charley, I don't do a lot of work down here in Jackson. Most of my work is up around Yazoo City, in the delta. I know how things work there and I think I know how things work here too. But I want to be careful. When we get in the room with Shawn, I'm gonna talk him through all the legal mumbo-jumbo of his arraignment. As I'm doin' that, I want you to pass him this note and some paper and pencil."

At Edsel's prompting, Charley opened the note.

Can't be sure who's listening. Write down anything you want me to know or the names and numbers of anyone you want me to contact. Don't say anything you don't want the authorities to know.

Walcott continued after Charley had read it. "Put his notes in your briefcase when we leave."

"But the security cameras ... "

"Oh, yeah, they'll see him writing and passing you the note. But the deputies can't mess with that. They tried it a few years back. But guess who upset their fuckin' apple cart ... ol' Burl Smythe found for the defense. It was landmark 'round these parts. For the sheriff or any law enforcement agency in Mississippi, for that matter, to confiscate notes from an attorney and/or said attorney's client is a clear violation of the attorney-client relationship. They can't touch your notes to Shawn or Shawn's notes to you."

"But you think they've got the interview room bugged? Listening in like that is a clear violation of our client's ... "

Walcott held up a hand as he interrupted, "Charley, maybe they are. Maybe they ain't. We won't take a chance."

Charley thought, *Thank you, Radford Cox, for recommending Edsel Walcott.*

An hour later both attorneys sat across from their client. Shawn's feet were shackled as were his hands and the chain connecting the hand shackles was run through a steel eyebolt screwed securely to the table's top, which made writing difficult, but not impossible. Shawn read the note and nodded. Edsel began talking and Shawn began writing.

Call Robbie Blackmon. 757 479-2470. He's a friend with the CIA. Any info Robbie has he should feel free to share with Radford Cox. The two of them should talk. I think Senator Robert Luckridge may have had Smythe killed. I think Radford can get to the bottom of this. Cooperate fully with him and his boys.

That afternoon, Shawn O'Toole was arraigned and charged with first degree murder in the death of Chief Justice Burl Smythe. The evidence was sketchy. All they had was Shawn's presence at the courthouse over several days and Burl Smythe's body. The murder weapon was missing, but the prosecutor had referred to it as "a high-powered rifle of currently unknown caliber." He'd spent some time elaborating on Shawn's military experience with similar weapons as an Army Ranger and Special Forces operator. He closed with, "I'm sure we will eventually find the murder weapon, Your Honor." In another place at another time, this might have been insufficient to bind someone over for trial, but this was Jackson, Mississippi, and one of their own, a prominent one at that, had been mercilessly gunned down. As he left the courthouse that afternoon, the cocky, young prosecutor talked with a group of reporters. "We have arraigned Shawn O'Toole on first degree murder charges. We continue to investigate this heinous crime. I assure the citizens of Jackson and Hinds County, this crime will not go unpunished. I intend to seek the death penalty for what Mr. O'Toole has done."

Before boarding the NetJets plane for the return flight to Manistee, Michigan, Charley DeBooker called Robbie

Blackmon. After explaining exactly who he was, he gave Robbie Radford Cox's telephone number. "He's expecting your call."

"Yes, sir. I have some new information. Luckridge talked with Smythe the day before he turned up dead. Luckridge also talked on a burner with someone in Santa Rosa Beach, Florida. Don't know who this was, but likely Mr. Cox can get to the bottom of that. We've had two calls involving the Santa Rosa Beach location. The one from Luckridge was the day before Smythe was shot. The one from Santa Rosa Beach to Luckridge was late in the day of the murder. Both of the calls were on burners and I don't think the timing is coincidental."

Buzzer Bradford, the former Special Forces operator who'd challenged Shawn that night at Radford Cox's bar outside of Eufaula, Alabama, stood up a little straighter in front of Radford and Radford liked that. "So tell me, Buzzer, how the fuck did you get that nickname?"

Bradford smiled, rubbed his chin and began, "My team was runnin' an op in one of Fallujah's fuckin' ghettoes. We were lookin' for this guy. He was supposedly playin' both sides against the middle. Spoke good English, so he was workin' for us, but then some things started to go south, and it seemed every time he'd get a certain piece of info, our guys would start takin' fire as soon as they got to where they were goin'. Kind of like, the fuckers knew we were comin', Mr. Cox. It didn't take us very long to put two and two together. This guy was gettin' paid by both sides. We went after him. We got to his front door, but when we looked around us, there were a bunch of hadjis watchin'. We assumed most of 'em were unfriendlies. We didn't want to just knock the door down. That would have been like pokin' a mama bear tryin' to get to her cubs. So, here's five or six of us just standin' around scratchin' our asses tryin' to figure out the best way to gain entry. So, I just stepped up and pushed his doorbell. It made a kind of a buzzin' sound. A minute later the guy we're lookin' for answers the door. Fuckin' idiot." He shrugged his shoulders and threw his hands up in the air. "Anyhow, that's how I got the nickname."

Cox laughed and asked, "What did you do with the guy?"

"Shit, sir, we had him so fuckin' scared. When we left, he was in the middle of us, and it looked like we were all goin' out for a beer or somethin'. Got his sorry ass back to base and last I knew he was locked up in some prison someplace. Sorry mother fucker."

"So, you ready for an assignment, kind of like the one you got your fuckin' nickname from?"

"Yes, sir, Mr. Cox. What can I do?"

"First off, you need to know that this is going to help Shawn O'Toole."

"Mr. Cox, you know ... "

"Buzzer, I don't give a rat's ass what you think he did to you. You're wrong. If he wanted to stick it to you, he would have reported what you did to that family. Did he do that?"

Bradford shook his head.

"He buried that picture, didn't he?"

Bradford nodded. "I s'pose so."

"So quit bein' a baby 'bout this. Shawn needs our help. Some rat fuckers are tryin' to frame him with this murder of that judge over in Mississippi. Truth be known, I should have shot that uppity mother myself when I had the chance, but I got took in. Ain't gonna happen again."

"Yes, sir, Mr. Cox. What do you need me to do?"

"That's better, Buzzer. Got an address in Santa Rosa Beach. Lookin' for an assassin and a high-powered rifle, likely with a scope on it. This needs to be a very quiet in and out. Understand?"

"Yes, sir. What do you want me to do with this person and the gun, when I get them?"

"Bring 'em both back to me ... as little damage to both as possible, Buzzer, especially the man or woman who owns the gun. He or she ain't no good to me or Shawn dead."

"Yes, sir."

"Here's the address. Big fuckin' estate or sumthin' down there on the panhandle. Make sure this cocksucker got no clue where he's goin' or how he got here. I want him to be so fuckin' confused that he won't know his ass from a hole in the ground. Here's a phone number too. It's Shawn O'Toole's CIA contact—guy's name is Robbie ... Robbie Blackmon. Feel free to contact him. Can you leave straight away?"

"Yes, sir, Mr. Cox. I'm good as gone."

CHAPTER THIRTY-ONE

I've never met a murderer who wasn't vain... It's their vanity that leads to their undoing, nine times out of ten. They may be frightened of being caught, but they can't help strutting and boasting and usually they're sure they've been far too clever to be caught.

—*Agatha Christie, Crooked House*

It was a short four-hour drive from Eufaula to Santa Rosa Beach, Florida, for Buzzer Bradford. Parked in a Tom Thumb gas station along Florida State Road 30A, about fifteen miles west of Panama City Beach, he placed a call. "I'm here. You're sure this is the place? I've been sent to the wrong fuckin' place more 'n once by you intel guys. Ain't no fun kickin' in a door and findin' out there ain't nothin' there, 'cept some mother and her kids that we've just scared half out of their wits."

"Iraq or Afghanistan?" Robbie Blackmon queried.

"Both. Take your pick. Happened both places."

"Listen, man, I'm sorry. Intel isn't a perfect science. And all I can give you is this address. Shawn and I have a friend ... works in anti-terrorism. She's fuckin' good at what she does. Normally she can wiretap, but we can't use that technology in this case. This job has to be on the down-low because of who's involved ... "

"Luckridge?"

The name surprised Robbie. "Don't know how you know that and I don't need to know, but yes, that's the guy. Certain people around here find out we're investigating him and the situation turns political. This is CIA headquarters and things in Washington are different now. Know what I mean?"

"Yeah, okay. So, comes back to my original question. You sure about this location?"

Robbie swallowed hard, then said, "Yes. It's a big parcel of land. We triangulated a series of calls coming and going from there. We don't know what was said, but Luckridge was in on them. This guy and Luckridge are connected and I ... we ... think, the guy in Florida is the guy who shot Smythe. I wouldn't be recommending to Radford that he send you in there if I weren't sure ... and if Shawn O'Toole's life didn't depend on it."

There was a long pause, and then, "Okay, man. Don't suppose you got a name do you?"

"Property records say it belongs to Mr. Richard Fortino."

"Okay, thanks. I got it from here."

Rick Fortino lived the good life on Florida's Emerald Coast. His home, all seven thousand square feet of it, sprawled on a parcel of land that measured between four and five acres, all of it ocean front. He'd been offered ten times as much for the land as he had in the house, but he'd adamantly refused. Privacy was what he wanted ... what he needed ... and the land around the house was his shield against the large numbers of tourists that seasonally moved between the various planned communities bordering each side of SR 30A. As he watched the news, he was pleased to see that somebody else had been arrested for the murder of Judge Burl Smythe. He could not fathom how this person had been implicated, but Rick Fortino was good with it, as long as it wasn't him sitting in the Hinds County Jail.

His latest girlfriend was away caring for her sick mother in Sandestin, just down the road. He was hungry for her, as he usually was after a successful "hunt," but not so hungry as to want to drive the twenty-five miles to see her in the heavy traffic he knew he'd find this time of the evening during this time of the year. Besides, he figured once he got there, she wouldn't give him what he wanted anyway. Her mother's care required her complete attention. Instead he glanced at his watch, slipped on a jacket and decided to head out to a nearby restaurant he particularly enjoyed, The Local Catch. It would be crowded, but he was hungry, and there was a cute little waitress there he liked flirting with ... maybe tonight, after she got off work ... *You never know,* he thought.

Buzzer was on his way back to the address he'd been given. His plan was to recon the property, determine his way in, way out, determine how many people were living there, see if he could determine what security systems a place like this might have ... he suspected there would be several ... and then decide how he was going to make the snatch. He was just short of the driveway when he saw lights come on atop two large stone columns on either side of the driveway's entrance. As he drove past, he saw a late model SUV waiting just inside two massive iron gates that were swinging open. With no one behind him, he slowed. In his rearview mirror he saw the SUV turn onto the road behind him heading in the same direction. A mile or so further, Buzzer swung into a convenience store parking lot, allowed the SUV to pass, and then fell in behind it at a respectable distance. In less than a mile, it pulled into a restaurant parking lot. The place was crowded, parking spaces were few and that allowed Buzzer to slowly drive past the SUV. As the driver got out, he got a good look at him.

Once inside The Local Catch, Buzzer took a seat at the

bar, ordered a beer and stared across the room at his mark, sitting at a table, alone. It was now just a waiting game.

Buzzer watched—dinner, dessert, coffee—Buzzer checked his watch, *Guy's not in any kind of a hurry*— an after-dinner drink—it all took the better part of two hours. *Finally.* He watched Fortino pick up his cell phone, pull on the coat he wore to head off the winter chill from the strong offshore winds that were blowing in from the Gulf, and walk to the men's room. Buzzer, who'd long ago paid his bar bill, went outside to the parking lot.

During his time in the Army one of the things that had tried his patience were the hours and hours spent in meticulously planning the special operations he'd participated in. Much of it, he thought, was pointless. As he stood in the parking lot, in the chill dark of a moonless coastal evening, he tried to recall a single op that had ever gone exactly as planned. There was always some overlooked detail, some circumstance that had changed, some door that was locked, but should have been unlocked, some person lurking where there should have been no one—literally a thousand things, any one of which caused the plan to change. Buzzer's original plan called for him to snatch this guy inside his home, but the restaurant's crowd had thinned extensively. Only eight to ten cars remained in the parking lot. Maybe this was an opportunity that could not have been foreseen. This could be one of those changes, though unanticipated, that could work out for the best. It would have to be fast. He would have to decide right now to do this or not.

Buzzer hid in the shadows of his car parked about fifty feet away and behind Fortino's SUV. He watched him exit the restaurant. Quickly scanning the area, he could see no one else in sight. Anyone else present would have scrapped the whole thing. Fortino did not show a key as he stepped to the driver's side door. Buzzer's mind flew through what he was observing. *It's a new car ... no keys, start button, unlocks itself when the owner approaches with the fob in his pocket.* The mark neither heard nor saw Buzzer come up from behind and soundly rap him with a pistol butt directly on the crown of his head. Before he could drop to the ground, Buzzer caught him and dragged him to the passenger side. *Was I right about the fob?* He breathed a sigh of relief as the passenger door opened. He piled his mark into the front seat, fastened his seat belt, wrapped his hands and feet together with duct tape and slapped two wraps of the stuff around his eyes. Buzzer removed the hat he was wearing and put it on his mark with the bill pulled down in the front. Then he got in behind the wheel and the two of them departed The Local Catch for Fortino's estate.

Halfway there, Fortino came to, groggy at first, but it didn't take him more than a few seconds or so to determine his hands and feet were useless. "What the fuck?"

"Hey, Mr. Fortino, welcome back to planet Earth."

"Who the fuck are you?"

"Sorry, we won't be exchanging introductory information. All that's important is that you know that I know who you are."

"What do you want?"

"All in due time ... all in due time."

As they pulled into the estate's driveway, the gates loomed in front of them. "How do these work?" He pointed to the gates for the moment forgetting that he'd blindfolded him. "The gates at your house ... how do I open them?"

Fortino smirked. "Fuck you."

It was awkward. He was seated and there was a console between them. But Buzzer had worked extensively with weights. He was strong, muscular, athletic and tipped the scales at two hundred thirty pounds. Pushing himself up in his seat, he came around with a left-hand punch that caught Fortino in the left side of his rib cage with sufficient power that it forced him to exhale every ounce of breath he had in his lungs. It sounded like a small balloon bursting. For a few seconds, he couldn't breathe and when he did, it was labored. "Oh, shit, I bet that hurt," Buzzer said, laughing. "So, know this, mister—I got a lot more of those left in me. We can sit here all night and I can keep beatin' on you or you can tell me how these fuckin' gates open."

Fortino just sat there and Buzzer obliged his obstinacy with another gut punch made all the worse because his victim could not see it coming. He watched as Fortino took a few minutes to recover and then, "How do these gates open?"

Still gasping, Fortino managed to mutter, "Remote. In the console."

"That's more like it," Buzzer said as he opened the console and found the remote. The gates swung open. Before they proceeded, Buzzer asked, "Who else is here?"

When Fortino didn't answer immediately, Buzzer balled up his fist and raised his arm. Fortino, apparently able to hear or perhaps feel his movement, gasped and then stammered, "No one ... just me."

"Security?"

Fortino nodded.

"Okay, listen to me. We're goin' in the house. Whatever security you got in there, you will disarm it just like you'd do if you was comin' home. If you fuck with me on this, there will be hell to pay. I got a Zodiak down at the shore," Buzzer lied. "If I hear a siren or see a patrol car come down in here, I'm gonna put two rounds in each of your knees. Then I'll disappear on my little boat. Yeah, you'll heal up from the wounds, but I'll place those rounds so that you likely won't ever walk again ... " he paused for the proper effect and then added, "And the other thing you'll have to worry about is when will I be back. Not *if* I'll be back, but *when*. Do we understand each other?"

Again, Fortino nodded. They parked in front of the

three-car garage attached to the main house. Buzzer got out, cut the tape binding Fortino's feet together, but linked his arm through Fortino's, guiding him to the front door. The door was locked, a keyless entry, requiring a code. "What's the front door code?" Fortino, fearing another gut punch, gave it to him. Once inside, the alarm system's warning beeps ended a second after Fortino gave him the last number. "Okay, good boy." Buzzer patted Fortino on the back like someone petting their dog. "Now, where's the rifle?"

"I don't know what the fuck you're talkin' about."

Still blinded by the duct tape over his eyes, Buzzer led him to the kitchen. "You left- or right-handed?" he asked as he turned on the water and then the garbage disposal. He saw Fortino's body stiffen. "It's the rifle or one of your hands. Which is it gonna be, Mr. Fortino?" He continued to run the water and the disposal. "So, where's the fuckin' rifle you used to kill Judge Smythe?"

Beach-front homes typically don't have basements. The water table is just too high. But people of means often have a secret interior room built into their homes where they keep their more valuable possessions. Fortino's home was one such house.

"Take the duct tape off my eyes and I'll show you."

It seemed a reasonable request, but Buzzer warned, "Remember, fuck with me and ... "

Fortino led him into the master bedroom and then into a spacious walk-in closet. He held up his bound hands as if asking for the bindings to be cut.

"Uh, that ain't happenin' there, Mr. Fortino. So, tell me why am I standin' in your fuckin' closet?"

Fortino hesitated momentarily, but as soon as he saw Buzzer ball up his fist he quickly said, "Back wall, on the left, button about halfway up."

Buzzer located the button, pushed it and the rear wall of the closet slid open. Inside was an arsenal of various weapons, but on a table, in the center of this armory, Buzzer immediately recognized what he was looking for. "So, this is it, Mr. Fortino, isn't it? SR-25, Stoner sniper rifle. I'll give you this much. You picked the right weapon for the job. Be interested in knowing what your standoff distance was when you pulled the trigger."

Fortino remained silent.

"Okay. Just curious. Not a piece of information I *have* to have."

"Listen, kid ... "

Buzzer pulled on a pair of thin plastic gloves and picked up the Stoner. It still held a magazine and he could tell by the weight of it, the magazine still contained ammo. He chambered a round and leveled the weapon at Fortino. He looked hard at his mark, whose fear was palpable, "I ain't no kid, Mr. Fortino ... not no more anyhow."

"Listen, I got money. Lots of it. Can't we work something out?"

"Mr. Fortino," Buzzer's look softened as he lowered the rifle, "maybe we could have when I was a kid, but, like I said, I ain't no kid anymore. C'mon we gettin' outta here." But as they exited the hidden room, Buzzer had a thought. He led Fortino to the bedroom, pushed him down on the bed and said, "Don't make a move." He pulled his phone out of a hip pocket and punched up Robbie Blackmon's number. "Blackmon, it's Bradford. Listen I've got the prick that shot Smythe. Lookin' at him right now and I'm holdin' the sniper rifle he used. But I got a question for you." Buzzer could hear a sigh of relief on the other end of the line.

"Go ahead. I'm listening."

"Radford wanted me to bring the gun with me, but I'm not so sure I should do that. Maybe I should just leave it here and let the cops find it right where I did. This fucker's got a secret room that looks like an armory. It was in there, lyin' on a table right in the middle of the fuckin' place. Not even the cops could miss it." Robbie didn't answer right away. Buzzer continued, "I sure the fuck ain't no lawyer, but there's this thing called *probable cause* ... seems to me we might fuck that up if I take the rifle with me. I mean, how the fuck are we gonna explain how we got our hands on it. We can't just hand it to 'em and say here's the Smythe murder weapon. They'll wanna know how we come by it. How we gonna answer that, Robbie?"

"I ... I ... don't know. You make a good point. I don't know how we'll get it into their hands, but I think you're right, it would be best if we could let them find it in this guy's house. So, leave it ... " Robbie paused momentarily and then confirmed, "Yeah, I say leave it."

"Yeah, I think so too. Ol' Radford will have my ass, but it wouldn't be the first time. I think leavin' it here is the best thing to do. We can work on how we go about tippin' off the cops. Thanks, Robbie." He disconnected the call and turned his attention to Fortino. They returned the rifle to the hidden room and then Buzzer asked, "You got video surveillance on this place?" Fortino was slow to answer and it earned him another quick shot at the same spot on his left rib cage. Buzzer let him roll around on the floor for a minute as he tried to catch his breath. "Get up." Fortino recovered to all fours. "Once again, asshole, does this place have video surveillance?"

This time Fortino nodded.

"How many days does it record before it dumps? Before you consider lyin' to me, you best know that we are on our way to meet a man that kinda rules the roost where we goin'. He won't like it if someone comes looking for me because they saw my picture in a surveillance video. It won't go easy for you. Clear, Mr. Fortino?"

"Seven days. It recycles itself every seven days."

"Anyone else gonna be here in the next seven days."

"Maybe my girlfriend."

277

"Where's she?"

"Sandestin. She's takin' care of her mother."

"Well, here's what we gonna do 'bout that. Where's your cell phone?"

Fortino replied, "Jacket pocket."

Buzzer reached in, pulled it out and said. "We gonna call her. You gonna tell her you'll be out of town for the next two weeks. If it don't sound convincin' to me, I'll fuckin' put a bullet in your knees right here and now. Tell her you're gettin' some work done on the house and she won't want to be here while the workers are at it. Understand?"

Fortino nodded.

"What's her name?" Fortino gave it to him and Buzzer looked her up on the cell phone's directory. Fortino did exactly as he was directed.

It was after midnight when they returned to the Local Catch's parking lot. Buzzer's truck was the only vehicle there. They parked Fortino's SUV at the farthest end of the lot and walked to the truck. Once he had him strapped in, Buzzer re-taped Fortino's feet, slapped two wraps of duct tape around his eyes, and put his hat on Fortino's head with the bill down low, so passersby wouldn't see the duct tape. "Don't get no ideas 'bout tryin' to 'scape."

They drove the four hours back to Eufaula, Alabama, arriving at Radford Cox's farm in the early morning hours. The cattle gate blocking the two-track leading to the farmhouse was unlocked. Buzzer and Fortino were expected.

Radford Cox dialed Charley DeBooker's number. "Charley, got a guy here name of Fortino. Ever heard of him?"

"No, can't say that I have."

"Yeah, well, he's an employee of Senator Robert Luckridge. Seems Mr. Fortino's a hitman. He's done three jobs recently for the senator; first was a car salesman up your way in Yankeeland, then another car salesman down here—read about that one in the local Dothan paper. His most recent victim was Judge Burl Smythe of the good state of Mississippi."

"He's admitted this?"

"Yep. Well, he was under some duress, but nothin' that won't heal up fine and dandy in a week or two. My boy that fetched him laid eyes on the murder weapon, but left it where it was. At first I wanted to thump him one for not bringin' it back here, but he 'splained he'd talked to Robbie Blackmon who thought it best to leave the weapon where it is."

"Where's that?" Charley asked.

"Seems Mr. Fortino's got a secret room in his house down there on the panhandle. My boy says it's like a fuckin' armory. Now that we've discussed it, it does seem like the right thing to have done. I'll bet the farm on findin' Fortino's prints all over it and ballistics tests will prove it was the gun used to kill Smythe."

"So, the trick is how do we get that murder weapon into the hands of the authorities?"

"Zactly," Cox replied. "You're right up to speed there, Charley. So, how do you think we should play it from here? My guess is that Robert Luckridge is feelin' right smug about now. He's gotten away with murder not just once, but three times, and Shawn's sittin' in the jailhouse charged with the most recent one. We could fuckin' rock his world if he found out we got his assassin confessin' to all three jobs, don'tcha' think?"

There was a pause and then DeBooker replied, "We should get this guy to the authorities and let him tell his story to them. I know the big fish here is Luckridge, but I'm thinking of Shawn O'Toole cooling his heels in that Mississippi lockup facing the death sentence as well. What if there was some way we could turn the guy you got over to the authorities and let him tell them he was working for Luckridge. That would trigger the FBI getting involved in looking at the senator and it would exonerate Shawn at the same time." There was a longer pause. DeBooker could hear what sounded like pigs squealing in the background. "Where are you, Radford?"

"Oh, just took a break from our friend and stepped out of the barn to slop a few pigs. Needed to clear my head a bit." Cox threw another bucket of slop into the pen and the pigs squealed louder. Cox continued, "Let me give Edsel Walcott a call. I'll see what he thinks."

"Radford, I know he's Shawn's lawyer, but be careful who you tell about this Fortino character. After all we did transport him against his will over state lines. Up here that's called kidnapping and I'm pretty sure that definition holds true in Alabama as well."

"Hey, no worries, Charley. I'd trust Edsel with my life. Besides, he's my lawyer too ... so we got that thing you call attorney-client privilege, right?"

"That's what they call it. Let me know what Edsel thinks."

"Sure will, Charley. Don't worry, we ain't gonna let that rat fucker Luckridge sneak by. I'll be in touch."

It was two weeks before Christmas, 2017. Mr. Rick Fortino had been Radford Cox's guest for the last three days and life had not been easy for him. It was a cool, but beautifully sunny day in Eufaula when Radford Cox and Buzzer Bradford walked into the barn where Rick Fortino sat bound to a folding chair, blindfolded and gagged. Both men could see him tense up as he heard them enter the barn.

Radford said, "Saw on your Florida driver's license that

your full name is Richard L. Fortino. So, what do they call you? ... Rich? ... Rick?" A rag was in his mouth with duct tape over that; there was no way he could possibly answer. Radford chuckled as he ripped the duct tape off Fortino's eyes along with a generous amount of his hair, causing him to grunt loudly through the gag. Cox bent down in front of his squinting victim, "Don't matter. I'm gonna call you, *Dick*, Dick, 'cause that's pretty much what the fuck you are."

Buzzer laughed.

"So, Dick, ever see a man die by lethal injection?" Cox paused, letting that sit there for a minute. "As things stand right now, you gonna die one way or the other. I might let Buzzer here," he threw a thumb in Bradford's direction, "finish you off and we'll feed you to them hogs out there. They'll eat pretty much any damned thing, ya know, Dick, and that includes your sorry ass. And the nice part about that is there won't be no body that could be dug up. Them pigs'll just turn you into pig shit. Why I've thrown animal carcasses in their pen before and they eat everythin', even the bones." He paused for effect, and then continued. "Or the State of Mississippi will stick a needle in your arm. That can go either way. Heard sometimes them poor boys on death row jus' go to sleep, nice and peaceful when the drugs take effect. Then I heard other times somethin' goes wrong. Heard one guy right here in Alabama suffered terrible, strapped down there on the table, twitchin' and shit. Guess he's awake the whole time. The warden and the guards all runnin' around like chickens with they heads cut off, not knowin' what to do, what went wrong. Took the poor fucker some three hours to pass on to his reward. Know what I mean, Dick?" Cox laughed, then added, "Personally, I'd like to see you lower my hog-feed bill." He reached down and stripped the duct tape from Fortino's mouth in one quick motion. Then he reached for a long set of barbecue tongs from a nearby shelf. "Gotta use these to fish that fuckin' rag outta your mouth. Some fella' bit me a few years back when I did it with my fingers. Ain't fallin' inta' that trap twice. Hold still." Cox grabbed a corner of the cloth with the tongs and yanked it free of Fortino's mouth. "So, tell me, Dick, how do you want to die?"

Buzzer had seen it before, Fortino's fear was palpable, "I ... I ... I don't want to die."

"Yeah, yeah, yeah, Dick. None of us *want to.*" Radford bent over in front of him and in his deepest, best Sunday-preachin'-at-church voice, quoting Philippians, said, "*I am hard pressed between the two. My desire is to depart and be with Christ, for that is far better. But to remain in this flesh is more necessary on your account.* Are you hard pressed, Dick? 'Spect you probably won't be depar-tin' to be with Christ though. 'Spect you be spendin' time with that other feller, 'stead. That's cause you're a dick, Dick!" Buzzer stood back with his arms across his chest and smiled.

"Listen, I got money ... "

"Now, see there, Dick. That's a mistake on your part. You assumin' I can be bought off." Radford Cox rubbed a rough hand over his chin. "And in most cases, you'd be 'bout right. But not in this case. Nope, you gonna die, either right here on this farm or in Parchman Prison."

Fortino broke down, sobbing. He kept repeating, "I don't wanna die ... I don't wanna die ... "

Cox and Bradford stood there staring at him. They had him exactly where they wanted.

Later that afternoon Cox placed a call to Edsel Walcott, Shawn's attorney-of-record, to tell him that Rick Fortino had decided to turn state's evidence in the matter of the murder of Judge Burl Smythe and to ask how he'd like to meet his new client.

CHAPTER THIRTY-TWO

Many blush to confess their faults, who never blush to commit them.

—William Seker

Anna Shane stood in front of Charley DeBooker's desk with rage in her voice. She was as angry as he'd ever seen her. "I hope they execute him three times; once for each person he's killed."

DeBooker remained calm and in his best professional baritone said, "Well, he's likely killed a lot more than that, but you should know that's not the deal we've offered Fortino, Anna."

She plopped down in the leather chair in front of his desk, took a deep breath and asked, "Okay ... okay ... I know how this works. We get Shawn back, Fortino ... what? ...goes to jail? For how long, Charley? And what about that shameless bastard, Luckridge? What happens to him?"

Charley held up both his hands, again trying his best to be reassuring. "We get Shawn back. That's the most important thing, wouldn't you agree?"

She nodded.

"Given who Fortino killed, the chief justice of the Mississippi Supreme Court, and how he did it, in front of his family like that, he's going to get life—that's the deal, *life instead of death.* He'll be incarcerated in Parchman Prison. Have you heard of it?"

She shook her head, still angry, but some of her rage settling out of her.

"Not a good place to be."

"What about Luckridge?"

"Remains to be seen. I'll know more after today. Walcott's taking Fortino to the authorities in Jackson today. We have a plan. Now we just have to wait and see how it all plays out."

At 10:00 a.m., on Monday, December 18, Edsel Walcott entered the Jackson, Mississippi Police Headquarters with a disheveled Rick Fortino next to him. Before they went in, Walcott pointed out Buzzer and two other tough-looking guys in a parked car just across the street. Walcott cautioned his client, "Don't fuck this up, Rick. You do that and Radford Cox will hunt you down and make you beg to die."

Standing in front of a thick, bulletproof window, the attorney spoke into the slotted opening, "I'd like to see the detectives handling the Burl Smythe murder."

The desk sergeant looked at Walcott and then at Fortino, "You are?"

"Edsel Walcott, attorney representing Mr. Richard Fortino."

"And what does Mr. Fortino have to do with the murder of Judge Smythe?"

"He's admitted to murdering the judge. So, you've got the wrong guy in jail for it right now."

The desk sergeant rolled his eyes. "Have a seat. I'll see if either of the detectives is available ... "

Walcott bristled, noting the rank on the desk sergeant's shirtsleeve, "Listen, Sarge, I ain't gonna go over there and take a seat. I also represent Shawn O'Toole. You jerk me around on this and we'll file a suit against the Jackson Police Department so fast, it'll make your head swim. But all of that will be after I've marched down to *The Clarion Ledger* and let a reporter talk with my client. Is that what you want?"

The sergeant picked up the phone and punched in an extension. Walcott couldn't hear what he was saying, but a couple of minutes later a detective took the two upstairs to an interrogation room where they were met by another detective who started the questioning.

"What happened to your client?"

Walcott answered coolly, "I don't see where my client's appearance is particularly relevant to what he has to say. So let's just leave it at, 'he's had a rough couple of days'."

"Yeah, I'll bet." He turned his attention to Fortino, "So, let's hear your story." Without interrupting him, the detectives let him spill his guts about Smythe's murder, but omitting any reference to Senator Robert Luckridge per his instructions from Edsel Walcott. When Fortino finished, one of them asked, "So, why are you confessing?"

Walcott laid a hand on his client's arm and answered for him, "Not sure why that's any more relevant than my client's appearance. Mr. Fortino has given you an address, security system codes to get inside and information on what you will find there."

The detectives, both of them, left them sitting there. Every fifteen minutes, Edsel would step out into the hallway looking for someone to give him a status report. It was as if they'd been abandoned in the interrogation room. Then, two hours after they'd left, the two detectives returned. "Walton County Sheriff's Department reports they found a Stoner sniper rifle at Mr. Fortino's property. They also verified he is the owner of the property."

Walcott smiled at the two of them and then nodded at Fortino. "Okay, then here's what I want you to do. Get the prosecuting attorney's office over here ASAP. This case is about to get bigger than just Jackson, Mississippi, and the murder of the state's Supreme Court Chief Justice."

On Tuesday, December 19, Shawn O'Toole walked out of the Hinds County jail a free man, and Edsel Walcott was recorded as the defense attorney-of-record for Richard Fortino who was about to be arraigned on first degree murder charges. On Wednesday, December 20, agents from the Jackson field office of the Federal Bureau of Investigation gleaned some startling information from Fortino about the involvement of a sitting US Senator, Robert Luckridge, in a murder-for-hire scheme to eliminate three men who were involved in something called The Brotherhood of American Loyalists. To back up his story, Fortino turned over information on all of his offshore accounts that together totaled over ten million dollars. That information was, in turn, given to the Bureau's forensic accountants who held some leverage over small countries like Switzerland, the Bahamas, the Cayman Islands, etc. There were some rules that had to be followed, but Fortino had given them complete access to his accounts. He'd also given them dates of his murders for Luckridge. Once they'd looked in Fortino's accounts and seen large deposits near those dates, they were free to demand information as to where those deposits had come from since such payments were likely linked to the commission of a felony. Their search led them on a dizzying trail of shell companies, shadowy organizations, and shady individuals, but once that first link was found, the rest of it unraveled like pulling at a loose thread until the seam comes completely undone. Looking at who sat on boards of directors, who could access accounts, who could make deposits and withdrawals, Luckridge's name was there, buried deep enough that casual observation wouldn't raise any eyebrows, but add in dates, times, amounts and match them up against murders Fortino had admitted to and the pattern was damning.

Senator Robert Luckridge tried to be his usual self, as he attended early Christmas Eve services at Grace Cathedral, not far from his historic home in Charleston, South Carolina's Battery district. Inside, however, he was frothing discontent. His chief of staff had phoned him earlier to tell him he'd received a call from a friend at the Department of Justice. The FBI was investigating his involvement in the Burl Smythe murder. Luckridge's subsequent calls to Fortino's burners had gone unanswered.

Twilight was fading as the Christmas Eve service came to an end. Between the cathedral's front door and his car, Luckridge schmoozed and shook hands with a dozen or so constituents. At the car, he opened the passenger-side door for his wife to get in and closed her door behind her. As he stepped around the back of the car, a loud crack split the air.

Memories of the massacre at Mother Emanuel African Methodist Episcopal Church, not that far away from Grace Cathedral in downtown Charleston, though two years in the past, weren't lost on the hundreds of Christmas Eve worshippers leaving the service. The shot sent panic sweeping through them like wildfire. Everyone ducked, children were swept up in the arms of parents, those outside the cathedral fled in all directions, those in the doorway and those behind them, still in the sanctuary, froze and looked around frantically. Everyone waited for more gunfire.

Inside the plush Mercedes Benz SUV, Beatrice Luckridge mistook the shot as the muffled, distant sound of a car backfiring. She waited for her husband to open the driver's side door and when he didn't she began looking around. She noticed the panic occurring around the church's entrance. She got out and called, "Bob." She couldn't see him, nor did he respond to her call. Then she stepped around the front of the car to find her husband lying in a pool of blood near the driver's-side rear tire. As she knelt, she could see the gaping hole in the front of his head where his forehead should be, and she began screaming at the top of her lungs.

CHAPTER THIRTY-THREE

Death isn't the end, it's the beginning.

> *—Jennifer Love Hewitt ... and a bunch
> of other people as philosophical as she is,
> just not as famous!*

High Bluff House was hosting its first Christmas Eve gathering. There would be thirty-five to forty people attending. That size group was just a bit too small for the common dining area, so Anna, wanting the evening to be more intimate, decided to transform the library's main sitting area into a dining room. Along the north wall, a fire blazed in the floor-to-ceiling fireplace. Sofas and easy chairs had been arranged in front of it for those who preferred to sit and sip their before-dinner cocktails. Radford Cox sat ensconced in the easy chair closest to the fireplace. "Miss Anna, that flight up here on that private jet was amazin'. It's been nice finally meetin' y'all." He held his hands out toward the fire and rubbed them together. "But, us southerin' boys can't take this here notherin' cold. Nonetheless, I thank ya for havin' me. Buzzer says he's sorry he can't be here." He tossed Anna a sly look, "But he's got a girl he's courtin' and ya know how that is."

Anna patted him on the shoulder, "Just glad you could make it, Radford. Sorry about the cold weather, but it just goes with the holiday season for us Yankees." They laughed and Anna added, "I can't thank you enough for what you did for Shawn."

"No thanks, necessary, Miss Anna."

She'd already told him a dozen times to just call her Anna, but finally gave up on that effort and she found his name for her quite charming in the style of great, old southern chivalry.

"I liked Shawn first time I met him."

That wasn't exactly how Anna had heard about it from Shawn, but she let the contradiction slide.

Across the room, Shawn and Mark O'Toole, Charley DeBooker, Robbie Blackmon, Nora Schneider, Jenny and her ever-present companion, Rusty, were clustered together. Robbie said to Shawn, "Sorry Gail couldn't make it tonight. Her mother and father had planned for a long time on coming to DC for Christmas and she couldn't disappoint them."

Shawn said, "Yeah, I was really looking forward to meeting her. What she did was key." Glancing at Robbie, he asked, "She gonna be okay? I mean there's no way anyone will ever know how much she helped us pinpoint Luckridge, right?"

Reassuringly Robbie nodded, "She's good, Shawn. No worries."

Nora looked at Shawn, "I'm not trying to make the holidays go any faster than they always do, but how much longer will we be able to enjoy your company around here?"

Shawn had been back in Frankfort for four days following his time spent in the Hinds County Jail. His first stop upon his return was to find Nora and explain everything to her. She had at first been cool toward him, resenting somewhat what she took as his lack of faith in her, but now she was asking how much longer he'd be in town. *This is good. Maybe she'd soon be moving in the direction of forgiveness*, he thought. He knelt down to give Rusty an ear rub and looked up at her. "I'm in no rush. Right now the only thing calling me back to Utah is my neighbor, the sheep rancher. He left me a message. He's got another border collie he's lookin' to get rid of. This one is younger than Rusty. She's hurt a front leg. Vet says she'll ... "

Jenny interrupted, "*She*?" It's a girl? Oh, you've got to save her, Shawn. Maybe she and Rusty could have ... "

Nora jumped in with both feet. "Whoa! Hold up there, little girl. You're getting way ahead of yourself here." Everyone chuckled.

Nora smiled warmly at him and said, "So, you've got to get back there and save her?"

Shawn said, "Well, yeah, if she's anywhere near as good a dog as ol' Rusty here," he pointed to the dog whose ears perked at the mention of his name. "But the rancher said he'd keep her until I can get back. Despite his gruffness, he does seem to have a heart for these dogs even though he'd never admit to that." Shawn nodded in the direction of Anna and Radford in front of the fireplace, "Kinda like ol' Radford over there, I guess."

By now the other guests for the evening were filtering into the library. There were now six families living at High Bluff House, residents of Angels' Overwatch. Nora took care of introductions as best she could, and Anna picked up the slack when the numbers became overwhelming. As Anna and Nora had talked and made the difficult decisions about which families would be invited to stay at High Bluff House, there was never any discussion of race, gender or quotas. Decisions were based upon need. However, both of them were pleased that the current population reflected diversity. Two of the families were black, one was Latino. Anna, who'd actually grown to like Radford Cox, nevertheless, felt there was a point she needed to make with him, so she made sure she was the one to introduce him to these minority families.

After the third introduction, he said to her, "I see what you're doin' here, Miss Anna."

"That transparent, huh?"

"Yeah." He rubbed a hand over his cheek. "But I guess I can't blame you."

"Radford, you are an enigma wrapped in a contradiction to me," she said, placing a hand on his shoulder. "Before all of this started with Shawn, I would have said you boys down there were nothing more than an extension of the Klan—just a bunch of *crackers*. But what you did for Shawn ... well, it just defies description for me."

He looked hard at her at first, but quickly softened. "I guess I can see where you might draw that conclusion. And I got to admit, the membership ain't very diverse, if you know what I mean." Then he quickly added, "But we got women that come out and shoot and train with us. Yes, ma'am, we got some pretty good women shooters among us, Miss Anna." He paused for a long time. Anna let him have the time to think. "We don't want to be about overthrowin' the gobment nor nothin' like that. We know we got to have gobment; we just don't want big gobment. I have to admit, I got a little greedy when Burl Smythe came up in our parts and started offerin' me money. He wasn't real clear what he wanted us to do, but eventually, I read between the lines. He wanted us to be his enforcer down in Alabama, Georgia and Florida. Didn't set real well with me then and it sure don't sit well now. Yeah, I'm gonna be thinkin' about some structural changes to my organization when I get back home. That might not set very well with some of them ol' peckerheads ... " Radford Cox blushed, "I'm sorry Miss Anna, I shouldn't have said ... "

Anna smiled and said, "It's okay, Radford. Call it like it is. A peckerhead's a peckerhead."

"Yes, ma'am, they sure are, and I guess my peckerheads are gonna have to become part of the solution 'stead of bein' a part of the problem. Know what I mean, Miss Anna?"

"I do, Radford. I do."

"So, these here families are all widows of American soldiers?"

"They represent all of the services, Radford. No Coast Guard yet, but there will be, sooner or later."

"You know I was a soldier once."

"I do know that. You served in Vietnam. You were awarded the Silver Star and Purple Heart."

Cox looked over in the direction of Shawn and Robbie Blackmon and pointed to them, "They tell you that?"

"A good reporter won't divulge her sources, Radford. Thanks for your service, though."

"Thank you. It's wonderful what you're doin' with your money, Miss Anna," Cox said as he swatted something from the corner of his eye as a bear would take a swipe at a pesky fly. "These families deserve it for their sacrifice."

One of the facility's full-time cooks came up to her and whispered in her ear.

"Thank you, Dana. I'll let everyone know. Excuse me, Radford, but dinner is ready." Anna went to one of the tables, picked up a spoon, and tapped the side of a water glass. The room soon quieted. "I'd like to welcome everyone to High Bluff House and to our first celebration to be held here. It only seems appropriate that we should be celebrating the founding of Angels' Overwatch at Christmas, the most joyous time of year. Dinner is served. It's buffet style, so help yourselves and then return here and find your seat. Welcome, everyone!" After a round of cheers and applause, she led the way to the buffet line.

Dinner was followed by a visit from Santa, gifts for the children and quiet conversation among the adults. Anna, who'd been looking for the opportunity to speak to Nora ever since she'd seen Nora, Shawn and Jenny sitting together at dinner, finally found the chance to ask her, "So, how long is he staying."

Nora blushed. "I'm not exactly sure, but I think he's planning on being here through the New Year. He has to go back and rescue another dog from his neighbor, but he doesn't seem to be in any big hurry to get that done. He's worked something out with the guy."

"That's wonderful, Nora."

Likewise, Nora had been looking for a chance to speak to Anna. "Are you okay with what had to be done?"

Anna nodded and a long pause drew out between them. "It was vigilante justice. I knew that, and if Ed would have been alive, he would never have allowed it. But he was dead, and to be honest, I didn't care what Shawn might have to do. I wanted to see Charlotte dead for what she did to Mom and Ed—Ephraim too. I was stuck in my own grief and not thinking of anyone else. Then when Charley told me about Shawn's situation, I began to feel really guilty about putting him a position where ... " her voice trailed off.

Nora said, "I know. I have been pretty rough on him the last few days myself, but I'm coming to grips with it. He didn't kill them, Anna. He gave them a chance, which is a helluva lot more than either of them did with your mother, Ed and—if not for Shawn—you and Charley. Shawn isn't ... I mean if I thought he was some kind of a monster, I'd never want to be near him, much less let Jenny be around him. But ... " again the pause drew out. "I really enjoy his company, and Jenny—well, all I hear is Shawn this and Shawn that. I know part of it is because he gave Rusty to her, but ... I know her and she's really becoming quite fond of him."

Anna wrapped her arms around Nora and softly said, "I believe he's a really good man that has had to deal with a lot of misery and sorrow. I see how the two of you look at one another and it makes me happy—it truly makes me happy."

The rest of the evening wound down slowly. The residents of High Bluff House retreated to their apartments. The kitchen staff had cleaned up and gone home to their families. Nora had put Jenny and Rusty to bed. She'd left their apartment door ajar in case Rusty decided he wanted to join the adults after Jenny fell asleep. When she returned to the library she found the group sitting around the fireplace rehashing the events of the last few months. Anna, Mark, Charley, Radford, Robbie and Shawn were enjoying a libation of sixteen-year-old single malt scotch Charley had brought. The doorbell's ring came as a surprise. Anna and Nora looked at one another and shrugged. Shawn asked, "Anyone expecting visitors?" His question went unanswered as Nora headed to the door.

Standing on the covered porch was a thirty-something black woman and an elderly couple. "I ... I'm sorry. I know it's late, but I'm looking for Robbie Blackmon. Is he here?"

"He is," Nora said. "Please come in out of the cold!"

Once they were inside, Nora said, "Robbie, there's someone here to see you."

He looked up, surprised. "Gail? My God, girl, what are you doing here?

With some distress in her voice she said, "I'm sorry, Robbie. We've been driving since very early this morning. I didn't know what else to do."

"What is it?"

Gail Prudhomme introduced her parents and then asked, "Have you seen the news this evening?"

He shook his head, "No."

"Robbie. I'm scared."

By now, Anna and Shawn had filtered over to the front door. After introductions, Robbie tried to reassure her, "Gail, what is it? What's goin' on?"

She looked at her parents and then back to Robbie, "Someone shot Robert Luckridge tonight in Charleston. He's dead."

Nora went to turn on a TV amid a mixed chorus of *What the hell* and other more profane expletives that spewed out of various mouths.

"There's more."

Anna suggested that they all move in toward the fireplace and have a seat. As the group moved in that direction, Shawn took their coats, Robbie offered them a shot of scotch to help warm them. Gail's father, Frank, was the only taker.

Then Gail began, "I ... I made a mistake ... "

Shawn and Robbie exchanged glances as Robbie asked, "What happened?"

Gail took a deep breath, looked at her parents and then began, "I used a system to get some information. It was one of the systems that require me to log in."

"What system was that?" Robbie asked.

"It's called PHONETRAK. We can access personal call information. We're not supposed to use it unless a warrant has been issued." She paused and then added, "But I needed to know who specifically Luckridge was talking to." She turned to Shawn, "I know I should have shut the whole thing down after you were released, but I didn't."

Shawn said, "It's okay, Gail. Tell us what happened."

"About 6:00 this morning, I checked our system ... the one I invented to triangulate the calls they were making on these burners. At 1:00 this morning, Luckridge had gotten a call on a burner phone. It was a single call. The call lasted five minutes."

Robbie perked up, "So, it's like he was expecting a call on that burner?"

"Exactly," Gail responded.

Anna said, "I'm confused."

Shawn explained, "This isn't the normal call pattern. Normally, one burner calls another. There's no answer, no voice mail, no text, but the called burner records the number. Then at some point later, usually a few hours at least, the called party checks the burner, sees there was a call and returns it, usually on a different burner. It's only efficiency is that these calls are nearly impossible to intercept." Anna nodded.

Gail continued, "So, I used our system to triangulate where the burner call to Luckridge came from."

Robbie asked, "And?"

"You aren't going to like the answer. It came from somewhere on the grounds at 1600 Pennsylvania Avenue."

For the next thirty seconds or so, you could hear a pin drop, the only noise the occasional crackle of the dying fire in the fireplace.

Gail swallowed hard and said, "That's when I made a decision. I knew the possible consequences, but I ... " She began to cry.

Shawn tried to reassure her, "Gail, we couldn't have done what we've done in the past months without your help. All of us trust your judgment. So, it's okay."

She nodded and continued, "So, I wanted to know more. I wanted to see if Luckridge had received any calls from the White House in advance of the burner call. I went into PHONETRAK, entered some bogus warrant information and I put in Luckridge's personal cell phone number. Like I said, I had to log on to do that. I knew the risk, but ... "

Shawn glanced at Robbie. Robbie shook his head.

Gail saw that exchange of looks and added, "I never would have taken the risk, but now the White House seems to be involved in all of this somehow."

Shawn looked at her and then at her parents. "Don't worry. You're safe now."

"I took a look at Luckridge's cell phone records for the past twenty-four hours. There it was ... Luckridge got a call at 12:56 a.m."

Shawn had put two and two together. "So, four minutes

before the five-minute burner call, Luckridge got a call on his personal cell phone, probably telling him a call was going to come in and he'd better answer it."

Gail nodded, "That's exactly what I'm thinking."

Robbie asked, "So, Gail, this system you guys have at the Bureau—this PHONETRAK—it allows you to pinpoint the caller's phone?"

"Yes." She looked toward Robbie. "I was going to call you with what I'd found out, but it was too early. Then, around 7:00 a.m., I got a call from my boss at the Bureau. I didn't answer it, but he left a voicemail." There was an ominous pause and then Gail added, "He wants to know what I was doing in that system ... and that's when I got scared. I woke Mom and Dad up, told them to pack and we got the hell out of town. I'm as good as done at the FBI."

Shawn hung his head. "This is exactly what I feared might happen. You were trying to help me." He paused, then said, "I don't know what to say, Gail."

Robbie was the one who stayed on task. "Gail, so you know exactly where that call to Luckridge's personal cell phone came from?"

She nodded, "The Office of White House Counsel." Silence permeated the room as everyone evaluated the gravity of what they'd just been told. Gail broke the silence, "Robbie, you know what Washington's like right now. The president is hunting leakers. I don't know if he's directly involved in this, but that call came from ... " No one said anything giving Gail time to compose herself. "All I could see happening this morning is the White House, the Bureau and the Department of Justice lining up to come after me. Then about six this evening, we were somewhere between Cleveland and Toledo, I heard on the news Luckridge had been shot and killed. It isn't just about losing my job now. Luckridge was murdered. I could be next." She glanced at her parents, who'd remained silent throughout this entire explanation because Gail had already gone over the scenario with them. "Whoever is responsible for Luckridge's death likely already knows I tapped into his personal cell phone records." She dabbed at a tear as her mother began to cry.

Gail's father added, "So, she said she knew Robbie was here ... said she'd been invited, but turned it down because we were comin' to DC for Christmas. I was the one suggested we drive out here and see you," he looked at Shawn, "thinkin' maybe you could help us. Seems to me we gotta hide out for a while."

Shawn nodded and turned to Nora, "Can we get these folks a room and maybe something to eat?"

"Certainly."

Nora put her arm around Gail's shoulders. "You and your mother and father come with me. Let's get you settled in for the evening. Do you have things in the car?" Everyone nodded. Nora turned to Radford and Mark who were standing next to one another. "Could you two see to their things? Please bring them up to the second floor."

It was just before midnight, Christmas Eve as Shawn, Robbie, Charley, Mark, Radford, Nora, and Anna reconvened in front of the fireplace where embers still smoldered. Anna asked the first question, "Any ideas?"

Shawn said to Robbie, "You know they are going to look at Gail's cell phone records to see who she's been talking to. How did the two of you communicate?"

Robbie hung his head. "On our cell phones."

"Yeah, that's what I thought. So, you know they are going to be coming to ask you questions; *what's your connection to Gail Prudhomme? Etcetera, etcetera.*" Robbie nodded. Shawn continued, "Someone ordered Luckridge killed. I don't think it's safe for you to go back to Langley." Again, Robbie nodded.

Radford Cox cut right to the chase, "So, we need to hide four people."

Shawn said, "I don't know. Things will really hit the fan when they can't find Gail. Then when they can't find Robbie ... "

Cox said, "You know one of the last fuckin' ... oh, shit ... I mean ... I'm sorry, Miss Anna, Miss Nora."

"It's okay, Radford. We've heard it all before," Anna said.

"Uh ... yeah ... well, then in that case, here goes ... one of the last fuckin' places they'd ever come looking for three black people is my peanut farm down there in Eufaula. Most everyone around those parts thinks I'm a real redneck—last place they'd ever look for a black person is on my farm. What do ya' think?"

Shawn asked, "What happens if they find out you're harborin' ... "

"Ain't no one comes nor goes off that farm lessen I let 'em. You know that, Shawn. My folks'll do what I tell them to do. They'll lock the place down so tight it'll look like a bull's ass at fly time."

Shawn discussed some rules with Radford and Robbie, who didn't seem too disappointed that he was going to have to be locked down with Gail. "No credit cards, no cell phones. You can't take Gail's car. They'll be looking for it. We'll get you a car to make the trip, but once you get to Eufaula, you never leave the farm, not until either Radford or I tell you it's safe. Okay?" Robbie nodded. Shawn turned to Radford, "I still have the money from Charlotte's and Swain's accounts. I can transfer some of that to—"

Cox held up a big, weathered hand, "No need, Shawn. We'll give these folks the finest southerin' hospitality around." Shawn smiled at him and nodded. Cox then turned his attention to Robbie and said, "If I didn't know better, I'd say you're kinda lookin' forward to this here lockdown." A few seconds passed and then Radford added, "Yep, just look at that boy blushin'."

Shawn said, "Sorry to spoil Christmas, but I think it's best you all got the hell out of here and headed for Alabama tomorrow. Anna, can we get a car?"

"There's an entire stable of them in the garage. There are a few full-sized SUVs. They can take their pick."

They were just about to break up for the evening when Cox's cell phone rang. He glanced at it and then announced, "It's Edsel Walcott." He put the phone on speaker. "Edsel, you up on speaker. Shawn, Charley, Mark, Robbie, we all here. What you got?"

"Radford, sumthin's up. First, Luckridge gets killed in Charleston. Now, I just got a call from the Hinds County Jail that Rick Fortino's dead. Someone slit his throat ... another inmate. I got his name, but had to pull in a few favors. Sheriff's office ain't talkin' to nobody 'bout it, it seems."

Radford let it rip, "Jesus H. fuckin' Christ! Them fuckin' rednecks in Mississippi couldn't guard a dirty diaper without fuckin' it up. What happened?"

"Don't know for sure, but I got my suspicions. Did a little checkin' around. The guy that did it just got sentenced to two forty-year sentences to be served consecutively. He was on his way to Parchman Prison in a few days. He 'bout fifty years old or so and parole ain't a possibility till he's served about sixty of them eighty years ... so, it's a life sentence and he ain't got nothin' to lose. I'm told he's got a girlfriend and supposedly they got a kid 'tween 'em. My bet is a couple of months from now, after all this drops off the news cycle, she'll start spendin' like she's hit the lottery. Seen it happen before."

"Dammit," Radford cursed.

"Well, at least Fortino got some information to the feds. I got it all in my notes. I was there when he talked to them."

Alarms went off with nearly everyone at High Bluff House. Shawn was the first to speak. "Edsel, it's Shawn. Where are you now?"

"Hey, Shawn. Merry Christmas. Wife and I are home, but headin' over to our daughter's tomorrow in Tupelo for Christmas with the grandkids."

Cox interrupted, "Edsel, listen to me. You're in some danger—'cause of what you know and all. In the next coupla hours there're gonna be five, maybe six of my boys comin' your way to keep an eye on you and your family. I'll tell them to make sure they touch base with you, but I'd 'preciate it if you'd listen to what they tell you to do. Don't want nothin' happenin' to you over all of this."

For the first time, they could detect some concern in Edsel's voice, "Well, uh, okay, Radford, if you think that's important, then I'll keep an eye out for 'em."

Anna spoke up. "Edsel, this is Anna Shane. I'm a reporter with *The Washington Post*. I was also a target for murder by this bunch that has killed your client. If Radford thinks you might be in danger, then it's important you believe him."

"Yes, ma'am."

"Also, it appears that someone at a very high level in the government may be trying to suppress the investigation of Luckridge's involvement in The Brotherhood of American Loyalists. So far, there's not been anything in print about what's going on in that regard. I intend to change that, but I'm going to need your support. May I count on that?"

Charley DeBooker started to say, "Anna, I don't—" She held up her hand and he stopped.

"Yes, ma'am. I'll do what I can."

"Thank you, Edsel. I'll be in touch."

Radford said, "Watch for my boys. They'll be there quick. Gonna call 'em as soon as we get off this call."

While Radford placed his calls to line up Edsel Walcott's security detail, Charley DeBooker sat next to Anna on the sofa in front of the fireplace. "You know it's dangerous, don't you? Look, they've killed two people in less than twenty-four hours."

She reached over and took his hand in hers, but her fury was building. "Charley, there are some really bad actors in this world. Charlotte, Ephraim, Luckridge are the ones we know about. Now it appears there are more. If they or anyone else thinks they can get away with killing my mother and my husband, then they're going to find the complete power of the press coming down on their fucking heads."

DeBooker knew not to try to reason with her.

"The FBI's keeping quiet on what they have. I've seen it before. The bullshit, 'We cannot comment on an on-going investigation.' Well, that may be true for the Bureau, but it sure isn't true for me. If no media outlet has picked up on the FBI's investigation of Luckridge's dealings with a white supremacy group within the next twenty-four hours, then *The Washington Post* will break the story under my byline."

"But you quit at *The Post.*"

"Not to worry. *The Post* is always looking for breaking news and, boy, do I have a story for them!"

In the kitchen, Nora found Shawn pouring himself a cup of strong black coffee left over from dinner. As he placed it in the microwave to heat, she asked, "You okay?"

"No, not really. I've just ruined a couple of lives tonight ... Gail's and Robbie's."

She smiled as she replied, "Yeah, well, I don't know what you saw when you told Robbie he'd best go to Eufaula with Gail and her parents, but Radford and I picked up on it. I think he's got a thing for her and this will be a good chance for them to see if there's anything there."

"Yeah, maybe."

Nora reached out and took his hand. "Listen, Shawn, Anna Shane is alive because of you; Charley too. Robert

Luckridge's conspiracy will be exposed because of you. I know we aren't at the end of all of this, but whoever is behind it has got to be running scared and it's because of you."

He held her hand tighter. "Yeah, I know, but I ... I was kind of hoping ... "

Her heart raced. She thought she knew what he was trying to say, so she decided that now was the perfect time to put her feelings for him out there in plain view. "I was kind of hoping that Jenny and I would see a lot more of you now that this was coming to an end. I hope tonight's revelations don't change any of that."

"Listen, Nora, it's been a long time since I've had any kind of feelings for ... for someone like you and Jenny. My life before didn't allow for it and now, after all that's happened ... "

Interrupting him she said, "You don't think you deserve to have a good life, am I right?"

He nodded.

"Nothing could be further from the truth." Nora reached up, laid a hand gently across his cheek and kissed him softly.

As they stood there in the kitchen, looking at each other, Rusty wandered in, sat and looked up at them. Shawn pulled Nora close to him and gently said, "I'm not going anywhere." Rusty stood, whined and headed for the kitchen door. "I know it's cold outside, but would you like to take a walk with us?"

"I'd love to."

THE WASHINGTON POST
WASHINGTON, DC 28 DECEMBER 2017

LUCKRIDGE IMPLICATED IN JUDGE'S MURDER

Anna Shane, National Political Editor

The Washington Post has learned that the late Senator Robert Luckridge, who was murdered Christmas Eve in Charleston, South Carolina, has been implicated in an FBI investigation into the death of Mississippi State Supreme Court Chief Justice, Burl Smythe. Further, he is believed to be involved in a secret society calling themselves The Brotherhood of American Loyalists, an ultra-right-wing organization with white supremacy leanings. Sources reveal the FBI has forensic accountants who can link other influential politicians and businessmen to this brotherhood. Other sources reveal that Luckridge received a phone call from The Office of White House Counsel very early on the day of his assassination ....

Anna and Nora sat at a table in the common dining area at High Bluff House with the paper in front of them as Shawn walked in. He got a cup of coffee and, as he joined them, he noticed the headline. "Holy shit! The cat's out of the bag now, isn't it?"

Nora nodded as Anna said, "Sure is. My old boss called me this morning. They've hired me on a consulting basis to keep working this story, but don't want me back in Washington. He said to work from here. Thought I'd be safer. They asked if I'd let them send some extra security out here to keep an eye on me, just in case."

"What'd you tell 'em?" Shawn inquired.

"Told 'em it wasn't necessary. Charley's already arranged it. Two of Radford's guys, I guess. They'll be here this afternoon. Radford told Charley his boys would be better than a couple of rent-a-cops. Can't say I disagree."

Pointing to the paper, Nora asked, "So, what happens next?"

"Since this article broke, I've already gotten requests for interviews from ABC, NBC, CBS, CNN, MSNBC—hell, even FOX wants me to sit down with them."

"So what are you going to do?"

"I've been thinking about that. I think I'm going to lay low. This story's too big for just me to be covering it. What it needs are a lot more reporters asking a lot more questions of a lot of people back in Washington. There are at least a couple of dozen reporters at a dozen major media outlets. Some of them have been calling. I told them I didn't think they needed to be asking me. Ask the FBI, the DOJ and the White House."

"So, you're going to stay here in Frankfort?" Anna nodded. Nora asked, "Here at High Bluff or at your mother's?"

Anna smiled at her, "I think I'll stay at Mom's, but I've got a lot of work to do here. Brian Gilbert is coming over tomorrow. We're going to take a look at a generic design for other Angels' Overwatch buildings. We can't always expect to find an old abandoned mansion waiting to be renovated like this one. He can get a jump on some of the preliminary architectural drawings. After that Charley and I are going to start thinking about other locations."

Nora reached over and took her hand, "Sounds like you're going to be very busy."

Shawn looked at Nora, "When does Jenny go back to school?"

Nora thought for a second and said, "January 2. Why do you ask?"

"So, we've got a few days on our hands?"

She liked the sound of it ... 'having a few days on *our* hands.' "Um, well, yes. What did you have in mind?"

Last night had been wonderful for her ... for them. After she was sure Jenny and Rusty were asleep, she had sneaked down the hallway to the apartment Shawn was staying in. Her only excuse was she'd wanted to talk. But as he held her close just inside the closed door, she'd recalled Mary Sullivan's diary entry of the first night she and Liam had made love in his small apartment in Manistee ... *his touch was so gentle and warm that I consented to his desire comfortably and without regret. I am in love with this man and he is in love with me.* All the nights of loneliness during her widowhood were over. Their coming together was so very serendipitous.

Shawn asked, "Have you and Jenny ever been to Koosharem, Utah?"

Nora looked at Anna who was smiling and nodding. "Shawn ... I ... I have some applications ... "

Anna interrupted her, "No one's going to be moving in between now and the new year, Nora. There's nothing here that can't wait until then."

"The mountains are beautiful this time of year. I was thinking the three of us could travel out, pick up the other dog ... did you know Jenny's already given her a name? Sydney."

"When did she come up—"

"Yesterday. You and Anna were working on something. So, she and I went for a walk with Rusty. I kinda like it. Sydney ... it has a certain ring to it, don't you think? Anyway, we could give the two dogs a couple of days to adjust to one another, I can show the both of you around Koosharem and then we can head back here in time for her to be in school on the 2nd."

Nora looked at Anna who was smiling and nodding her obvious approval.

Shawn took Nora's hand in his, "Yeah, I know, it's kind of sudden. I'll understand if you aren't ... "

"No ... no ... I can't think of anything else Jenny and I would rather do than go to Koosharem with you. Does Jenny know?"

"No."

"Then let's go find her and tell her we are going to pick up Sydney as soon as she can get ready."

ACKNOWLEDGMENTS

I truly enjoy the challenge of writing current, compelling fiction. It is not for the faint of heart. One has to be willing to literally live, day and night, with the characters one is creating, in settings that are sometimes familiar, sometimes not, and along the way have them do things that most of us wouldn't ever dare. Such has certainly been the case with *The Widow and the Warrior*.

As a writer, one must like the editing part of the writing process otherwise it can become tedious, tiring and frustrating. I have always enjoyed the editing part of each of my, now, four books. However, I admit that in the case of this book, I have enjoyed the editing even more than I enjoyed the creation of the original manuscript. Maybe that's because this manuscript needed more of it than the other three did.

Whatever the case may be, in my life, I am blessed to have a wonderful family and many friends whom I hold in deep and abiding respect. Thirteen of these have been very helpful in honing this story. They are:

DR. ROLLA BAUMGARTNER, a voracious reader of all types of literature, has been a beta reader of all of my books and a great friend for over 20 years. His comments are always cogent.

HEATHER SHAW, a gifted writer in her own right, a principal at Mission Point Press and the designer of each my book covers. Her comments on The Widow and the Warrior were eye-opening.

FRED MEYER, a first-time beta reader whose enthusiasm is boundless and comments spot on.

COLONEL (USA, RET) TOM JOHNSON and his wonderful wife, CATHY, two of my oldest friends, who now live in Mississippi. They reshaped this Yankee's view of their state, and in doing so, reshaped a couple of the book's characters.

WYNNE BAUMGARTNER, a first-time beta reader and Mississippi native, whose comments helped me flesh out a relationship important to the book's ending.

PATRICK MURPHY, a fellow writer and good friend, with a keen wit and the ability to turn a phrase. Both of us are fans of good dialogue and he is quick to see the best, and more importantly, the worst of it in a manuscript.

MARIE SHOWERS, my sister-in-law, who helped me see that the original manuscript was actually two books. One she liked. One she didn't.

BRYNN MONTESANTI, my daughter, who's very busy now being a town clerk, mom, teacher, wife and rookie gardener/farm girl. She gets me!

JENNIFER CARROLL, a successful newspaper woman in her own right, whose endorsement of this book is a treasure.

MICHELLE GRAVES, Editor of *The Manistee News Advocate*. A busy editor of a daily newspaper serving a community that depends upon the paper for its timely news. Her endorsement means the world to me. I can't thank her enough for taking the time to read and comment on my work..

SUSANNE DUNLAP, my editor with Mission Point Press and a professional editor without equal. Working with you was like taking a graduate-level creative writing class. Just to say "thanks" seems wholly inadequate.

C.D DAHLQUIST, my copy-editor whose keen ear for words and keener eye for detail is like a master jeweler. She has taken a gemstone and polished it, placed it in the perfect setting to produce a beautiful piece. Thanks, C.D.!

And, finally, DIANE, my wife, whose faith in me is boundless. She is my first and last editor always. I wouldn't want to do this with anyone but you.

I cannot thank each of you enough for what you've done to help me make *The Widow and the Warrior* the best read it could be.

ABOUT THE AUTHOR

John Wemlinger is a retired U.S. Army colonel with 27 years of service. The author of four novels, he lives now in Onekama, Michigan, with his wife, Diane, close to the Lake Michigan shore. When he and their border collie, Sydney, aren't roaming the beaches or nearby hiking trails, he is writing, playing golf or creating unusual pieces of original art from the driftwood, rocks and beach glass that he finds along the shoreline. One of the true joys of his life is talking with people about his books and his art. He can be contacted at www.johnwemlinger.com or follow him on Facebook.

AWARD-WINNING BOOKS ALSO BY JOHN WEMLINGER

Winter's Bloom

Operation Light Switch

Before the Snow Flies

John Wemlinger has written a powerful novel about a veteran suffering from PTSD and the unlikely path that leads to his salvation. Winter's Bloom is a poignant tale of loss, love and redemption that will keep you turning the pages.

— Frank P. Slaughter, author of *The Veteran* and *Brotherhood of Iron*

FOR OVER THREE DECADES, Rock Graham has carried the physical and emotional scars from a tour in Vietnam. He is a decorated war hero, but guilt from what happened one dark night in a steaming southeast Asia jungle is always lying in ambush, waiting for an unguarded moment to set his demons free. When he tries to find solitude at a cottage on Lake Michigan in the dead of winter, a chance encounter on the desolate, frozen shoreline changes his life forever.

John Wemlinger has written a fast-moving and compelling story of overcoming a grave injustice with the help of family, friends, caring military professionals, and sheer guts.

—Ron Christmas, Lieutenant General, USMC (Ret)

Wemlinger gets it. The nimbleness of our armed forces is as important today as its fire power.

—Mike Kelleher, Brigadier General, US Army (Ret)

CLEVELAND SPIRES, a respected and highly decorated soldier, lost his career, his family, and much of his pride when he was sent to prison for a crime he did not commit. Now he's out, and after returning to his hometown, he stumbles onto a clue that might prove his innocence. That clue leads him to Bangkok, Thailand, where he finds himself thrust into the middle of an international conspiracy that will rock the global economy. What he does next will take all of his courage and an unflinching faith in a system that once failed him.

MAJOR DAVID KELLER was well on his way to becoming a general when a roadside bomb in Afghanistan took his legs. Angry, grieving, and carrying a loaded gun, David returns home to mend a few fences before using that gun to end his life. But before the snow flies, his family, his community and Maggie McCall, someone he tried to forget, will prove to him that life in the small town of Onekama, Michigan, can be great once again—if he will only let it...and if murder doesn't get in the way.

CPSIA information can be obtained
at www.ICGtesting.com
Printed in the USA
FSHW012039160920
73861FS